MISTRESS of NIGHT & DAWN

Vina Jackson

An Orion paperback

First published in Great Britain in 2013
by Orion Books Ltd,
Orion House, 5 Upper St Martin's Lane,
London WC2H 9EA

An Hachette UK company

5 7 9 10 8 6 4

A CIP catalogue record for this book
is available from the British Library.

ISBN (Paperback) 978 1 4091 4747 3
ISBN (Ebook) 978 1 4091 4746 6

Typeset at The Spartan Press Ltd,
Lymington, Hants

Printed in Great Britain by Clays Ltd, St Ives plc

The Orion Publishing Group's policy is to use papers that
are natural, renewable and recyclable products and
made from wood grown in sustainable forests. The logging
and manufacturing processes are expected to conform to
the environmental regulations of the country of origin.

www.orionbooks.co.uk

MISTRESS of
NIGHT & DAWN

MISTRESS of
NIGHT & DAWN

Prologue

A Child by The Lake

The child was sleeping.

A sliver of moonlight peered through the motel room window while the hushed, liquid sounds of the nearby lake were carried on a carpet of night towards them. They lay motionless on the narrow bed. Both the Engineer and the Mistress-in-Waiting were silent, absorbed in thought, listening to the regular rhythm of the baby's breath as it cruised alongside the background chatter of the cicadas.

'I didn't know cicadas sang at night,' she remarked.

'It could be because of the light on the jetty,' the Engineer said. 'Or the heatwave.'

'Yes, it is hot . . .' She instinctively smoothed the sheet that covered their bodies with her damp hands, as if ironing out the creases would alleviate the suffocating heat. 'Or maybe they're crickets or katydids,' she added.

'No, definitely cicadas,' the Engineer informed her. 'It's a distinctive chorus. I recognise it.'

The young woman fell silent and turned towards him, allowing her fingers to brush against his skin.

The Engineer sighed, overcome by an uncontrollable feeling of gratitude swelling inside his chest. They were side by side, eyes wide open, the baby's basket set on the floor at her side where she could keep an eye on it and

I

reach its handle without having to move more than an inch.

He turned towards her. His wife.

Of two weeks only.

Her blond hair spilling freely over the cushion, golden, regal.

In his mind, he replayed the short wedding ceremony in the town hall of the picturesque village where they had first found refuge after fleeing the Ball. The same village where their child had come into the world. Their shelter from the storm, a small community in a distant valley dotted with lakes, which they had stumbled upon by chance.

They had debated furiously whether this was the right place to hide, a pretty but touristy gathering of picture-postcard cottages, gift shops and a circle of cabins surrounding a partly isolated minor lake, but it had felt right. Hiding in plain sight amongst the ever-changing flow of visitors. It had been late spring and her pregnancy was due to come to term in early summer. They had noticed a small hospital on the outskirts of the village as the Greyhound bus they were travelling on had driven by and they knew they couldn't run for ever. It was as good a place as any, they had reckoned.

The ceremony hadn't been much of a ceremony. The official had worn a black suit with a dark tie and their witnesses had been the local midwife who had presided over the baby's arrival and the owner of the bed and breakfast where they had initially taken refuge. They knew no one else in town. It was all over in ten minutes and the only touch of colour had been a few bouquets of red roses the Engineer had scraped together at the last minute. In her Moses basket, the child had remained silent through the proceedings as they exchanged vows, parroted all the right words and ended up so quickly as man and wife.

The Engineer extended his hand and passed his fingers through her long hair, like travelling through silk, a sensation he found both arousing and soothing. He took a deep breath in an attempt to immerse himself in the moment, to make it last.

Had the child been a boy, he knew, there might have been an opportunity to remain here for a while, or somewhere else, and maybe settle down, to get away from the road and their headless flight. But that opportunity was now denied them. The Ball would never allow the offspring of a Mistress-in-Waiting to escape her destiny.

'You can't sleep, can you?' his wife asked him.

'No.'

She shifted nearer to him, effortlessly sliding over the central dip in the mattress, the imprint created by the hundreds of couples who had preceded them in this bed before they had inherited it, and snuggled up against his side. He slept naked, and she usually wore a thin cotton nightgown, which had now bunched up at her waist.

The contact was electric. It always was. Since the first time their bodies had met, when they both worked at the Ball on a summer's night a whole year ago.

Their lips made contact.

Just as they had on that fateful evening as the fireworks roared through the sky in the distant fields setting a signal for the bacchanalia to begin, a rainbow palette of fire, sparkles and flames bathing the landscape in a blanket of magic.

Their hearts beating in unison.

Then and now.

The Engineer took his wife in his arms, banishing the imagined sounds of the final Ball they had participated in. Remembering how they had relished that first embrace, how it had seemed to go on for ever and everything around them had somehow disappeared, leaving them at the centre of a cocoon of silence and affection, in sway to each other, suspended in the fleeting breeze of their breaths, the softness of their skins, the yearning in their eyes.

And they had both known, in an instant, that this was what they had been waiting for all their lives.

She had said his name softly, as if shielding it from the ears of others. The Engineer had whispered hers, lingering on every syllable, caressing every sound.

Still holding on to each other as if their lives depended on it, they had looked at each other, searching for words, the right words, the wrong words, something to hang onto.

'It's wrong,' she had said, but wouldn't let go of him. 'Us.' She shivered. 'You know what is happening at dawn, don't you?'

'I do,' the Engineer had confessed. He had designed the ceremonial console. There was no way he could pretend not to know.

The first time she would be inscribed.

Marking her once and for all as the Mistress-in-Waiting.

And they had fled.

Knowing they would inevitably be pursued.

To the ends of the earth.

'Hold me,' his wife said, and his mind was returned to the present. To the suffocating bedroom where the wide open windows brought no relief from the curtain of leaden heat. His fingers lingered in the wake of her hair and tiptoed down to her bare shoulders. Her skin was damp.

Her small hand glided across his bare back, her nails gently trailing across his skin, pulling him tighter against her. His heartbeat accelerated. They hadn't made love since the child's birth. It wasn't something they had discussed, it had just happened. Waiting for the right time.

That morning, he had watched her shower when she had left the door to the bathroom half-open. The porcelain white of her body had shone under the pearling water like a jewel and the Engineer had felt his chest tightening in response. He was overrun by the soothing familiarity of his desire for her. Knowing it would never die.

There was a muffled sound. The baby had burped or hiccupped.

Their bodies parted.

'Is she waking?'

His wife looked over the side of the bed.

'No. It's still a bit too early, I think.'

Right then, as if responding mischievously to her mother's statement, the baby opened her eyes wide, revealing dark-brown orbs that lit up her chubby face.

Her parents smiled.

The baby peered out at them, silent, querying.

'Hungry?' her mother asked the child, pulling down her nightgown's strap and uncovering her swollen breast and its delicately pink nipple. The expression on her face unaltered, the baby began sucking.

'She always is,' the Engineer said.

His wife leaned over the side of the bed, picked up the baby and brought the child to her chest.

'We still haven't given her a name,' he said.

So far they affectionately called her 'dumpling', but hadn't settled on the right forename. Every time they tentatively agreed on one, they ended up discarding it the following morning as uninteresting, inappropriate, banal or downright wrong.

'We'll come up with something,' the Engineer stated and kept on watching his wife and new-born child with unerring fascination.

Fed and changed, the baby quickly fell asleep again.

'She's good for a few hours now,' his wife said.

Dawn was peering through the cabin's wide-open windows, bathing the room with shimmering light. Already, the temperature was rising and the monotonous sound of the cicadas was growing in crescendo.

In her basket, the child appeared unaffected, not even sweating, at peace, her thin trails of dark hair unevenly distributed across her small head, her breath reassuringly regular.

'I need some fresh air,' his wife remarked, wiping the dampness away from her forehead.

'I don't think it's any less stifling outside,' the Engineer pointed out.

'By the lake, maybe?' she suggested, her eyes casting a longing glance in the direction of the calm spread of water beyond the wall of trees that enclosed the perimeter of the motel and its circle of cottages. There wasn't a single vehicle in the car park at the front. They were the only visitors today.

He looked down at the baby's basket on the floor

between the unmade bed and the wall. 'What about the child?'

'She's just eaten,' his wife observed. 'She'll sleep until midday, at least eleven,' she added. 'She'll be okay. We don't have to stay more than an hour at most.'

'Okay,' the Engineer reluctantly agreed.

As if seeking absolution for their temporary desertion, they both leaned over the basket and kissed the baby's forehead before walking out and jogging the few hundred yards or so to the lake.

'We're close enough that we'll hear her if she cries. She has powerful lungs, our little one,' the Mistress-in-Waiting remarked as they held each other's hands and trampled barefoot through the grass and across the patchy curtain of tall oak trees before emerging onto the dry mud bank of the small lake. A small, rickety jetty extended into the peaceful waters, and a weak, gossamer breeze rose magically from the water's shallow depths and brushed against their skin, weakly diverting the mounting heat of the new day.

The irregular wooden planks felt warm under their feet and they walked a length away from the pontoon's edge.

At this distance from the trees and the fields, the insistent sound of the cicadas singing had faded away, and the young couple were bathed in an eerie stasis of silence.

Skimming across the roof of the trees behind them a gust of wind rose, born out of nowhere, and the sudden sound of branches creaking and leaves shaking in its wake reached the Engineer's ears. Out of instinct, he swiftly looked back, and thought he saw a shadow run between two of the trees, before disappearing out of sight like a ghost. His heart dropped.

'What is it?' she asked him, sensing him tense at her side.

'I don't know,' he said. 'I thought for a moment there was somebody in the trees, watching us.'

'Your paranoia, again,' she said. 'And, anyway, who cares if we are seen? We're married, remember, and it wouldn't be the first time we'd been seen naked, would it?'

His gaze lingered, fixed on the thin gap between the trees, and he then turned back to her. 'It's nothing. Don't worry.'

He hadn't told her that the previous day when he had walked into the village to pick up fresh milk and provisions, he had come across a couple of strangers whose attire was unlike that of the customary tourists who visited the area. And, out of the corner of his eye, he'd caught a glimpse of the woman looking at him somewhat quizzically. However, neither she nor the man accompanying her was familiar to him from his time at the Ball. He'd quickly dismissed the idea they might be acolytes tasked with running them down, but the kernel of the thought had embedded itself in his mind and suddenly returned.

'I love you,' the Engineer said.

His wife turned to him and smiled in that way that always melted his heart and, almost as if in slow motion, pulled the straps of her nightgown to the side and allowed the flimsy garment to fall to her feet. She was naked underneath. The early rays of the sun ran through her long blond tresses, crowning the strands of gold with a delicate haze.

Riven to the spot by the beauty of his wife as she stood, feet slightly apart in a pause of expectation, the Engineer held his breath, his attention locked on every single detail of her unveiled body, the indescribable shades of pink of her nipples, the trace of her rib cage beneath the white skin, the dark yellow fire of her thatch, the elegant curve of her hips, the exquisitely thin circle of her ankle and the gold chain he had always known her to wear there. Then he looked up and their eyes met and his soul plunged into the green depths of her life.

He went to her and kissed her, abandoning himself to the cushioned softness of her lips, her bare skin wrapping itself around his own. This seemed to go on for ever, time around them falling to a standstill.

Finally, she broke away. His eyes were closed.

The sun was rising over the trembling horizon behind him, growing stronger with every passing minute, its fierce rays washing over his bare back and, for a brief moment, he felt dizzy, unsure what was hotter, the slow, sharp fire travelling across his shoulders or the cauldron of her mouth as she wrapped herself around him and teased and played with him as only she knew best.

The Engineer gasped. 'Not now. Not like this,' he protested. 'I want to be inside you.' It would be the first time they would make love since the birth and he wanted to enjoy it to the full, make it unforgettable.

His wife detached herself from him and he joined her on his knees, the rough texture of the jetty's wooden planks an unwelcome burst of reality and discomfort. He stretched out and reached her discarded nightgown and spread it out on the jetty floor and then delicately positioned her across it and parted her legs.

Her arms stretched out from her side and her body opened like a cross, preparing herself for his imminent but welcome invasion.

*

They were sprawled out on the wooden jetty, spent, exhausted. The sun was rising over the trembling horizon behind them, growing stronger with every passing minute, its fierce rays washing over their bodies.

'Come on,' she chided him, getting to her feet. 'What are you waiting for?'

And with that she faced the end of the jetty and took flight, causing a thousand ripples to shimmer across the broken surface of the lake's dormant waters as she dived in.

The sound of her laughter echoed through the air.

The Engineer hesitated briefly and then followed her in, the impact of his body creating a further galaxy of concentric circles to race wildly across the already rippling skin of the lake.

The cool water felt invigorating and they splashed around like wild children in a playground, enjoying the way their hot skin was bathed with relief with every successive moment that passed.

'Catch me,' his wife called out, swimming towards the centre of the lake.

Seeing him approach, she jumped up and plunged under the water to hide from him, prolonging the game they were playing.

By the time he reached the spot where she had submerged herself, she hadn't returned to the surface. He realised this was the deepest part of the lake, unlike the shallow edges where they had set off from. He waited for a moment but, overcome by a rush of fear, he lowered himself fully in the waters, below the surface. It took an agonisingly long time for his eyes to adjust to the submarine murk and he had to force himself to keep them open, against all his instincts.

Spinning around in panic in an attempt to see where she might be, he could feel his lungs bursting as he attempted to hold the air inside and not be expelled. He thrashed uncontrollably, the lake around him tightening its grip like hard wool around his body.

Finally, just as he was about to launch himself upwards to the surface of the lake in a bid to take in fresh air and make a further attempt, he noticed a blurred form floating just a few arms away from him. It was her. His wife.

Fixed in time. Her eyes were wide open and pleading. Her golden hair floating like an explosion above her head, her arms beating a metronomic rhythm by her sides. He knew she could see him. He made an attempt to reach her but the weight in his chest became unbearable and felt like it would saw him in two.

He looked down. Her ankle was caught in a jungle of weeds on the floor of the lake and she was frantically trying to set it loose but her energy was visibly waning and every successive tug only appeared to tighten the plant's hold on her leg.

He was only half-conscious by the time he reached her and was unable to summon the physical will to untangle her from the weeds in which her ankle was held captive.

He gave her a last look and he knew she understood.

As resignation engulfed him, he first thought with a sense of relief that what was happening was not the fault of the Ball, and his final one was for his daughter who was sleeping peacefully just a stone's throw away.

Slowed by the sheer weight of the water, he struggled to

raise a hand and reach her cheek in a final gesture of tenderness but he failed to do so and his fingers grazed her left nipple. Then everything grew black around him.

East of the lake, a cloud passed across the sun.

In the cabin, the child had woken up and was now crying.

I

Hunting Ghosts

They were surrounded by noises, smells, movement and light. It felt like this early part of the night was merely a prelude to even bigger and strangely wonderful events.

Siv turned to Aurelia.

'Isn't this magical?' she asked her friend.

'It's better than magical,' Aurelia replied, glancing around in wonder as one strange thing after another caught her attention. There was something a touch askew about the evening, as if the atmosphere they were bathed in was having an insidious effect on her mind.

The ordinarily plain stretch of grass had been transformed and was now peppered with tents, each of them brighter and more flamboyantly decorated than the last.

From close up Aurelia could see that the temporary structures that housed the fair's attractions were made of simple canvas and steel and that the flashes of red and yellow and blue that flicked into the sky from the roofs of the big-tops like dozens of fluorescent tongues were simply fabric streamers. But from afar it appeared as though a plague of rainbow-coloured mushrooms had sprouted all over the heath overnight and she half suspected that the whole thing might disappear again just as quickly right before their eyes as if the fair had grown out of nowhere and not been placed there by design.

The toffee apples that they had purchased at the ticket gate were the size of small pumpkins and the candyfloss that she had sampled from Siv's paper bag was so light and fluffy it could easily have blown away before she managed to get it into her mouth.

Children, their faces half lit by the fairy lights that were woven over everything, ran unsupervised between the tent poles like pixies on a rampage. Even the sounds of sausages sizzling and machinery whirring and popcorn popping seemed sharper than usual.

Once they had passed through the hedgerow that marked the funfair's entrance, everything had been magnified, right down to the feathery touch of the gentle breeze that wafted over Aurelia's skin and sent a pleasant shiver all the way up her spine.

Aurelia felt on edge, both elated and terribly curious. Like tiptoeing on the edge of intoxication even though she hadn't yet had a drop to drink.

Which was not the case for Siv, who had brought along one of her father's thin silver hip flasks, which she had filled with gin and some mixer before they left the house and had regularly refreshed herself from it on the train taking them to London.

'When I grow up,' Siv remarked, 'I think I might run away with a circus.'

'You *are* grown up,' Aurelia replied. They would both be celebrating their eighteenth birthdays soon, just a few weeks apart.

'I mean properly grown up, and all that,' Siv responded,

as they walked past a stall selling cheap souvenirs and glow sticks. The old woman running it hailed them as they passed, loudly advertising her wares, but they ignored her and continued towards the circular marquee where the dodgems had been set up and loud sounds of mechanical mayhem and laughter rose all the way to the plastic roof.

A gaggle of teenage boys rushed past them, running in the opposite direction, still exhilarated from their turn on the cars. The smallest of the group, who could not have been more than thirteen and wore a combination of school blazer, blue Chelsea FC football shirt, ripped jeans and heavy steel-capped working man's boots, brushed against Siv as they passed.

'Watch it,' Siv shouted.

The boy froze in his steps and gave her a dirty look, struggling for the right riposte but the sight of Siv standing there, legs apart in a confrontational pose, her tight denim shorts stretched against her thick black tights, an expression of provocative rage spreading across her lips, silenced him.

Although small in size, Siv, with her blond hair cut short, oozed menace. It was as if she was itching for a fight. The boy lowered his eyes and moved on, running after his companions to escape her stern gaze.

Once again Siv and Aurelia were blanketed by the sounds of the fun fair in full flow. Laughter, shouts, muffled melodies of antediluvian pop tunes duelling between the steady thwacks emanating from the coconut shy and the hiss of flames meeting paraffin as a man juggling fire sticks stopped to refuel and gave them a theatrical flourish. Aurelia winked at him and was rewarded with a wide grin before he returned to painting the night sky with streaks of light.

'No need to be so aggressive,' Aurelia chided Siv, who was still glaring after the boy. Aurelia had long grown used to her friend's bursts of temper. There was a core of revolt lurking inside Siv, her against the world; it had been present since their first years together in primary school, an anger against the status quo, the state of things, that Siv used to compensate for her size and deceptive frailty. As a result, and although Aurelia had always been taller, now by almost a full head, Siv had from that early stage assigned herself the role of protector to her friend, and would have fought to the death on her behalf had any bullies crossed their path. Which they never did, as Siv's pugnacious reputation rapidly began to precede her.

Aurelia remembered an occasion, just under ten years ago, when she had been wrongly accused of some minor misdemeanour in class, and tiny Siv had stood up with a roar of indignation and confronted the teacher, red in the face, crying out 'That's not fair!', which had landed both of them in detention. The event had cemented their friendship once and for all.

'Can't let these uncouth Londoners get the better of us country girls, can we?' Siv said with a grin.

Aurelia smiled back at her but deliberately left the question unanswered, not wanting to let a spat interrupt the happy mood of the afternoon. They'd been planning this for ages, the culmination of their half-term break, and they'd mulled over at least a dozen celebratory possibilities before deciding to travel to London for the day and then spend the evening at the fun fair on Hampstead Heath.

They had promised Siv's parents that they would arrive home by midnight. Although they were old enough to stay out as late as they liked, together they had developed a reputation for mischief and both Aurelia and Siv had long ago learned that their home lives were more pleasant when they kept their parents pacified or at least informed about the length of their intended absences.

Other girls from their class had been to the fair over the Christmas break the previous year and sung its praises but, before Aurelia had arrived, she couldn't imagine that it would be any different to the various fairs she had on occasion visited on the south coast and nearer to home. Maybe the Ferris wheel would be larger, the carousels faster and the rides more colourful, but none of that could explain the overwhelming desire she'd had to visit the fair on the heath rather than go dancing at a string of clubs in the West End with the ID cards that Siv had borrowed from friends who had already turned eighteen. So why in her heart and the pit of her stomach could she feel that sense of excitement and repressed expectation?

They reached the dodgems pay kiosk manned by a sullen white-haired man dressed all in black and Siv purchased tokens for three rides with coins fished loose from her pocket. Then they waited for their turn to embark on the car they had picked out, metal red and gleaming, bruised steel, parked at the other end of the floor, unreachable until the current session ended.

Aurelia was lost in a daydream, the sounds of Taylor Swift's 'I Knew You Were Trouble' punctuating the regular rhythm of random dodgem collisions unfolding in front of her eyes.

'Those boys are staring,' she heard Siv say, although at

first it felt as if her friend's voice was coming from behind a padded mirror. She snapped to attention.

'Which ones?' she asked, distracted and quite unconcerned by the attention they might be getting.

'Over there? Can't you see?'

Aurelia followed Siv's nod of the chin. Three skinny teenagers at the opposite end of the track, all wearing jeans and flannel lumberjack shirts in various combinations of colours and cleanliness, were gazing at them with undisguised hunger in their eyes.

'Oh . . .' Aurelia said.

'I like the one in the middle,' Siv pointed out. He was the scruffiest and was slouching in a rakish way. His two friends were shorter and unremarkable, both holding bottles in their hands.

'Not my type,' Aurelia said.

'They're never your type,' Siv interjected. 'You don't seem to have a type.'

Aurelia knew that Siv had, on several occasions, been with men. She'd had to listen to the fascinating if excruciating details with a mixture of awe and amusement. Of course, she sometimes felt attracted to boys, but never those whom Siv chose for her and she had always shied from moving any step further than holding hands or a formal goodnight kiss on the cheek. It was a combination of shyness and the simple fact that every time she had been involved in any kind of romance things had gone awry in often embarrassing ways.

The music ground to a halt and with it the deliberate whirlwind of dodgem cars sliding across the steel floor of the attraction.

Taking her eyes off the admiring boys, Siv seized Aurelia's hand and led her to the metal red car they had spotted earlier and they sank into it, squeezing themselves onto the driving seat.

Aurelia noticed out of the corner of her eye two of the boys who had been watching them earlier make a beeline for a blue car full of dents. The third one had remained in place, and was now smoking a cigarette. As Siv took the simple steering wheel in both her hands, Aurelia detected a touch of malice in the watching boy's eyes.

The loudspeakers roared into life again, the music beginning slowly, as if stretched like an elastic band until it reached a full crescendo. It was the same Taylor Swift song. The dodgem car twitched and Siv put her foot down on the pedal and it took off as if stung by a bee.

Siv glanced around her as she gripped the steering wheel, seeking out possible targets. But there were only half a dozen somewhat forlorn cars spread along the steel floor of the attraction. Before she could select a victim, there was a heavy jolt as the dented blue car driven by the two boys from earlier made a crunching contact with theirs, and their aggressors let out a whoop of frantic laughter.

'Women drivers!' exclaimed one of them, with a pronounced Brummie accent.

Siv quickly manoeuvred herself into reverse and with one deft movement swung around and before the boys could respond again she had pressed her foot flat onto the pedal, slamming the blue car against the side of the track. Aurelia lurched forward in her seat as Siv chortled and raced away again, the boys hot in pursuit. She managed to evade them for the rest of the ride, which came to a halt much earlier than they'd expected.

Extricating herself from the car, Siv extended her hand to Aurelia to help her out. 'That'll teach them,' she said proudly, glancing back at the car to check the two boys' reaction. They remained in place, already seeking out their next targets when the ride came to life again and apparently impervious to Siv's attempts to get their attention. The third boy, the observer, had already faded away, seemingly bored with watching them.

Siv frowned, visibly losing interest in the dodgems as her target spun off in another direction without a backward glance. 'We'll use the other tokens later,' she said. 'Let's see some of the other attractions.'

Siv and Aurelia stepped onto the grass. Away from the noisy cars, it now felt colder. Aurelia sniffed the air.

'I think the weather is turning,' she said.

Within a few minutes, the wind was rising in gusts and battering the tents that covered the green fields, sending the strings of beads that covered the nearby tarot reader's awning clattering against each other in a tangle of multi-coloured plastic. The Ferris wheel creaked and strained like an ancient behemoth struggling to tear itself out of the bolts that held its iron arms together and escape, octopus-like, across the open areas of the heath.

Aurelia raised a hand to her face and brushed away the strands of auburn hair that had uncurled from her hair band and were whipping out into the breeze like reeds in a stream. The wind felt like a cool pane of glass against her cheek. She fought the urge to lean against it, relax, and let it catch her or send her falling straight to the ground. Instead she turned her face into the cool air and opened her arms as if embracing the tempest that swept against them. She laughed.

'Can you feel it?' she shouted to Siv over the weather. 'There's something loose in the air tonight. It feels like Halloween.'

Siv laughed with her. The sound caught in the current and turned into a whistle. She hadn't bothered to gel her cropped blond hair and the wind had pushed it up into tufts on her head so that she looked even more gamine than usual. Any other girl might have been offended by the number of people who mistook her for a boy. Not Siv. She delighted in her androgyny.

'Let's get back indoors,' Aurelia added. 'It's going to rain.' She dropped her arms to her sides and pulled her fringed black shawl tightly around her shoulders, though the thin fabric did little to protect her from the elements.

'Come on then,' Siv took Aurelia by the hand, pulling her along as was her habit, and they entered the nearest tent, an enormous dark-green tower that, despite its size, blended into its surroundings so well that they nearly walked straight past it. The canvas door flapped open and then closed again immediately behind them, swallowing them up.

Unpleasant smells of sweat and damp and month-old candy permeated the cavernous structure and left a bitter, metallic taste in Aurelia's mouth, as if she had been sucking a penny.

'Is there anyone here?' Aurelia whispered into the dark. A light bulb crackled and flashed. Both girls jumped and clung onto the other's hand tightly.

'Sorry,' said a young man who was now visible at the counter. 'Mechanical failure. With the light, not the ride,' he added hastily. 'Do you want tickets?'

A green rubber monster's mask was pushed onto the top of his head and his messy ginger hair fell across his forehead. The elastic band that was designed to hold the mask in place over his face dug into his chin, leaving an angry red welt. Aurelia wanted to reach out and loosen it, but instead, she dug into her tote bag and withdrew the quilted coin purse with the gold clip that she had received from her godmother for her birthday.

'What ride is it?' she asked. The inside of the tent was bereft of signs or any other identifying information. They could have been anywhere.

'The ghost train,' replied the young man, in a perfunctory manner, as if he were announcing the departure of the next express service to London.

He stared at Aurelia's fingertips as she counted out the change for two tickets. She had painted them that morning, a dark, rich navy blue that gleamed against her pale skin. Siv's were bright green, the colour of the fresh limes she liked to add to her gin when she wasn't drinking it straight from a hip flask.

Aurelia took the ticket stubs between her fingers. The young man held onto the slips of white paper a fraction too long before letting go. The nails of his right hand were bitten to the quick. The nails on his left hand were of ordinary length, and neatly filed. Aurelia was a keen observer of people, and she noted this snippet of information with interest. She wondered what other parts of the boy were frayed at the edges on only one side.

'Through that door,' the boy said, pointing to a thin black veil behind him, without taking his eyes from Aurelia for a moment. A grinning plastic skeleton hung over the opening; its once white bones now discoloured from old age and overuse. It emitted a mechanical wail when Siv pushed it impatiently to one side to let them through.

'He likes you,' she said matter-of-factly, punctuating her statement with another swig from the silver flask and nodding her head towards the ticket collector whose faint outline was still visible through the thin curtain, as if to confirm that she was referring to him and not the skeleton.

Aurelia shrugged. It wasn't that boys made her nervous. She just happened to find the idea of romance uninteresting, and the few times that she had tried it, always as a result of Siv's meddling, things had gone wrong in ways that seemed unbelievable in retrospect.

The first boy who had ever tried to kiss her had tripped as he had moved in to make contact, fallen flat on his face and broken his nose on the pavement outside her house. And only last year, at the school's end-of-term disco, her date had managed to inadvertently lock himself in a broom cupboard, and hadn't been discovered until the caretaker cleaned the hall the following morning.

Siv joked that she had Cupid's nemesis resting on her shoulder and batting away the arrows of love. And if that were true, Aurelia didn't mind. She was not unaware that sometimes men looked at her, or tried to strike up a conversation. She was simply ambivalent.

'And he wasn't bad looking,' Siv added. 'Ginger, but still cute. I think you should talk to him.'

'I did talk to him.'

A single cart sat empty at the top of a gentle slope. It didn't appear to be fixed onto rails. Aurelia waited for some sign to indicate what they should do next.

'Do we sit in that, do you think?'

'I meant *talk* to him,' Siv replied. 'And who cares, these rides are all stupid anyway. Is anyone else even in here?'

The sound of muffled voices and brash laughter reached them through the thin veil that blocked the ride's starting point from the ticket collector.

'Shhh,' Siv said. 'Someone's coming.'

'The cart's not big enough for all of you!' came the voice of the young ginger-haired man from behind the counter. 'You'll have to wait for me to set up another one.'

'Hurry up then,' a deeper voice replied.

'Boys! The ones from the dodgems,' Siv hissed joyfully. 'Come on.'

She grabbed Aurelia's hand and pulled her into the darkness of the tunnel, pushing aside the rubber spiders that fell down from the rooftop as they set off the motion sensors. Stale popcorn crunched beneath their shoes, crushed to fragments by the heavy weight of Siv's favourite shiny purple Doc Marten boots with their garish black and yellow laces and barely touched by the soft tread of Aurelia's ballet pumps.

The cart clicked and whirred into life behind them.

'Quick!' cried Siv, as the boys bundled in, and pushed away the attentions of the red-haired ticket collector who was frantically insisting that they buckle up their seat belts. 'Let's hide.'

The tent seemed to go off for miles in all directions. It hadn't seemed so wide from the outside. They found the metal rails that the carts ran along, and raced down along-side the track looking for a place large enough for the two of them to crawl into or disappear behind.

'Here,' Siv said, when they nearly toppled straight over a pair of elderly-looking vampires who were sitting precariously atop a fake-blood-covered rock.

They crouched down as the cart came rushing towards them, faster than they had expected.

The faces of the two vampires morphed into snarls as the cart set off the pressure switch, caught in the glare of a beam of light that flashed on, just in time to cast a vivid glow onto the twin moons of Siv's buttocks as she leapt up and pulled down her shorts and tights, flashing her arse.

A boy shouted in surprise. 'Hey! I think that was a girl,' he cried behind him. The cart's occupants tried to swivel around but it was too late, they had been whisked around the corner before they could catch another glance or identify the perpetrator.

Siv chuckled as she re-fastened the button on her jean shorts.

'Are you quite finished?' Aurelia asked her friend, between peals of laughter.

Siv snickered again in response. 'No,' she said, 'I was hoping I'd make them crash.'

She pushed the silver flask into Aurelia's hand. 'Here, settle yourself down with a swig of this. And let's keep exploring.'

Aurelia took a sip, and grimaced.

'Ugh,' she said, 'I thought you said you were going to mix it?'

'Not enough room in the bottle,' Siv replied. 'I didn't want to waste the space.'

'This place is huge,' Aurelia marvelled, as they edged along another corridor. 'And it doesn't feel like a tent.' She ran her hand along the nearest wall. It was as cool and damp to the touch as a stone in a river. Again she had a strange sense of excitement about the night, as if the fun fair was a place that sat somewhere on the fringes of reality, part of the world but not subject to its ordinary rules.

They continued walking. Aurelia had taken the lead this time, stepping into the dark with one hand still caressing the wall and the other holding Siv who trailed a step behind. By now the two girls were lost in the darkness, their movements under the canvas and along the elusive tracks no longer setting off the motion sensors, most of which had only been calibrated for the passage of the carts.

'Use your phone. It'll give us some light.'

It was like being in an obscure labyrinth. They could hear the faint sounds of the fair beyond the walls but were unable to orientate themselves and find the exit, the brightness at the end of the tunnel.

Aurelia squeezed Siv's palm. She could sense her friend's bravado diminishing as the darkness stretched out ahead of them and they both became apprehensive.

The track vibrated and a rumble neared them as a metal cart swam towards them out of the relative night of the ghost train ride. Above its clanky metallic din, there was a murmur of voices. She switched her phone off.

'I swear she had her pants down,' one of the boys said.

'She had a good arse, even for a ghost,' the other boy in the cart mused.

'If we hunted her down, maybe she'd show us more than just her arse,' the first one replied.

Siv giggled quietly.

'Do you think I should give them an extra flash?' she whispered, her fingers moving to the waistband of her shorts.

'I don't think they deserve it,' Aurelia said. 'Let's scare them instead.' She looked around for a suitable prop that she could hold up and jump out in front of them with, but before she had time the cart raced by, the outline of the boys' heads visible in the penumbra and once it turned the corner. The two young women followed the tracks and finally made for the exit, once they had given the car a few minutes' lead so that the boys could disperse.

A curtain of plastic skulls and bones rose and Aurelia, quite impervious to its effect, brushed it aside and they were assailed by the colourful lights and din of the surrounding fun fair.

'That was dangerous,' a voice said. He had been waiting for them at the ride's exit. 'And I was getting worried something might have happened to you inside there.' The attendant with the ginger hair and the green rubber monster mask perched atop his untidy mop of hair lounged against the side of the tent, arms folded.

'We didn't do any harm,' Siv insisted, standing her ground, almost provoking him. 'Honest.'

'It's usually guys who cause problems,' he said. 'I didn't expect it from you two.' He looked Siv up and down, and his eyes flitted from her to Aurelia.

Siv laughed, and slipped her fingers through her short

hair, something she always instinctively did when she was flirting, Aurelia knew.

'And do you have a problem with girls who cause trouble?' she baited him, standing with her slim legs apart, in a defiant stance, holding herself straight at full height, her modest chest jutting towards him.

Confused by Siv's odd mix of flirtatious aggression, he glanced at Aurelia, but recognising the indifference in her eyes, quickly turned his attention back to Siv.

'Come on, Siv, let's go,' Aurelia suggested. She was beginning to feel sorry for the ticket collector who seemed sweet enough beneath the shadow of his monster mask, unlike the boys from the dodgems who were all run-of-the-mill teenagers, fuelled with testosterone and otherwise entirely dull to everyone besides Siv, who seemed to be interested in them all.

But her friend refused to back down.

'I just meant to say you shouldn't have walked into the tent on foot. Something could have happened and I always get the blame for everything,' he sighed.

'You're not the boss?' Siv asked.

'Do I look like I own the place?' Ginger said. 'It's just a job. Not a very fun one at that. And I only came out here to make sure you got out okay, not to fight with you.'

He took a step back, waiting for them to leave.

Siv continued to stand and stare at him, but quickly realised that her efforts to provoke him had failed, and switched to another tactic. Aurelia stood quietly beside her. She'd seen her friend in this mood enough times before to know that trying to talk her out of it was a pointless exercise.

Eventually, Siv's expression softened.

'Listen,' she suddenly said, 'we're sorry, okay? We were just having a bit of fun.' She looked down at the ground and scratched her boot along the dirt. A bright bolt of red swept over her cheeks. Siv was unaccustomed to apologising. Aurelia could barely believe her ears.

The boy looked up and grinned. His features transformed when he smiled, becoming infinitely more handsome, a fact that was not lost on Siv.

'All right,' he said. 'No harm done.'

'Can we make it up to you? Buy you a drink or something?' she continued gruffly.

'Yes. Thanks. That would be good.'

He didn't talk like any other boy Aurelia had known. She looked at him curiously, but his attention was now politely fixed on Siv, who had extended the invitation.

'I have to get back to the till. But I get off in half an hour.'

Siv looked up at Aurelia, a grin spreading across her face, silently seeking approval.

'Fine by me,' she said. She could use a nicer drink to wash away the taste of Siv's gin.

'Great,' the ticket collector replied. 'See over there, the large tent with the red canvas roof. That's where the main bar is. Thirty minutes, okay?'

'It's a deal, Ginger,' Siv said.

'I have a name,' he protested. 'It's—'

'Shhhh . . .' Siv interrupted him quickly. 'I don't want to know. To me you're Ginger. And get rid of the monster mask. I never kiss men wearing masks . . .'

She took hold of Aurelia's hand and they walked away towards the heart of the fair.

The wind had fallen.

'Could we try the fortune-teller now?' Aurelia suggested.

'No way. Didn't think you believed in all that mumbo-jumbo hippy magic. I want to fire a gun. Let's go to the target range.'

Aurelia agreed, but made a mental note to seek out the fortune-teller another time. She'd go alone, if Siv wouldn't accompany her. All of a sudden, she had felt a strong compulsion to know what the future held for her, although, like Siv, she ordinarily had no truck for the irrational and its gaudy trappings.

Siv was a good shot and ended up just a mere target away from the giant teddy bear grand prize, but was lumbered instead with a yellow and orange plastic duck, which she brought along to their assignation, flushed with pride.

They had briefly debated whether to go, and Siv had first made certain that Aurelia had no personal interest in the ghost train attendant.

'I'm sure that, given a choice, he would prefer you, you know . . .'

'Not my type.'

'You'll still be a virgin by the time you're twenty-five at this rate,' Siv said.

'I don't care.' Aurelia shrugged. She didn't disapprove of Siv's behaviour for any moral reason, but neither did she feel any kind of obligation to strike up a flirtation with someone she didn't really fancy just for the sake of it.

Siv nodded.

'Well, I like him, and I'm not too proud to give him a try even if he did fancy you first. They all do, anyway.' It was merely a statement of fact, not a complaint. Aurelia was the prettier of the two and always the one that men radiated to first, even if they soon learned that it was Siv who was inevitably the interested party.

They entered the bar tent and began to pick their way through a sea of dropped plastic cups to the front where a line of customers, three bodies deep, were queuing for pints of cheap beer.

They spotted Ginger, who was trying to hold a place for them near the front. There were rips in his jeans but he had ditched the rubber mask and even combed his hair into some semblance of tidiness. When he saw the two young women approaching at the appointed time, he smiled broadly, as if relieved they had come, not having believed until this moment they would actually do so.

'Hi, Ginger.'

'Hey, you made it.' He offered them a flirtatious sideways smile. 'I thought you might bail.'

'We're women of our words,' Siv shot back.

'So what are your names?'

'She's Tall and I'm Short. Will that do? No need to complicate things, surely?' Siv said.

A long trestle table with a red and white checked table-cloth had been set up against the far wall and they walked over, holding their plastic cups. Aurelia and Siv had chosen cider and Ginger ordered lemonade. 'I have to drive home later,' he explained, as Siv stared pointedly at his non-alcoholic drink.

On closer inspection Aurelia reckoned the artfully dishevelled fair worker must be in his mid-twenties. Despite the difference in age, it was quite obvious the diminutive Siv was in charge.

*

One hour later, on the pretext of getting some fresh air, Siv had lured Ginger to a patch of unlit grass under the shadow of a tall oak tree on the outskirts of the fun fair. Aurelia, bored to death, had left them to it and wandered off. But she had stopped ten yards away, enjoying the cool of the night air after the heat and noise of the bar tent.

She glanced across and saw the couple by the tree were now frantically kissing, Ginger bending down to reach Siv's lips, their hands manically exploring each other under the layers of clothes. Aurelia couldn't help but be fascinated as she observed their animated fumblings, half shocked and half envious, knowing from the yearning look she had seen in his eyes that he would have much preferred if Aurelia had been willing to go with him instead.

She wondered what he was thinking as his hand briefly delved under Siv's shorts before she peremptorily nudged him away without breaking off their embrace.

Aurelia felt as if she should look away, but her curiosity was getting the better of her. The reflections of the strings of multicoloured bulbs on the line of poles illuminating the nearby fun fair trickled through the tree branches when the now quietened breeze abated, offering her a clearer view before the darkness washed over the couple again. For a rapid moment, she glimpsed a flash of white skin. Surely Siv hadn't lowered her shorts, as she had done in the ghost train tent? Not here, in almost full public view.

There was a faint sound to her left and, alerted, Aurelia swung round. Some distance away, someone was urinating against the back of one of the long trailers. Her heart jumped as she recognised the familiar sound. Then the shadow moved away in the opposite direction, unaware of her presence or that of Siv and Ginger.

She turned her attention back to her friend. The light shifted and she caught a clearer view of the couple. It wasn't Siv's white buttocks on view but Ginger's. His jeans were bunched around his ankles. His arse was firm and muscular. Evidently he did not spend all of his time stuck behind a desk at the fun fair. And Siv was on her knees in front of him, her small hands resting gently on his thighs and her head moving up and down in perpetual motion.

Aurelia held her breath.

But also held her gaze.

It was one thing listening to Siv's lurid stories about the shape and taste of the men she had been with, but another thing altogether watching her in action, the slow, deliberate way she moved her lips up and down his shaft and the way that he clenched his fists in an obvious attempt to maintain his control. Aurelia's throat tightened.

A cloud slid across the half-full moon and for a second or so the couple were caught in a natural spotlight. At the same moment, Ginger turned his head slightly in Aurelia's direction and his eyes met hers. Aurelia blushed as he saw her watching them. 'I wish it were you,' she felt he might be trying to say to her. Then new clouds wrapped themselves across the moon and her view was once again obscured. She looked down to the ground, her heart beating like a drum inside her.

From the corner of her eye she saw Siv rise to her feet and move towards her, Ginger following, fastening his belt as he walked.

'There you are,' Siv called to Aurelia.

Ginger cleared his throat, searching for some way to change the subject and alleviate his embarrassment.

'I can take you to another place,' he said. 'Strictly speaking it's just for the workers. But no one will complain about you two, especially as you're with me.'

Siv's attention was immediately roused at the mention of another location that they weren't allowed into.

'Shouldn't we be going?' asked Aurelia. 'What about your parents?'

'We can tell them there was a hold-up on the Tube, or something. Just a little longer,' she pleaded.

They agreed and Ginger set off, his red hair glinting in the moonlight, with Siv at his side and Aurelia following behind.

Aurelia observed the two of them together. Ginger was quite tall and seemed particularly so in contrast with Siv. They made an odd couple. Although, she realised, so did she and Siv in the eyes of others.

The tent that Ginger took them to was much smaller than the main bar, which had been set up for the punters. The interior was completely decked out with fairy lights that some creative individual had set up to resemble a solar system, so the ceiling appeared to be much higher than it was. Each time Aurelia looked up, she felt as though she was under the night sky somewhere outside London and closer to her home by the coast where the stars were visible and not blanked out by pollution and city lights.

In the middle of the tent, a make-shift bar had been set up out of large wooden barrels. The smells emanating from this area were unlike any that Aurelia had noticed in a bar before. She sniffed the air and her mouth began to water.

'Chocolate,' said Ginger, watching her response and smiling. 'It's hot chocolate. The best you've ever tasted. The tarot-reader makes it. Says she took the recipe from a customer's head and it would be immoral to share his secrets with anyone, so we don't know what she puts in it. She makes a fortune selling the stuff . . . wait, and I'll get some.'

He joined the queue at the counter and Siv set off after him to help carry the drinks back, leaving Aurelia standing alone in a corner, the subject of more than a few curious glances.

She stood silently waiting, avoiding the temptation to kill time by playing with her phone, knowing that it would soon be full of missed calls and messages from either Siv's parents or her godparents when they did not arrive home at midnight.

With nothing but the make-believe stars to keep her company, Aurelia became aware of the thoughts that flitted through her mind and each small sensation passing through her body. A new and unusual feeling had wrapped itself around her chest. She felt for a moment that time had stood still, and everything in the tent seemed all at once louder, brighter, more vivid. The chatter of the tent's patrons fell away and she noticed the song playing in the background. 'Missing' by Everything But the Girl. The music made her lonesome, as if the lyrics were a premonition.

Another scent assailed her senses, joining the blend of ginger and cinnamon that flavoured the tarot-reader's hot chocolate. She turned her head and concentrated, but could not identify its source.

It became stronger, and suddenly she was aware of the body of a man at her side.

Aurelia started. She hadn't noticed him approach. The room seemed somehow to grow darker, and she couldn't make out his features, just the bulk of his presence and an overwhelming sense that she was safe, no longer alone in the company of strangers.

'Oh, it's you,' she said, as if she had known him all along. The words had slipped through her lips of their own accord.

'Yes,' replied the man, his voice deep and full of humour. 'It's me.'

Her whole body reacted in a curious fashion, as if his breath, his words, had surrounded her with an invisible cocoon, a shield of tenderness and unsaid safety.

The feeling that she was alone here, just her and this man, this stranger whose presence every nerve in her body could sense but whose face she couldn't see properly.

He lifted his hand and brushed it through her hair. His palm was cool against her face. She remembered how she had felt soothed by the gusts of wind by the ghost train, and she leaned against him and relaxed.

He bent his head down to hers and kissed her. The feeling of his lips against hers blanked out every other thought in her mind and every sense in her body. There was no tent, no Siv, no Ginger, no stars and no fun fair. There was only her mouth and his, and nothing else in the world mattered but that.

2

Great Expectations

And in the next moment he was gone.

Ginger and Siv returned and before Aurelia could speak, or even grab hold of the man's hand, he had vanished. The lingering taste of his mouth on hers was replaced by the sweet and slightly smoky flavour of the tarot-reader's hot chocolate as Siv handed her a delicate white china teacup with a matching saucer, like something that Alice would drink from in Wonderland.

'Chilli, I think,' Ginger said as he took a sip.

'No, paprika,' Siv replied firmly. 'I'm one quarter Hungarian. I know the flavour,' she added to give weight to her assertion.

'Love,' Aurelia said dreamily. 'It tastes like love.' She touched her fingertips to her lips.

'Have you lost it?' asked Siv, staring at her. 'Maybe we should get home . . .' She glanced at her watch. 'Shit! It's nearly midnight.'

The girls fled from the fair in such a rush that neither of them had a moment to remark upon the subtle changes that they each observed as they passed through the wide arches that marked the exit. Outside, the air was a little cooler, the light a little duller and the scent in the air a little sour, particularly in comparison with the heady aroma of cocoa and spices that had filled the employees' bar.

Siv squinted momentarily to find her bearings, looking for a sign that would point them in the direction of the Northern Line and Aurelia cursed gently under her breath when she realised that she had misplaced her gloves. Both of them disregarded the sudden tightness in their chests and the catch in their throats and the heaviness that had taken hold of their legs. It was as if they were pulling on invisible threads that still connected them to the centre of the fun fair and did not want to let them go.

They ran down the platform hollering, 'hold the doors!' and leaped aboard the last train to Leigh-on-Sea no more than a moment before its departure from Liverpool Street station. Siv sat down with a thump of relief and promptly fell asleep, spending the rest of the journey snoring softly on Aurelia's lap, whilst Aurelia ignored the drunk and rowdy late-night passengers who mumbled 'All right, love' at her as they stumbled through the narrow carriage, leaving a trail of burger wrappers and half-eaten chips in their wake.

She stepped from the carriage and inhaled the sea air so deeply that the salt stung her nostrils. As the train rumbled off into the morning, Aurelia had the sense that in some inexplicable way her life had changed, and she would never be the same again.

Much to their surprise, neither Aurelia's godparents nor Siv's parents had been as upset by their late arrival as the girls had feared.

'You're grown up now, I suppose,' Siv's dad said to them

as they'd stumbled downstairs the morning after the fair. There was a note of sadness in his voice, though on later occasions he had cause to mutter under his breath at the fickleness of teenagers.

After that, both Aurelia and Siv were given tacit permission to stay out late at night or even not come home at all, but neither of the girls was inclined to use it.

The truth of it was that the fair had changed them both, in small but noticeable ways. Siv became more focused and almost studious, albeit in a physical rather than an academic sense, with all of her spare time and energy devoted to practising 'tricks'. She continued to date the ticket collector who was now officially courting her in an old-fashioned manner, commuting down to the coast whenever he had free time. His name, as it turned out, was Harry, but the girls continued to call him Ginger, and he would still mostly refer to Siv as Short. Aurelia was always just Aurelia. She had never been the sort of girl who suited nicknames.

Ginger had some skill with rigging, and Siv had convinced him to set up a practice trapeze in her parents' garage, where she swung from beam to beam and rope to rope like a jungle creature. Accidents were inevitable and Ginger spent a good deal of his time patching her up and grumbling that her father would think him a wife beater if he continued to send her back into the house with bruises. But Siv gradually grew stronger and her once slight shoulders, though not bulky, became distinctly toned.

The exercise suited Siv, and gave a focus to the bubbling pool of aggression that she carried inside so that soon she rarely snapped at anyone, even the young skateboarders who came whizzing along the footpath by the estuary too close to the girls' ankles as they walked past the pier.

Aurelia, too, had been preoccupied since that day and night spent on the heath, though her thoughts turned in a distinctly different direction, and always returned with predictable inevitability to the stranger and his kiss.

At first she had simply replayed the feeling of his lips against hers over and over, but when those thoughts became tired she began to imagine how his mouth would feel on other parts of her body until, eventually, she wasn't sure which parts of her daydreams were memory and which parts invented. Sometimes she felt that she had dreamed the whole thing and other times she thought that it must have been more than a kiss, but that she had somehow forgotten the rest. Her memory of the event was in some respects so absolutely keen and clear, and in other respects impossible to get straight in her mind. Thinking about it was like trying to find the edge of water.

When she was alone, Aurelia's thoughts were always accompanied by self-pleasure. She went about her routine with the slow, concentrated languidness with which she approached everything that she set her mind to. Often, she ran a bath, surrounded the rim with a hundred or more tea-light candles nestled side by side and lay in the water touching herself until it turned cold hours later. She rarely came, preferring instead to enjoy the residual feeling of sexual frustration that permeated her being for days.

She had, of course, told Siv about the kiss. Siv initially reacted with eager interest. It was the first time she'd known her friend to have a crush. But as time went by and Aurelia continued to be fixated with the stranger, Siv grew bored and stopped asking her to try to at least remember what he had looked like or what he had been wearing.

The only thing Aurelia recalled with any certainty was his scent.

'Pomegranate,' she told Siv.

'Pomegranate?' Siv scoffed. 'Men don't smell like pomegranate.'

Aurelia began to eat the flesh of the deep-red fruits for breakfast most mornings. She was surprised by the bitter aftertaste, but soon began to enjoy the contradiction of the harsh and woody tang that followed the initial sweetness of each mouthful. And she liked to run her tongue over the seeds and think of the stranger.

Eventually, though, the fun fair became just another memory, and the girls returned to their usual routine of school interspersed with drama and dance classes, Aurelia's part-time job at the florist in Old Leigh and Siv's Saturday mornings behind the till selling playing cards and whoopee cushions at a local emporium. Sundays were reserved for spending their wages and socialising. Life continued in much the same vein for several months. Exams came, were duly ticked off, and a time for decisions was nearing for both of them.

The weekend following their final exams, both Siv and Aurelia managed to get monumentally drunk on a pub crawl they had unadvisedly joined with friends from school. That night, at Siv's inebriated insistence that she finally find herself a proper boyfriend, Aurelia had flirted heavily with Kevin, a good-looking if somewhat vacuous student from the nearby academy.

By then, the memory of the stranger's kiss at the fun fair

was fading fast and, after a few hours, Aurelia had agreed to go back to Kevin's house, only for him to stumble as they made their way to his car, hand in hand. He fell badly on his wrist, breaking it, and had to go to A and E, which put a dampener on any further activities of a sexual nature.

Aurelia was beginning to think her love life was cursed. Or, thinking of some of the more lucky escapes she'd had in her teens, that maybe she had some kind of guardian angel. She quickly dismissed the idea, despite that odd feeling she'd had for some time now that she was being watched. It was unnerving, but every time she looked around to investigate there was no one to be seen.

And then the letter arrived.

In a thick, brown envelope that screamed bureaucracy it fell onto the mat below the door's flap with a heavy thud alongside the usual assortment of household bills, a couple of magazines and a handful of circulars.

Aurelia was in the first-floor bathroom brushing her teeth. She heard Laura's steps in the hall and her customary grunt as she bent down to pick up the mail. Her godmother was suffering from arthritis in her joints and, these days, her movements were all too often punctuated by sighs and sounds of mild protest at the way her body was reacting to her physical needs.

Laura was a decade older than her godfather, John, and Aurelia had always been amazed that two people who seemed so different had managed to stick together for so long. John was a serious, practical man who worked as an architect on dull corporate building projects in the City of London. Whereas Laura was an artist who specialised in blowing glass into delicate birdlike shapes, as far removed from the sturdy steel structures that John designed as one could imagine.

They had met twenty years earlier on the Tube, when Laura had been carrying one of her creations to an exhibition and had dropped it at his feet where the glass had shattered into a million pieces. Their hands had touched as Laura had knelt down to gather up the fragments and John had tried to help her. The rest, as they often said, was history. And, despite the apparent contrast in their personalities, they remained as much in love now as they had been the first year they met.

Aurelia had never known her own parents. She was only a baby when they both died in an accident in America and she had been raised by John, who had been a friend of her father's at university, and his wife Laura, who was unable to conceive children of her own.

Aurelia was grateful to them for taking her in, but despite their kindless she had never quite managed to think of them as Mum and Dad, and so their relationship remained a strange mix of affection and distance.

Her godparents had always been somewhat furtive about the details of her parents' deaths and eventually Aurelia presumed they simply didn't know anything more. So she stopped asking questions, but she never stopped wondering what sort of people her parents had been, exactly how they had died and whether or not she was growing into their likeness.

There was a shuffle of paper from the hall and then Laura's voice.

'Aurelia dear, there's some mail for you.'

She rinsed her mouth and acknowledged her

godmother's shout out. In all likelihood something totally unimportant. Aurelia couldn't remember the last time she'd received any actual mail in the post. All her communications were through email and text messages, with Siv and the other friends in their circle, and she had no recollection of setting pen to paper aside from sending the occasional birthday card. She rushed back to her bedroom, slipped on a pair of jeans and ran downstairs.

Laura had moved to the kitchen where she was busying herself with preparing breakfast. Gentle hissing sounds from the coffee maker were punctuated by the steady rhythm of the wooden spoon turning in the pan, stirring the porridge oats to keep them from burning. A soft light fell through the large bay windows and lit up the jars of marmalade and pickles that were stacked on wooden shelves alongside the larder. John was still upstairs reading in bed, his customary weekend indulgence.

The mail had been picked up from the mat and the letter addressed to her was propped up on the dining table, resting against a large jug of tulips, imported from the hot houses in Holland and just beginning to open, their pale-pink buds unfurling with surprising swiftness and adding an early spring note to the late winter morning.

Aurelia peered down at the envelope. It was indeed her name typed in a traditional font across the rectangular white label.

Rather than tear it open right there and then, she decided to take it up to her room and read it at her leisure. Sitting cross-legged on her bed, she carefully inserted her tweezers into the corner of the brown envelope and ripped it open.

It was a letter from a lawyer asking her to attend a

meeting at the firm's offices in London's Inns of Court at the earliest possible opportunity. Aurelia's first reaction was that they had sent the letter to the wrong person and she checked over the envelope again, studiously scrutinising her name and the address, but there was no mistaking the details. Reading the brief text a second time, she was struck by the fact that it required her to visit the lawyers on her own and that she should not be accompanied. There was no explanation of the circumstances or a reason.

She Googled the company and it appeared to be legitimate, with a website listing partners and associates with a plethora of initials following their names.

Aurelia instinctively resisted informing John and Laura of the letter's contents and pretended to them when asked later by her godmother that it had only been junk mail.

'I really haven't a clue what it might be about,' she told Siv when they met up later that day in a small cafe on the seafront where they often whiled the time away when they were idle. Harry was up in the Midlands with the fun fair and unable to come down to the seaside to join them as he often tried to do. 'Why don't you phone them?' Siv suggested. 'Ask them why?'

'They wouldn't be working on a Saturday,' Aurelia pointed out to her friend.

'Maybe they are. Have a go.'

The number went unanswered, as she expected.

All weekend Aurelia attempted to ignore the curious summons. They went to see the latest Michael Fassbender movie at the local Cineworld, which failed to please Siv as the actor, whom she doted on, kept his shirt on throughout, but the appearance of the letter kept on nagging at Aurelia's mind.

As soon as their Monday-morning classes broke up for lunch, she dashed to the sports field where she knew she would be guaranteed some privacy and rang the law firm in London. She was unable to speak to the lawyer who had signed the letter and was told by his female assistant that the first available slot for a meeting was the following week on the Tuesday. She was not in a position to inform Aurelia what the matter was about and she would be advised in due time. Aurelia accepted the appointment immediately, even though she knew it would mean her having to play truant from school that day.

The whole week and the following weekend dragged on as she tried to blank the trip to London from her thoughts and made an effort to concentrate on her final batch of coursework which was due just a month or so away. She had good predictions and had already been accepted by a couple of decent universities depending on her results, although the thought of her further education failed to fire her. She had given much thought to the subject laying in bed at night while seeking the solace of sleep and come to the conclusion that, unlike most of her classmates, she simply lacked any career ambition and the prospect of moving away from home and being more independent was not much of an incentive.

And when she wasn't thinking back with a bitter sense of yearning to that magical kiss, and the myriad smells and colours it evoked inside her, her thoughts would travel to the idea of seeing America somehow. Her birthplace. She had no particular desire to leave the protective wing of her godparents, who were both pretty relaxed and uncontrolling, but she longed for the fresh energy of younger shores. Aurelia often felt that she didn't quite fit here in England.

But always her thoughts would drift to the stranger at the fun fair and the feeling of his mouth against hers, and she would sink into her pillows and touch her fingertips to her lips before moving down her body to her nub, where she would try in vain to pretend that the hand that brought her such pleasure was not her own. Deep in her heart, Aurelia could not shake the feeling that he would return to her again, and she feared that if she moved so far away, he might not be able to find her.

'What should I wear to visit a lawyer?' she asked Siv over the phone the evening before her appointment. From her top-floor open window she could see the last rays of sunset melting across the horizon and over the cobbled streets and clapboard cottages and a sliver of dark sea to the left. The night air was sharp and invigorating.

'Something elegant. And simple,' her friend suggested.

'My best jeans and the blazer?' she asked Siv.

'No. You can't wear denim. A dress maybe? Shows you're a serious kind of person.'

She settled for the mauve pencil skirt she had worn for the shotgun wedding of a classmate who had fallen pregnant six months earlier, together with a white silk blouse that screamed demure from six paces. And opted for flat shoes as a concession to comfort. Siv had agreed to cover for her at school; it was a study day and maybe she wouldn't be missed. She knew, however, she would feel self-conscious all day dressed like that.

The commuter train to the city was full and she hung on

to the straps for the whole journey, feeling slightly nauseous in anticipation of her meeting with the lawyer. The carriage ground to a halt and disgorged its human cargo onto the platform and Aurelia felt as if she was being dragged along with the flow, a totally insignificant drop in a vast current of people all racing to their important jobs and morning meetings. She had a whole hour to spare and decided to walk from Liverpool Street Station to Holborn rather than take the tube, first stopping to buy a coffee from the two Italian coffee vendors on Brushfield Street, their sales patter and bright orange umbrella providing the one spot of colour on a grey morning.

Leaving the City behind, the crowds thinned as the rush hour passed and Aurelia's attention turned to her surroundings, observing the stone walls of the ancient buildings, smooth and pale in stark contrast with the gaudy flower pots that hung from the awnings of the pubs geared for tourists.

Waiting at a set of traffic lights by Holborn Circus, leading down to Fetter Lane, Aurelia paused, holding her dark-green cape coat tight to her chest, watching the traffic and three tall red buses riding bumper to bumper as they crawled along the road, and glimpsed a faint reflection of movement in one of the bus's windows. She quickly turned round and thought she caught a shadow darting across the corner of a large office block into a side alley, as if fleeing from her quicksilver glance. Her heart fluttered and she accelerated her pace and headed for the Thames, looking back at regular intervals to see if she could spot any anomalies in the milling crowds, but was unable to do so.

She entered the Inns of Court, sprawled like a peaceful oasis in the heart of the urban closeness, and relaxed. A gentle breeze was coasting in from the nearby river and animating the tree branches as she spotted the building she was searching for. A receptionist who looked like a carbon copy of her headmistress noted her name down in a register and led her to a waiting room.

'Mr Irving is expecting you,' the older woman said. 'He shouldn't be long.' The airy and brightly lit room was like a doctor's antechamber but without the traditional well-thumbed collection of out-of-date magazines. A carefully trimmed small bonsai tree sat on a thin glass shelf on the far wall. Aurelia adjusted her tight skirt and tried to compose herself, her eyes darting across the room in an attempt to take in all its details.

The wait was a short one as a middle-aged man in a pin-striped suit, dark-blue shirt, silver tie, red braces and polished black shoes walked in briskly and offered his hand. He was medium height and wore glasses and his grey hair stood in sharp contrast to the rest of his appearance, halfway down to his shoulders, lustrous, combed back, studiously inappropriate for his profession and age.

'Gwillam Irving,' he said, his hand firmly shaking hers. His palm was unusually cool to the touch.

'Aurelia . . .' she answered. 'Aurelia Carter.' She had chosen to use her godparents' name a few years back, and not her birth name. They had brought her up and been so kind to her it had felt like both an acknowledgement and a vote of thanks.

'I know,' the lawyer said and, with his extended arm, indicated for her to follow him.

His office was across from the reception area and so much smaller than she expected, crowded with piles of dossiers, papers and law magazines attracting dust on every surface. He bid her to sit down, after clearing some stray folders from the old leather swivel chair facing his cluttered desk. There was a quaint, benevolent kindness in his smile as he sat and faced her.

He cleared his throat and gazed at Aurelia. 'I have been instructed to contact you and make you an offer, Miss Carter,' he said. 'However, I regret to advise you I will be unable to answer any of the obvious questions that, I am sure, you will wish to ask later, and I apologise in advance. My instructions are quite clear.'

Aurelia, puzzled, remained silent.

'You have a very generous benefactor,' Gwillam Irving said, sitting ramrod in his own chair.

'A benefactor?'

'I think that's the best way of putting it,' he answered.

'I'm not sure what you mean,' Aurelia replied.

'Irving, Irving and Irving, of which I am a senior partner, have been retained to set up a trust fund to be established in your name, which runs to a not inconsiderable sum, if I may say so. The principal will be available to you in full on your twenty-first birthday, although adequate amounts can be disbursed to you beforehand on certain conditions pertaining to your continuing your higher education.'

Aurelia sat silently, processing the information.

As she was about to open her mouth and begin asking a litany of questions, the grey-haired lawyer continued.

'I am unable to reveal the identity of our client who has requested to remain anonymous.' He awaited her reaction.

Her mind was in a whirl. There was just no one she could think of who could have come up with such a scheme. Her godparents were always careful with money, but they only had a small pot of savings, and she had no other relatives she was aware of.

'How much?' she queried.

The sum he quoted silenced her for a moment.

Seeing her lost for words, Gwillam Irving added, 'The interest alone, and we will be careful to arrange for the best possible interest to accrue until your twenty-first, will suffice to cover your cost of living through university and much more, I can assure you.'

'This is crazy,' Aurelia protested.

'There are two important conditions attached, I am obliged to point out – and I will of course provide you with a written copy of the proposed arrangements before we part – and they are that you begin your university education, in a place of your choice, before the aforementioned twenty-first birthday and also that you . . .' He hesitated. Aurelia stared hard at him. '. . . that you should not enter into marriage before that date.'

Aurelia felt her throat tighten. This was all so absurd. Not that she had any intention of entering into wedlock for the foreseeable future; there was not even a man, a boy, anywhere in her life.

'Were any of those conditions broken, the trust fund set up in your name would automatically be rescinded, I must make it clear.'

Her mind was crowded with questions but she already knew each and everyone of them would be pointless and that the lawyer would not prove forthcoming.

Irving talked her through the minutiae of the fund that would now be hers and the arrangements awaiting her agreement for the way it would be set up. She signed pages and pages of legal documents in a daze, not even bothering to read most of the details.

The lawyer escorted her to the door of the chambers and shook her hand.

'Congratulations, Miss Carter. You are a very lucky young woman.'

The breeze from the river had lifted, the leaves on the trees dotted geometrically along the Inns of Court barely fluttered now, and the whole world felt unreal to Aurelia.

She retraced her steps to the train station, moving in a daze through the busy London streets and crossed into the City. On the corner of Bishopsgate, she felt a pang of hunger in her stomach and stopped at one of the fruit stalls that dotted the street and picked up a punnet of strawberries. As she did so, she once again felt someone's eyes on her, drilling into the back of her neck. She abruptly turned round, submerged by that unsettling if illogical feeling she was being followed or watched. But there was nothing she could focus on. She bit into one of the plump red fruits, still observing the passers-by with uncommon attention. This was real life, not a thriller, no one could be following her, surely. Why would they?

She tucked the remainder of the berries into her handbag and walked down the steps into the train station.

Her train to the coast was already on the platform and half empty. Aurelia settled in and reviewed the morning in her mind in an attempt to make sense of it all. There was an announcement on the Tannoy, the carriage's doors closed and the train rumbled off. She glanced through the window and noticed the dark silhouette of a man standing at the entrance to the platform, receding in the distance with every passing second.

Aurelia looked away distractedly, and hunted through her purse for a tissue. The tips of her fingers were still red, stained with the juice from her strawberry.

Aurelia began to spend more and more time walking along the estuary. She had not yet told her godparents of her new wealth. Perhaps it was her way of clinging to the past, knowing that change was now inevitable. Siv often joined her, and it became their regular Sunday-afternoon jaunt. They would walk along the waterfront to Old Leigh and stop for fish and chips and an ice cream in a cone and sit together looking out at the white sails that dotted the gentle waves and the thread of smoke that bloomed into the sky from the Canvey oil refinery across the water.

They talked about the future, but never with any particular certainty. The topic often turned to Aurelia's trust fund, and what she might do with it. Siv tossed possibilities into the air at random like a juggler.

'You could buy a zoo,' she said. 'And become a lion tamer. Or a big yacht,' she added, 'and we could sail to Madagascar. I'll be your first mate, of course.'

Aurelia paused with her chip halfway to her mouth and pursed her lips, considering these fantastic new suggestions, never quite sure whether her friend was being serious.

'I'm not allowed the money, though, until I finish my education.'

'You're allowed to spend some of it on your education, right?'

'Yes, that's what the lawyer said. Part of it is for university and then once I've finished that, I'm allowed the rest, to do what I like with.'

'Well then. You'll have to have an extra extravagant education. The School of Rock? Space Camp? Why not somewhere abroad?'

Aurelia shrugged. 'I suppose so. I like it here, though. I'd miss the sea.'

Siv sighed. 'The money is wasted on you,' she said. 'You couldn't care less, could you?'

'Well, what would you do with it?'

'Circus school. There's one in America. But, even if I could afford it, my parents would never let me. They want me to do something practical. My mum thinks I should be a nurse.'

Aurelia snorted. 'You'd make the worst nurse in the world. Ginger could be a nurse. He already is, isn't he?' She glanced pointedly down at Siv's palms and knees, which bore the proof of multiple falls from her makeshift trapeze.

Siv ignored the jibe. 'Why don't you come with me? You've always said that you wanted to go to America. See where you were born.'

Aurelia fell silent.

'Oh, for Christ's sake,' Siv said, guessing correctly that her friend's thoughts were still fixated on the stranger from the fun fair. 'You didn't even see what he looked like, never mind get his number.' She kicked a rock into the ocean, hard, to emphasise her frustration.

It was Ginger, in the end, who unknown to either of the girls suggested to Siv's parents that Siv might have a chance at entry to the School of Performing Arts in

Berkeley. Though she was new to swinging on a trapeze, years of forced ballet and tap dancing lessons had given her the necessary prerequisites and if she could come up with a unique enough act for the audition, she might scoop a scholarship place.

Ginger had given up the fascination that he had first held for Aurelia the moment he had seen Siv take her first sip of hot chocolate, leaving a cocoa moustache on her top lip. He had leaned forward and kissed it from her mouth, and when all of his senses were overwhelmed by the taste of cinnamon and spices, he was smitten, and he had silently agreed with Aurelia, who had said that the drink tasted of love.

Siv was the girl for Ginger. There was an essential vitality in her that attracted him, a magical quality to her physical movement, as if she were part person and part sprite. He suspected that if Siv were cut open, doctors would find that her blood ran hotter and redder than the average human. But he sensed her restlessness, and he knew that all the things he loved about her would be the things that would take her away from him. She was far too full of life to spend the rest of it in a drowsy village by the coast.

Aurelia was the opposite. There was a coolness to her, a softness and languor that was evident in everything from the pallor of her skin to the auburn tone of her hair that ran like water straight down her back. The two of them together were like Yin and Yang.

And so began a long series of discussions between Siv's parents and Aurelia's godparents, and it was decided that if they did not encourage Siv to go, she was likely to take off anyway, and that if Siv was to go, Aurelia ought to go with her.

One month later, the girls' tickets were bought and their cases were packed. They planned to take a gap year, after which it was expected that Aurelia would finally settle on a subject that she wished to study, and Siv would apply to audition at the School of Performing Arts. Her parents gave her one chance to make it, and agreed that if she were unsuccessful she would enroll in medical school, or another, 'practical' subject of her choice.

Board for both girls and extra tuition for Siv was arranged in the San Francisco suburbs with a retired dance teacher who Ginger knew of through his funfair connections, and who had once tutored at the prestigious School of Art and Dance in St Petersburg. Aurelia and Siv would contribute to their stay by assisting with providing lessons to the teacher's few remaining pupils, and taking care of the old mansion that she lived in, on the Oakland outskirts.

Siv sniffed. They were in her parents' garage, where Ginger was working on carving a series of tiny figurines from pieces of scrap wood, and Siv was hanging upside down from a thick rope like a bat. The air was fragrant with the scent of wood shavings.

'Are you going to come with me to San Fran?' she asked him. A tear was trying to run down her cheek, but gravity and her upside-down position sent the salt water flowing back into her eyes. She blinked.

Ginger paused and tightened his grip on the brass-handled pocket knife that he held in his left hand.

'We talked about this,' he said.

'You could catch a boat,' she replied.

'We'll see,' he answered, and continued to chip delicately away on the face of his wooden model.

Ginger was utterly terrified of heights. He had never left England, and nor had he any desire to take the path that most of his friends in the funfair did and move from ticket collecting to either performing on stilts or working on the highly paid maintenance crews who looked after the Ferris wheels and other machinery whilst balancing on cherry pickers or dangling from harnesses in mid-air.

It was this fear that drove him to improve his skill working with rigging, but only from the safety of the ground. He was an expert with knots and with tossing coils of rope to his colleagues who worked above him.

'Some friends of mine from the fair are having a party next weekend. In Bristol,' Ginger continued, adeptly changing the subject. 'A few performers who studied in America will be there. They're doing a UK tour. Why don't you both come? And you could make it a sort of farewell party, also?'

Siv began flipping her legs back and forward rhythmically so that the rope began to swing.

'I'm not sure that being around funfair people would help Aurelia,' Siv replied. 'It will just make her think of Mr No Name.'

Without school to distract her, and with work only on Saturday mornings and one afternoon during the week, Aurelia had gradually sunk further and further into a sort of lethargic depression. She feared worrying her godparents by telling them about her mystery benefactor, so instead she had arranged for Gwillam Irving, the lawyer, to call Laura and John and convince them that they had inherited a sum of money from a much distant, now-deceased relative from a side of the family Aurelia knew they had both totally lost contact with. It was a white lie, possibly not even far from the truth. On learning the news, the elated pair had immediately set aside a substantial part of the money for Aurelia's travel and university fees, and cancelled their plans to remortgage to cover the expense of sending her abroad.

The kindly old lawyer had been delighted to carry out the deception, and the trick had cemented Aurelia in his mind as his favourite client. Not only was she young and pretty and the whole situation intriguing, but the girl was a refreshing change from the usual egotistic, stuffy bores that he normally dealt with when tasked with the tedious problem of administrating wealth to heirs and other beneficiaries.

Aurelia, though, was uncomfortable about lying to her godparents, and she continued to flit indecisively between excitement at the upcoming trip abroad and an unsettling feeling that she should stay in England, as if the stranger's kiss had somehow anchored her here.

'Do you think the two are connected in some way?' Siv asked Ginger when Aurelia was out of earshot. Besides Siv, Ginger was the only person who knew about both Aurelia's mystery windfall and the kiss.

'But surely the money must have been donated by a relative,' he replied. 'Her real parents, perhaps. And that would make the kissing guy her . . . well, that just wouldn't be right. At any rate,' he concluded, 'it would do her good to take her mind off it all.'

Siv agreed, and Aurelia allowed herself to be talked into

attending the party, although she was still feeling strangely out of sorts.

It was already dark when they left for Bristol. Both had spent considerable time packing their chosen outfits, as it was to be fancy dress.

'Fairy tales? What kind of theme is that for a bunch of dudes?' Siv had asked Ginger, when he had advised her of the dress code.

'They're not your typical dudes,' Ginger replied.

Siv had gone as one of the Lost Boys from *Peter Pan*, in a pair of cut off-brown leggings and her short hair gelled up into a mohawk. Aurelia had opted for Little Red Riding Hood, although it had taken her most of the afternoon to curl her hair into ringlets.

'Damn,' she said, frowning at the mirror, 'I look more like Goldilocks.' The heat seemed to have brought the blond out of her normally auburn hair. Or perhaps it was a trick of the light that made her curls appear to be a paler shade.

'I could have been one of the three bears,' Siv replied, 'but that wouldn't have been nearly as much fun.' She pulled open the window and fired one of her fake arrows towards Ginger's rickety old car as he pulled into the driveway to collect them. He had travelled down from London to pick them up and they had planned to take a scenic route, mostly by the south coast, to their destination, making the whole weekend something of a special event.

'Hey, careful with that thing,' he shouted. 'I know how good your aim is.'

'I missed you on purpose,' she replied, as he bent down to pick up the shaft that had landed just short of his car.

Aurelia rarely travelled by car. Her godparents, both committed environmentalists, refused to own one, preferring to cycle or take the train everywhere. She quickly fell into a doze as the busy streets disappeared behind them and began to murmur and twitch as her mind filled with shadows, unnoticed by Siv and Ginger who were both lost in the heavy dubstep beat playing on the stereo.

She started with a cry when Siv shook her.

'We're here, honey. Are you okay?'

'Yes, of course,' Aurelia replied, forcing a smile. Her sense that she was being watched had grown stronger, and now she had the feeling that her dreams were also being invaded. Clearly the events of the past few months had begun to addle her brain.

Her lips were dry. She passed her tongue across them and tasted pomegranate.

And remembered the kiss.

France 1788

Unrest was spreading fast across the country as the incequalities in French society had begun tearing at its social fabric.

The Ball Council had initially planned to set the celebrations in a small castle, just an hour's ride from Paris, owned by a relative of one of the Council members, but influential advisers at the king's Court had suggested a more distant location might prove more suitable so as not to draw too much attention. They had settled on a property in the south situated by the river downstream from Avignon's ruined bridge. It was the summer residence of a distant cousin of the royal family and had been put at the full disposal of the Council, with all its attending servants given leave for several weeks and replaced by Ball functionaries so that a necessary veil of secrecy could be drawn on what would happen there.

It was both sufficiently isolated and opulent, its grounds bordered by high walls crawling with vines and other hot-weather vegetation, that the influx of visitors, performers, guests and set-up workers would not be unduly noticed in the nearby town during the course of the necessary preparations for the big night.

Some months ahead, Oriole had been brought to Avignon and installed in the house of Ball sympathisers, a stone's throw from the imposing bulk of the Palais des Papes, and her training and grooming had intensified in preparation for the night of the autumn equinox when, as part of its annual ritual immemorially set on a day when day and night were the same length, the Ball would take place.

The legend persisted to this day that this tradition went all the way back to ancient Egypt and the times of Cleopatra, but no one now involved with it truly knew the origins of the Ball, whether it had begun as a religious ritual initiated by rogue priests in one of the many temples scattered across the deserts or as a heathen, pagan celebration of quite another nature.

Whenever Oriole was not being prepared for the Ball, she spent her free time embroidering or playing the harpsichord. In both of these enterprises, she had countless instructors, and like the shadowy, mostly silent, folk who supervised her around the house and the clock for the fateful day which was fast approaching, they were invariably masked. It was a matter of intense frustration to Oriole that none of these attendants ever allowed themselves to grow close to her in any way, beyond the essential communication of instruction, advice and education. She felt lonely, her childhood and the whole life she had enjoyed before she had been chosen fading into distant memories.

From the day of her arrival here she had been ordered always to dress in her best finery; heavy dresses with elaborate embroidery and gold stitching, tight corsets seizing her waist in a vice and forcing her to stand straight at all times, even at leisure. Her hair fell across her shoulders in a shower of gold ringlets which took the servants hours every morning to arrange after the hundred and more strokes of the brush she swept through her hair before she went to bed the previous evenings.

It was as if she was constantly on show, about to be presented at court. The tight leather ankle boots she also had to wear on a permanent basis were an inconvenience, elegant but uncomfortable. There were days when, if left to her own devices, she would have so much preferred to gambol around on bare feet, her tall, elongated frame liberated from all its restrictions, her slight breasts unconfined.

Why would they not answer all the insidious questions that were nagging at her mind? Why had her parents consented to the whole enterprise and delivered her into the hands of the Ball's attendants?

Her nights were full of strange and disturbing dreams the shape of which she had never experienced before, as if something in the food or drink she was being given was manipulating her thoughts, directing them into new, previously unfathomable directions. Oriole would wake in the early hours of morning, sweat still wetting the collar of her nightshirt, images of ice, fire and raging suns still bright in her mind, her thoughts running frantically in circles, losing contact with the comfort of reality.

But there was seldom time enough to catch her breath or dwell on the images and swirls of terror of the night, before the morning attendants would invariably enter her chamber and wordlessly pull the covers away, undress her, bath her, feed her, dress her in her now customary uniforms of gold and silk, billowing folds and delicate white stockings that reached to halfway up her creamy thighs, and escort her to the rooms where the training took place. And she had to concentrate again on every element of the ritual.

And day followed day.

Until the equinox.

Oriole had lost all sense of time and when she woke up that morning, her initial surprise was that it had unexpectedly proven a night empty of dreams, a welcome oasis of peace. She opened her eyes, squinted at the sunlight rushing through the half-open windows, realising someone had already pulled the heavy curtains apart. A shadow briefly obscured the light and her vision sharpened. The Matron, head of all the other attendants. Dressed in all her finery.

'The day has come,' the Matron said. 'You must do us proud.'

Oriole blinked.

'We've been told that the Marquis himself has designed this year's ceremonial ritual. It's a great honour,' she continued.

Oriole had vaguely heard rumours of the Marquis. Not all favourable. Many said he was twisted and perverse.

'Rise.'

The bed covers were pulled away and Oriole's skin felt the clean caress of the morning breeze as it wound its way through the windows and awakened her senses. The sky outside was unbroken blue. She shivered briefly.

Under the gaze of the Matron and the masked attendants, she inelegantly crawled out of the bed. The moment she was on her feet, the silent women surrounded her and tugged at her night gown as she raised her hands to the ceiling to facilitate its removal.

She was led, naked, out of the door into the adjoining chamber where the copper bathtub stood at the centre of the room, coils of steam rising upward from its hot, perfumed contents. She carefully dipped a toe and tested that the heat was just on the right edge of warm and invigorating and her two legs willingly followed. Oriole closed her eyes and, with a shudder and an intake of breath, waited for the maids to pour the cleansing water over her shoulders and let it flow across the hills and valleys of her body.

As the two expert sets of hands proceeded to soap and massage the flow of water into her bare flesh, Oriole opened her eyes and saw the Matron examining her, in judgement, appraising the firmness of her nudity and the pleasing harmony of her curves, lines and pallor.

There was a shuffle, a movement behind, her and she heard another set of steps entering the chamber. She instinctively wanted to look round to see who it might be, but the Matron's stern gaze drilled into her eyes, forbidding any attempt at movement. The stranger entered and she felt a hand cup her buttocks and then draw a line from the tip of her shoulders all the way down to the thin alley that parted her cheeks. Like a merchant assessing his merchandise. It must be a man's hand. He coughed approvingly and turned her to face him as the maids wiped the final layer of soap away. It was her uncle, the man who had been appointed her custodian after her selection.

Oriole was shocked and briefly panicked, wanting to shield her breasts and sex from his view, but she knew that the regulations prohibited her from concealing any part of her nudity. She felt her face redden and a knot in her stomach clench.

Her uncle now stood next to the Matron, both of them watching her intently, silently, an ambiguous smile spreading across his thin lips. He wore his best wig and his military uniform, with the medals from the Spanish campaign.

The servants proceeded to dry her and she stood frozen under the steady, impersonal examination. Satisfied by her appearance, both her current guardians suddenly walked out, leaving her in the care of the busy maids who now proceeded to powder her body from neck to bottom, until she stood like a porcelain statue, her feet still loosely gripped by the now lukewarm water at the bottom of the copper tub.

A nudge to her shoulder indicated she should exit the bath and return to the bedroom where she was instructed to sit on a damask-print chair, still bare-bottomed, and another set of servants, their faces partly obscured by black domino masks, proceeded to brush her hair upwards until it looked like an almighty explosion of blond curls standing like a throne above her delicate features, puffed up with the help of lotions and cream into a bee's nest of regal splendour, not unlike how the Queen, Marie-Antoinette, had appeared on that one occasion her parents had taken her to court a few years ago and she had set eyes on the monarch from half a room away.

The maids seemed to work in shifts, fine-tuning her appearance throughout the morning, layering her naked body with further white, fragrant powders until the fierce coats of snow felt like another skin, an evanescent form of clothing. She was fed rosewater syrup, but no actual food, and then they proceeded to rouge the tips of her breasts, and, after plucking her eyebrows into a perfect accent, the women then moved down to her sex and carefully shaped and trimmed the hair there.

Oriole abandoned herself to their ministrations, her mind

wandering idly as she tried to distract herself, not thinking of the night that lay ahead, banishing the occasional stab of pain seizing her with every successive pluck in that delicate area of her intimacy.

She was handed a cup of aromatic tea and ordered to drink it.

'This will help you sleep,' she was told. Something she now craved for after the hours of cleansing and preparations, her whole body now painted, shaped, every single nerve attuned, expectant, vibrating somehow.

The beverage had a curious taste, Oriole realised, as she was gently carried to the bed and quickly fell into a deep sleep.

At the back of her mind, she knew that as night fell she had been lifted from her slumber, wrapped with warm and soft cloth and transported in a carriage across a short distance. All as if in a distant dream in which she was both herself and another.

She wiped the drowsiness from her eyes.

The stone hall was immense, illuminated by a concentric ring of torches burning bright all across its perimeter, shedding a flickering light on the spectacle unfolding below. She was sprawled across a velvet-covered divan placed on one of the balconies that overlooked the vast well. As sleep methodically ebbed away, Oriole felt a sharp, tight pressure stabbing both her nipples and, a moment later, her sex. She quickly parted the diaphanous silk robe wrapped around her body and, with a jolt of shock, noticed that she had been adorned in all her sensitive parts with small dark-orange stones. Amber, she realised. At first, she feared they had been forcibly pierced into her flesh but rapidly observed with a sigh of relief that they were actually attached by sharp clips that bit painfully into the skin where it was at its most delicate. They had never warned her about this.

As her senses gradually returned – how long had she slept? – Oriole concentrated on the pain as she had been taught and it slowly morphed into an alien form of pleasure, a deep sigh of satisfaction coursing from the tip of her breasts and sex, opening all the way down through the pit of her stomach and up to her chest, then her lips, and finally her mind, sharpening each nerve end in her body. She shuddered. Then she realised, with the garment wide open, that she was fully exposed. But no one below was looking at her and she was alone on the balcony. She pulled the material together. It was almost transparent anyway, and she knew this was no occasion for modesty. She was aware that her total nudity, later, was unavoidable. The weeks of training had readied her.

Music floated upwards from the well of the stone hall.

She raised herself, sat upright and looked down as the sound of musical instruments being tuned reached her ears.

In a far corner of the hall, a stage had been set up and a string quartet sat. To Oriole's surprise, each of the musicians was quite naked. She noticed that they all wore oriental-like flat slippers to shield their feet from the cold stone floor and then realised she was wearing the same. Her attention was inevitably drawn, at a distance, to the members of the two male musicians, darker than the rest of their bodies, dangling provocatively between their thighs, but too far from her to see clearly. Oriole stretched her upper body and leaned over to see better and watched as the tuning ceased and the musicians froze into position, the female cellist with luxuriant red hair clutching her heavy instrument between her thighs.

The sounds of the music began, the melody, foreign and initially unfamiliar, slow, soothing her senses and cushioning the atmosphere with a cloak of seduction. It was nothing like the music that would normally be played at court, or in the parlours her parents frequented and sometimes took her to. It sounded slightly Oriental.

There was the muffled sound of dragging feet below and she rose from the divan and peered below the balcony. A dozen couples were shuffling their way across the floor, dancing, the women in extravagant pink skirts layered from the waist down like ruffled pyramids, the men in matching-coloured tight leggings. All wore nothing from the waist upwards aside from thin straps of material holding their garments up. Oriole drew her breath as she followed their hieratic movements, as they drew intricate patterns across the stone floor, a carefully designed geometry of courtship and ritual. One moment the couples were whirling wildly, hands, fingers making fleeting contact, and then the next they were separating and circling each other, like predators surveying their prey, almost mouth to mouth, breath to breath, before parting again. The sound of the music rose and the dance quickened.

Just then, the fog of sleep finally parted fully in Oriole's mind and she remembered what was to happen first and what her part would be.

Out of nowhere, a masked servant appeared at her side, handing her a crystal glass full of wine. She brought it to her lips. It was heavy, earthy and, as it ran down her throat, sharp and heady. Once the liquid reached her stomach, the warmth inside became like a fire brewing slightly and the background pain of the bejewelled clamps began to morph into pleasure. The servant floated away and, once again, Oriole's attention was drawn to the floor of the grand hall below.

The dancers moved languidly, but with every new phase appeared to be retreating towards the circle of the walls, leaving the centre of the hall empty.

A new woman broke through the line of the dancers and, step by step, moved to the centre of the circle they had gradually vacated. She was uncommonly tall compared to all the other dancers Oriole had been following with her gaze, covered from head to feet in a black, perilously thin silk loose gown that swam like moving water around her body, its waves shimmering with every movement she made. Once in her assigned position, she stood, her legs firmly apart, at the geometrical heart of the hall and raised her arms. Her face was lined but still incomparably beautiful, full of serenity and wisdom.

The musicians came to a halt, but stayed in place, now just spectators.

A door opened at the opposite end of the hall, which Oriole hadn't previously noticed, the darkness of the wood blending effortlessly with the texture of the stone wall. Six domino-masked servants trooped out onto the floor, escorting the imposing silhouette of a man. Even from her distant vantage point, Oriole could recognise the richness of his clothes. The gold threads, expensive materials and the sheer delicacy of the tailoring were equalled by the nobility of his bearing. He wore a crown on his veiled head, over his powdered wig. Surely this was heresy, Oriole briefly thought, only the King was allowed a crown. Then she noted the narrow crown was not made of gold or precious metal, but of wood, diminutive white flowers and leaves, like a pagan headdress, all its elements delicately woven together.

The man radiated power and strength, even though his face was concealed from view. He took position at the centre of the hall, facing the tall woman clad in black.

As he did so, Oriole saw a series of smaller doors opening, dotted across the circumference of the stone hall, and a multitude of folk streaming into the room, arranging themselves around the circle of the wall. Again, their clothes were exquisite and elaborate. She thought for a second she recognised her father and mother amongst them, but her attention was soon captured by the woman in black's movements.

Her raised arms alighted on the man's shoulders, as if blessing him, or greeting him.

On this signal, the six servants surrounded him like a shield of bodies and slowly began attending to him.

First, one of the girls stood on tiptoe and reverently picked up his crown and held it in place while another servant relieved him of the powdery white wig, and then the improvised crown was returned to his head. Throughout the operation, the veil obscuring his face was left untouched.

Yet another servant approached him and began undoing his collar and then his shirt and was succeeded by a servant who pulled it away from his body, uncovering a wool vest. A hush fell over the audience.

One of the serving women moved to face him, placing herself between the woman in black and the man and got down on her knees and applied herself to untying his breeches and ceremonially pulled them down, his immense cock springing to attention. Oriole's heart stopped and she thought she heard muffled gasps from the spectators below.

The man now stood motionless as he allowed one of the servants to pull the wool vest above his head, leaving him naked, apart from his knee-high boots polished to within an inch of shining glass in the light of the flickering torches of the hall.

Oriole swallowed. There was something both regal and animal, feral even, about the Master of Ceremonies. Her heartbeat was quickening by the minute.

The woman in black, the Mistress of the Ball, clapped her hands and the servants crept away.

She approached the man and Oriole perceived the sharp intake of the crowd's breath.

The red-haired cello player's bow initiated a languorous caress of the instrument's strings and a deep, melancholy tone filled the air.

The Mistress took the Master's cock into her hands and it hardened instantly, growing to an even more daunting size between her fingers.

Oriole could not draw her eyes away.

Then the woman in black moved closer and took the man into her mouth.

Oriole gasped.

There was a tap on her shoulder and she turned round, although her whole soul was captivated by the spectacle below and she felt she couldn't afford to miss a single moment of the ritual.

It was the Marquis. She recognised him from the small

portraits adoring the title pages of some of the books he had written, some whilst imprisoned, and which the Matron had recently instructed her to read, to complete her sexual education. They had left her both disgusted and fascinated, and overall profoundly disturbed.

He was dressed like an Italian Polichinelle, in bright colours, his outfit much too tight for his rotundity.

'Now,' he whispered. 'The time has come.'

Oriole rose. She blushed as she watched his eyes travel across her barely concealed nudity below the transparent gown.

He offered his hand to guide her, but she declined and opted to follow him.

Past the door to the balcony parapet where she had been installed, down a long, winding circular stone staircase, torches flickering like night fires along their passage, and finally reaching an oval antechamber where the Marquis left her.

'Wait here.'

Oriole stood in silence, shivered. Her ears strained for the sound of the cello, but it had faded away behind the thickness of the stone wall that now separated her from the main hall.

Finally, the door facing her opened slowly and the crowds parted and allowed her a vision of the woman in black kneeling at the feet of the man and pleasuring him with ardour and assiduity.

There was a pat on her back and Oriole advanced.

As she crossed the threshold of the room, the diaphanous silk robe she had been wearing was pulled from her and she stepped ahead, naked but for the soft slippers and the jewellery provocatively decorating her private parts.

As much as she wanted, she was unable to look anywhere but ahead, remembering all the lessons of the past months, the instructions, the reasons for the ritual, how her destiny had been revealed to her, leaving her both expectant and apprehensive.

'Now,' someone whispered behind her and the word was carried along a hundred or so lips, like a twisted choir, '*Now.*'

She had reached the couple and the Mistress stepped back, exposing the man's cock. Up close it was beautiful and fierce, dark, strong, dangerous, inviting.

Four of the male dancers she had witnessed earlier in full ceremonial movement approached her from behind as the Mistress retreated from her frame of vision, leaving only the Master, in all his splendour.

Each dancer took hold of her at the same moment, two at the shoulders and another two seizing her calves and Oriole was lifted in the air. Her legs were parted and, her face blushing like it had never done before, she realised how wet she was.

The Master moved into position and the dancers lowered her onto him.

Impaled, Oriole felt as if he had become a part of her and every muscle in her strained to embrace him. She was filled and it was unlike anything she had expected, both an invasion and a surrender. She closed her eyes, and abandoned herself to every sensation that passed through her body.

The attendants who had placed her into the initial pose of penetration let go of her and she felt the Master's hands holding her, cupping her buttocks, and he began to move inside her, methodical, relentless. She welcomed every successive thrust.

The music rose from the sorrow of the cello to a crescendo of screeching violins and the ensemble took flight on wings of melody until every note paralleled one of the Master's thrusts.

Oriole didn't know how long it lasted but eventually, a sound rose inside her and rushed to the surface and, unable to control her drowned senses, she screamed.

It was a scream of pleasure.

She was attached to the Master, his hands no longer supporting her. She wanted to faint as her orgasm tore through her, but instead she looked up at him. His veil was no longer present and his face appeared to her for the first time. It was handsome, feral, and kind.

Later, he would pull her off him and say, 'It is done, Oriole, you will be the new Mistress. But first, the Inking.'

The following year, revolution swept the land and the Ball would not return to French shores or war-torn Europe for several decades.

3

A Prick of Blood

'Is that a church?' Aurelia asked Siv as they approached the heavy timber door and Ginger pulled on the cord of an archaic bell to announce their arrival. The sound of raucous laughter and loud music was audible from the street and formed a strange juxtaposition with the sonorous clang of the brass.

'It's a converted chapel,' Ginger answered, as the door swung open. 'Cool, huh?'

'Welcome! And great costumes . . . Just what we needed,' said the man who greeted them. He was shorter than Ginger, but the exuberance of his manner took up more space than his physical body and made him seem larger in stature than he actually was. The tips of his hair were dyed a brilliant purple colour, which was barely visible through the lace cap that covered his head. He was wearing a sundress and a frilled apron, and holding a wooden spoon aloft as if it were a wizard's staff.

'Come in, come in,' he said to Aurelia with a broad smile. 'I'm the grandmother, and this is the wolf.' He gestured to a young man standing alongside him who was dressed in the least fearsome wolf costume that Aurelia could imagine; a brown felt onesie with a large oval white spot on his belly. A few tufts of dark-brown hair stuck out from the hood, which was decorated with a floppy pair of felt ears and fangs.

The wolf smiled at Aurelia, displaying a pair of incisors that were infinitesimally longer than his other teeth, a fact that was more noticeable as his hood obscured part of the rest of his face, giving him an air of danger despite the cartoon nature of his costume.

'Wow,' Siv said, 'you really do have very big teeth!'

'All the better to smile at you with,' the wolf replied, widening his grin even more.

Aurelia suppressed a shiver. It was cold in the chapel, and she had dressed for effect and not for comfort, in a thin white lace blouse, with a matching skirt and a light cotton red cape that fastened with a brooch around her neck but left her arms bare unless she pulled the material tightly around her body. Even then it wasn't thick enough to keep out the chill. She now regretted ignoring Siv's suggestion of slipping tights on beneath her skirt. Once the party got into its swing no one would notice who was in full costume and who wasn't, Siv had said. But Aurelia was always attentive to detail, and so she had worn bare legs with small white socks and her pale-pink ballet flats.

Siv was half naked in comparison, in her outfit of ripped brown leggings and a black bra worn beneath a denim vest that she had borrowed from Ginger and then artfully distressed despite his protestations. Her arms, calves and torso were totally exposed to the elements and yet she was not sporting so much as a single goose pimple and could easily have passed for a miniature Rambo rather than one of the Lost Boys as she intended.

'What's in your basket?' asked the wolf.

'Flowers,' Aurelia replied, lifting the lid of her god-mother's wicker picnic hamper to display a mixture of roses and tulips that she had bought from the market that morning.

The wolf bent his head down and sniffed. 'Lovely,' he said.

The flowers had crushed a little on the journey, concentrating the heady scent that wafted out so Aurelia felt as though she were carrying her own private garden.

'Do I spy another Lost Boy?' a voice interrupted. The voice came from the stairwell behind them where a young man was hanging upside down with his knees over the balustrade. He was dressed entirely in different shades of green and wore a hat on his head with a bell on the end that tinkled as he swung around the stair rail and dropped onto the floor below with a soft thud. He was barefoot and his finger and toenails were painted in vivid lime, a colour that Siv often wore.

'I'm PJ,' he said, directing his attention entirely at Siv.

'I'm Short,' Siv replied, using the nickname that Ginger still endearingly used for her.

'I'm getting a drink,' Ginger interjected, pushing his way past Peter Pan and the wolf to find the kitchen. Siv and the crowd that had gathered in the hallway to greet them followed his lead and went in search of the rest of the party.

No longer the centre of attention, Aurelia was left to explore. She tucked her basket under her arm and pushed open the door to the living room, where various other characters from Aurelia's childhood tales were reclining in all manner of poses.

The room was enormous, with a ceiling easily twice the

height of any ordinary home. It was split into the area that would have once held the congregation who came to worship, and a raised smaller area at the back that was once a pulpit but had since been filled with colourful rugs, bookshelves and a piano.

A red-haired mermaid was perched on a blue stool in the corner of the pulpit, her legs stretched out in front of her and encased in a tight diamanté sheath that glittered when it caught the light. She was resting her head on a large golden harp. The costume suited her so well that it took Aurelia a moment to notice that from the waist up she was entirely naked. Her breasts were thick and large and decorated with a silvery powder that gave her skin a fish-like appearance to match the sheen of her tail.

First Aid Kit's 'King of the World' boomed from a stereo system set into an alcove where the church organ would once have been played and added a jolly folk feel to the ambience. Three young men were dancing a jig in the room's centre. They were light on their feet and so quick and lithe that it was the sound of tapping from their steps, rather than their movement that indicated all three of them were hooved. Each of them wore curled horns on their heads that were extraordinarily thick and large in comparison with the delicacy of their facial features. In the dim light they could have passed for satyrs rather than men in costume. Aurelia crept closer to take a better look.

Suddenly a candle stuttered and started again and Aurelia jumped as a dark shade flew up the wall alongside her, before she realised that it was her own shadow. She laughed and shook her head at the fancy that had come over her. Of course the dancers must be people in costume and nothing else. This was real life and not a fairy tale. Aurelia gasped when she realised that, besides their horns, hooves and tails, all three men were fully naked.

Siv and PJ reappeared next to her, each holding a large goblet filled with a deep crimson liquid. Siv passed a spare glass to Aurelia, who took the glass and sniffed its contents suspiciously. The drink smelled like the flowers in her basket, and not like anything that she might previously have considered drinkable.

'It's some kind of syrup,' Siv said, 'made from rose petals and star anise.' She threw her head back theatrically and took a large gulp of her own glass, and then poked out her tongue as if to demonstrate that it was not poisoned. 'Isn't this amazing?' she said, waving an arm at the naked dancing men. 'It feels like the funfair, but better. We're going to do some tricks later,' she added, throwing her arm around PJ's shoulders and giving him a squeeze.

'Where's Ginger?' Aurelia asked.

'Gone to check the rigging,' she replied.

Aurelia looked up at the ceiling and whistled between her teeth. Thick ropes twisted over and under beams and rigging points, forming a complicated web.

'It's awfully high,' Aurelia remarked, drawing her brows together in worry.

'PJ will be with me, and he's an expert at this stuff, don't worry.'

'It's true,' PJ said. 'I feel safer in the air than I do on the ground.'

'Does the P stand for Peter?' Aurelia asked him.

'No,' he replied. 'Persephone. Persephone John. Percy

sounds too much like a name for a pig, so everyone calls me PJ.'

'PJ went to the circus school in San Francisco,' Siv explained. 'And he says he'll help me plan my audition.'

Aurelia looked at Siv suspiciously. She had removed her arm from PJ's shoulders, but showed all the other signs of an intense flirtation. The mohawk that she had spent hours gelling into pointy perfection had already been misplaced into a mess of tufts on her head, as she absent-mindedly ran her fingers through her hair, a habit that she developed whenever she had a crush on someone.

Siv and Aurelia had spent hours discussing the problem of what to do with Ginger since he would not be coming with them abroad. He had said that he was too afraid of flying, and Siv had taken his fear as a personal affront. If he had truly loved her, Siv said, he would have found a way to follow, even if it had involved swimming across the ocean. Perhaps now Siv was simply angry with him, or maybe the speed at which she had seemingly discarded her feelings for Ginger was just a sign of her eminent practicality. Siv was a straightforward sort of person who was unencumbered by notions of sentimentality. She simply got on with the way things were, without worrying about how they might have been.

'We're going to find somewhere to practise,' Siv said, and she took PJ by the hand and together they skipped over the stone floor to the stairwell and then disappeared from Aurelia's sight.

Aurelia took a small sip of her drink. It tasted sweet and woody. She took another mouthful. The longer she swirled each sip, the more the flavour developed on her tongue.

Before she knew it her glass was empty and she suddenly felt an urgent craving for more.

She clutched her glass tightly and prepared to cross the room to the kitchen in search of a jug of the red liquid, but the music had gathered pace and the partygoers who had previously been lounging on cushions scattered across the room were now on their feet dancing alongside the three horned men to the rhythm of a heavy drum beat that grew faster and faster with each passing moment until Aurelia felt as though she were trapped in a whirlwind of bodies rather than a party.

Even the mermaid had lost her melancholy expression and had abandoned her harp for the dance floor but, incredibly rather than dancing on her feet, she was walking on her hands with her ankles in the air, still bound together beneath the tight sheath of her tail. Her bright-red hair trailed behind her as she moved like a tongue of fire snaking across the cool grey stone floor of the chapel.

From the corner of her eye, Aurelia noticed another shadow moving in the candlelight, the only individual present who hadn't joined the dancing.

He stepped into the light.

'The suit is a bit hot for dancing,' the wolf explained. He was holding a jug of the red drink. Aurelia's throat cracked as she spoke.

'May I?' she asked.

'Of course, please.'

He filled her glass to the brim, and Aurelia dropped her head back and gulped it down. Again she was overcome by an overpowering thirst. Again he refilled her glass.

'I made this,' he said. 'It's my mother's recipe. I'm pleased you like it.'

'Yes,' she said. 'It's delicious.'

Aurelia licked her lips. The music had slowed again, and along with it, all the dancers had stopped their twirling and begun to sway in unison to the gentle but steady beat of a chant, 'Hoof and Horn', that pounded so heavily from the stereo system the beat seemed to be coming up through the floors and pouring from the ground up into her legs that were now beginning to twitch.

'Take off your shoes, you'll feel it more,' cried a girl who wore a white blouse with a bluebell-coloured full skirt overtop and a curved staff in one hand. She grabbed Aurelia by the waist and spun her around so that her red cape flew out like a sheet in the wind. The girl laughed and twirled her staff.

She too, like everyone else at the party, was barefoot. Of course, it was simply polite and commonplace to remove one's shoes before entering another's house as a visitor, so perhaps this should not have been surprising. But at all the parties Aurelia had been to, most of the other girls, particularly the shorter and the plumper ones, wore high heels. Aurelia was self-conscious of her height and preferred not to stand out when she could avoid it, so she tended to wear ballet pumps. Such a large number of bare-footed people in a room, half of them at least partially unclothed, made Aurelia feel as though she wasn't at a party at all but rather in the woods and surrounded by nymphs or other creatures who were only partially human.

'Who are you?' Aurelia asked breathlessly, as she tugged off her socks and slippers and tossed them into a corner.

'Little Bo Peep, of course,' replied the girl who continued to spin without showing any signs at all of dizziness. She was obviously naked beneath her blouse and as she moved her breasts swung like pendulums in time with the music. Her nipples were clearly visible through the sheer fabric and were a deep, rich brown, the same shade as her hair and her eyes.

Aurelia planted both feet onto the stone floor and spread her toes. As the music reverberated through her, she felt her body moving entirely of its own accord. She joined the other dancers, lifting her arms over her head and allowing whoever was nearest to take her by the waist and spin her so that her skirt flew out and her cape twisted and turned, even catching on one of the horned boys' heads and tearing, but Aurelia didn't care, so long as the music continued.

Another track came on with a faster beat and the room began to spin again and the candles flickered and the shadows on the walls grew and Aurelia began to tire and grow dizzy. Had she stopped to think about it, she would have noticed that she felt completely intoxicated, although she hadn't tasted a drop of alcohol in the rose-petal-flavoured drink. She was hot and thirsty, but the wolf had disappeared and taken his jug with him. Aurelia tried to push her way through the crowd to at least find a glass of water, but she was stuck.

She turned the other way and found herself facing a thick wooden door. Aurelia pushed it open and a bracing gust of cool night air refreshed her skin and ruffled her hair. The curls had all but fallen out now and her locks were returning to their usual resolute straightness. The wind was strong but applied a pressure to her body that she enjoyed. Ever since the night of the funfair, and the stranger's kiss, she had found the weight of the wind comforting, even when it blew in harshly from the sea as it was prone to do in Leigh.

Aurelia stepped from the back porch onto the grass. As her toes sank into the wet dew, she briefly considered returning to find her shoes but one swift glance back at the mass of hot, contorting bodies that she would need to pick her way through dissuaded her. That was if she could even remember where she had tossed them.

A sliver of moon cut a sharp arc across the sky. It was a new moon, and made the night feel young and full of possibilities.

She spied a smaller building in the distance and strode towards it to investigate. It seemed to be a replica of the chapel. An even smaller church than the first. Aurelia squinted into the dark beyond it to see if she could see another, half expecting a row of them to appear, like a series of nested Russian dolls, but behind the stone walls of this one was simply a tall wooden fence.

The church was surrounded by small trees and shrubs and, amongst the moving leaves, Aurelia could hear shuffling and scraping sounds. The noises of the night, she tried to tell herself. Nothing more than wind and hedgehogs. But she could not restrain a brief glance over her shoulder to check that she was still alone. Spectres danced all around her still, just as they had when she was inside and the shadows of the dancing partygoers had moved like a Chinese theatre across every wall. Outside in the dark, though, every movement seemed ominous to Aurelia and she quickened her step until she reached the smaller building and then pushed against the door.

She was surprised and relieved when it opened easily without so much as a rusty-hinged squeak. Aurelia fumbled for a light switch but found none, and as she groped uselessly in the dark for any sign of a lamp, she began to panic, until eventually she simply sat down on the cold stone floor with her back against a wall and curled her arms around her knees to calm herself and allow her eyes to adjust to the darkness.

The stone was cool against her feet. It had that feeling of peace that very old things do, as though the slabs that made up the floor had been there so long they had become a part of the world and were no longer wrestling to stay upright. They simply belonged.

Aurelia relaxed against the wall. Time slowed. She found that the longer she was still and silent, the more acute her senses became. She ran her hands gently over the stones beneath her and reveled in their roughness against the pads of her fingertips. She noticed that the air temperature was layered, and she basked in the occasional pockets of warmth that caressed her skin. It was as if the room was breathing, and warming her with each out-breath. The noises that she had noticed outside faded away. There was nothing besides this room and her body within it, the steady pulse of her heart in her chest and the air brushing her body. She was unusually warm, as if the heat from the dancers had ebbed into the earth and continued to warm her even though she had left the dance floor.

She became aware of the restriction of her clothing. The cape was fastened too tightly around her neck. She reached up a hand and unclipped the jewelled brooch, decorated with two cherries, that held it together. The seams of her blouse dug into her arms. Her lace skirt, which had seemed so light and delicate when she had slipped it on, in comparison to her usual denim jeans, now scratched the tops of her calves. Aurelia longed to feel the peaceful calm of the stones against all of her skin. She raised her fingertips to her throat and, one by one, slipped the buttons through their buttonholes. Each one felt like a tiny globe beneath her fingertips, round and smooth and warm. She unhooked the waist fastening of her skirt and lowered the zip, then raised her hips and pulled the fabric off at her feet. Gingerly, she lowered herself down again, noticing each minute crumb of grit as it rubbed against her buttocks.

Her legs were cramped. Aurelia was possessed by a desire to feel the stones against every part of her body. She turned and lowered herself onto her front and eased herself down, pressing her breasts against the firm grasp of the stone floor. She turned her cheek and spread her arms out in the shape of a crucifixion.

A small part of Aurelia's mind wondered how it might look to people who knew her if they were to come in and find her spread out naked on the floor. That same part of her was surprised that she hadn't thought to blush, or to hesitate as she removed her clothing and exposed herself fully to the night air. But that small voice quickly faded. Aurelia didn't care. She was comfortable lying naked on the floor. It reminded her of the long baths that she regularly took at home and in her mind she pictured lighting her tea lights. She closed her eyes and imagined the scratch of the match against the matchbox, and the sudden puff of a flame bursting into life, and the care that she took to keep that one flame alive as she lit one candle after another.

As Aurelia remembered the excitement that always overtook her as the flame hurried down the match, closer and closer to her fingertips, she noticed a similar spark within her own body, but instead of running down, it ran up. A warmth ran into her belly and between her breasts. Her small nipples hardened, but not in response to the temperature, which if anything seemed to be getting warmer. As the spark travelled to her arms and into her fingertips and down her legs and into her toes, Aurelia smiled. And she raised her right hand from the floor and squeezed her right breast, and then took her nipple between her thumb and her forefinger and pinched. Aurelia let out a soft sigh of pleasure, and allowed her hand to continue its gradual journey downwards, running between her breasts and then over the soft skin of her belly and down to the even softer folds between her legs.

She wetted her fingers and laid them back on her sex, expertly turning the pad of her finger in tiny concentric circles. As she did so, her mind began to travel, as it always did, back to the funfair, and the stranger, and his kiss. Her mouth parted and she licked her lips. The same burning thirst that had possessed her on the dance floor returned. She wriggled and pressed her body into the stone, as if she could absorb some of the damp through her skin and into her throat. Her tongue was dry and each bump of her taste buds was cracked and parched. But her cunt was flooded, as if all of the moisture in her body had travelled there. She could not recall having ever been so wet.

Hot liquid ran over her lips and down the flesh of her thighs. She dipped her finger inside her opening and then lifted it to her lips. Yet again pomegranate, as if that distinctive taste reigned over her, pursued her.

At first it was just a hint of the familiar sweetness of the juice and the bitter woody aftertaste that filled her mouth when she crunched on the seeds. Aurelia dipped two fingers inside herself and brought them to her mouth and tasted again. She was so eager to taste more that she almost gagged, pressing her fingers into her mouth all the way to her knuckles. Still the terrible thirst overwhelmed her. She added another finger, and tasted again and again, but it was as if her mouth became even drier with each taste of her own wetness.

And then, suddenly, she felt the wonderful pressure of another mouth against her own and a flood of sweet liquid trickled between her lips. She responded without thinking, thrusting her tongue eagerly into the other's mouth, seeking to quench her powerful thirst.

The mouth drew away and a finger was pressed to her lips.

'Shhh,' a voice whispered into her ear. 'There's plenty more.' A man's voice.

'It's you again,' Aurelia replied.

The sound of his words quelled every nerve in her body. It was like the feeling of being a child again, and having her godmother enter her room and pull a blanket over her to soothe a bad dream.

'Yes,' he replied. 'It's me again.'

She raised her hand to caress the line of his face, but he caught her fingers in his own and stopped her.

'Fold up your clothes,' he whispered. 'They're getting creased.'

Not a single window or even a crack beneath the door provided so much as a sliver of light for Aurelia to see by. The darkness was absolute. But she knew that she had not moved far, and her clothes were nearby, so she stretched out her arm until she felt the brush of soft cotton and stiff lace. She folded each garment into a tidy square and set them gently to the side.

'Good girl,' he said softly.

Her cape was further away, she knew, but instinctively she did not want to move away from the presence of the stranger. Near him she felt soothed and calm and she feared breaking that spell so she stretched every muscle in her body until she was able to reach the corner of her cape and then she grasped and tugged the material towards her, piercing her forefinger sharply on the clasp of her cherry brooch as she did so, breaking her skin. A bead of hot blood pooled onto her fingertip.

'Ow!' she gasped.

'Are you hurt?'

'My finger,' she said.

And then she felt the pressure of his forearm against her back, and the other beneath her knees as he scooped her into his arms and she was airborne, her head nestling against his chest. He took her bloody finger between his lips and sucked, and the warmth of his mouth took all of the pain away.

The stranger carried her through the darkness to another place. An alcove just across the room that she had not previously noticed in the darkness. Her skin touched velvet as he laid her down again. The space was narrow but filled with sumptuous fabrics and cushions and Aurelia luxuriated in the welcome feeling of softness against her skin after the roughness of the stone. She began to writhe against it, like an animal confined indoors who has been released onto the grass.

'I interrupted you,' he said. 'Please continue.'

It took Aurelia a moment to realise what he meant, but once she did, she complied immediately. It felt entirely natural to her that the stranger should sit alongside her as she masturbated. She had fantasised about that very thing almost nightly since the first time that their lips had met and she had tasted the sweetness of his mouth.

Her fingers travelled downwards and resumed their place, but this time it wasn't enough. She could hear his breathing in the dark and the warmth of his body so close to hers served only to remind her more bitterly that her hand wasn't his.

'Help me,' she whispered.

He lifted his hand to her mouth and gently inserted his finger between her lips. She began to suck. He removed his finger and then trailed downward, following the path that she had traced earlier. He cupped her breasts, squeezing one nipple and then the other. The stranger twisted harder than Aurelia had, and she gasped, and then moaned, as a sharp jolt of pain bloomed in each breast and then faded into warmth.

As he stroked her belly, he grabbed a handful of her flesh in his fingers and Aurelia lifted up her buttocks and pressed herself against his open palm. She spread her legs open wider and groaned, hoping that he would hurry up and push something inside her because if she had to wait any longer she felt that the waiting might actually kill her. Death would begin with the disintegration of her mind and would be followed by her body shattering into pieces, no longer able to sustain the storm of desire he had unleashed that now raged so powerfully within her she felt as though she might break like a wave crashing upon the shore of his body.

Aurelia groaned when he merely brushed his fingertips over her mound and did not travel any lower. She clawed at the surface beneath her and grasped handfuls of the fabrics that she lay on and gripped and pulled in an effort to release the tension that continued to fill her. Then she took hold of his head in her hands, and drew him against her, pulling his mouth to her own. She touched his face, tugged at the stiff collar of his shirt so that she could reach his shoulders, wrestled his buttons through their buttonholes with shaking fingers so that she could run her hands over the muscles of his back. He briefly pulled away and she heard the rustling of cotton and denim as he quickly disrobed and tossed his clothing aside.

'Oh, Aurelia,' he said. His voice cracked with sadness. He held himself above her, far enough so that their skin did not touch unless Aurelia raised herself to meet him, but close enough so that she could feel every hair on his body. She felt like asking 'How do you know my name?' but even that thought quickly faded as she abandoned herself to the moment.

'More,' she replied. It was now an effort for her to articulate any words at all. She simply wrapped her hands firmly around his neck and raised her head and parted her lips and again he pressed his mouth to hers and released the sweet liquid that quenched her burning thirst.

But it was not enough. Aurelia felt instinctively that nothing would ever be enough, could ever fill her enough besides the body of this man inside her. Her need for him was violent, and she knew it was irrational. She wanted to tear at his skin and feel him tearing at hers until they could crawl into each other and never be parted.

Instead she positioned herself below him, shuffling down and exploring his body with her hands until she gripped the firmness of his buttocks and then the hardness of his cock. It was the first time that Aurelia had ever felt one and she was momentarily surprised by the softness and silkiness of its skin. He moaned as she ran her hand over his shaft, investigating each crevice and furrow and then gently squeezing his balls, enjoying the warmth and weight as they rested in the palm of her hand.

The stranger bowed his head and kissed her and at the same moment she arched her back and pulled him towards her by the hips until he slid inside her and their bodies joined. They rocked together in perpetual motion, but it was still not enough for Aurelia. She hissed with the pain of his first entry, but with the sting came the wonderful and overwhelming sensation that he was inside her at last and filling not just her body but also her heart and her mind. And her soul.

How was it possible that two people who barely knew each other at all – had never even once made eye contact – could be so physically at home with each other? Mentally she knew that the whole thing was downright crazy. But her body sensed instinctively that she and the stranger were two pieces of one jigsaw puzzle and they fitted together as if they had never been apart, as if each of them could only be whole when connected to the other.

And then her mind went blank, as the stranger placed one hand on either side of her hips and unceremoniously flipped her over. He covered her body with his own. He was so much larger than she was. His thighs were thick and his shoulders broad and when he pressed his torso against her back and pulled back her hair and nestled his jaw against her shoulder, she felt cocooned in his presence, as if the earth had stopped moving on its axis and nothing existed besides this moment that contained them and their two bodies moving in unison.

Her cheek was wet. She flicked out her tongue and tasted salt.

'Why are you crying?' she asked him.

'Because I want to see you. But it has to be this way,' he replied.

'Then feel me,' Aurelia said to him, as she struggled to slip her hand beneath the combined weight of their bodies to guide him inside her again.

The stranger drew back onto his knees and raised Aurelia up with him so that she was resting on all fours. He threw his weight behind his first thrust as if he were trying to drill all the way through her.

Aurelia cried out in shock and then with joy as the violence of his motion satisfied her craving to be owned by him, filled by him, joined with him, part of him. She pushed herself up with her hands so that she could press back and feel him even deeper inside her, but in one swift motion he caught her wrists and pinned her arms behind her back. With his other hand he caught her before she fell and so Aurelia found herself balanced in his hands and on his cock. She allowed her body to surrender, knowing that she was entirely at the mercy of his movements, but also utterly safe with him. He would not allow her to fall, and neither would he thrust too hard. She could not imagine any movement that could possibly be unpleasant or too much for her. Even if he somehow managed to split her in two, it would not be deep or hard enough.

He took a length of her hair and twisted it around his wrist, pressing her forward into the cushions with one hand as he raised her head with the other so that her body stretched like an archer's bow. His other hand slipped down to her neck and he encircled her throat. Aurelia pressed herself against him, allowing him to clasp her, basking in this expression of her vulnerability and her total surrender to him. *Take me* she wanted to cry out. *Own me, use me, I am yours*, she thought, but fearing that speaking would break the spell of their bodies in speechless and instinctive communion she kept silent, just allowing herself a murmur, a low groan of pleasure escaping between her lips.

When he lifted his hand from her throat she felt as though he had removed his hand from her heart. It was more than a caress when he touched her there like that. It was a gesture of giving and of taking, of safety and of violence, of belonging and of ownership, of surrender and of dominance.

Then his touch snaked lower, and Aurelia's momentary grief was overtaken by new and immensely pleasurable sensations. He had wrapped his arm around her and pulled her back against him so that she could lean on his chest as he squeezed her breasts and then stroked her stomach and then his hand slid further south.

As he slipped his finger into her opening, they moaned together, he at the wonderful sensation of her fiery warmth and she at the sheer joy of feeling him inside her again. He moved upwards until he found her clitoris and he began to pleasure her in just the same way that she pleasured herself, brushing his finger around and around in perfect rhythm. He hugged Aurelia so tightly that she could feel his heart beating against her back, faster and faster in time with the motion of his other hand against her sex until suddenly she cried out and collapsed back against him, overwhelmed by the release of her orgasm.

Aurelia's eyes slid closed and she breathed out a sigh of

happiness as the stranger lifted her up and cradled her in his arms. He kissed her forehead gently and smoothed back the stray tendrils of hair that clung to her face. She felt his thigh muscles clench briefly and it occurred to her that the stranger had still not enjoyed the pleasure of his own release. But he did not seem to mind, and Aurelia drifted into a heavy slumber in his arms, enjoying the luxury of peaceful dreams free from the dark shadows that had plagued her thoughts ever since his lips had first touched hers at the funfair.

He held her tight until the night became dawn.

At the first sign of daybreak, the stranger pressed his lips against the smooth mound of Aurelia's cunt and the mark of his visit that had appeared as she slept and would change her for ever, although it would be some time before she knew it. He kissed her mouth once more.

And then he left.

'Aurelia! Aurelia!' cried Siv. Her friend groaned, fluttered her eyelids for the briefest of moments and then fell back into sleep.

Siv took hold of Aurelia's shoulders and shook her. Hard.

'Aurelia!' she shouted again. 'Ginger took off with the fun-fair crowd. He's not coming back. And I don't want to hang around here all day. There's a train in half an hour . . .'

Aurelia woke with a start.

'Hello?' she mumbled. She brought her fingers to her lips and felt the ghost of another mouth on her own. 'Are you there?' Aurelia asked in a daze.

'Of course I'm here, you silly bint! Whatever has come over you? Let's go. Now.' Siv shook her again. 'And for

God's sake put your clothes on before you catch your death of cold.'

Aurelia hastily crossed her arms over her breasts. She shook her head briefly to clear the cobwebs from her mind.

'I had the strangest dream . . .' she said. Her eyes darted around the room, taking stock of her surroundings. She could barely remember arriving in the strange stone church, never mind falling asleep here without so much as a cushion or a covering to keep her warm.

Her eyes landed upon her white blouse and skirt, which were folded neatly and tucked into the corner. She drew her brows together in a gesture of concentration, flipping through her memories like a Rolodex, but striving to grasp the memory of undressing was like snatching at a puff of smoke. The harder she tried to remember, the more the memory eluded her. She stood up and hastily slipped her clothes back on again, pausing when she noticed a darker speck of red on her previously pristine cape. Then she spied the open point of her cherry brooch, and her finger began to throb.

Had she raised her eyes, she might have noticed the alcove in which she had lain with the stranger and the single white rose that he had left there for her, its pale petals in stark contrast to the dark red and purple velvets and cushions that had supported their lovemaking, not that either of them had needed the comfort of fabric when locked in the embrace of the other.

But Aurelia didn't notice. She quickly gathered up her things and hurried with Siv to the station, leaving the cold stone walls and her memories behind her.

4

The New World

A gentle wind was rising in the bay, dragging grey clouds along in its invisible wake, an initial taste of autumn, or fall as they preferred to call it here.

Aurelia had expected California to be an eternally sunny place and now realised how little she had prepared for this venture overseas. San Francisco's climate, so far, had proven more European than tropical. She felt angry with herself for not having done any research once the subject had arisen in conversation with Siv and they had hastily decided on northern California. Whose idea had it been anyway? If she'd been seeking rain and dull, damp mornings, they could have travelled to London instead, or stayed home, surely?

Even though she had been born in the USA, Aurelia had been shipped back to her godparents in England following the death of her parents and this was the first time since then that she had been back there. Siv had visited New York and Florida for vacations, but neither of them had been to the West Coast and their prior knowledge had been distorted by the intake of too many films and TV shows.

They'd arrived a week ago at night and the city had already been in darkness. The cab drive to Oakland had seemed to take an eternity and, as the car had driven across the bridge, both the hills ahead and the peninsula behind had been enveloped in a foggy shroud through which barely a constellation of distant lights could be seen. This had proven particularly disorienting after the endless flight, and by the time they reached the sprawling cottage that would be their new home with its front lawn cut into a perfect handkerchief, they were in no mood to make conversation.

Edyta, the old woman who ran a small ballet school from the building where they would be boarding, had met them at the door. She was long and lean like a grasshopper, her dance training still evident in her bearing.

Ginger had helped arrange their accommodation through his connections as a parting gift to Siv. He claimed to have no idea of Edyta's age and Siv and Aurelia didn't dare ask, but suspected that she was probably in her seventies, though she might have been older and particularly well kept.

Siv and Ginger had sworn to keep in touch with each other, although Aurelia sensed the relationship would now come to an inevitable end as a result of their move to America.

A cream silk robe with a floral pattern was wrapped tightly around Edyta's body and her feet were tucked into bright-red slippers. She wore a little gloss on her lips and her grey hair was cut into a short bob, coloured with a faint lilac tint and tucked neatly behind her ears. Her earlobes were long and hung even lower due to the weight of a pair of heavy ruby stud earrings.

She showed them straight to their bedrooms, all white walls and sparsely furnished in frugal but elegant clean lines, and pointed out the shower and the kettle and other necessities before allowing them to crash into bed and sleep off the stresses of the journey.

On the following day they had an opportunity to explore

the cottage and learn what their duties would be. Aurelia, even though she was relying on her windfall to cover her board, had volunteered to assist with some of the paperwork one afternoon per week for the sake of gaining work experience and Siv, who was working for her room and suppers, would be tutoring dance lessons every weekday afternoon and helping with keeping the cottage clean. They were given a whole week off to settle in before beginning their chores.

That initial week had proven a blur and Aurelia had journeyed through it in a daze. She knew it was not only jetlag or the unsettling feeling a new environment often causes. As she adapted to the new house, the new city, the new country, juggled the accents, the curious customs, the layout of the local streets and nearby convenience stores, together with the strange state of being that a separation from home seemed to cause, she was conscious of the fact she was only partly here. Half of her mind, and maybe even all of her body – in a challenge to the laws of physical reality – was still back in Bristol, naked on the stone cold floor in the early hours of a bleak, coastal morning.

Her fugue on awakening and the strange stupor that had initially overtaken her mind when Siv had found her and she had hurriedly dressed and they had rushed to Temple Meads train station had gradually lifted over the days following the party in Bristol. Ginger had decided to stay on as his next job was in Wales.

Then Aurelia began to remember. At first, her memories were not like memories at all but rather brief flashes of feeling and of emotion so acute and so real that it seemed as if she had been transported straight back to the stone church, as if moments from that night had somehow been frozen in time and she was replaying them at random and sometimes totally inappropriate intervals. There would be occasions when she was walking down the street with brown paper bags full of shopping and her mind totally distracted thinking of the most banal of activities and suddenly she would feel the stranger's hot breath on her cheek and taste his mouth on hers and feel the pressure of his fingertips caressing her clitoris and she would be almost overcome by great crashing waves of desire so strong that she needed to pause in her step, lower her bags of groceries to the pavement and stand still and breathe until it passed and she was able to continue.

But gradually the events of that night had arranged themselves in an orderly fashion in her mind, although she still had no idea who he was or what it all meant and this time she had not shared her experience with Siv. It felt too private. And altogether too confusing and crazy to explain to another, even her best friend.

There were moments when Aurelia wondered if she had lost her mind entirely. But no matter how much she struggled to apply a modicum of logic and rational thinking to her emotions, Aurelia could not argue away the fact that every thought of him was accompanied by the twin sensations of arousal and safety. Whatever had happened that night, she knew that she had been safe – protected, even – in the stranger's arms.

Other things had got in the way, though, and she had been forced to put all of her questions, thoughts and desires on hold as they had rushed to organise their trip to America. It had been like a film in fast forward: the packing, the last-minute details, the emotional farewells and then the mini cab to Gatwick and the plane to San Francisco. As if the rest of her life had conspired to prevent her thinking about the night and the stranger and her deflowering until now.

Today was their final day of freedom before Siv began working for her keep and they would both start their new lives in San Francisco properly, as bona fide residents rather than visitors.

Aurelia looked down at her finger. There was no longer any mark there where she had pierced herself with the sharp pin of her brooch and there was, of course, no outward sign of the comfort that he had given her when she had briefly cried out in pain, or the press of his lips on her injured skin.

The mark inside her, however, was still present. Indelible. One she would cherish for ever.

The wonderful stranger.

His touch.

His caresses.

The way he had made love to her. How her untrained body had so effortlessly blended with his. And the emptiness that she had felt that morning when she awoke so acutely aware of his absence before she had even remembered he had ever been there at all.

Aurelia heard the slamming of the front door, and checked her bedside clock. It was still only seven in the morning. She sighed, remembering with an undertow of irritation that Siv had to go into the city to pick up the obligatory application forms for the upcoming circus school audition and to get her original documents photocopied. She followed the sound of her friend's steps as she ran down the road to catch the municipal bus.

She stretched, her limbs lazily unfurling from the broken angles of sleep under the crisp bed covers, her toes grazing the end of the quilt, and exhaled loudly in the knowledge she was now alone in the house. This was the first occasion since their arrival that she and Siv had been apart. And as much as she enjoyed spending time with her friend, Aurelia now welcomed the opportunity to laze about with no particular task in mind and spend some time on her own.

Not that there weren't things to do. She had promised to send a long email to her godparents in Leigh-on-Sea to let them know all was well, but somehow she couldn't summon the energy even to pull her iPad from her luggage, where it still rested alongside most of the clothes she had not yet bothered to hang up in her bedroom closet. There was washing to do, and shopping at the local mall as the provisions they had hastily stocked up on at the corner convenience store on their first day were running low, but nothing that couldn't wait.

Aurelia closed her eyes and allowed her stiff muscles to relax. One part of her mind was prompting her just to remain in bed and do nothing while the other, more responsible half, was studiously making to-do lists.

Anyway, this was no civilised time to get up. Much too early, she concluded.

She kept her eyes shut, although the light streaming through the curtains created a white background to the screen formed by her eyelids and a constant distraction.

The scattered sounds of birds welcoming the morning outside reached her at irregular intervals, somehow evoking long half-forgotten memories she couldn't quite identify, like a form of Morse code that only her DNA could interpret. Finally, she couldn't resist and peered slowly at the corner of sky visible through the window. A greyish blue, uncertain colour.

And knew she wouldn't be able to get back to sleep now.

She swore under her breath and pushed the quilt to the side. Against her will, she was now wide awake and feeling a hollow pang in her stomach. Slipping sideways out of the bed, she walked barefoot to the kitchen. The old promotional rock 'n' roll T-shirt advertising an Arcade Fire European tour that she had been wearing in bed, along with a pair of cotton knickers, barely reached her midriff and Aurelia shivered. It was chilly and the stains of blue in the sky beyond the windows conveyed a false impression of warmth. Siv had left a jar of peanut butter on the table and she grabbed hold of it and rushed back to the comfort of her bed. Then realised she hadn't taken a spoon. Dammit, her fingers would have to do. She dived between the covers holding the glass container aloft.

Ten minutes later, licking her fingers clean, Aurelia dropped the now half-empty jar on the bedside table and screwed its plastic lid on. Again she considered getting up and beginning her chores or arranging some kind of touristic activity, but it was just too early in the day and the multitude of available possibilities offered her too many choices.

Instead, she turned over and buried her face into the warm softness of the pillow and welcomed darkness in the comfort of the material. Her arms were still uncovered and she pulled up the blanket and was now left with a decision to either lay her limbs over the top or tuck them under the cover alongside her body where the heat was now captured. She opted for the latter.

Her fingers were flattened against her inner thighs as she adjusted her position for a maximum of comfort.

A nail grazed the skin of her thigh in passing and Aurelia shuddered, her memory flooding with images and feelings as if a box of secrets had just been opened.

The stranger's touch.

The way his fingers had moved across her skin, sometimes soft and sometimes firm.

How he had made her his on that mad evening that was still imprinted on her mind like an incomprehensible hieroglyph.

A whirlpool of emotions stirred inside her and she retreated into her private world, blanking the room, the faint noises reaching her through the window, transporting herself away on wings of deliberate magic from the Oakland suburb to a dark vaulted space in Bristol, seeking with increasing hunger to recreate every single movement that had passed between them, the smells, the touches, the contact, the static.

She licked her lips. And again she tasted pomegranate.

As if the delicate and fleeting echoes of the fruit had been conjured out of nowhere by the force of her will, her yearning.

Her heart jumped and she moved a finger nearer to her sex.

Her eyes still closed shut, she tried to imagine her fingers were his and he was again exploring her, travelling like an intrepid pioneer of unknown lands across the pale plains of her flesh, approaching the fire, the volcano, that defined her sexual heart. How had it felt to him?

The finger inched its way towards her opening, the heat radiating towards it, reaching it by infinitesimal increments, every hesitation a further degree upwards, an extra step towards the subterranean blaze that kept her alive, feeding the internal engine that regulated her senses.

She arched her back, deliberately slowed her movement. Patient, delaying the inevitable.

But there was so little ground over which her finger could drag itself without coming to a total stop and, all too soon, as Aurelia attempted to prolong the expectation, explore the apprehension, expand time to new proportions, the finger made contact with her lips.

She was wet, her body responding of its own volition to the complex feelings rushing around in circles in her mind.

The moistness of the labia she brushed against was velvety soft and, for a brief moment, Aurelia pretended she was blind and imagined a whole world she would only ever perceive through the nerve endings on the tip of her fingers, a new universe in which one only survived by the power of touch.

The probing finger dipped inside her – as his once had – weighing her, mapping her, now immersed fully in her raging heat, wrapped in the fiery blanket of her lust. When the stranger had similarly been inside her, Aurelia couldn't help wondering what it had felt to him to be gripped by such transcendent heat and wished she could once be a man, if only for a day, just to know.

The temptation to introduce another finger was all-encompassing, but it was not the way she preferred to fulfil her pleasure. She retreated and turned over onto her back. Parting her legs wide, her right arm now leveraged into position, her forefinger found the hardened nub of her clit and began a rough symphony of concentric caresses while her free fingers dipped smoothly between her damp lips, their slight movements in studied, clever harmony.

She took a deep breath, all the time watching behind her eyelids a confused movie in which memories of that night in Bristol blended with elements of dreams and nightmares and nothing and no one was quite clear enough to recognise, plunging in and out of focus. Fuck, if only it hadn't been so dark, then she might have remembered more about it all, the details of his face, the colour of his eyes, every line and crevice and blemish on his skin, and not just his voice, his smell, and the mechanics of the sex they had shared, however wonderful it had been.

The tectonic plates of her lust began to move, silently, inside her, subtle shifts in her equilibrium, as her cravings and her emptiness met on an upward path that zigzagged between her heart and brain and Aurelia now abandoned herself fully to the rise of the powerful sensations that had now taken hold of her whole body and mind.

She was melting into the bed, drowning on a sea of acceptance, primed for the terrible explosion that would blow her whole being apart, sunder her into a million pieces for the briefest of moments, a state of blissful nothingness during which life collided with death before the scattered clusters of her soul came back together again and she could breathe anew.

Yes, just another microscopic movement and she would be there. Reaching utter blankness and joy, Aurelia held her breath, every single sense following the progress of the mighty tide as it washed through her body and reached its culmination.

Yes.

Her back arched as if she had been stabbed, and then she fell back, her long auburn hair settling like a shroud against the pillow, like a crown of sun around her flushed, ecstatic face.

Yes.

She breathed again, feeling the lightness spread along her limbs, her mind clear, her body relax.

Aurelia sighed.

She had never felt an orgasm so strongly before.

Could it be because she had now been made love to by a man, that man, the stranger? Had it elevated the power of her orgasm to another level? Or was it just the craving for him that now filled her night and day and the way it blended uneasily with the memories that night?

Once again, her mind was all over the place.

'I think too much,' she concluded. Why couldn't she just enjoy the moment?

As she lay sprawled out on the bed for what seemed like ages, Aurelia basked in the inner glow the orgasm had triggered, both welcoming and fighting the sensations, left breathless by the sheer strength of the sexual seizure and struggling with the deep well of the yearning for the name-less man who had unwittingly caused it, or at any rate, multiplied the intensity of the moment to a factor of in-finity.

She tried unsuccessfully to censor her thoughts and return to reality.

Through the window, against the roof of the sky, she could see that blue was winning the battle against grey and the room was now beginning to feel warmer.

She needed a shower. Or she would fall asleep again and waste most of the day lingering in the comfort of the bed.

She stretched her legs and slipped a foot out from the quilt. Her toes tingled. The ends of her fingers too. Her body was suffused with lightness as she stepped towards the bathroom, her bare feet shuffling across the cottage's wooden floor.

Splashing cold water against her face as she leaned over the cracked porcelain of the sink in the exiguous bathroom, Aurelia felt her mind revive although all her nerve endings still buzzed with uncommon energy. She turned on the shower tap, testing the gushing cascade that poured from the showerhead until it was the right temperature and would neither freeze her nor scald her and turned, pulling her T-shirt above her head and letting it fall to the tiled floor and stepping out of her knickers. As she did so and was about to step under the water, she caught a brief glimpse of her pale, elongated body in the tall mirror covering the inside of the bathroom door.

She noticed with the faintest of smiles that her dark-pink nipples were still hard and how her orgasmic flush continued to linger, spreading its pastel colours across the top of her chest.

She moved to dive under the shower's flow and then did a double take. Something had caught her eye. She moved back an inch and looked at her body and its sinuous, pale length reflected in the bathroom mirror. A touch of colour. She looked down. Squinted as the steam from the shower was rising in the small space and the glass was beginning to mist up.

A bruise? A stain?

An indistinct shape just half a finger's length away from her opening.

Aurelia instinctively passed her fingers over the area, as if expecting mild pain. She didn't recall having recently hurt herself there or having bumped into a sharp corner of furniture or anything. There was no sensation.

She reached for the shower controls and interrupted the water and, with the back of her hand, wiped the surface of the mirror clean to get a better view of the small image that now stood out on her skin in such an intimate place, her puzzlement tempered with rising fear.

A fine red shape.

The mirror came into focus.

The image of a small heart.

Her breath halted.

Her body was now barely an inch from the mirror and as she looked down at her pelvic area, there was no longer any doubt. It was a minuscule heart, shrouded by thin tendrils of fire in the same sharp shade of red.

Her real heart was beating out of control in her chest.

A tattoo?

Impossible.

She looked again, her gaze fully captured by the small heart etched into her skin.

She passed a couple of fingers over it, as if half-hoping its texture might prove different from the rest of her uncovered flesh, to prove it was artificial, temporary, a mistake. But it felt no different, fully a part of her.

A fake? A joke somehow organised by Siv, while she was sleeping? But Siv wouldn't do something like that in such an intimate place, surely?

She soaped her fingers and aggressively rubbed against the newly formed heart. It didn't budge.

Aurelia stood there, naked, no longer aware of her surroundings, her mind in a daze.

All she could think of was the stranger and the way she had fallen asleep against him after they had made love. Passed out? Surely she hadn't. And she would certainly have roused again. Tattoos were painful and the equipment must be noisy. She could not have slept through such a thing. Could she?

It couldn't have happened then. It was impossible.

Because she knew for certain the flaming heart had not been there after Bristol: she remembered how, the following day back at home, she had examined her body in every single detail, as if trying to check if she was still the same person now she had been fully penetrated by a man, almost wishing to look different. And then, once in Oakland on the previous days when she had showered and routinely shaved her pubic hair with care and precision to ensure that she did not cut herself there had been nothing to see. No heart. How could it appear out of nowhere?

For a moment Aurelia felt short of breath.

How could a tattoo just appear on her body? She was far more open minded than Siv when it came to matters of tarot-readers, fortune-tellers and the existence of ghosts and guardian angels, and she often dreamed there was magic in this world she was living in. But not this sort.

She looked down again at her pubis and its now faintly illustrated landscape.

The red of the heart was almost scarlet, but its fierce shade was in perfect harmony with the pallor of her skin. The combination was like strawberries and cream, fire and ice. A tell-tale miniature heart, exquisitely chiselled across her skin. Again she touched it. It was painless, as if it wasn't there.

Aurelia sighed. Nothing made sense.

She ran back to her bedroom, and snuggled between the sheets and the quilt, as if seeking refuge, her mind pouring over every single possibility, however fantastical it might be, until the sheer process of thinking in circles, in a maddening loop, exhausted her and she fell asleep for a few hours, comforted by the warmth and softness of the bed.

It was almost midday when she woke up. Her initial reaction was to pull the covers away and quickly look at the red heart.

She felt faint: it was no longer there. The area of skin where she had witnessed it was now pure as snow, the customary porcelain white of her body.

Aurelia knew she wasn't crazy. It had been there. It hadn't been a dream.

And now it was gone.

A wind of panic swept over her. And with it, the faint smell of fruit in the room. Like a leitmotiv evoking the man in Bristol and the taste of his lips.

She resisted the impulse for a few minutes but the smell, the taste persisted, somewhere at the back of her brain rather than on her lips, and she allowed her hand to move down and willed her fingers to begin caressing her again.

After she came, her mind shattered anew by the unholy strength of the sensation, she couldn't help looking down at the bottom half of her body again.

The blazing heart had reappeared.

In response to her lust.

Aurelia spent the rest of the early afternoon curled up in bed waiting for Siv to return home. As crazy as she knew the whole story would sound, she had to tell someone.

Every one of her senses strained to hear Siv's familiar footfall and the tinkle of the bell that rang when the front door opened or closed to alert anyone in the cottage to a visitor.

Her eyes kept darting to her bedside clock, but it seemed that the more often she checked how many minutes or hours had passed since her last glance, the slower that time travelled. It had been hours now. Surely Siv couldn't still be collecting her audition forms? Perhaps she had decided to catch the tourist boat to Alcatraz as she had talked about doing.

Every few minutes Aurelia would lift the covers and examine herself again. The tattoo had now disappeared and her skin had resumed its usual appearance. Through a process of elimination she was now certain that the tattoo appeared when she orgasmed. But it was not as simple as that. After she had come and noticed the tattoo for the second time she had tried again, but this time her thoughts and actions were perfunctory. She deliberately cleared her mind of the stranger, switched on her iPad and searched for the most banal pornographic clip that she could find and then touched herself in a manner that she knew would fulfil her most basic needs quickly and efficiently but nothing more.

The tattoo did not appear.

She tried once more. This time she deliberately summoned every memory she had of that night. His scent. His touch. The roughness of the stones beneath her fingertips when her hands had accidentally grazed the floor, seeking the satisfaction of their mutual passion and uncaring of physical discomfort. She touched herself the way his hands had roamed across her skin and allowed her mind to travel back to that room. Her fantasy was so lifelike it felt almost real, as though he were there in her room in leafy Oakland, or a shade of him at least. With one hand under the covers engaged in seeking pleasure, her other hand lifted without thinking, searching for the contours of his cheek, his hair, his jaw, but she reached nothing but air.

Again she came with her thoughts full of him and her body wracked by contractions so fierce she shook the bed. Aurelia lay still, basking in the aftershocks as she waited for the final waves of lust to crash over her and subside.

Then she remembered the tattoo. Tore off the covers. Again it was there, more vivid than ever before.

She carefully arranged her limbs into the least pornographic pose that she could manage and took a picture of the tattoo on her phone with the lens zoomed in for modesty's sake, so only a patch of her skin that might have been anywhere on her body and the red heart with its fiery tendrils were visible in the snapshot.

Then she watched it fade. First each of the vine-like coils

that snaked out like the rays of a miniature sun receded, and then the heart itself gradually turned paler until it was gone altogether. It was like watching a flower close its petals in fast forward motion.

Despite her fear and confusion at the sheer madness of it all and what it might mean, Aurelia could not suppress a brief smile of satisfaction.

He had left a mark on her after all, and not just on her mind and soul.

The front door bell tolling Siv's arrival pulled Aurelia out of her reverie. Though she had spent all afternoon clock-watching and waiting for her return, now that her friend was back Aurelia realised that she still didn't have the faintest clue how she would even begin to explain what had happened.

Aurelia waited for Siv to burst into her bedroom and regale her with all her news of the day, but Siv wandered straight by without so much as a tap on her bedroom door to see if she was in.

Aurelia threw back the covers with a disgruntled huff and followed the sound of Siv's footsteps into the kitchen, where she found Siv standing in front of the open fridge door and drinking milk straight from the carton.

'We all have to use that, you know,' Aurelia complained.

Siv pulled the carton away from her lips and wiped the milk moustache from her mouth with the back of her hand.

'Wow, someone got out of the wrong side of the bed today,' Siv replied, purposefully taking another long glug straight from the carton as if to confirm that the rules of ordinary behaviour did not apply to her and she did not care who knew it.

'Actually,' Aurelia said, 'I got a tattoo.' She was tired of her friend acting as though she was the only rebel in the world.

Siv choked and milk sprayed from her mouth and nose onto the floor. Her eyes streamed.

'That'll teach you,' Aurelia added smugly as Siv continued to cough and struggled to catch her breath. Aurelia relented, stepped closer and gently patted her back. 'Water?' she asked.

'No, no, it's okay. You were joking, right? About the tattoo? Good one . . .'

Aurelia remained silent.

'Fuck, you weren't joking! When? How? And I thought that my day was going to surprise you . . .'

Aurelia opened her mouth like a fish and then closed it again when the words didn't come.

'It's a bit of a long story. And I think you're going to want to sit down to hear it,' she finally said. 'Shall we go out for a drink?'

It wasn't until they arrived at the bar on the corner Broadway and West Grand that they remembered neither of them were old enough to drink in America. Had they thought of it in advance, they would have bothered to put on make-up and more fashionable clothes and tried to pass for twenty-one, but Siv was wearing her usual uniform of short shorts over tights and Aurelia had slipped into a pair of jeans and ballet pumps and simply pulled her long hair into a ponytail. If anything they probably looked younger than their nineteen years, so they had opted for a nearby diner instead.

'Damn puritans,' Siv grumbled, as an exuberant and in

Aurelia's opinion, overly cheerful, waitress returned to their table with two malted milkshakes and a bowl of French fries slathered with so much bubbling hot cheese that the dish resembled some kind of alien life form that might leap from the plate and wobble across the table towards them at any moment.

Siv tentatively extracted one of the fries from beneath its gluey yellow topping and popped it into her mouth.

'Not bad,' she announced. She picked up the ketchup bottle with both hands and squeezed a tsunami of tomato sauce over the top. Aurelia, who preferred her chips served in paper, with vinegar, by the seaside, ignored the bowl and sipped at her drink. It was cool and creamy, and in her opinion, far tastier than beer anyway.

They had slid into the same side of one of the red vinyl-covered booth seats so that they could talk in low voices without fearing that their conversation would be overheard by the other diners.

'Well then,' Siv announced. 'Show it to me.'

Aurelia removed her phone and pulled up the picture that she had taken a few hours earlier.

Siv squinted at the screen. 'Nice,' she observed uncertainly. 'But where is it?' she asked, pointing at the unidentifiable patch of bare skin that surrounded the tattoo. 'Is that your boob? Or somewhere else that you can't show me in here?' She winked mischievously at her friend.

The questions continued to stream out and Aurelia was unable to answer most of them. She couldn't suppress a blush when it came to the topic of making the tattoo appear.

Siv's reaction was both joyful and resentful. On one hand she was delighted that her best friend had finally found pleasure with a man, although on the other she was more than a touch annoyed that she had not been informed of the momentous event when it happened. But it was nothing like her curiosity at the seemingly ensuing consequences.

'So, it's only when you come hard? Or only when you think of this mystery guy? Or both?' Siv questioned. 'Oh, for God's sake,' she added, when Aurelia's cheeks turned as red as the diner's vinyl seat covers. 'We all do it. I just didn't realise you did it so often.' Siv raised her eyebrows and snickered. 'You always surprise me, Aurelia, it's one of the reasons that I like you so much.'

'I'm not sure exactly how it works,' Aurelia replied. 'I only just discovered it today. But it's always when I think of him that my orgasm is more . . . intense. So it's impossible to say for sure.'

'And you didn't see him? That night at the chapel? Not even a flash of his face? Did he leave a note?'

'It was so dark. And we were mostly lying down.'

Siv snickered again. 'Not just lying down, I'll bet . . .' she teased.

'I mean, I'm not even sure how tall he was. Taller than me, I think. Definitely not fat. But I don't know the colour of his hair or eyes or anything. Only that he tastes of pomegranate. And it's not like a cologne or perfume. More like the flavour of his skin, and his lips . . .' She trailed away with a dreamy expression on her face.

'You do realise that this makes absolutely no sense at all,' Siv replied. 'If I didn't know you so well, I'd think you had finally cracked. Do you think he could have put something in your drink?'

'No,' Aurelia insisted. 'He's not like that. I know it.'

'You don't know him at all, really.'

'Even so. We drank all the same thing. Everyone did. And if that were true, it still doesn't explain how this mark appears and disappears. No drug causes that.'

'Invisible ink that reacts to your body temperature?' Siv hazarded a guess.

'No such thing,' Aurelia ruled.

They each continued to think aloud, batting ideas back and forth until they had exhausted every possibility both plausible and implausible, eventually shifting effortlessly into a comfortable silence, the mark of a true and easy friendship. The fries on the table had long turned cold and Aurelia was now onto her second milkshake as Siv's mouth had been occupied by doing most of the talking.

Aurelia broke the silence. 'Sorry,' she said at last. 'I didn't ask you how it went at the circus school. Did you get your forms? Why did it take so long? Where have you been all day?'

'Well,' Siv announced proudly. 'I've got a job.'

'What? How? Doing what? Does your visa even allow you to work?'

Siv took another loud slurp of her shake.

'It's cash in hand. I'll be working as a nude model.'

Aurelia coughed and snorted her mouthful of malt.

Siv's eyes narrowed. 'That right there is karma, my friend. Teach you for laughing at me earlier. And my announcement is a lot less shocking than yours, I'm sure you'll admit.'

'Less shocking than mine?' Aurelia hissed. 'I didn't choose the tattoo. It just arrived. What do you mean a nude model? Tell me you're not doing porn.'

Aurelia remembered the film clips that she had viewed earlier that day to aid her arousal and the way the women had been so completely on display with nothing at all left to the imagination. She winced. Surely her friend would not want to be a part of that?

'No, no. Not that I haven't considered it, I'll admit, but I know it's too risky to be onscreen. Future career prospects, parents and all that. I'll show you the ad.'

She reached into the pocket of her jeans shorts and pulled out a crumpled piece of paper. It was from one of those fliers that appear on lamp posts with tentacle-like tear-off slips hanging from the bottom with the advertiser's number. The advertisement had been handwritten in a deliberately artful font, almost calligraphic in style. It read:

Nude models wanted. Any sort.
Good rates, no funny business. Call Walter *******

'And you called this guy?' Aurelia asked.

'Yes. And it happened that I was right near his studio. So I went there and modelled for him.'

'You went to his house? Alone? Are you bonkers? You might have been killed, Siv.'

'I haven't said that it was a him, yet. And I had a good feeling about it. No harm done.' she shrugged. 'And now I'm getting the bill.'

She proudly fished a thin wad of notes from her pocket.

'You're doing this for money? You know I have enough to pay for everything. And your parents would send more if they thought you need it. Especially if they knew you were going into nude modelling . . .'

'I hate taking money from you. And you know that

helping with the ballet classes is only covering board and hardly anything more. I want to be able to travel and party and buy things, not live like a pauper for months on end. Besides, it was fun.'

'You took your clothes off for him?'

'Yes. But do you want to hear the most amazing part of it all?'

Siv had lowered her voice to a whisper and leaned closer to her friend's ear as if she was about to share a secret.

'He's blind,' Siv said.

'So he touched you?' Aurelia asked. 'Siv, this sounds like a set-up.'

'No, he didn't lay a finger on me. It was like he was looking at me but not seeing me, but somehow he was able to sense my body . . . I've never felt so "seen" before. It was as if he could read my mind, my thoughts, see my soul. Or something like that.'

Aurelia snorted. 'And you're worried that *I've* lost the plot?'

'I have to go back, of course. We barely got started today. But he paid me up front, which is equally odd. I could just scarper with the money. But somehow I think that he knows that I won't.'

'Listen to us,' Aurelia said. 'I feel like we're living in a fairy tale. Or someone else's dream.'

'Oh, I almost forgot. He's having an exhibition, and invited me to pose for him there. You should come. Check it out for yourself, and stop acting like my mother . . .'

She produced another flier from her other pocket. This one was printed on glossy white card that Siv had carefully folded up into a small square. The writing was in the same font, in thick black ink. The letters were crafted so perfectly that it was impossible to tell whether the lettering had been printed or painted. It simply read:

Exhibition: by invitation only.

Aurelia picked up the card and examined it carefully. She turned it over, but the back was blank. There was no sign of an address or any other instructions or explanation of the event.

'This gets stranger by the minute,' she said.

Venice 1847

He had been told that more rats than human beings lived in Venice.

The gondola glided down the Grand Canal past the Scalzi Bridge as night fell. Ange's cape was thin and the cold wind from the lagoon chilled his ageing bones. The water's surface spread out in a million ripples in their wake, a subtle arrangement of waves, eddies, concentric rings and fluttering droplets through which their embarkation and dozens of nearby thin, elongated boats silently made their way.

By his side, Formetta had wrapped himself inside a thick brown blanket and gazed ahead with a distant look in his eyes. Soon the canal widened as they passed St Mark's Place and the open waters of the basin beyond the Punta della Dogana beckoned.

The gondolier, shrouded in darkness, his features invisible, veered to the right, in the direction of the Isola di San Giorgio Maggiore.

Ange Desclos had travelled from Bohemia to the shores of the Adriatic in search of a manuscript. On her deathbed, his mother, who had once worked as a maid to Count von Waldstein at the Castle of Dux, had finally announced that the unknown father Ange spent his life speculating about had been none other than the notorious Casanova, who had been the count's librarian until his own death in 1798.

Not only this, but she had revealed the existence of several unpublished chapters of his controversial memoirs. It was well known that the rest of the book, published in Germany back in 1822, had been heavily censored, but there was also evidence of huge, unexplained gaps in the lengthy story. Ange had also become a librarian, possibly unwittingly following in his father's footsteps. This quest for the missing part of Casanova's narrative was not only a task of bibliophilia, but also a way of coming to terms with the man who he believed had been his father.

His research spread across many years in dusty archives in Prague, Paris and Berlin and had eventually led Ange to Venice, Casanova's birthplace and the setting for many of his adventures.

Eventually he had come across it while poring through his notes in the dull light of the common room of the Pensione Tronca in the Cannaregio sestiere. An anomaly. A period of six months in 1788 where Casanova's locations and doings were seemingly missing. And a few brief lines years later describing enigmatic events at a magnificent celebration in a castle near Avignon in the south of France.

Why was there no further mention of this throughout the thousands of pages of the narrative? The few remaining survivors of Casanova's days he had managed to track down and speak to could shed no light on the mystery but vague rumours whispered in public houses and the ghosts of memories that Ange had encouraged to the fore with small bribes, fine brandy or simple wheedling, had finally thrown up the name of Formetta. Today's meeting was his final avenue of investigation. The ultimate name on his list, and now Ange could no longer recall when or why the elderly dancer's name had even been passed on to him.

How could he have known that Formetta would turn out to be deaf and dumb, and whatever secrets he harboured would prove nigh impossible to release? He had, exaggerating his gestures, indicated to the old man that he could write his questions down but the desiccated, white-haired retiree, had gestured him away as if the effort of doing so was beneath him.

'Casanova, the Chevalier de Seingalt? A Ball? A manuscript?' Ange had shouted out, louder than he had wanted, as if raising his voice would have made a bigger impression on his interlocutor. But the elderly dignitary had just stood there with an enigmatic smile on his narrow lips, brushing a mote of dust away from his hand, as they had both faced each other in the sonorous antechamber of the small palazzo where he lived close by the Ponte dell'Accademia and to which Ange had been dispatched.

Following a half hour of unsuccessful attempts to communicate, Ange had been ready to take his leave when Formetta had unexpectedly summoned a servant, who had brought him a blanket, and led the way to a pontoon at the back of the palazzo where the gondola had been stationed, indicating that Ange should follow him onto the boat.

And now night had fallen over the lagoon, and approaching the island, Ange was surprised by the myriad lights illuminating the horizon of churches and domes, a hundred torches burning bright on walls, parapets and in windows. A strong waft of flowers, fragrances and random spices reached his nose as the embarkation was carefully man-oeuvred against the wooden quay.

A liveried servant extended a hand to assist his rise from the boat. Ange was helped onto *terra firma*. He looked back, expecting Formetta to follow him, but the gondola was already drifting away into the black waters of the lagoon. The elderly man was waving at him, a gesture of farewell.

'Damn!' Ange muttered under his breath.

Ahead of him, a path of flickering torches cut through the night. He followed the attendant to a tall, semi-circular wooden door that led into a cavernous building squeezed between the island's monastery and the San Giorgio church, but hitherto almost hidden from the eyes through some clever architectural artifice. Music rose from the building as he approached.

He walked solemnly across the threshold and entered a vast cupola-shaped cavern where light literally dripped from the undulating ceiling like a curtain of fire, blinding him at first until he squinted to filter the assault and slowly made sense of the environment he had emerged into.

Beyond the wall of white light an orgy of colours surged through, an otherworldly palette screaming of opulence and excess.

The hall was busy with an assortment of people in the most extravagant attires and plumage, as if denizens of previous centuries had returned for the occasion festooned in every shade and variation thereof of the rainbow and more, every length of fabric more extravagant than the one before, wisps of cloth, cotton and silk draped with care and ingenuity along and across bodies, both male and female. A veritable carnival of the visual senses.

For a brief moment, Ange felt terribly self-conscious at the modesty and drabness of his own suit, but the busy crowd seemed impervious to his presence and not a single glance questioning the suitability of his attire was cast his way. Shielded from the night air, his body was finally warming as his curiosity mounted.

A murmur inside his head whispered that this was indeed the famous Ball that Casanova had supposedly once written about. The grail he had been tracking for what now felt like most of his life.

Voices rose from the crowd like wild streamers in a variety of languages, most of which he could not comprehend, a blanket of sound that hummed and buzzed in a hypnotic manner, making him feel even more of a stranger in a strange country.

Black-cloaked attendants, their powdered white faces peering anonymously through the opening in their tight hoods, moved between the guests dispensing tall blue glasses filled with sweet wine. After savouring his first glass, Ange quickly chased another of the circulating servants and helped himself to a second one, which he greedily downed in a single gulp. It was exquisite, caressing his throat as its warmth spread inside his body. His senses immediately heightened, focused on the exotic outfits of the many guests. He paused to catch his bearings.

The crowd ebbed and flowed, moving through the large high-ceilinged room like the streams of a river sinuously seeking its source, colours blending, merging, melting into each other to create new shades and variations of impossible tints like paint flowing freely on a shimmering liquid surface.

Ange felt blissfully light-headed.

The throng parted in front of him and a group of tall women whose bejewelled gowns all freely exposed their bare shoulders and an avalanche of voluptuous curves, their skin whiter than white in echoes of porcelain, rushed through, the delicate texture of their crinoline brushing momentarily against the hand he held against his side. As if aspirated by their wake, Ange felt obliged to follow them as they wound their way through the milling crowds and passed through an immense vaulted door that led into another, even larger, chamber. The door clamorously closed behind him.

He looked ahead and held his breath. At the centre of the room stood an immense water tank, its glass walls exquisitely streaked at regular intervals with streams of blue and scarlet, like liquid volcanic flows within the glass. The impressive construction, which towered heads above the spectators who now circled it, must have been designed on the nearby island of Murano by its world-famous glassmakers, he reckoned.

The water inside the tank shimmered in the light of the ring of torches illuminating the room, burning bright and casting a diorama of fire and shadows across its empty contents. Busy taking in the bizarre reservoir that had been installed here, mentally attempting to calibrate his response to the incongruous situation he now found himself in, Ange heard the sound of water splashing and turned to witness a group of six women diving through the water behind the thick glass, the nakedness of their pale bodies somehow magnified by the transparent wall now separating them and the water from the onlookers and the rest of the room.

It was the group of women he had followed into the

chamber. He looked down and saw the dresses they had shed scattered haphazardly across the stone floor.

'The night begins,' a basso profundo voice behind him proclaimed. A man's. But Ange's attention could not bear to be diverted from the spectacle unfolding before him and he did not look back.

'Could it be the zodiac this year? I hear it's been over a hundred years since it was used as a theme for the Ball,' a woman said in response, her voice high-pitched and he questioning.

'Pisces, maybe?' someone else said, blurrily pitched between man and woman at the limits of Ange's hearing.

The nude women disposed themselves around the circumference of the immense water tank, their shapely legs fluttering in position, stirring the water into small whirlpools that rose around them, circling their limbs. Ange couldn't take his eyes away from them. Their bodies were all so perfect, as if sculpted from precious marble, skin like a taut canvas, every detail of their regal anatomies magnified by the glass. How could they breathe, he wondered? Small bubbles of water pearled through their lips and drifted to the surface of the glass tank at regular intervals. Were they mermaids? Or just fish turned human in appearance by unfathomable instruments of magic?

Behind him, Ange could sense the room filling and a dull rumour of expectation rise through the crowd of spectators. Even if he had wanted to, there was no way now he could move away, surrounded as he was by a rush of bodies. He stood rooted to the spot.

A reverent silence spread across the room, all voices

stilling, a supernatural hush, the sound of a hundred breaths held back.

And then, an almighty exhalation.

A trap door had opened at the very centre of the floor of the glass tank and a winding line of naked swimmers, all male, he counted twelve in all, emerged from unknown, hidden depths, like arrows through the water, rising swiftly to the surface before diving again and separating into half a dozen pairs, each now making a beeline towards one of the women fluttering on the outer wall of the water tank like butterflies pinned against its glass walls.

Each man was likewise perfect in body and shape, muscled, defined, sculpted, oozing power and intent as they approached their prey.

'The rams,' someone close to Ange whispered in his ear. 'Aries.'

Ange felt giddy. Something in the sweet wine? He brushed sweat from his forehead and watched, transfixed, as each pairing of men wrapped itself around one of the women in the water and proceeded to impale her from front and back in rapid, rehearsed motion. Until all eighteen bodies were dancing a shameless dance of lust in the water, thrashing wildly and wantonly in place. Yes, a ballet, but a beautiful and uncommon submarine one, bodies in communion, interlinked, joined, married to each other in metronomic motion, a slow, steady swirl of flesh in water, flesh against water. A celebration.

His throat felt dry and painful.

'Until dawn,' a cry of liberation, resonating through the chamber, words flying above their heads, the water tank, the Ball.

As reluctant as he was to take his eyes off the spectacle unfolding in the translucent water, Ange couldn't help but notice men and women in the crowd surrounding him beginning to disrobe, bodies, white, tanned and olive-skinned in all shapes, sizes and ages, proudly revealed, clothing casually dropping to the floor, corsets unhurriedly being unlaced, shirts parting from skin, breeches dropping, shoes being cast aside.

Behind him, someone tugged on his shirt, gently but firmly, as if to assist him.

At the same moment, streams of coloured rope unfurled from somewhere in the heights of cavernous chamber and fell, dangling just inches away from the shimmering surface of the water tank, and out of nowhere, a group of naked aerialists began their descent, each wearing a thin crown of flowers and matching ankle chains in shades of gold, stopping their acrobatic arc just before their feet reached the water. As they did so the conjoined couples circling the periphery of the enormous bowl, each a sublime two-backed beast lost to the throes of pleasure, began a slow drift to the surface where, as if in slow motion, they reached the open arms of the nude acrobats and were taken into the safe harbour of their strong arms and each respective trio ascended to the roof where Ange and the other spectators lost sight of them.

Catching his breath, Ange felt unknown hands fumbling around his waist, undoing his leather belt and with a gentle tug on his cotton trousers pulling them down to the ground and realised he was also now naked, his cock hard as rock as it hadn't been in ages. In itself a remarkable feat as the pleasures of the flesh were but a distant memory in the ascetic life of a scholar he had been leading for as long as he remembered.

At first, he thought the water tank was now empty as the water swirled in front of him behind the thick glass of the container, like a whirlpool still hungry for the presence of the now departed bodies, but then, in the periphery of his vision, he caught sight of a quicksilver shadow racing inside the water which then unblurred as the new, solitary swimmer slowed and paused.

It was a woman. Either she was the tallest specimen of her kind or the water bowl was distorting her proportions. If the previous maidens had been perfect, then this new apparition was beyond perfection. Her red mane floated upon the water, wave upon wave of fire settling with grace between the interstices of the submarine currents she seductively swam through with a haughty elegance. Her alabaster skin shone as if lit from inside and her limbs extended in all directions like Medusa's hair.

Her eyes were the colour of deepest coal, dark pits of knowledge paradoxically illuminating the beauty of her face, where cheekbones, lips, eyebrows and mouth formed a balance like no other. Her body was a symphony of equilibrium, long neck conjugating with small, shapely breasts impervious to the water's currents, standing firm and high on her chest, before the valley of her stomach descended with geometrical precision towards her sex, smooth, like a desirable scar delicately carved into her flesh and outlining the holy of her opening.

A hand gently took hold of his cock. Soft and caring. A woman's. Not that it would have mattered had it not been as Ange was so transfixed by the vision of the woman in the water. Bodies bunched around him, skin against skin, heat against heat, as if he was no longer a single entity but a mere working part in a massive, heaving organism made of flesh, through which the winds of lust blew.

'Virgo?' he whispered.

'No,' a nearby voice replied. 'Aquarius,' correcting his ignorance. 'Virgo comes at dawn . . .'

He was still trying to process the information when there was a loud splash in the water at the very top of the giant glass bowl, and a similarly perfect man, brooding with intense power and seemingly carved out of granite emerged from the whirlpool and began swimming towards the red-haired siren.

A wave of shuddering strength raced through the spectators as they bunched up even closer to each other. Had Ange fainted, he knew, he would not have even fallen to the ground and would have been held up by the massed bodies now pressing against him in all directions.

A warm, wet mouth took him in and his whole body nervously trembled as the lips enveloped him and a tongue darted across his sensitive glans. But still he couldn't look away from the spectacle unfurling in front of his eyes.

'The bull,' someone said breathlessly.

The beautiful woman was now at the centre of the bowl, head back, lying back on an invisible bed of emptiness, as she parted her legs open. As she did so, Ange focused on the porcelain pallor of her flat stomach and its one irregularity: a bold black number 1 written on the skin, situated at an equal distance from her navel and the straight, darker line of her cunt.

The swimming bull reached the woman and fitted inside

her open thighs with mechanical exactitude. As he did so, her mouth opened wide and a tower of tiny bubbles floated to the surface of the water bowl.

How could they even breathe? Ange wondered distractedly.

The two bodies, now fucking in earnest, buckled and a new ballet began.

Like gladiators fighting, every single movement a poetic and minutely rehearsed concerto of thrust and defence, attack and surrender, acceptance and exacerbated desire.

Somehow the mouth sucking him with infinite skill and appetite worked in coordinated unison with the savage lovemaking he was witnessing, orchestrating the slow but inevitable rise of his desire, the awakening of his body, the battlefield of his aroused senses.

Time stood still.

The couple in the water, sealed in a cocoon of explosive passion, finally shuddered in mutual ecstasy and their joined bodies rolled and jolted as they rocketed to the surface of the bowl in search of air. At the same moment, Ange came. Sighing deeply, his legs almost turning to jelly in shock, he at last looked down to see who had been relieving him in such exquisite fashion, but all he could see was a dark-haired head retreating backwards through a jumble of legs and bodies. He wanted to call her back, but couldn't summon the right words. He looked around at the bacchanalia still in progress around him and smiled.

Later, he left the chamber and moved through the building.

Each room had been conceived as a different environment. He trampled the grass of a glade, waded through forest and marvelled at the ingenuity and invention of whoever the Ball's organisers were and also came to the realisation that the absent part of Casanova's manuscript, if it existed, could only have been about a preceding incarnation of the Ball. Of this he no longer had any doubt.

He witnessed the twins of Gemini and their ritual seduction of the archer of Sagittarius, who was masquerading tonight as a centaur.

He marvelled at the spectacle of the sea-goat of Capricorn wrestling in daring obscenity with the water-bearer of Aquarius.

And in the bedrooms, each one like a remembrance of things past, from carpeted walls of a *Thousand and One Nights* Arabian cavern to the rough-hewn recreation of a prehistoric cave or a silk-laden medieval four-poster bed of delights, he followed the lovemaking of Cancer and countless others, participants and spectators alike in a wondrous series of combinations allying the graceful and the forbidden, until his eyes and senses were properly saturated.

Towards morning, feeling his sexual powers awakening again, his energy regrouping, his blood hot and lustful, Ange wandered into an area empty of crowds and stumbled through a recessed door.

It was a small room, sparsely decorated and furnished. A divan stood at its centre, on which a young woman sat. Liveried attendants stood on either side of her, as if protecting her. She wore a diaphanous robe through which the gentle curves of her body could be glimpsed. She was small but perfectly proportioned, her skin powdered to an approximation of snow, her lips and the evanescent spectacle of her nipples standing out in deep-scarlet painted tones.

As he entered the room, Ange became conscious of his own nudity and visible arousal, and made a rapid gesture to cover himself. But the gentle smile of the woman disarmed him. There was a kindness and maturity in her face that soothed his raging senses within an instant.

He felt he should talk to her, excuse his nudity, the vulgarity of his appearance, but was not given the time. A crowd of Ball officials trouped past, ignoring his presence, and approached the woman on the divan.

'Dawn has come,' one of them solemnly proclaimed.

She rose.

Ange's heartbeat slowed.

Her faint smile changed, although he was unable to decipher how the kindness morphed into lust and desire.

Her two attendants at her side, she walked towards the newcomers, passing Ange without a final glance and followed the officials.

He trailed the newly formed procession.

And he watched as the young woman was first bedded at the stroke of dawn by the man in a lion cloak and saw how her smile so quickly turned to lust and joy.

Ange had somehow completed the whole circle of the signs of the zodiac.

And then witnessed the Inking.

He departed Venice the following day and gave up his search for the missing manuscript. But he would never forget the Ball.

5

The Fantastic Aerialists

Had it not been located on a busy suburban street corner just off the main thoroughfare and surrounded by ordinary homes, shops and restaurants, the building that loomed over them could have passed for a castle.

'Not very friendly-looking, is it?' Siv remarked to Aurelia as the two young women stared up at the monstrous brick walls and even taller towers that stood at each corner of an edifice that was so vast it seemed to cover two whole blocks.

'No,' Aurelia agreed. 'Sort of looks like a cross between a dungeon and a church.'

'More like a fortress, I'd say,' Siv replied.

They continued to dawdle at the front entrance, neither of them willing to make the first move to enter. It was still daytime and somehow the final rays of late-afternoon sun made the structure seem even more oppressive, as if the building was better suited to darkness.

Siv hooked her thumb into the belt loop above the pocket of her denim shorts and absent-mindedly began to run her fingertips over the folded edges of the thick white card that Walter, the blind sculptor, had given her by way of invitation to the exhibition. Aurelia glanced at her friend, alerted by the movement of Siv's hand against her hip, and frowned.

It was now late Saturday afternoon and just a few days

had passed since Siv's brief foray into nude modelling and Aurelia's discovery of her tattoo.

Aurelia had been preoccupied, of course, with thoughts of the stranger and the mystery of her disappearing and reappearing mark, but as she had already completed her one afternoon of household duties for Edyta that week and had been largely idle the rest of the time, she had plenty of opportunities to observe the subtle changes in Siv's behaviour that had occurred since she had met Walter.

On the afternoons that Siv spent teaching, she had asked Aurelia to watch her phone like a hawk in case he called to arrange a follow-up session. Aurelia had agreed to do so, but thought that the arrangement was a little over the top: surely he could simply leave a message, and Siv could call him back?

Aurelia had also noticed that Siv had become totally preoccupied by this mysterious exhibition that Walter had invited her to attend. The thick white card, bereft of a date, time, location or any other useful instructions, had been taken out of Siv's pocket, unfolded and returned so many times that the writing was now barely legible.

Siv had suggested all manner of crazy things to draw more information from the invitation and Aurelia, who knew that her own thoughts and behaviour had been anything but rational lately, had reluctantly gone along with it all, holding the thick card up to an electric light, over a candle flame, even standing on the front porch under a moonbeam, an idea that had occurred to Siv after watching the latest Peter Jackson fantasy movie.

'Well, it can't be Elvish, then,' she complained dismally as the worn black writing continued to simply say 'Exhibition:

by invitation only,' and the white space surrounding it was entirely free of hieroglyphics, invisible ink or any other clues.

In the end, Siv had responded to Aurelia's repeated badgering and simply dug out the original advertisement that she had applied to and phoned him.

'Oh sorry,' said Walter, at the other end of the line, 'I forgot to give you directions.' Siv motioned frantically for a pen and paper and Aurelia groaned and rolled her eyes as she noted down the time of the event and a quite ordinary-sounding address.

'We've got to stop this believing-in-magic nonsense,' Aurelia said when Siv ended the call. 'It's not doing either of us any good.' She stared pointedly at the tufty mohawk that Siv had created on her head by running her fingers through her fringe during the call, the habit that she took up whenever she was stressed, flirting or both. Now that Siv so often wore her customary teaching uniform of ballet tights and a colourful vest top, she looked even more than ever like a pixie with her short locks poking straight up on top of her head.

Siv had nodded her head vigorously in agreement, but despite the fact that the two of them had vowed to take a rational approach to the unusual events that had befallen them they still hesitated when they arrived at the Exhibition's apparent entrance. Aurelia was loath to acknowledge the strange feeling that surrounded her. She felt that if she walked through the venue's doors she might enter yet another strange new world where even more bizarre and unexplainable events might occur.

'It's like somewhere a witch might imprison Rapunzel,' Aurelia said at last, staring up at one of the four towers that seemed to go up into the sky for miles, like open fingers on a giant palm ready to snatch her up.

'I'll be your knight in shining armour,' Siv replied. 'Come on.' She took Aurelia's hand in her own and they stepped towards the heavy door.

It swung open silently in front of them as they approached.

'Come in then,' said a woman from within. The tone of her voice was halfway between a sultry purr and an angry growl.

She was sitting inside the darkened corridor that lay just beyond the doorway, behind a heavy wooden table upon which a small pile of dollar bills and coins rested along with an ink pad and heavy stamp, and a folded-over piece of card that bore the name 'Lauralynn' in the same calligraphic font that had decorated the invitation. Her long blond locks were fixed into pigtails that stuck out on either side of her head in Japanese schoolgirl style. The youthful nature of her hairstyle was in stark contrast with her ramrod-straight back, authoritarian posture and the wry expression that suffused her features. She was so tall and her back so straight and the table so low that she resembled a young queen reigning over the limited territory of the foyer.

They approached the counter and Siv insisted on covering the small entry charge.

'No bags?' she asked, raising one perfectly groomed pale eyebrow and staring pointedly at Aurelia's small purse and Siv's empty hands. She looked them up and down. 'You didn't bring a change of clothes?'

'I told you that you should have asked about a dress code,' Aurelia whispered to Siv.

'He's blind, how would he know what to wear?' Siv hissed back.

'Ah,' said Lauralynn. 'Walter invited you. Did he tell you what kind of exhibition it is?'

'An art exhibition, isn't it?' Siv replied. 'He just gave me this.' She fished the invitation out of her pocket and passed it over the table.

'I told him this wouldn't do . . .' Lauralynn sighed. 'Come with me then. It's an erotic art exhibition. Mostly performance-based. And we ask all attendees to dress the part for the sake of atmosphere. Normally I'd just turn you away, but since Walter invited you . . . come out back and we'll find something that will do the job.'

She stood up from behind the counter revealing the rest of her frame. Her tightly laced stiletto ankle boots were about seven inches tall, Aurelia reckoned, which made her already long legs seemingly go on for miles. Even in regular clothes, Lauralynn could never have passed as anything but extraordinary. The rest of her outfit was in accord with her hair-do, but her white blouse and short pleated skirt did not manage to imply a semblance of innocence. She seemed like such a simmering powerhouse beneath her clothing that her school uniform costume gave her the appearance of a superhero unsuccessfully feigning harmlessness on an off day.

Aurelia stared closely at the way the strange rubbery fabric of Lauralynn's outfit clung to her skin and shone in the light. She had never seen anything like it before.

'Latex,' Siv whispered, as they followed Lauralynn to the storeroom. She fished a long chain with a brass key attached to the end from between her breasts with the air of a VIP banker about to open a very important safe.

The room was packed with outfits of all descriptions, most in shades of red, purple and black and many of them, in Aurelia's opinion, either tasteless or frightening, or both.

'Are they expecting a nuclear war, do you think?' she asked Siv as she spied a rack of gas masks hanging against one wall.

Lauralynn stared at them and shook her head. 'Where did he drag you two in from, I wonder?' she mumbled to herself as she pulled out a rail of clothing from behind a pile of boxes that were brimming with skimpy bras and frilly knickers.

'You'll be all right in these,' she said to Siv, handing over a heavy pile of garments tied together with a ribbon. 'And this will suit you, Missy,' she added, trying to throw a bundle of black fabric towards Aurelia and stopping short when she realised that it was too diaphanous to travel through the air and stepping forward and passing it to her instead.

Aurelia grasped the slippery bundle in her hands and held it slightly away from her as if it was a hot potato. What was wrong with her clothes anyway? They were only going to look at things and it wasn't even dark yet. Surely only posh restaurants and nightclubs had dress codes. She put off undressing, hoping that Siv would be in agreement and they could either leave or convince Lauralynn to let them through as they were, but Siv had already begun to strip off and shimmy into the garments that had been picked out for her. Once fully dressed she swivelled on one toe, executing a perfect pirouette to display her new threads.

Siv's opaque tights had been replaced with skin-revealing fishnets and her short shorts with an even tinier pair that cupped her arse so tightly her cheeks, already firm and toned from all the dance practice, were perfectly delineated, perhaps even lifted slightly and imperceptibly spread apart. She had managed to wriggle into a stiff but flexible basque that was decorated with a series of satin and stretch-lace panels with a square-cut neckline that simultaneously flattened her small breasts entirely so that her chest resembled a boy's but was low enough to reveal just a hint of each of her pink nipples.

The whole outfit was cream-coloured and had been purposefully distressed with rips, burn marks and theatre dust to give it an aged appearance. Siv had laced her purple Dr Martens over the fishnets and the heavy boots made the top of her calves and thighs look even shapelier than usual.

Aurelia's breath caught in her throat. A sharp dart of arousal throbbed within her and caught her by surprise. She had never felt that way about another girl and certainly not about Siv.

She hurriedly glanced away and took a closer look at her own outfit to distract herself. At first glance the dress that she had been handed appeared to be totally sheer and she carefully picked up each of the thin straps and unravelled it to its full length with some trepidation. It was made of a sort of soft, stretchy fine mesh with a pattern of fine diamanté beads that ran in a snake-like pattern down the front, assiduously placed to cover the wearer's most intimate parts.

Aurelia let out a sigh of relief. Since her response to Siv's very minor nudity had brought her such a sharp pang of arousal, she was concerned that somehow her tattoo might appear suddenly in front of onlookers and she dreaded the explaining that might be necessary if it were to become visible through a sheer dress.

'Come on then, try it on,' Siv pestered. 'Though I have to say, I'm not quite sure it's really you. It's a little "stage show" with all those sequins.'

'It once belonged to a burlesque dancer in London, apparently,' Lauralynn explained. 'But it's the right length for you.'

Aurelia felt her cheeks warming under the combined gaze of the two women but she complied in the most modest way that she could by quickly unbuttoning her blouse and pulling the dress on over the top and then slipping her jeans off underneath.

Siv stared at her with a critical eye. 'It doesn't look right with a bra on,' she said. 'That'll have to go. And your knickers, too, I think. You have VPL. Only one way to get rid of it.'

Lauralynn nodded her agreement. The mischievous half-smile that she had previously sported had turned into a wide grin that transformed her expression into fully fledged devilish.

Aurelia grimaced but did as they suggested, slipping her knickers down to her ankles and kicking them off, then she reached behind her back and unhooked the hook and eyes that held her bra together and slipped a thin strap over each of her shoulders, carefully fishing her brassiere out from beneath the dress.

Bralessness was an uncommon feeling for Aurelia, who was accustomed to wearing an underwired bra every day as a matter of course. It was a sensation that she enjoyed, although only when alone in her bedroom or on a particularly lazy weekend day when she lounged around the house in just her old Arcade Fire band T-shirt and a pair of boxer shorts.

The fine mesh of the dress brushed against her chest and her nipples involuntarily hardened in response.

'I can't walk out in this,' Aurelia hissed at Siv. 'I've got practically nothing on.'

'It's not as revealing as you think, honestly. Take a look in the mirror.'

She turned and gasped when she saw her reflection. Even in the unflattering electric lighting of the storeroom, Aurelia was a picture. Black was a colour that she rarely wore as her skin was so pale she worried that it made her look closer to dead than fashionable, but the sheer fabric allowed some of her colouring to show through so that the effect was striking but not harsh, and the shimmering diamanté highlighted the greenish-blue colour of her eyes.

Aurelia had always been tall for her age and she suspected that Siv's reputation for aggression had been the only thing that prevented her from being teased for her height at school. She hd always been longer and leaner than the other girls and her perceived difference had led her to drop out of the dance classes that Siv had persisted with as she had always felt like such a clunky giant.

Now she rarely gave her body shape much thought, but she would probably describe herself as lanky rather than shapely. She had long ago given up on the idea that her breasts might grow larger or her hips fuller as she grew older. Curvaceousness was certainly not an adjective that she would ever have ascribed to herself.

But the linear pattern somehow highlighted the natural curve of her waist and hips and because the dress fell all the way to the floor even though she looked even taller than usual, she still had her ballet flats on.

'Here, try this as well,' Lauralynn said, passing her a slim, pale-wooden circlet that was threaded with tiny, lifelike silk flowers. Aurelia balanced it carefully on top of her head. With her auburn hair rippling over her bare shoulders and the floral wreath resting on the crown of her head, she looked like a pagan goddess.

She stood in front of the mirror and closed her eyes, frightened by her own image. In her mind's eye another picture leaped forward – the vision was of her, but another her. In it she was sheathed in a white dress, and standing with her face to the wind. Her hair was loose but had morphed into a nest of copper-coloured snakes that writhed sinuously against the sides of her face and hissed with each breath of air that caressed her skin. The terrible fierceness of the serpents was matched only by the ferocity Aurelia saw reflected in her own eyes.

'See? It's only if you're standing right in the light that anyone will notice you've got nothing on underneath.'

Siv's voice shook Aurelia out of her daydream. She was standing in front of her own reflection once more, but this time the dress was just a dress and her hair hung as still and lifeless as it ought to.

'And there's a whole load of people wearing a lot less than you two, believe me,' Lauralynn added. Her arm was stretched straight out in front of her, dangling a pair of strappy black stiletto shoes beneath Aurelia's nose. The heels were six inches high and each was decorated with a bronze serpent that ran up from the base of the heel so its open jaw would rest against the wearer's ankle.

Aurelia glanced at the shoes and shivered.

'No thanks,' she insisted. 'I'm a flat-shoe kind of girl. Especially if we're going to be walking around, and I'm betting there's lots of stairs.'

'Suit yourself,' Lauralynn replied with a shrug, before walking out ahead of them and beckoning for the two girls to follow. She was so stable in her own towering heels, she might have come out of her mother's womb wearing them.

Aurelia was mesmerised by the swaying of Lauralynn's hips beneath her short skirt and briefly she wondered how the blond woman's skin might feel beneath her fingertips in contrast with the smooth, rubbery material of her latex hold-ups. She imagined her hand sliding between Lauralynn's legs and all the way up her thighs and briefly caressing her. She felt her own lips moistening and she was immensely grateful for the protective covering of the sequins that would prevent anyone from noticing her tattoo if it should suddenly appear again.

Aurelia shook her head. What on earth had come over her? Lately she had been experiencing the uncomfortable sense that she was somehow changing, but her conscious thoughts hadn't quite caught up with the instinctive responses of her body or the fleeting images that darted into her mind like fireflies and disappeared again just as quickly.

Lauralynn caught her eye as they reached the main desk again and winked at her as if she had been reading Aurelia's thoughts all along. 'Enjoy yourselves,' she said. 'There's all sorts of displays up there so make sure you have a good look around.'

'Come on,' Aurelia said to Siv. 'Let's go and get this over with.' She feigned reluctance because she did not want to own up to the spark that she felt igniting within her and the corresponding flush of excitement that crept from her toes all the way to her scalp. On each occasion that the stranger had visited her she had been in a place like this and surrounded by that strange sense of having found another world. The same energy that had imbued the air at the fun-fair and at the chapel was present here, as if something magical were about to happen and perhaps that something magical might involve another visit from the man who had left his mark on her in Bristol.

When they reached the base of the long flight of stairs that Lauralynn indicated led up to the exhibition, Aurelia gripped the winding iron stair rail eagerly. It wasn't until she reached the top and discovered what lay ahead that she began to wonder what she had got herself into.

They had arrived at a long passageway that was peppered with closed wooden doors and further passageways that branched off the main corridor. There was no sign of any other people or any indication of where they should go next though Aurelia could hear the murmuring of voices and the occasional clatter of high heels. As she strained to catch the source of the sounds, she observed a strange whistling noise, rhythmic thudding and the occasional loud 'crack', a sym-phony of aural vibrations bouncing like balls from the stones so that it was impossible to pinpoint where the noises originated.

They picked a bricked archway at random and wandered through it. Shadows crept up the walls around them. Torches had been set into the walls and the flames hissed and stuttered. The air was warm and smelled faintly like paraffin, leaving a bitter, acrid taste in Aurelia's mouth.

'It doesn't feel like America, does it?' Siv remarked.

'No,' Aurelia agreed, 'it feels more like England.' The place was a maze, and she felt just as she had when she'd been stuck with Siv in the ghost train, but now she could not separate her increasing foreboding from her sense that the stranger might appear again here, just as he had at the funfair.

They passed by several adjoining rooms, each of them either open and empty or closed and firmly locked, and were about to give up on the idea of finding Walter or any kind of art display when they reached another stone staircase.

'You'd think they'd at least have elevators,' Siv complained.

'They probably do,' Aurelia agreed. 'We must be in the wrong place.'

She took one step up and narrowed her eyes, looking for some sign of what lay around the corner, but she couldn't see anything. Then there was movement in the shadows ahead of her and a strange scraping sound and she turned her head and squinted again through the poor lighting. She thought she had seen someone with an animal on a lead. Perhaps it was Walter, with a guide dog. There was definitely something, or someone, crawling along the stone steps above them, but unless her mind was playing tricks on her again she was sure that she had caught a glimpse of a bare arse and a long, slim pair of legs disappearing behind the bend in the staircase. Surely not a person on a lead?

'There's nothing up here,' Aurelia called back to Siv, who was still poking around in the corridor behind them. She was lying, of course, but she couldn't think of any way to explain her natural distrust of the sculptor. She knew that if

Siv got any inkling at all that she didn't like the idea of tracking him down, then every rebellious bone in Siv's body would respond by redoubling her detective efforts.

'It's okay,' Siv called back, 'come down here, I've found something.'

Aurelia followed the sound of Siv's voice down the winding passageway and past all the other locked doors.

The room that Siv had discovered was small but appeared larger because every flat surface had recently been painted white. A small window, barred like a prison cell, provided the only light, but the white paint reflected each ray so effectively that the walls seemed to glow.

Aurelia opened her mouth to speak when she caught sight of the display inside, but Siv had drawn her finger to her lips to indicate that they should be silent.

A woman was hanging from an elaborate series of pale-pink ropes that were fixed in place in various points on the ceiling. She was positioned like a ballerina in mid-*grand jeté*, with her arms raised above her head and bound at the wrist, her back arched and her legs spread wide apart, her back leg raised higher than her front as if she had reached the highest point of a leap and was now on her way down again. Rope had been wrapped, tied and cinched around her ankles and just above her knees, and then clipped onto the lengths that hung from the roof. She wore a rope harness that wrapped around her hips, inner thighs and buttocks and supported the majority of her weight.

Her expression was peaceful, as if she found serenity in having been caught in flight. If anything, it seemed that the effect of the rope was to prolong her airborne freedom rather than to restrain her. She remained perfectly still and at ease in her bonds and did not move or make a sound to acknowledge the presence of the two young women.

In the corner of the room a man sat on a stool alongside a small workbench. He was not looking at the suspended woman, but Aurelia had the impression that he was analysing her somehow. His head was slightly cocked to one side as if he were seeing her by listening rather than looking. With his hands he was deftly shaping a clay figurine.

She recognised the man that Siv was so taken with.

This must be Walter.

Aurelia peered at him. He was wearing a strange combination of clothes. A pair of cream-coloured hemp trousers and a long-sleeved, collarless purple shirt made from the same fabric, which was thick and looked rough to the touch. Perhaps, in the absence of vision, he enjoyed the texture of things, which would explain both his outfit and his chosen art form.

Up close, his hair was snow white and cropped close to his head. Aurelia noted his features but found them unremarkable. A square jaw and high cheekbones gave him a somewhat animal appearance, an effect that was magnified by the way that he moved and responded to touch and sound rather than to sight. His loose-fitting clothing did not reveal much in the way of muscles or lack of them, but it was obvious that he was of slim build and his straight-backed spine suggested the kind of good posture that comes with fitness.

To Aurelia, he simply looked like an old man. Not an unattractive one, certainly, but far beyond the age that she considered eligible. He must be in his sixties, she thought, at least forty years Siv's senior. Did her friend really feel that way about him as she had with the now long-jettisoned Ginger? She turned and gazed at Siv.

Siv was standing with her feet spread solidly apart and her thumbs tucked through the belt loops of her severely abbreviated shorts with her fingers in her pockets. She was staring at Walter, transfixed. Aurelia followed the line of her gaze. Siv was not looking at the side profile of his face that was visible to them, but rather she was totally entranced by the movement of his hands as he shaped the clay. Aurelia took a step closer to her friend and pinched her arm to get her attention but Siv had drifted into a sort of daze and was totally oblivious to everything around her – Aurelia, the room, the woman hanging from the ceiling. For a moment, Siv looked as if she was blind as he was.

'Siv!' Aurelia whispered under her breath. Siv ignored her. Aurelia waved a hand in front of her face. Finally she broke her gaze from the movement of the sculptor's hands.

'What?' Siv hissed back.

The sculptor did not turn at the sound of their voices. Most likely, Aurelia thought, he had known that they were there all along.

'Let's go,' she said. Siv's reaction to the sculptor made her hair stand on end. She had never seen her usually straightforward and rational friend behave this way and it made her uneasy.

Siv shifted her weight from one foot to the other but did not make any move to leave.

'We'll distract him if we stay here,' Aurelia added. This had the desired effect. Siv took one more wistful look at the sculptor and then reluctantly began to head towards the door.

Aurelia watched Siv walk. Her steps were slow and heavy, as if her friend were somehow attached by invisible threads to Walter and was having trouble leaving him behind. Again Aurelia felt a strange itching sensation on her skin, the same feeling that she had when she occasionally watched thriller films and wanted to scream a warning at the TV set when the heroine opened a squeaky door or headed down the rickety stairs to the basement.

Why was she so troubled by Siv's interest in the sculptor? Aurelia hadn't seen any of his finished pieces but, regardless of the quality, the fact that he could create visual art at all without the ability to see was remarkable, but besides that he seemed fairly ordinary and unfrightening. It was Siv's reaction to him that was so strange. She couldn't quite put her finger on it, but something about her friend was different. She seemed consumed by her thoughts of this man.

No different to me then, Aurelia thought with a wry smile. Likely it was a passing crush or a phase caused by his unusual talent and Siv would snap out of it.

'Whoa,' said Siv, coming to a halt in the corridor ahead of her. Aurelia hurried to catch up with her and see inside whatever new display it was that had now caught Siv's attention. Some of the doors that had previously been locked were now open and within the first was one of the most alarming sights that Aurelia had ever set her eyes on, but yet she could not pull her gaze away. It all seemed to be happening in slow motion like a film stuck in freeze frame.

A young woman – probably around the same age they were, Aurelia guessed – was leaning against a wall with her arms and legs spread in starfish style. This woman too was bound, but only with very thin white ribbons that were wrapped around her ankles and wrists. The fragility of the restraints that bound her only served to highlight the fragility of her wrists and ankles and the delicacy of her frame. Her long hair was jet black and hung loosely around her shoulders and face so that even her profile was obscured. She was standing in perfect *en pointe* in a pair of peach-coloured ballet slippers. Her lacy knickers were the same shade and had been pulled halfway down her thighs, exposing a pert, naked arse. Clearly visible on each cheek was a bright-red handprint.

A man stood behind her with his arm raised. He paused at the top of his swing like a baseball pitcher gathering speed and power for a throw and then brought his hand down onto her buttock with what seemed to be all of his strength. The girl cried out, releasing a guttural sound that suggested pain but was not accompanied by any attempt to escape her situation. She involuntarily jolted forward, tugging on the ribbons that bound her, but she managed to remain on her tiptoes. Aurelia, though, knew from her own limited experience of ballet that retaining that posture under such circumstances must have taken extraordinary balance and strength of will.

The first moment of impact passed and the girl relaxed again. The man had switched from his heavy blow to a soft caress, cupping her arse cheek in his hand with absolute gentleness as if he was stroking the delicate petals of a flower. A look of total satisfaction crossed his face as she leaned back against his palm. Then his eyes flashed and his smile turned cruel as he raised his hand again and brought it down with a thud onto her other cheek. She hissed between her teeth in pain, jolted forward again and then relaxed once more into his hand. This time his finger slid briefly between her legs and he traced a line from her sex lips up to the cleft of her arse. In response she strained against the ribbons that bound her ankles so that she could shift her legs further apart, inviting him in.

Totally unbidden, Aurelia felt her own body responding. A familiar warm sensation began to buzz between her legs and she felt a strong desire to pleasure herself. She closed her eyes momentarily to try to ward off the feeling and keep her mind in the present, but the moment that she did so the images that had been in front of her now appeared behind her eyelids, but in her imagination she had transformed into the dancer with her wrists and ankles restrained and it was the stranger from Bristol who stood behind her with his arm raised, preparing to strike her. The thought made her wet and her mental vision seemed even more real because with her eyes closed she could not prevent the rhythmic sound of smacking and the girl's cries from filtering through her ears. Every rational thought in her head told her that this was wrong. And yet, and yet . . . she was so aroused.

Aurelia's eyes snapped open. She tugged Siv's arm.

'Mmm?' Siv mumbled.

'Let's keep looking,' Aurelia said. Truthfully, she wasn't sure if she could handle seeing anything more like this. An internal battle between curiosity, arousal and disgust was raging within her with no clear victor in sight and the conflict that resulted was making her feel horribly confused and uncomfortable.

Was this even legal? she wondered. Fancy being too young to drink beer at a bar, but being old enough to attend events like this. But she knew that it hadn't been advertised. Even if an interested person had got hold of a ticket, they would still need someone to provide them with the time and address. So perhaps it was entirely underground. That thought gave her a little more courage. She liked the idea of being part of a secret.

Her eyes darted around the room and she noticed that a steady stream of people were heading in the same direction like eddies in a river flowing into one another and heading upstream.

'The show is starting,' a slim man in a stiff, starched shirt said to another man who was so much his double they might have been twins. They were both wearing dark-blue ties patterned with love hearts and dancing satyrs.

Aurelia and Siv fell in behind the two men and followed them all the way down another corridor.

'Bloody hell,' said Siv when they were finally released from the bowels of the endless passageways that were spread like veins running from a giant heart and into the main hall.

The room was enormous and covered with a huge domed ceiling. Orange and red rays from the setting sun fell through the long rectangular windows that were inset into the brickwork at one end of the building and cast a hazy glow over all of the room's inhabitants, as if they were standing near the dying flames of a bonfire. The domed roof was supported by numerous curved steel arches, each of which was further reinforced by a network of shorter pipes so that the ceiling resembled a huge metal spider's web.

Seven trapezes dangled from equally placed points across the ceiling and at the end of the trapezes, with their feet just a few tantalising inches from the floor, hung seven pale-skinned, red-haired women who were entirely naked besides their vivid purple ballet slippers with satin laces that formed a hatched pattern all the way up their legs to their hips where the satin strips wrapped around their waists and then threaded between their buttocks. They were each gripping the trapeze bars tightly with their fingers, but also appeared to be locked to them with delicate silver chains that were attached to slim bracelets fastened around their wrists and onto the bar above so that they resembled prisoners hanging with their wrists in irons. Their heads were covered with gossamer thin violet-coloured gauze hoods that were fastened around their throats beneath a silver band. Their necks were relaxed with their chins resting on their chests. If it had not been apparent that their muscles were tensed and their toes pointed sharply downwards in a perfect *en pointe* that sharply emphasised the firmness of their buttocks and the chiselled musculature of their legs, then they might have been sleeping.

Half a dozen silver rings were threaded through each of their outer labia and clipped onto the ribbons at their thighs, pulling their sex lips wide apart so that the women's arousal was obvious and dampened the ribbon that was bound tightly between each of their legs. A thick knot was tied into place tightly over their clitorises and from it another long, thin satin ribbon was attached, matching a similar long length that was bound to larger rings that decorated each of their nipples.

The threads looped across the room to a platform in the centre that was situated above the women but was clearly visible to the audience and on top of the platform stood a man who held each of the lengths of ribbon in his hands.

Walter.

He was now entirely naked besides a purple pouch, which might have looked ridiculous were it not for the natural aura of dignity that was evident in his bearing.

'It's him again,' Siv whispered excitedly in Aurelia's ear. 'Doesn't he look quite extraordinary?'

'But he's blind,' Aurelia responded, as if the knowledge of his infirmity made the whole scene impossible, even though she had already witnessed him creating the likeness of a model that he couldn't possibly see.

'I know,' Siv sort of sighed.

Onlookers in various states of dress and undress surrounded the strange web, waiting for something to happen.

Aurelia stood alongside Siv from their vantage point near the front of the crowd and stared as the scene in front of her unfolded. It was only good manners that prevented her from covering her mouth in shock. Were these women prisoners? Marionettes? She was no prude and certainly saw nothing wrong with nudity in general or in art. The fact that the other models she had seen so far had been naked had not shocked her particularly. But there was something specific about the sight of women who had their heads covered but their private parts spread open that seemed nuder than nude. She knew this was a performance, and the women were clearly complicit. She could not quite put her finger on what it was that made her feel at once so uncomfortable and yet on the other hand so captivated. Her heart was racing in her chest, an undercurrent of excitement pulsing through her body.

Music began to play. It was classical, a genre that Aurelia never listened to by choice, but only occasionally overheard when John played his collection of records on full blast as he read or did the hoovering upstairs.

'Strauss,' Siv whispered in her ear. ' "The Dance of the Seven Veils".' Siv was a punk chick at heart, but her ballet training had given her some exposure to classical music.

As the music came to life, so did the dancers. They each moved in time to the music in perfect synchronicity, though it quickly became apparent that they were not the ones leading the dance. Walter, who oversaw them all behind his personal walls of darkness, was tugging on the threads that were bound to their piercings just as the conductor of an orchestra would change the rhythm of a piece by virtue of his movements behind the rostrum. Each pull on a ribbon signified a new instruction and in response the women would spin, twirl or spread their legs apart in a perfect airborne split that displayed their private parts – naked besides the thin satin harnesses that rubbed between their legs – to all those who watched.

Sometimes Walter would pull fiercely on a ribbon that was attached to a nipple and cause a dancer to arch her back in pain but just as swiftly he would release the piercing and tug the thread that corresponded to the knot that stimulated the dancer's clitoris. Though the faces of the women were partially obscured, it seemed to Aurelia that she could follow their expressions of pain or of pleasure as they responded to the pressure that was applied to the point of each piercing. Their desires and emotions were visible through their bodies in the tautness of their muscles or the way in which they either resisted against or surrendered to the pull of the ropes that bound them.

His eyes were closed throughout most of the performance

as if he was reading the dancers' responses purely through the tug and release of the ribbons. Which Aurelia knew he was. And he was not intent on wholly delivering pain.

Siv pinched Aurelia's arm.

'Look,' she hissed, 'he's making them come.'

Aurelia turned her gaze from Walter back to the women who surrounded him. Siv was right. Their movements still matched the beat of the music, but they were no longer dancing the same steps. It was as if the sculptor was playing a different tune on each of their bodies, providing each woman with precisely the right combination of pleasure and pain that would take her to the edge of ecstasy and keep her there until the moment that he applied the final stroke of pressure and she spasmed in obvious orgasm. The woman closest to them was so wet that glistening droplets ran down the inside of her thigh and left a dark mark on the length of purple ribbon that decorated her leg.

When each of the women had come, they resumed their initial position of stillness like wind-up toys that had finally wound down and then together they were slowly lowered until their feet reached the floor and they fell into the waiting arms of the exhibition's assistants who unlocked the chains that bound their wrists to the trapeze bar but left the hoods fastened over their heads. They were led away, presumably to a dressing room, but seemed to be in such a trance-like state that they were unable to move of their own accord. A tuxedoed attendant walked over and led Walter off.

Aurelia was captivated and horrified in equal measure. Every conscious thought in her body told her that this was the work of madness. This wasn't art; it was abuse. She looked around the audience. Almost without exception those watching looked aroused, excited or bored. None seemed shocked. After a round of applause, some of it enthusiastic and some of it obligatory, the circle of onlookers that had gathered around the scene broke away and began to chatter amongst themselves.

Siv had fallen silent. Aurelia wondered how this spectacle had affected her friend. Surely she would now not want to pursue Walter any longer.

'Are you okay?' she asked Siv.

Siv shrugged, feigning nonchalance, but the hand that she rapidly brushed through her already messy hair and the urgency that filled her movements betrayed her.

'I wish it could have been me. Up there. I really do,' Siv confessed in a dejected tone.

Stunned by Siv's admission, for a moment Aurelia tried to imagine herself in her friend's place. How would she feel if she were hanging up there like that with the stranger on the platform above, sensing even the tiniest change in her flow of arousal, orchestrating her every move like a puppet master? She closed her eyes. That one thought was like throwing gasoline onto the spark of excitement that had been brewing inside her ever since they arrived. It was as if an ember inside her had burst into flame and a shock of arousal burned through her body like a wildfire. Fuck! She was going to come in front of Siv, in her see-through dress in front of all these people with the vision of Walter and his marionettes still sharp in her mind's eye. She fought the sensation. Not here. Not now, not like this.

'Let's get out of here,' Aurelia whispered. Her head was spinning and she needed some fresh air to make sense of it all. She didn't want to know what was behind any of the other open doors or what was creating the strange cracks and thuds that emanated from the other rooms through the corridors. But was that because she feared that what she saw might disgust her, or because she feared that what she saw might turn her on?

Nothing made sense any more.

6

A Beating Heart

After that day, Aurelia often tried to raise the topic of the exhibition, Walter, his strange marionettes and the way that Siv had responded to the whole thing, but her friend would simply shrug her shoulders and change the subject or hurry away and busy herself with some other task.

Soon Aurelia began to feel as if a wall had been somehow erected between the two of them. On the surface they remained friends as they always had been, but the invisible glacier that protected Siv's unspoken emotions about the sculptor and the reactions that his performance had elicited proved impossible to penetrate.

A month passed.

Aurelia began to wonder if she should have enrolled in college, rather than taking a year off. Siv was now so often out of the house and busy, attending to mysterious errands that she supposedly ran for Edyta but never discussed, her waking life so full of sundry activities, while she lingered back in Oakland, sitting in her room alone most of the day, with just the sound of the dancing routines and hushed conversations, instructions and occasional laughter rising towards her through the floorboards from Edyta's basement studio below.

It was as if her mind had been parked on a sidetrack and

left to its own devices. Idle, and prone to thoughts she would rather repress. The mysterious trust fund and its benefactor; blurry, imagined memories of her parents assembled from the few facts she had been provided with and a half-dozen fading photographs of them, like total strangers; the deep impact of the scenes she had witnessed at the exhibition; bittersweet evocations of the man she had coupled with in the Bristol chapel, the taste of his kiss, the softness of his lips, the welcome hardness of his cock and, crowning everything, a strange sense of despondency and confusion.

She should be exploring. She and Siv had talked about hiring a car and driving off to Los Angeles to discover the sunnier side of the Californian mirage, maybe heading for the desert and investigating Las Vegas, the Grand Canyon, the Hoover Dam and so many places she had once dreamed of. But they had discovered their age precluded them from renting a vehicle in the USA despite the fact they both had driving licences.

Now she couldn't summon the interest in even thinking of alternative ways of travelling. She was becoming lazy, indifferent. And she felt resentful at the way Siv had managed to busy herself so quickly and adapt to their new environment.

She missed their shared silences and the closeness that had often been unexpressed but still present between them until the day of the exhibition.

Nights were exhausting, full of conflicting dreams and stray thoughts, and by the time she woke Aurelia invariably felt she needed a half-day at least to overcome the sheer tiredness that had spread throughout her body, the tightness in her muscles and limbs, the crab-like apathy gripping her mind.

Part of her knew there was a whole world out there waiting for her, almost expecting her, but right now she was held back. By fear of the truth, personal demons?

All too often she would pull up the hem of her nightdress and peer down at her midriff, the pale white plain broken by the delicate, narrow crevice of her cunt, searching in vain for the coloured heart. She would hope against hope for its return but it remained invisible, defying her by its absence, sowing seeds of confusion, almost suggesting it had never been there and her mind was unhinged. She would repeatedly touch herself, dip inside the moistness of her opening, play with herself in an attempt to revive the fire, but it was always in vain. Sometimes she thought she felt a buzz, experienced the feather breath of an itch in the precise area where the heart and its thin tendrils had once appeared, but when she looked the skin was uninterrupted, at peace, unmarked, and the feeling was like an echo, an emptiness where once there was a fullness.

And then at unwanted moments, in the kitchen emptying the dishwasher or catching up with overdue ironing, her thoughts would return to the exhibition. The image of a flat hand making fierce contact with a white arse, and the pink, spreading stain occasioned by the impact calmly flowing like water across the landscape of soft flesh would scratch away at the scab of her perceptions and that buzz would begin to resonate and Aurelia would abandon herself to its approaches in the hope of resurrecting the flaming heart.

She had never given any thought to spanking or being

tied up before that fateful evening a month ago. In fact, the prospect of welcoming minor pain was anything but attractive to her senses and even felt a tad ridiculous at first sight. And then she would remember all the other episodes she had watched with rapt eyes, the sight of the veiled woman and the way that Walter had so authoritatively controlled the movements of their bodies. How on edge she had been, curious, then piqued, then deeply disturbed.

Aurelia closed her eyes. Evoked the hard pad of the stranger's fingers in the darkness of the Bristol chapel and how he had so decisively seized the pliant flesh of her buttocks as he buried himself inside her. Or the way he had at some stage in the whirlpool of emotions in which she had been drowning, taken hold of her wrists to hold her in place while he thrust inside her and she had welcomed his authority, his dominance. Would it have felt the same if he had bound her wrists with a length of white rope? Her feet? Immobilised her?

She shuddered.

Was this what her soul yearned for? Surely not. But the more the images she had stored away at the back of her mind kept returning behind the screen of her eyes, the more she felt that secret vibration playing with her nerve endings, insidiously toying with her, flirting with taboos she never knew she had kept hidden.

Yet again, her legs opened wide and she allowed her hand to burrow under the covers. The strains of the 'Nutcracker Suite' wafted through the floor from the basement studio below. It was morning, a junior class, all the little toddlers in pink tutus and displaying gap-filled smiles.

Before reaching the lips of her sex her finger lingered over the skin where the heart sometimes resided and glided across its silkiness. Out of nowhere, heat seized her heart and rushed down to her midriff like a train out of control. Aurelia gasped. She hurriedly pulled her arm out from between the covers. Jumped out of bed and headed for the bathroom. She was on fire, needed a cool shower to calm down, push her senses into retreat. Throwing off her flimsy nightgown, she turned on the water and caught a glimpse of herself in the tall mirror.

The heart was visible again. Sharp. Carved into her flesh. Its thin, imperceptible tendrils extending out, alive. And the more she peered down at the impossible tattoo, the more she pictured herself in a stone hall, bound hands and feet and at the mercy of a whip, a paddle, hands, men, a man, her man. The stranger. The taste of pomegranate filled her mouth, half sweet, half bitter.

This is not me, she thought, seized by an overwhelming sense of panic. But the images in her mind refused to retreat, and as the heart pumped with frantic abandon, she came. Just standing there. Not even touching herself.

Aurelia knocked on Siv's door the following morning, hoping to find her friend back to her normal chatty, open-hearted self, but the room was empty and the bed had not been slept in.

Her initial reaction was one of both disapproval and envy. Tinged with apprehension. And sadness.

Was this what they had come to? Could Siv really have met a new man and plan to spend the night with him and not even mention it? And was it a new man? Aurelia remembered the way that Siv had responded to Walter.

The look that had passed over Siv's face when she had watched him moulding the clay body of the dancer that he was sculpting, or the desire that Siv had expressed to be one of his marionettes.

A pang of guilt struck her as she recalled how disapproving and suspicious she had been of her friend's attraction to the sculptor. Her disapproval had simply been a way of masking the confusion she felt about her own cravings, she knew that now, but she couldn't take it back.

Aurelia tried to push her worry and hurt away. After all, it was Siv's life, she told herself, and there was no need for her to be censorious and not allow her friend to enjoy life to the fullest as long as she didn't get hurt. Hadn't that been the idea behind coming to the USA and the once fabled streets of San Francisco?

As she set to ticking off the daily chores at the cottage and covering for her friend, she attempted to phone Siv on successive occasions but her calls were never answered. The following day, when Siv had still not reappeared, she slipped into her bedroom again to check her belongings. All Siv's clothes were still there and nothing appeared to be missing, although she did come upon Siv's phone charger in a drawer, which might explain why she was not responding.

Edyta commented on Siv's absence when Aurelia went to her to pay their rent and willingly covered her friend's share.

'I wouldn't worry,' the gaunt ballet teacher said, a twinkle of light in her eyes accompanying the ironic turn of her thin lips. 'She must have a reason . . .' And she nodded approvingly.

Aurelia wanted to tell her that Siv was probably involved

with a blind, older man, but felt it would be betraying Siv to reveal her secret.

A week went by and Siv had still not given any sign of life and Aurelia became more concerned. She Googled Walter but could find no trace of him or any mention of a sculptor famous for working blind on the web. She visited the venue where the exhibition had been held, only to be politely informed at the door that the 'party' had been a private hire and they were not allowed to reveal the name of the client.

Yes, the thin-lipped, bespectacled receptionist told her, other similar events might occur in the future and some of the same guests or event staff might be present, but this could not be guaranteed, nor any calendar of private events be released.

Dreading a telephone call from Siv's family and the prospect of having to lie to them about her whereabouts, Aurelia was wavering as to whether she should get in touch with the local police when, in uncanny response to her concern, she received an email out of the blue. It was from Siv.

i'm ok. i'm happy. don't worry for me. one day you'll understand. love ya.

Her family never called, so Aurelia assumed Siv had also made contact with them along similar lines.

Although the news provided some relief, it also made her feel angry. Siv had let her down. Been incredibly selfish, she reckoned.

Why couldn't she have come to the Oakland cottage to explain herself, pick up her belongings before shacking up with Walter or whoever she had now taken a shine to?

It was so damn inconsiderate. Not the sort of thing real friends should do.

Meanwhile, to compound her foul mood, she had received a letter from the lawyer, Gwillam Irving, ambiguously asking after her and reminding her of her obligations to the trust fund. Did he know that Aurelia had still not taken a single step towards enrolling at Berkeley as she had agreed to? In addition, every attempt since Siv's fugue to make the heart reappear, by touching herself or evoking the Bristol stranger's touch in her jumbled mind, had failed abysmally.

She resolved to do something about it.

Aurelia knew it was irrational, dangerous even. But she had come to the conclusion that she had to find out whether the heart would come to the surface again if she made love with another man. It was as if the invisible tattoo had created a hole inside her, a vortex that was sucking all her thoughts into it, and she was desperate for answers.

Even though she looked older than her age, she knew that American barmen and staff were still likely to ask for some form of ID, so a bar was out of the question. Where to go?

Prompted by the letter from Irving, Irving & Irving, she had finally resolved to visit the campus at Berkeley and investigate the earliest possible opportunity to enrol for the courses she had planned while still back in Leigh-on-Sea. She deliberately chose to wear her shortest skirt – a tweedy patterned thing that reached barely halfway down to her knees, showing off her long legs – along with the tightest of crewneck white T-shirts and Siv's black leather jacket, which had been left behind by her friend. Not a studious out-fit by a long stretch of the imagination, nor one that left much to the same imagination in revealing her tall, slim body.

Aurelia had never gone out of her way to attract the gaze of men, and felt very self-conscious dressing in this manner. She picked up the thick folder of variously sized forms at the admissions office, and wandered across the main campus, failing to attract undue attention amongst the milling crowds of equally tall, blond but suspiciously tanned girls already present. Chilled by the breeze that wrapped itself around her bare legs, setting off goose pimples, she found refuge in the library.

The tall-ceilinged reading room was all burnished wood panelling and long benches. Aurelia gathered a pile of books, found a seat by one of the vast bay windows and gazed out at the ever-fluttering leaves on the branches of the trees surrounding the building. She hadn't planned to actually study, but just picked up various volumes at random, mostly novels she had heard about but never got round to reading. Perhaps if she leafed through a few pages she might find herself hooked and spend a few peaceful hours in the warmth with her mind at peace.

She arranged a tall pile of books in front of her – a wall to block out the distracting view from the windows – and was left with a single book. A novel by Haruki Murakami. She'd never read anything by the Japanese author, but what she had heard had somehow attracted her: a heady cocktail of twisted love stories, cats and jazz, she'd heard some commentator on a late-night TV programme describe them. And the covers in England looked cool. This edition was a hardcover and didn't have a dust jacket, though.

Aurelia was twenty pages or so in when she felt a curious itch spread across the back of her neck, as if she was being watched. The last time the sensation had been so acute had been when she had run for the train in London, she remembered. She was about to turn her head and check out the room when she heard a voice from the other side of the reading bench, behind the small wall of books she had built to ensure her privacy and a lack of distractions. She experienced a brief sense of disorientation, like being observed, hemmed in from two separate directions. Out of instinct, her nostrils flared, in an attempt to recognise a familiar fragrance. Pomegranate? But there was nothing there to smell. But, for no reason, her lips felt wet. She licked them.

'Good book, eh?'

She moved her pile by a few inches to see who her interlocutor was.

It was a young man in his mid-twenties. He had light-brown hair which fell down over his forehead in a fringe. He wore dark horn-rimmed glasses, and Aurelia couldn't help noticing how his ears stuck out from the darker arrows of luxuriant sideburns that stopped halfway down the line of his jaw. Faint freckles dotted the bridge of his nose and the upper half of his cheeks, below a set of sharp cheekbones that any girl would have been jealous of.

The moment Aurelia set her eyes on him, she was reminded of the mental picture she'd formed the first time she'd read Mark Twain as an assigned book in school. The young man was the living image of an older Tom Sawyer. She couldn't help herself from smiling.

'I'm only a few chapters into it,' she said.

'Wow. You're English!' he exclaimed, his open mouth showing off a vista of whiter-than-white teeth.

Aurelia chuckled. 'Is it that obvious?'

His smile grew even wider, his eyes lighting up.

'It's a great book,' he continued. 'I envy you reading it for the first time.'

'Why?' Aurelia asked.

'Oh, I don't want to spoil it for you. You must read it to the end to find out.'

'I suppose so.'

'My name's Huck,' he said.

Aurelia burst out with irrepressible laughter.

'Not Huck Sawyer?'

'No. Name's Huck Johnson . . .'

She introduced herself.

He was from the Midwest and it was his second year at Berkeley, where he was studying for a Masters in anthropology. His parents were doctors. The thick volumes on his side of the reading table were all text books, but he loved modern fiction, he told her. Was even working on a novel of his own, he confessed. Had dreams of becoming a writer one day.

'I'd love to read it,' Aurelia politely suggested.

'It's anything but ready.' He lowered his eyes, as if embarrassed. 'So what brings you here?' he asked, less than artfully moving the conversation on.

Half an hour later, Huck suggested they might have a coffee. There was a decent cafeteria in the basement of the library, it seemed. Aurelia accepted.

When he rose from the bench she noted with surprise

that he happened to be surprisingly tall, towering half a head over her at well over six feet and more. For a while now she'd had a nagging feeling that she didn't even know how tall the man in the Bristol chapel had been. The sudden thought caused a knot to form in her stomach, eating at her insides.

Over terrible coffee and half-decent cupcakes and cookies, she forced herself to speculate what Huck body's looked like under his baggy lumberjack shirt and formless slacks. He looked younger than he was, which failed to turn her on. But she'd noted the gentle signs of desire in his eyes when he had looked lingeringly at her after she had risen from the library bench, her long, bare legs an unavoidable focus point, and how, even now, in the cafeteria, sitting side by side, his glance would unavoidably move to her uncovered thighs on occasion.

From time to time she allowed her tight tweed skirt to ride up to mid-thigh, maybe inadvertently allowing him a furtive glimpse of her white cotton knickers before she pulled the skirt down again. It felt like a game, and he was the perfect subject, and while the old Aurelia would have been downright dismissive at the way she was pulling his strings, the new post-crazy-heart Aurelia knew exactly what she was doing and was beginning to relish her new-found power. Were all men so easy to manipulate?

Huck was crashing on a friend's couch near the Haight, waiting for a share in a house closer to the campus to become available and there was no way that Aurelia's room above the ballet school basement could be used, so they agreed to split the cost of a motel room.

The young man's decrepit Japanese compact was a mess of crumpled, unwashed clothes he had been meaning to get to a laundry for ages, discarded sweet wrappers, old magazines and newspapers and empty coffee cups. He hurriedly cleared the front seat for Aurelia and she fitted her long frame into the narrow space and they roared off in search of the motel he claimed to remember. Aurelia wondered how many times he had been there with other girls. She quickly felt nauseous and rolled her window down as the car's petrol fumes assaulted her.

The drive was a silent one as she reflected on the turn of events and how she had ended up suggesting they sleep together. She knew unsentimentally that the young American was just a means to an end and felt unsure whether she liked herself for being so calculating and selfish.

Curtains drawn and a weak lamplight casting an eerie glow on the room's interior, Aurelia undressed as soon as they parted from their initial kiss. Huck just stood there, with eyes wide open, watching her, unable to believe his luck, as she stepped out of the short tweed skirt, her tall frame and endless legs bathed in a flickering orange glow.

'Wow!' he said. 'Are all you English gals so forward?'

Aurelia laughed. 'I have to go to the bathroom. Get your stuff off and see you in bed,' she demanded, stepping past the thin door that led to the sink where she felt a compulsion to brush her teeth and hoped the motel room provided a complimentary toothbrush. It didn't. She vigorously rubbed her wet fingers against her teeth and hunted for a mint in her bag. She slipped off her underwear and watched the deformed image of her naked body in the cracked mirror. She couldn't help glancing down, searching for the scarlet heart. Not that she was expecting to see it. Yet.

By the time she walked back into the unheated bedroom, shivering slightly, Huck had switched the light off and was sheltering between the covers. Aurelia lifted them and joined him. His body was blissfully warm and he was already hard, his cock jutting sideways against her hip as she settled on her back, her eyes reading patterns of grey in the pocked ceiling of the room. He shifted slightly, moving to kiss her again, adjusting his position alongside her, as if embarrassed that his penis was brushing against her.

His breath tasted of stale cigarette smoke. Aurelia took a deep breath; only one man so far had conjured the sweet aroma of fruit.

Mid-kiss, she parted her knees, allowing Huck to move himself between her legs. He clumsily positioned himself, still wary of closing the distance between their bodies. Aurelia found his cock and gripped it between her fingers. Even though it was quite rigid, it was also surprisingly soft and velvety to the touch. And hot.

Just like the stranger's had been.

Did all men feel the same? Would it be so simple to drive the stranger from her mind? Her brain went into overdrive, processing the sensation and corresponding thoughts. His kisses became more halting. He moaned as her fingers travelled down his stem and her nails grazed his balls. Aurelia buckled invitingly and Huck collapsed onto her.

'Fuck me. Now,' she whispered in the young man's ear.

'Are you sure?' he asked, as if hesitant to go all the way so soon.

Aurelia's lips broke away from his. 'Yes,' she groaned.

Still not letting go of his cock, she firmly guided it towards her. She knew she was extremely wet. He was about to breach her when she pulled back, and moved away from him on the bed.

'Do you have a condom?' she asked him breathlessly, red-faced with both desire and annoyance at having so easily forgotten such a basic precaution. Something her god-parents and teachers had drummed into her until it felt like a broken record. Although she recalled, with a sudden spasm of panic, that the Bristol stranger had not actually appeared to have used protection from the few details she could now clearly remember. Since she had neither given birth nor experienced any health problems since then, she thought it was safe to say she'd got away with it.

Huck leaned over his side of the bed and fished inside the pocket of the slacks he had tidily folded onto a nearby chair and pulled out a blue-ish wrapper.

As he tore it open with his teeth, his lower body and aroused penis still coyly obscured from her view by the sheets, Aurelia felt a pang of regret at the way this was all turning out wrong: no magic, no romance, just the ordinariness of sex. His cock might feel the same in her hand as the stranger's had, but nothing else did.

Now sheathed, Huck resumed his previous position between her thighs – Aurelia had not moved an inch – dispensing a tender smile by way of excuse in her direction as he entered her, his wet lips nibbling affectionately at her ear.

After a moment's pause, he began to move inside her. Aurelia lowered her guard and gave in to that exquisite feeling of being filled, even though it felt so different this time, mechanical, and that tingling, indefinable buzz, was not being allowed to rise through her veins.

Huck was whispering terms of endearment, but Aurelia ignored them, concentrating on stirring up forgotten sensations, returning them to life, but she couldn't prevent herself from being distracted by the tobacco on his breath, the sweat on his back, the way his fringe of hair flopped against her cheek, the monotonous in and out movements of his body against and inside her.

It seemed to go on for ever.

Huck must have noticed her lack of enthusiasm. 'Are you all right?' he asked.

'It's okay,' Aurelia said.

'Sure?' His thrusts slowed.

A flash of images rushed like wildfire in front of her eyes.

'Harder,' she said.

'How?'

She threw her arms to the side. 'Hold down my wrists, you can be rougher if you want,' she suggested, memories of the events she had witnessed at the exhibition flooding back.

He gripped her, but there was no conviction in his movements. She was about to ask him to spank her, hurt her even, but hesitated, shocked by the cravings washing over her. She attempted to blank both the invasive memories and the sordid environment of the cheap motel room.

She looked up at Huck and their eyes met.

'It's not working,' Aurelia said, detaching herself from him and rushing to dress.

'What did I do wrong?' Huck asked, fumbling for his own clothes, his arousal quickly abating.

'Nothing.'

'What did you mean by "harder"?' he begged her to explain.

'Nothing,' she repeated.

A veil of anger now clouded his gaze.

'I just don't understand girls like you,' he said.

'What do you means by "girls like me"?'

'Girls who want to be hurt. It's not the way I was brought up. I thought that—'

'You thought what?' Aurelia was slipping her head through the white T-shirt's narrow collar.

'Bay Area girls here are often kinky. Somehow I thought that you being a Brit, you wouldn't . . .' He looked away.

'I'm not kinky,' Aurelia shouted and rushed out of the door, anger getting the better of her.

There were no cabs around and she was obliged to walk back to the ballet school cottage. It took her over an hour and a half and she ended up fighting tears all the way. She knew she was changing inside; it wasn't just Siv's departure or the appearance of the strange heart on her body. Something else was happening.

As she reached the corner of her street, she was seized yet again by the unsettling feeling that she was being followed. And not by Huck; she knew she would never see the young man again. She turned her head but the avenue was empty, just autumn leaves dancing in the wind. She wiped the tears from her cheek. There was no need to worry Edyta, but now that she had nearly arrived home she could not face another evening alone and worrying about her friend. She nipped inside and penned a quick note to explain her absence and left it on her bed.

Found Siv, she wrote. *Staying away. Nothing to worry about. Will be in touch soon.*

She wasn't sure what it was that made her lie. Perhaps superstition; that if she put the thought in writing it might come true.

A light mist was beginning to fall and at the last moment Aurelia ran back inside and picked up a change of under-wear, a fresh T-shirt and her shawl from the hook by the door and pulled it tightly around her shoulders. It was the same shawl that she had worn at the funfair, she realised, with a pang of sadness. How long ago that seemed. And where should she go now?

She wandered down to the diner and stared in the window at the booth seat where she and Siv had once shared a plate of chips and excitedly discussed the origin of her tattoo and Siv's afternoon of nude modelling. No amount of looking through the glass would be able to bring her friend back, though, she knew that. She had to think. Where could Siv have gone?

Walter.

Instinctively, she knew that her friend had taken off with the blind sculptor. She racked her brain for the umpteenth time for any scrap of information that Siv might have mentioned that would lend a clue to her whereabouts. Siv had met him on the day that she had picked up the forms for the performing arts school, and she had mentioned that his workshop was nearby. But she couldn't go knocking on all the nearby doors at this hour.

She flagged a passing taxi and instructed the driver to take her back to the imposing venue where the exhibition had been held. It was the only thing that she could think of. Maybe she would get lucky and find a young man on duty at the front desk who would respond to the sight of her still bare legs and give her the information that she was seeking.

The stone building did not seem nearly as imposing or as magical on her third visit. Her initial appreciation of the structure was now tempered by her feeling that the exhibition that had been held here had ultimately resulted in Siv's disappearance. She was tempted to kick the wall in frustration, but knew that would lead her nowhere but probably leave her with a sore foot, so she contented herself with savagely ringing the buzzer on the front door over and over again.

'For God's sake! We're closed. And I don't even work here . . .' hissed a husky female voice into the intercom.

Aurelia had long given up hope that anyone would answer and was so surprised by the response that it took her a moment to gather her thoughts. A dim memory struggled to rise to the surface in her mind.

'Lauralynn?' she asked.

'Yes?' replied the voice suspiciously.

'Please let me in,' Aurelia asked. 'You worked at the exhibition. You dressed us . . . my name is Aurelia, I was here with a friend and now she's disappeared and I need to find her urgently. I think she might be with Walter, the sculptor . . .' The words tumbled out of her mouth haphazardly.

The door swung open.

Lauralynn stood right behind it, with a large carrier bag in each hand. She was no longer wearing latex, and her hair was tied back in a simple ponytail instead of the schoolgirl plaits that she had last been sporting, but, un-costumed, she was just as imposing. In her high heels she was taller even than Aurelia and her legs were longer than she remembered and seemed even shapelier clad in skin-tight denim. She was obviously braless and Aurelia couldn't help but stare at her breasts, which were covered only by a thin white vest top, through which a pair of nipple rings were clearly visible.

'You had a problem?' Lauralynn asked. 'Or have you forgotten what it was now? You seem rather, err, distracted.' She grinned from ear to ear, displaying a mischievous white-toothed smile.

Aurelia flushed all the way to her roots.

'I was at the exhibition . . .' she stammered. 'You lent me a dress . . .'

'Yes, I know who you are,' Lauralynn replied. 'You looked great in the dress, too.'

Aurelia didn't think it was possible to blush any more deeply than she already had, but somehow she managed it.

'You can have it if you like,' Lauralynn continued, glancing down at one of the carrier bags that now lay by her side. 'You're lucky you caught me. Only reason I'm here. Taking all the costumes and things down to our headquarters in Seattle.' She looked at her right wrist, though she wore no watch there. 'You'll have to be quick, though, my flight leaves soon. I'm on my way to the airport.'

'My friend Siv,' Aurelia said. 'I think she could be with Walter. Do you know how to find him? Or her?'

Lauralynn raised an eyebrow. She seemed amused by this news rather than surprised or worried, which Aurelia supposed was a good thing. At least it was evident that

Lauralynn didn't think running away with Walter was any cause for concern, so the blind sculptor probably wasn't a psychopath.

'Run away with Walter, eh?' Lauralynn mused. 'He does seem to have a knack for spotting them.'

She seemed to be talking to herself.

'Spotting them?' Aurelia asked. 'Models, do you mean?'

'Not exactly,' Lauralynn replied. 'But I don't have time to explain now. I can't take you to Walter. But I can take you to someone who probably knows where he is. You'll have to come with me, though. Now.'

Lauralynn picked up her carrier bags and began to hurry through the door, barrelling Aurelia out of the way and waving her arm to hail a passing cab.

'Come on then,' she yelled pulling open the passenger door and throwing in her bags.

Aurelia leaped into the back seat a moment before the taxi sped away. This caused her skirt to ride all the way up to the tops of her thighs and she self-consciously tried to hitch it down again.

'No need to be modest on my account,' Lauralynn murmured. She was far more forward than any man Aurelia had ever flirted with, perhaps with the exception of the stranger, though their limited but intense exchanges could hardly be considered flirting, had in fact been virtually dialogue-free. Briefly Aurelia wondered if Lauralynn's confidence extended to other areas and immediately she felt a familiar pulse throb.

She had never been with a woman before, nor considered such a possibility with any seriousness. Until now. Aurelia spent the rest of the journey with her mind in a tangle caught halfway between worry for Siv, satisfaction that she finally had a lead and the mental picture of Lauralynn's breasts squeezed into her T-shirt and the metal loops that so clearly decorated her permanently hard nipples.

Occasionally her mind would drift back to her tattoo and thoughts of the stranger and the memories and fantasies that he always elicited in her. She was certain that somehow the mysterious Walter and Siv's disappearance had something to do with him, and he was the one that she truly longed for. But it had been so long now without a word from him. She could not spend her life waiting for a man that she had not even seen.

The cab crossed the bridge, driving back to Oakland but before it could reach her suburb, it took a sharp turn and Aurelia found herself disembarking at Oakland airport. Lauralynn swiftly took charge and purchased a ticket for Aurelia. She protested, insisted on paying, but Lauralynn just waved her proffered credit card away.

It was raining in Seattle, and nearly midnight by the time they arrived. Aurelia was freezing cold and bone weary as they picked up Lauralynn's car, a small Honda Civic, from the Tacoma International car park. She didn't pay any attention to anything at all as they journeyed along dark, wet highways besides remembering the hypnotic sway of Lauralynn's hips and arse and marvelling at the way she could seemingly stride along forever in her stiletto heels without exhibiting a moment's pause or pain in her feet.

'We're here,' Lauralynn whispered breathily against her ear. Aurelia lifted her head. She had fallen asleep on Lauralynn's shoulder as the blonde had been driving. Lauralynn laid a warm hand on her thigh to gently rouse her. Aurelia felt her heart thudding in her chest. 'Not far to go now. I called Tristan and told him to put the kettle on. He makes the best hot chocolate. Soon you'll be warm all the way to your bones.'

Lauralynn and Tristan were sharing a hotel suite, yet they didn't appear to be lovers. Aurelia watched the two of them busying themselves in the small kitchen and mini-bar area. Domesticity clearly did not come naturally to either of them. Lauralynn had still not removed her high heels, and even in her casual T-shirt and jeans it seemed clear that she was more used to being waited upon than doing the waiting.

As she watched Lauralynn inexpertly tear open a sachet of sugar and spill it over the carpet, she had the distinct impression that this was not Lauralynn's usual style. She was being wooed. Tristan was far too good-looking to be at home in a kitchen. He was tall and tanned and muscled and moved with a slow languor that suggested he would be more at home lying back on a cushioned litter with slaves attending to his every whim.

'So you two work together?' Aurelia asked. She was eager to get to news of Siv in case she fell asleep and Tristan disappeared before she could quiz him.

'Not exactly,' Tristan said as he passed her a tiny espresso cup and saucer filled with an aromatic, deep-brown liquid.

Aurelia took a sip. It was chocolate, hot and thick with a touch of spice. Immediately she felt her chill lift and a soothing sensation filled her all the way to her toes and her fingertips. 'But this is . . . I think I have had this before,' she said.

'Everyone's had hot chocolate before,' Lauralynn interjected, sliding into the spare seat alongside Aurelia before

Tristan had a chance to. 'Though he does make rather a special brew, I'll give him that.'

Aurelia took another long, hard look at Tristan. Could he be the stranger? The man that she had desired for so long? She didn't think so. He was attractive, beautiful even. But it was an unsettling sort of attraction: something physical welling up inside her. Something in her brain was warning her about an unquiet darkness surrounding him. But at the same time, that darkness beckoned to her, as if it was part of something greater, something he was part of. No, he was not the man she had given in to and gifted herself to, had willingly been taken by. Surely she would recognise 'him' somehow, even from a distance, would be able to feel the presence of the man who had stirred such strong passions within her that night and in so many of her waking fantasies since.

'Do you know where Siv is?' she asked him outright.

'I know where Walter is,' Tristan replied. 'Or at least, I know where he will be, two nights from now. And if your friend is with him as you believe, then she will be there too and I can help you find her.'

'What do you mean, she will be there? Where?' Aurelia grumbled. She was growing tired of all this secrecy.

'A very special party,' Lauralynn said. 'The Ball. It's our highlight of the year.'

'Our highlight of the year? Who is "Our"?'

'Probably best that you get some sleep before we tell you all about it,' Lauralynn soothed.

Aurelia's cup was taken away from her. She murmured her thanks to Tristan for the drink, but he had gone back to the mini-bar and she was alone with Lauralynn on the couch. The warm hand that had rested so gently on her thigh in the back of the taxi cab was pressing against her skin harder now and she shivered as Lauralynn's nails pressed against her skin, right at the seam of her knickers.

'I should take a shower . . .' Aurelia said sleepily, remembering that although it already felt like a lifetime ago, she was still wearing the same clothes that she had put back on again after her brief encounter with the Tom Sawyer look-alike from the university library.

'You can share mine,' Lauralynn replied, and then Aurelia felt the velvety softness of Lauralynn's mouth against her own and the flicker of a warm, wet tongue delving gently between her lips.

Lauralynn pulled her to her feet into the nearest bedroom. The last thing that Aurelia saw before the door was shut firmly behind them was Tristan's eyes boring into her own. Did she see a flicker of anger pass over his face? Or was it simply disappointment?

7

The Island of Doctor Wells

'It's a very exclusive party,' Tristan had said, 'but I believe your friend might be found there. I hear many circus folk and guys and gals from the arty crowd will be attending. Quite an event. It only comes round once a year and always somewhere different. And I mean really different. I went to one that was held in some underground caves and half the entertainers were dressed as bats and seemed to be flying. You won't ever attend a more incredible party.'

'You'll love it,' Lauralynn assured her, as they sipped their coffees in the sheltered courtyard of the hotel where she was staying off Pike Place Market.

It was the best coffee Aurelia had tasted since she had arrived in America. Warm, pungent, velvety, it spread across her throat as it travelled down, both soothing her senses and making them sharper. She took every sip as slowly as she could, to savour the taste better. Now she knew why Seattle was considered the coffee city of America.

Lauralynn winked at her.

'Nice?'

'Delicious.'

Tristan was looking intently at both of them and Aurelia wondered how much he knew, how close he was to Lauralynn. From the studied shape of his enigmatic smile, she guessed he knew everything. Aurelia blushed. She was anything but ashamed at having slept with Lauralynn; it had been an incredible experience. But she felt unsure about this undeniably attractive man being able to picture the way she had surrendered to pleasure in the arms of a woman.

His dark-green eyes alighted on her and she imagined him savouring the vision of their intertwined limbs. She drew a long breath. Even the way that he moved was hypnotic, and whenever she was in his presence she felt as though he was drawing her closer to him as if they were magnetised. He was difficult to read, though, and Aurelia was not convinced that she could trust him enough to let her guard down entirely. She would settle for admiring his physique from arm's length, at least for the moment.

'It's strictly by invitation only,' Tristan said. 'But I am allowed to bring guests. However, the location must remain a secret and you will have to accept wearing something over your eyes for the crossing,' he continued. 'just for an hour or so,' he added.

'An island?' Aurelia asked.

'An island, yes,' Tristan confirmed.

Aurelia was aware there were hundreds of islands in Puget Sound, so it would literally be a venture into the dark. Could she trust Tristan?

The others' eyes were on her, as if they were both conspirators and she was the outsider.

'I'm willing to go,' Aurelia said.

Arrangements were made for the following evening and Tristan left them.

Sitting alone with Lauralynn, Aurelia realised with a sense of panic she had nothing to wear for the Ball, having travelled to Seattle with just a change of T-shirt and under-wear.

'Don't worry,' Lauralynn assured her, a playful tone in her voice. 'Come back to my room. I'd certainly enjoy undressing you again and then we can even try some of my stuff on you. It'll be fine. We're almost the same height and as for size, did you know I'm a whizz with a needle and thread?'

Once they had boarded the ferry, a group of men in dark-blue sailor suits – Tristan among them – circulated amongst the guests and proceeded to restrict their vision, one by one, by blindfolding them with exquisitely soft silk night masks. Each mask was embroidered in silver thread with a symbol Aurelia was unable to recognise.

Lauralynn's sight had not been impaired, leading Aurelia to the conclusion that she officially held an invitation to the mysterious event and was actually in cahoots with Tristan, took her by the hand and led her below deck. A sharp, bitter breeze was rising from the west, zigzagging its way through the jigsaw puzzles of islands littering the Sound, and freezing Aurelia to the bones under the flimsy gown that Laura-lynn had altered to suit her: a mess of multicoloured chiffon that tied at her waist and a V-neck around her neck, barely covering her breasts and leaving her back and all the way to her belly button completely naked. When she spun, or if the fabric caught in the breeze, then the loose, full skirt flew up in all directions like a parachute, as if it that had been the designer's intention, and Aurelia guessed that it probably had. Lauralynn had dressed to outrank Tristan, in skin-tight latex captain's regalia complete with gold stripes on her sleeves and a blue and white hat that sat high on her head and made her just a few inches taller than he was. Aurelia had struggled to hide her amusement when she noticed Tristan's sulky response to Lauralynn's choice of attire. Lauralynn had caught her eye and winked, well aware that she had ruffled Tristan's sartorial feathers.

As promised, the hop to the island took under an hour, which came as a relief to Aurelia, who, despite having been brought up by the sea, had never had much in the way of sea legs and had been apprehensive about the crossing, fearful of being sick and ruining her dress in the process.

As the ferry docked, there was a rumour of voices on the bridge above them as instructions were called out and the pitter-patter of feet increased. They had been sitting in a corner below, huddled together in silence although Aurelia had been full of questions.

Lauralynn rose and took her hand again and Aurelia followed, still unaccustomed to the enforced darkness, taking care not to stumble when her feet came across steps. Arriving on deck into the open, it felt like night, a distinctive chill in the air, and her senses were assaulted by a complex swirl of fragrances; the aroma of the sea blending with an intoxicating palette of sweetness, spices, fruit and other notes that teased her senses. It felt as if the island they had landed on lived outside time and was not subject to the normal laws of humankind, bathing in a glow and an odour of its own, unlike any other.

Before Aurelia could fully absorb her new environment, she felt Lauralynn's hand let go of her and heard a whisper in her ear: 'Welcome to the island of Doctor Wells . . .'

It was Tristan's voice.

And then, from Lauralynn, 'I'll see you later, sweetie. I

have matters to attend to,' followed by the sound of departing footsteps.

She could hear the murmur of her fellow passengers welcoming their arrival and the gentle sound of the sea beneath her as a hand she guessed was Tristan's took hold of hers and guided her across the deck. She gingerly manoeuvred herself, with his help, onto the lowered walkway that descended towards *terra firma*.

She finally set foot on the island, felt others brushing against her and heard a chorus of sighs rising as the guests realised they had finally arrived at their destination.

Tristan's hand rose and loosened her mask.

Aurelia found herself just a stone's throw from the shore. There was no port, no building, just a shingle beach, a scarred line of wave-swept rocks and a thick wall of trees facing them. She shivered.

'What is this?' she asked Tristan, a hint of anxiety creeping into her voice. She had not anticipated an uninhabited island.

'Don't fret,' he replied. Through the cloud of night that surrounded them, she could see many of the other guests crowding around her and appearing similarly nonplussed by their situation.

'It's the reason this particular island was procured. Discretion.' He tugged on Aurelia's hand. He was wearing white leather gloves.

She followed his nudge and saw her fellow visitors being similarly prodded on by their minders. Stepping hesitantly, the small group broke through the line of trees and, in an instant, were rewarded by a flickering set of lights ahead, colours juggling with each other, bright reds and greens and every variation of the rainbow, like will-o'-the-wisps dotting the night.

Encouraged, their step quickened and the guests advanced in single file towards the illuminated area that was coming into focus.

As they got closer, it became apparent there was a forest inside the forest, with a group of outlying one-storey buildings dotted at irregular intervals along its periphery. A world within a world. They crossed the first row of lights and the ambient temperature rose as if by miracle, the night breeze magically fading away under the powerful attack of the hundreds of lights bathing the inner forest in warmth.

Broken shards of music threaded their way towards them from the distant heart of the woods – the sound of calliopes tinkling away, the melancholy strain of violins and the swing of entrancing melodies Aurelia was still unable to put a name to. The guests surrounding her purred with excitement and began to break ranks, drawn to the festivities and the line of lights with joyous abandon.

Aurelia wondered whether she should rush after them, seek out Lauralynn. Maybe Siv was somewhere ahead? But Tristan still gripped her hand and they came to a standstill as a multitude of guests emerging into the bay of bright lights overran them. Where had they all come from? There must have been several ferries disgorging them onto the island, not just the one she had travelled on, she guessed. Arriving from shores scattered up and down the Oregon coastline and further afield.

Her apprehension was melting away.

Aurelia glanced ahead at the exotically attired guests almost waltzing between the trees. She looked up and was struck by how extraordinarily green the branches were, every leaf impossibly hand-painted by some expert jeweller so it shone with a thousand shades of life. Like a stage set up in the middle of nowhere, both artificial and familiar, a theatre of dreams where the green of the tree leaves conjugated with the solar explosion of the artfully disposed lights bathing the centre of the island with a magic circle of enchantment.

'It's . . . beautiful,' she said in a hushed tone, the mere thought of being any louder an offence to the spectacle unfolding before her eyes.

'Isn't it?' Tristan replied, a benevolent look of self-satisfaction moving across his full lips. 'We plan every Ball for a whole year, with much attention to every single detail. It has to be unique. That's the only rule.'

'I don't know why,' Aurelia remarked, 'but it makes me think of Shakespeare. *A Midsummer's Night Dream*.'

'Oh yes, it is said Will once came to the Ball years ago.' Tristan nodded.

'Really?'

'We go back centuries,' Tristan said. 'But only the Network elders know the whole story . . . I'm only second generation.'

So he was now revealing himself. Contradicting what he had said a few days earlier. He was directly involved with the Ball, not just a guest.

Peels of nearby laughter reached their ears. Through the break between a clump of trees and tall bushes, a woman trailing a thin white veil ran barefoot, pursued by what looked like a faun. Aurelia blinked, but the couple had already moved away, just the echo of their laughter flickering.

'We can join the festivities later,' Tristan said. 'There is no rush.'

All Aurelia wanted was to run into the heart of the forest and experience its delights, to seek out Siv if this was where she now was, and to see Lauralynn again, but Tristan's voice held a quiet authority and he emanated that unsettling aura of curious attraction. Every time she looked into his green eyes, she couldn't help but be submerged in a multitude of feelings. She knew she couldn't truly trust him, but something inside her was strongly drawn to him, somehow perceiving that he could fill something hollow inside her and perhaps even answer many of those lingering questions that had trailed her like heavy baggage ever since she had been a child. Aurelia shuddered, a fine mist falling across her eyes. She felt dizzy. It was the intimation of imminent answers as well as a strange sense of déjà vu. A feeling of belonging.

As if reading her thoughts, Tristan said, 'You can feel it, can't you?'

'What?' Aurelia protested.

'We were born on the same day,' Tristan said.

'Were we?' Her mind was racing. 'How can you know that?'

'Come,' he suggested, indicating the small bungalow on their left. Her mind was spinning in a whirl. Fuck, was he about to reveal he was her long-lost twin, and she was trapped in the convoluted machinations of some Victorian novel? Aurelia began to feel there was a *deus ex machina* offstage, presiding over her life, tugging on invisible strings, manipulating her, and she was fast losing control.

'Come,' he said again.

But they did not enter the flat-roofed and shuttered wooden building; Tristan stopped once they had reached the deck and turned solemnly towards her. Aurelia read hesitation in his eyes. In the distance were the sounds of laughter and celebration spinning around the echoes of faltering melodies, beckoning them.

He stood there, gazing at her with both longing and, Aurelia felt, apprehension. He was the same height as her, broad-shouldered and narrow-hipped. A swimmer's build, she knew from days spent at the local pool back home, where she, Siv and their friends had often gossiped outrageously and giggled enviously about the bodies of the sportier boys from the neighbouring comprehensive. In their tight Speedos they paraded and dived self-consciously into the pool, showing off their compact bodies under the judgemental gaze of the teenage girls gathered on the other side in instinctive segregation.

Tristan reminded Aurelia of them, the perfect proportions of his body under the fluid material of his uniform not quite in sync with the hints of both shallowness and cruelty rising from his aura.

'So what's this all about?' Aurelia asked him.

'Don't you know?'

'No, I don't. Who are you and Lauralynn? How do you know who I am? How could you know when I was born?'

He ignored her questions.

'You are here for a reason. Don't you feel it? You're meant to be present at the Ball.'

For a brief, impulsive moment, Aurelia wanted to storm away, suffocated by a torrent of strange feelings, assaulted by memories she didn't know she had. That unexplained, faint smell of pomegranate reached her, the distinct song of distant cicadas, all like a film in terribly accelerated motion. Still giddy with a sense of disorientation, she felt unsure of herself. There was the sound of movement on the periphery of her consciousness and she abruptly turned round, overcome by the feeling they were being observed, but the night failed to unveil any shadows.

There was something, a kernel of lost information at the back of her brain. It floated there, suspended, unapproachable, but she couldn't get it into focus. Still, she was aware it was important.

And she also knew that Tristan, facing her with that look of severity and veneration, was willing her to remember.

Reality receded – the forest, the bright lights, the island all retreating – until she pictured herself within an impregnable cocoon of power where the whole world orbited around her, depended on her. And she was also on the outside looking in. Watching attentively as her tall silhouette stood still, clad in opaque gauze, her long limbs a harmony of flesh, the gentle curve of her small breasts, their high line stretching the thin material that barely clothed her, the rounded outline of the curve of her arse cleverly disturbing the melodic geometry of her body.

Aurelia drew her breath as, for the first time in ages, she felt the heart near her cunt pulsing away, a steady rhythm, a drumbeat of tension. She had no need to look down, to investigate under the shimmering dress Lauralynn had devised for her to confirm its reappearance. It was alive. More than ever. Pumping the blood of desire through her veins, reaching for every extremity of her body. She shuddered. She was unable to move, rooted to the spot, fire spreading along her limbs.

Tristan extended his arm in her direction, pulled up his sleeve and turned his wrist towards her.

Carved across his prominent, bulging veins, was a picture, the tattoo of a similar heart to hers, although its colours were fading, nowhere as sharp as the one she had lower down. It was smaller too.

A mark of recognition.

'I know where yours is . . .' he said, his voice trailing away through the intoxicating silence that surrounded them.

How could he know?

He moved towards Aurelia.

A gentle breeze enveloped her, and she watched as her dress rose all the way to her waist, uncovering her legs and lower stomach, as if being lifted by other hands. She was unable to look round and confirm if they had been joined on the bungalow's deck by others. The sweet fragrance of exotic fruit wafted across her face, carried like electricity along waves of night air. It was like being paralysed, although she welcomed her helplessness and had no desire to feel otherwise.

Tristan kneeled in front of her and reverently pulled her knickers down.

As he inevitably unveiled the tattoo of her heart, she saw a flash of recognition race across his green eyes.

With his hands on her thighs he inched his face nearer to her until the warmth of his lips radiated gently all the way to her labia, the hidden waves of his breath travelling across the ridge of her opening.

She felt his hands spreading her legs, his mouth

advancing towards her now intoxicatingly wet slit and finally experienced the subtle roughness of his tongue inside her as his hands now tenderly opened her up and he began to taste her, like a bee diving into a flower in search of honey, like an explorer searching for treasure.

Aurelia could no longer see Tristan's head as he began to lick and play with her. Her dress, against all laws of gravity, now floated in mid-air around her waist, forming an impenetrable cloud between them.

It was both similar and totally different to the way Lauralynn had aroused her, orchestrating the rise of her pleasure, masterfully riding the waves of her orgasm. Tristan was skilful, but there was also an element of worship in the way he delved inside her that Lauralynn had quite deliberately bypassed. She had been more savage, demanding, blissfully selfish. He was almost studious, as if he was holding back, respecting unsaid limits.

Why am I being so analytical? Aurelia asked herself. Comparing Lauralynn and Tristan was ridiculous. They were totally different experiences.

His tongue danced across the damp lips of her cunt, like a firefly; clever, sly, inquisitive, caressing her labia, darting here and there, seeking her out, drawing her pleasure, toying with her folds, nibbling her until she was unable to distinguish between pleasure and pain.

She closed her eyes and went into mental freefall as Tristan orchestrated her orgasm, swiftly and expertly, reading the journey of her lust as it travelled from pussy to heart to her fingertips to the pit of her stomach and then again to her heart.

As much as she enjoyed his ministrations, Aurelia

experienced a twinge of regret and knew deep inside her soul that what he was doing to her was not an unselfish act of love, but an elaborate ritual, another stage in her awakening and that she was not destined to be his, nor even Lauralynn's, who had toyed with her so well the night before. Against all logic, she was convinced there would be another. There must be. Soon. Who would know every note, every melody she could play, that could be played with her. A virtuoso. The one. Who would answer all the questions, the Ball, the tattoos, this strange journey she appeared to be undertaking like a puppet on a string.

She peaked, coming with a deep and pleasurable sigh.

Her perception returned and her body relaxed, abandoning its tenseness. She felt as though her mind had been momentarily wiped clean in that sublime second of non-existence, but now her consciousness returned and she regained awareness of her situation: the outlying bungalow, the forest nearby and all the joyful, drunken sounds rushing through the branches of the trees, the intense brightness of the artificial sky created by the canopy of multicoloured lights, the island.

Tristan was still on his knees, his head down. Her dress had floated down again and now covered her limbs and the still pulsating fire raging inside her. She knew the heart next to her smoothness kept on burning bright; she had no need to check.

Her paralysis swept away from her and, out of habit, she brought a hand up to brush away some strands of hair sweeping irritably across her forehead.

It came as yet another shock that she now displayed a second heart, smaller, less aggressive, but similar to the first one and Tristan's own, painted across the tight skin on the underside of her wrist. It was inert, not beating, like a years-old tattoo. She gazed at the new apparition delicately etched across her pale skin, uncomprehending, dazed.

'Take me to the ball,' Aurelia whispered.

A hundred steps from the deck of the low-lying bungalow. Aurelia counted each of them as if she was living in a fairy tale and there was a precise ritual to be followed for fear of breaking the enchantment. To the line of the trees through which a river of light illuminated the heart of the forest, crossing a veil of darkness shielding the spectacle like a moat. And then the world came alive.

The music, the laughter, the fragrant winds of spices, incense and perfume infusing the air like a palette of intoxicating wildness.

The voices of men and women rising up and down like a wave of sounds weaving a siren spell.

Her heart couldn't beat any faster. She looked round and saw that Tristan was no longer with her. Had she left him behind, or was it written in some legendary book of days (and nights?) that she should face the next part of this adventure alone?

A melody rose majestically through the canopy of branches, swooping down on her, the crystal tones of a violin in full flight, both caressing her senses and aggressively taunting them. The tune was familiar and, after a brief second of disorientation, it came to her: Vivaldi, *The Four Seasons*, although she was unsure which particular season this happened to be. The divine music soared and fell and carried her steps along a narrow path that led to a glade where the intensity of the light was almost blinding and she had to rub her eyes to acclimatise her vision.

The bright lights dotted amongst the branches of the hundreds of trees shone like a million multicoloured suns. People were running everywhere, every costume more elaborate and magical than the one before, floating along currents of heady joy. Materials shimmered, creased, swam in the air, heavy and courtly, light and evanescent, waves of movement blending into each other, sheer beauty in motion, with too many fleeting details and which she was unable to analyse or process in the magic of the moment.

Most here were human but others, passing too fast along Aurelia's visual horizon to make any lasting impression, were disguised in a semblance of the animal kingdom: fauns, birds with wild plumage, dogs (or wolves – it was difficult to tell them apart), horses, lions even, cats with sly masks and furry wraps, satyrs and all sort of mythological creatures she couldn't recall a specific name for. A bull moving proudly and with a distinct air of superiority along a path. Was it actually a bull? Aurelia hesitated as she spotted his horns. She saw a tall man in fearsome leather garb pulling a group of nude women with dark collars around their necks behind him, each with a number painted across her right buttock. Another uniformed warrior pulled a cart in which two bare-breasted mermaids were sprawling on a bed of water. They were followed by a centaur, half-horse, half-broad-chested man.

As Aurelia advanced, the participants of the Ball would invariably make space for her, opening a path, as if fully aware of her presence and marking her progress towards the heart of the burning forest. But no one would speak to her, let alone touch her along the way, as if all were part of a complicated scenario and there to facilitate her journey. As if this story had long been written and no one was even willing or capable of changing it now that Aurelia was actually present on the island and a guest of the Ball.

A circle of diminutive women was dancing, hand in hand, running in elaborate geometrical patterns, arms strung along like a daisy wheel; each woman was naked but for a garland of lilies wrapped around her hair. In the tumult of movement, Aurelia noted that every possible combination of hair shades was present: blondes, dark and light; brunettes, ranging from deepest ebony to the familiar colour of warm mud; redheads moving between flame and the comfort of auburn.

They moved with grace and complexity, carried on the joy of laughter, ever in motion. As she approached the group, Aurelia saw that each tiny woman was like a delicate miniature – breasts small with hard nipples denoting their maturity, limbs small but perfectly formed and subtle proportions and rounded hips, firm, high buttocks and flesh through which taut arrows of experience had long marked the territory of their sexuality. On closer viewing, their faces were quite adult, well-knowing, and etched sharply with experience of life. It was the exquisite balance of their bodies that had induced Aurelia to think they might have been considerably younger on first appearance. And their distinctive lack of pubic hair was no sign of pre-pubescence, but evidence of systematic epilation of a permanent nature that no longer had to rely on the blade of a razor.

'Our Mistress-in-Waiting is back,' a shrill, bird-like voice said and the circle of tiny dancers broke and welcomed

Aurelia in their midst, opening up like a shell to welcome her.

The tallest of the small women, by barely a wisp of hair, advanced towards Aurelia, knelt before her and, somehow out of nowhere, offered her a garland of flowers, indicating to Aurelia she should similarly place it around her own head. It fitted like a glove and as she adjusted her hair and swept a strand away from her forehead, the thin dress she had been wearing was gently but firmly pulled away from her body and Aurelia found herself naked but for the crown of flowers. Hers were dark red in sharp contrast to the peaceful white lilies of the tiny women.

They were all gazing at her with wonder. Why were they calling her a Mistress-in-Waiting? What did that mean?

Aurelia glanced down and saw that the two hearts – on the underside of her wrist and by her cunt – were now shining like fire, as if the countless lights in the trees were all pointing in her direction.

She also knew that familiar sensations were beginning to run through her body and she was unable to control them. But rather than feel vulnerable at being so naked and exposed in the open air – she wasn't cold at all, as if the whole area she was standing in did not answer to the normal call of nature, night and temperature – she felt curiously assured, dominant, expectant.

The circle of nymphets stepped back, opening up a new path for Aurelia and she moved ahead, the blazing fire of light in the heart of the forest ahead of her acting like a magnet. A warm, sensuous breeze floated against her bare skin like a never-ending caress.

In a large, central clearing over which an eruption of

multicoloured lights swam like an alien sun exploding in a thousand directions at once, stood a large clearing where the vast grass lawn was littered with a dozen or so canopies and tents, walls of white material fluttering like silk against limbs, at one with the gentle breeze. For a brief moment she felt like Alice in Wonderland and every tent opening was beckoning to her, begging her to enter, watch, taste whatever forbidden pleasures were concealed within.

Watch me.

Eat me.

Savour my juices.

Savour me.

Like telepathic voices coasting along invisible ley lines straight towards her brain.

It was like being drunk, even if Aurelia had precious little experience of ever being so. A curious sense of liberation, a light-headed giddiness that moved her feet and soul.

She peered inside the first tent, and laid eyes on a tangle of bodies in motion, embedded in each other, moving, undulating to the loud sounds of a beating heart, a raging tsunami of flesh and joy, a slow-motion earthquake whose inner rhythms and frenzied couplings called to her. A dizzying concert of voices, moans, frantic exhalations, sighs weighed down by all the memories of the world, the words become flesh.

Aurelia drew her breath, captivated by the spectacle, awe and wonder, unbridled lust and shock coursing through her at a rate of knots. Somehow she knew that if she stepped inside the tent, she would become its captive for ever and ever, like a fly in a spider's web, a prisoner deep in the amber depths of centuries of lust.

With difficulty she tore her eyes away.

She walked to the next open canopy where long tables laden with food, fruit and drink, each more exotic in appearance and likely in taste than the one before, initially blocked the entrance. Cakes lovingly carved into the shape of swollen Fabergé eggs, avocados from which the finest of caviar could be scooped, tender morsels of meat and fish, declawed lobster pincers, rows of identical oysters and clams on beds of crumpled ice.

She paused. Fleeting silhouettes ran like ghosts around her, overtaking her, passing her, in perpetual motion along roads of laughter as she gathered her wits and peered nervously beyond the tall tables and, out of the corner of her eye, she caught sight of the centaur she had crossed paths with earlier. He was sprawled across a confusion of silk cushions, his animal lower half now more obviously an artifice, his massive chest a swirl of dark curls, head back, legs wide apart, heavy-thighed. His mouth was wide open, and between his mighty legs a woman's dark-haired head could be seen moving up and down, her mouth wrapped across the thick meat of the rigid cock which strained through the opening in his costume. The woman was on all fours, her buttocks in the air. Aurelia had a jolt of recognition – something about the soft curve of the woman's arse, the way she moved – and she realized it was Siv.

She wanted to call out to her friend, but was hypnotised, silenced by the sheer beauty of the ritual, the evidenced slow reverence and hunger of Siv's oral ministrations.

Aurelia's heartbeat was dancing the light fantastic as she stood motionless, watching her friend and whoever the stranger was in oral congress, voyeuristically admiring the measured advance of the large penis's shaft deeper into Siv's mouth, and how a stream of profound pleasure animated her friend's bared skin, moving below its surface, illuminating it with an inner glow with every new, imperceptible movement.

Frozen in fascination, Aurelia could not tear herself away from the spot, barely noticing the other couples, threesomes and moresomes dotted across the area, all active and dancing to the sound of their own inner tunes, fucking, thrusting, bucking, struggling, advancing and retreating, like beautiful beasts lounging amongst the sea of silk cushions that littered the canopy's floor.

A shadow of fearsome light bounded across the room and the tangle of bodies almost changed colour. And then Aurelia noticed the presence of a solitary man, clothed, sitting squarely in a yoga-like position in a corner of the area: Walter. Between his hands was a lump of wet clay, which he was kneading and pummelling and twisting, an angelic smile on his lips, his dark, empty eyes darting from one copulating couple to another, capturing the essence of the action with the cleverness of his hands.

Aurelia began to realise that for every movement of his agile fingers, a couple somewhere under the night canopy also moved, providing him with a new angle, a new revelation, a new position. Walter was their conductor. A blind man leading an orchestra of unbound pleasure, leading each and every soul and body here towards their climax.

And what then? Aurelia wondered.

Siv stepped back slowly from the centaur's open thighs and looked round. As she did so, she noticed Aurelia standing there transfixed.

She smiled and Aurelia's heart froze.

Never had she witnessed such a blissful smile on her friend's face. It was a smile of deep happiness, of reassurance, of ultimate contentment. Their eyes made contact. Siv's shone with a terrible splendour.

I am home, the glint in her pupils seemed to say to her friend.

A deep sigh of relief washed over Aurelia. Siv was here. She was okay. She was happy even. But as she watched her friend lower herself slowly onto the centaur, Aurelia couldn't bear to look any longer for fear of bursting into tears. For she knew that from this moment onward, Siv now belonged to the Ball and its mysteries and they would never return to the life they had once shared.

She ran from the open canopy and found herself back in the open, trees scattered around her like slender barriers, grass under her feet, a tenuous and haphazard labyrinth of wood and leaves that felt alive to her senses. Her disorientation grew.

The lights from above the forest roof began to lower in intensity, and Aurelia imagined herself in the centre of a whirlpool, her feet unsteady, being washed from place to place between a welter of sounds, bare bodies brushing against her as they rushed by. She blinked and another tent appeared, dark against the wall of night, its silhouette carved against the fading lights. She had no doubt in her mind that this was her appointed destination, the ultimate reason she had been brought here. The funfair, the kiss, Gwillam Irving and his office, the inheritance – if inheritance it had been and not just a moneyed mirage to lure her here – the blind sculptor, that fateful night in the Bristol chapel, Lauralynn, Tristan, the new-found certainty rising inside her that nothing had been random.

It was like a fever marching through her, unstoppable, desired, fearsome.

Her apprehension grew and she raised her hand to brush her hair away under the garland of red flowers, the crown that only emphasised the pallor of her skin. She shivered. She was in an unknown wood, naked, vulnerable, lost.

As her limp hand fell, she caught sight of the image of the heart on her wrist. It was scarlet and now burned from the inside, a soothing fire, a source of heat and dull pleasure. She looked down and saw another tattoo now adorning her body, slightly off centre between her breasts, shadowing her real heart. Beating fiercely to their own rhythm, the heat like a blanket, a force field in which she was cocooned.

She looked up at the tent. A similar image of a fiery red heart stood out on the canvas where an opening lay, flaps of material shimmering in the night breeze.

Aurelia stepped forward.

Walked into darkness.

Stopped. Stood motionless.

As if by magic, the dark interior of the tent took on a blue, artificial hue and light slowly rose, illuminating her new surroundings.

There were no bodies in motion here, no tables bursting with food and wine, just an empty space in the centre of which an immensity of rich Arabian carpets were strewn. They made her think of Scheherazade and the *Thousand and One Nights*, brought to mind faint memories of the first time she had felt sexually aroused as a growing teenager when reading those exotic stories, and the guilt she had then experienced imagining herself as some sacrificial virgin to some dark and handsome sultan or adventurer.

A hand landed on her shoulder.

Aurelia emerged with a start from her reverie.

Turned.

Even before she set eyes on him, she smelled his scent, that unmistakable wind of fruit and musk and kindness and knew exactly who he was.

His voice was like honey, deep and tender.

'Welcome back to the Ball, Aurelia.'

He was standing straight and still, just half a head taller than her. His face was a perfect blend of narrow oval and square jaw, his lips full, his cheekbones pronounced and his hair a kindly mat of dark-auburn curls.

She held her breath, as if to make the moment last for ever.

He was dressed in a simple white shirt, open wide at the collar, and a pair of tight, dark breeches as if he was an acrobat. Her gaze could not help but linger in the area of his crotch as she, with a deep blush running across her cheeks, remembered the feel of him inside her.

'You . . .' she muttered.

'My name is Andrei,' he said, looking into her eyes.

Aurelia felt like fainting as surging waves of relief and joy fought inside her.

'You . . .' she repeated, losing all power of intelligible speech.

His hand moved from her naked shoulder, and the realisation that she was still naked while he was still clothed made her feel ever so vulnerable.

'It's been . . .' she attempted to say.

'A long time coming,' Andrei said.

New Orleans 1916

Thomas had been riding the rails with hoboes and their like for a couple of years since his arrival in the country, just before the war had broken out in Europe. It was a perilous thing to do, hiding inside the boxcars of trains and seldom knowing what his destination would turn out to be. He had become an expert in avoiding the greedy brakemen, at waiting at watering tanks and railroad yards for trains to slow down. He had grown accustomed to sharing journeys and stories with the flotsam and jetsam of the early century, fractured version of the American dream, but unlike them it wasn't hunger or despair that had forced him into this.

He had learned how to ride a blind and deck a train from experts like Josiah Flynt and Jack London and how to avoid getting locked inside a reefer by always carrying a piece of wood to keep the door from locking shut. He had also made good friends, suffered a few broken ribs and beatings by railroad thugs and fellow illegal passengers but, most of all, he had collected information. Piece by piece, word by word.

About the Ball.

It was five years since he had first heard of its shadowy existence. It had been one of countless extraordinary rumours that circulated freely amongst the students at Heidelberg University where he was studying English Language. But then the liberal consumption of alcohol and the dissipated ambience of the times encouraged such fantasies. Thomas had never lent much credence to the raft of apocryphal stories that spread like wildfire through the student community. People needed dreams to escape reality, Thomas reckoned, while he was a genuine realist and had no truck with illusions.

Like all students and professors, Thomas had been a regular in the brothels of the lower town. Not though, for all the reasons that his colleagues most likely suspected. He did not seek out whores because they were ever obliging, cheerful and truculent, or because for his first two years at Heidelberg he had needed a suitable release valve from the pressures of his studies in what was such a predominantly male environment, although those things helped too.

No. What Thomas sought was discretion.

Though he now lived as a man and could not remember a time when he had not thought of himself as one, regardless of the mechanics of his form or biological function, he could not escape the fact that he had been born a woman, no matter how hard he tried.

As a child, he had torn the frills from his dresses, ignored the dolls that he received as gifts from his grandparents, and sought pleasure in climbing trees instead of learning to bake or embroider. He had been indulged by a mother who didn't know what else to do with him and ignored by a father who, intent on rising through the ranks as a public servant, was rarely home and paid no attention to such matters. But when he had grown older and had shorn his thick, long brown curls from his head with his mother's sewing scissors and insisted on being called Thomas instead of Therese, things had reached a tipping point.

Fearful of how their small community might perceive even the smallest deviation from what they believed to be appropriate gender norms, his Protestant parents had packed Therese off to her grandparents for a time, where she supposedly married and moved abroad and Thomas had been created. His father had pulled some strings, fiddled with records and bribed an old friend who enrolled him in Heidelberg University as a male student.

Things were different in the larger centres, Berlin particularly, where the researcher Magnus Hirschfeld campaigned for gay and transgender rights and ran the 'Scientific-Humanitarian Committee', which was all good and well, but Thomas did not want his body or his desires to be picked apart by some well-meaning scientist, examined like a butterfly pinned to a table top. He simply wished to live as a man, because he was a man. It ought to have been simple, but as he had grown older he had realised that it was not simple. Berlin might still be the centre of sexual liberalism in Europe, but other voices were growing in power.

Prudence was the path of the rational man and Thomas had always been rational, and so he learned to hide. He bound his breasts and combed his hair just so and applied small touches of theatre make-up so that he passed muster as a very pretty boy, just.

Of course this meant that he often suffered the advances of male classmates and tutors. The university was teeming with homosexuals. He assiduously ignored their attempts to bed him and played out his heterosexuality by visiting the brothels. There the prostitutes who pretended straightness were only too happy to open their legs for his large wooden bird with its beak carved into the shape of a phallus that he had purchased from an old crone at a market along with a harness that held the device firmly against his hips so that he could fuck as well as any other man. Better, he thought, for the eager prostitutes seemed to love his silky skin and soft lips and his cock that never grew soft.

But the pleasure he took with them was fleeting. He wanted more, longed for the companionship of like-minded and like-bodied people, but outside the context of minority rights or scientific research or sexual liberalism. Thomas wanted to be ordinary in the company of extraordinary people instead of extraordinary in the company of the ordinary. He wanted to celebrate his manhood and welcome his strangeness and dance on the grave of a world that was only comfortable with binaries. He insisted upon developing an encyclopaedic knowledge of anyone who came in a shade of grey instead of black or white.

He was complaining, one inebriated night in a tavern, to Wolfgang, one of his younger tutors, as to how unfulfilled he felt with women when his companion, in a drunken stupor, had whispered in his ear that maybe he should visit the Ball, where the women were not only in a class above, but all manner of excesses were allowed that even the law would frown upon.

Thomas had dismissed this as an alcohol-generated boast rather than an indiscretion, but his curiosity had been piqued. However, when he queried Wolfie the following morning in the cold light of day, his tutor had shiftily pretended never to have said a word about the remarkable Ball.

Over the course of the succeeding months, Thomas had begun to enquire about the fabled event and, stray bits of information at a time, began to form an alluring whole. Images of young men in chains, restrained by strings of gold, noble women who offered themselves freely to one and all, persons who defied any clear definition but clothed themselves like nymphs or satyrs and fucked like animals, nude dancers and sexual rituals that couldn't help but excite his mind and senses predominated. There was even rumour that the Ball had taken place in one of Mad King Ludwig's castles in Bavaria barely a year ago. Soon, Thomas became a believer.

Sensing the approach of tides of war throughout the continent, his father penned him a note out of the blue and in vague tones that were no doubt designed to confuse any spying eyes, encouraged him to move to America for a few years. Thomas obliged, fully aware that the life of a soldier would be impossible for him, and was further spurred on by snippets of information obtained from a ship's chandler in Hamburg that the Ball had since moved to the New World.

By the time he reached Baton Rouge in Louisiana, most of his money had run out. There were no trains going south he could hitch a further ride on, so he arrived in New Orleans on foot.

He hadn't combed his hair for days, his clothes were dusty from the road and it was a day before the Spring Equinox. Along the way, he had ascertained that the Ball always occurred on an Equinox. Now all he had to do was to pin it down.

From early morning, when the sun rose above the horizon of the wide Mississippi, the air was full of heady, lingering smells. The scent of magnolia and bougainvillea twisted in the air like invisible plaits; spices surged across the narrow streets of Storyville from crawfish stewing in pots or vats of bubbling water in which immense prawns floated like survivors of a shipwreck, caught in an aromatic whirlpool that invariably set off pangs of hunger in Thomas's stomach as he walked by.

By midday the heat was oppressive and he had to hunt for shade beneath the trees of Jackson Square, with the Mississippi river unfurling lazily across his horizon just two hundred yards away.

Back in New York after his initial arrival in America, Thomas had encountered a sailor who claimed to have once worked for the Ball as both an acrobat and a builder. He had let slip that this year's event might be taking place on a river, but had clammed up when questioned further. Thomas hoped he had chosen the right one.

The jingle-jangle sound of a tune played on a calliope floated towards his ears, wafting in from the river bank, like a siren call. Thomas left the shelter of the branches and headed for the shore.

The most extravagant riverboat he'd ever seen sat in the muddy waters, towering above him, all wheels, narrow chimneys and turrets. On its flank, carved out in gold, was its name: *Natchez IX*. Thomas had read about the river's fabulous riverboats, but this sight exceeded all expectations. His breath was taken away.

Still wide-eyed with admiration, he noticed a steady file of sailors and workers moving up and down a set of wide narrow planks connecting the boat with the dock. Boxes, contraptions, barrels, large suitcases and all sorts of unknown cargo were being loaded onto the vessel.

Joining them was easy. Thomas was a master of disguise and knew all too well how most folk interpreted the outside world purely according to the internal restraints of their own expectations. Even when he made no attempt at all to hide some of his more feminine features, people presumed that he was a man simply because he was wearing trousers. He strode down to the dock, mimicking the hunched-over posture and downward stare of the workers, picked up a crate and simply walked straight onto the vessel.

Once aboard, finding a hiding place was simple. He put his crate down, shuffled towards the door again as if filing behind the rest of the crew to collect another load and then, at an opportune moment, slid sideways behind a large stack of crates in a dark corner and simply remained there. Time passed slowly but, nonetheless, it passed as time always does. Soon the shadows that the crates cast grew longer and the room grew darker as night fell and at last he heard the unmistakable purr of the paddle engine and felt the boat pull away from the dock.

A new batch of workers replaced the heavy lifters who had been in charge of bringing the cargo onboard. Thomas carefully shifted his position so that he could encourage the blood to flow through his cramped limbs and investigate the change in crew. Something was different about this bunch. They did not walk with the usual downbeat gait that affected most manual labourers. Their uniforms were not dusty, drab or worn, but quite the opposite. They were all clad in crimson trousers and jackets with bright brass buttons and jaunty peaked caps and looked more like porters in a luxury hotel than sailors or ship's lackeys. They were engaged in deep and furious conversation regarding the placement of various items of cargo and the decoration of the ship.

For the Ball, Thomas realised. His heart beat furiously in his chest. The rumours were true. The guests were now aboard and preparing in their cabins. The red-uniformed crew would be busily engaged for the next few hours finalising preparations, and the celebrations would begin at midnight and end at dawn in a mysterious ceremony that was discussed in hushed tones of reverence.

The workers laboured nearby for several more hours and Thomas was certain that his hiding place would be given away. When finally it became obvious that the crates that he had been hiding behind were about to be unpacked he had, at the last moment, scrambled behind a curtain. His eyes widened when he saw the contents of the final crate before it was carried away. The box was brimming with phalluses of every description. Wood, ivory, even one that looked as though it was made of gold. They were carved into the strangest shapes that Thomas had seen. Some took the form of monsters with ridges running down the sides of their bodies; others were shaped like beasts of the air and sea. One was carved into the shape of a human arm and fist and was just as large.

He was filled with the desire to use one of these implements on a willing body. He closed his eyes and surrendered to the pulse of arousal that throbbed through him, that made him feel so alive. He imagined a woman lying in front of him with her legs spread wide apart and perhaps tied to the sides of the bed, wet with anticipation, begging to be jammed full of whatever he wanted to thrust inside her.

Thomas loved to dominate women, to hear their cries of arousal as they abandoned themselves to pleasure. Because he was physically a woman but behaved as a man, they were more honest with him. Women confided in him their desires to be spread wide and fucked hard and savagely in a way that their husbands or other clients were unwilling or unable to do.

From the few snippets that he had picked up throughout his research, Thomas had a vague idea of how the party-goers would be dressed, but it had all sounded too incredible to be true and now that the moment had arrived his nerve began to fail him. He had packed with him only the most basic accessories. A clean, bright-yellow cravat. A brass pin in the shape of a peacock that he had found in a student's drawer and stolen. But he could not sneak in wearing his travel-weary, dusty trousers and shirt. He would be identi-fied as an outsider in a moment.

There was nothing else for it. When all the workers had departed, he sorted through the boxes that had been left behind in storage until he found a supply of clean red uniforms and one that fitted him near enough. That would have done the job, but Thomas was tired of hanging around the edges of life and he did not wish to spend the night as a servant.

It was midnight. The guests would have long ago left their rooms and headed for the top floor where the Ball was being held. He donned the uniform and then picked up a pile of clean bedding and took a set of stairs up to the next level where he presumed that the guests' quarters would be and from there he carefully jimmied a few doors until he had collected half a dozen items from different rooms. A pair of ankle-length grey trousers with a thick cuff. A double-breasted jacket with a wide collar and unflattened lapels. Unbelievably, a pair of canary-yellow socks that matched his cravat perfectly. It was a risk, of course, stealing so openly, but people who were this rich would be unlikely to notice and the chances of anyone accusing him to his face were slim. It was impossible to imagine that anyone would break into a room and wear another guest's own clothes to the same party, and therefore it was possible.

The rooms themselves were more richly decorated than anything that Thomas had ever seen. He stroked a hand over the wallpaper. Silk! And the chandeliers were like waterfalls of crystal cascading down from the ceilings. But he knew that by lingering here he was delaying the inevitable. He could hear the merry rhythm of a ragtime tune being played on a piano and the corresponding thud of dancing feet reverberating on the wooden floorboards above him.

He carefully parted his hair into its regulation style and slicked it back so that his long, wavy fringe swooped coquettishly over one eye. Then he topped it with a wide-brimmed straw hand angled rakishly to one side and decorated with the peacock pin, and then followed the sound of the dancing feet to the highest deck.

Two red-uniformed attendants stood on either side of a thick red velvet curtain, presiding over entry into the Ball.

'Good evening, sir,' said one of the attendants, without so much as a questioning glance at his stolen attire.

'Good evening,' he replied.

'We must warn you,' the attendant continued, 'do not be alarmed. All is as it should be.'

The attendant rose to his feet and pulled the curtain aside theatrically.

A wall of heat blasted towards them. Flames licked up the walls of the boat's interior and surrounded all of the riverboat's inhabitants in a savage, fiery glow.

Thomas gasped.

And then he stepped inside.

He caught the briefest glimpse of naked bodies, alone or in pairs, who appeared to be writhing in flames as if they had been set alight and then his eyes were covered and his hands were grasped and he was led forward. He stumbled and nearly fell, but other hands grasped him and pulled him up and along until he was lowered onto a soft divan. The jacket and trousers that he had gone to such pains to collect were swept from his shoulders and shimmied down to his ankles and removed before he could utter a single word of protest.

Had his ruse been discovered? Was he about to be thrown from the riverboat, or arrested? But the hands that attended to him were not rough in the slightest.

A pair of warm lips met his own and his mouth was prised apart gently by a tongue so soft and skilful that he thought it must belong to a woman. Fiery liquid dripped down his throat. He nearly choked, and his head was expertly pulled back and another mouthful of the liquid spat into his mouth. It was like nothing Thomas had ever tasted. Fruity and spicy and full of flavours that evoked exotic faraway lands and filled his body with a sudden surge of energy, as if he had eaten well and just awoken from a full night's sleep.

Finally the multiple hands that attended to him withdrew and he was able to open his eyes. He looked down. He was almost entirely naked. Even the plain cotton bandage that he used daily to bind his breasts had been removed and replaced by another binding made from the finest silk. His pubic hair had been decorated with a film of some kind of fine orange paint so that his crotch resembled a flame.

'Where am I?' he croaked. 'Who are you?'

'We have been waiting for you,' replied one of the women who attended to him. 'You are the Bull.'

'What?' Thomas asked.

The woman knelt down in front of him and opened the lid of a heavy wooden chest that had been placed at his feet. The interior was lined with sumptuous blue velvet and resting upon it was a harness made from the finest leather. Attached to it was a dildo carved from ivory. The device was lifted and placed into his hands. The dildo itself was easily as long and almost as thick as his forearm and it had been carved into the likeness of a horned bull's head, both beautiful and terrifying, and decorated with two ridged horns that Thomas knew had been designed to stimulate the inside of a woman, perhaps even to the point of pain. It was surprisingly easy to wield and the straps fastened around his thighs and waist as if the device had been fitted to him long in advance.

Thomas stood and thrust his hips forward to test the weight of the device. The woman who was still kneeling in front of him leaned forward and kissed the head of the bull-shaped phallus and then opened her mouth and began to suck eagerly on the end of it.

His breath caught in his throat.

It couldn't be. But it was.

He could feel the undeniable sensation of a soft tongue sweeping over the head of his cock. A pair of hands took hold of his shaft and began to stimulate his whole length in staccato rhythmic strokes until a glorious pressure began to rise within Thomas right from his base to his scalp and he felt as though at any moment his entire body was going to tear apart.

As if sensing that he was losing control, the woman pulled her mouth away.

'You must save your orgasm for the Mistress. The ceremony will be at dawn.' The sudden absence of her lips on his shaft was like the sensation of being plunged from light into darkness. The energy within him gradually reduced from a roaring fire to a painful but bearable throb.

The hands seized him again and he was lifted and carried on a human litter along a corridor and through a set of double doors that opened onto a hall that was easily three times as vast as the first room that he had entered. Again his skin met with that same uncanny heat, but this time it felt like an energy that warmed him from the inside, wakening every molecule in his body until even the hairs on his head wanted to dance.

A hush swept through the crowd like a wave as the people who were gathered inside the hall caught sight of him being carried along on the litter and parted to allow him through. Almost all of the guests were bereft of clothes and, instead of cloths and fabrics, their bodies were painted with the same glittering reddish-orange tint that had been applied to him.

Thomas tried to take it all in, to make sense of his surroundings. The walls in this room appeared to be on fire too. He was not in a position to properly investigate what strange theatre magic or feat of engineering had made this possible but, to the unschooled eye, it appeared that a raging fire had been lit behind a wall of thick glass that ran around the whole perimeter of the room. The servants who moved around the room carrying silver trays aloft were clothed in wisps of strange black and orange that caught and reflected the glow cast from the flames and the light from chandeliers that hung from the ceiling in such a way that they resembled human torches.

A gong sounded as his human carriage reached the middle of the great hall and he was placed down in the centre of a stage-like platform. Thomas looked down upon the people that had gathered around him. Their faces were suffused with excitement, expectation and the sort of reverence that he remembered on the faces of his parents when they were full of religious fervour. He examined their bodies. The glittering paint hid nothing but rather accentuated whatever features each guest had chosen to highlight. Some had painted flames upon their curved waists and breasts. Others had shaven their pubic hair and drawn tongues of fire in its place. Most of the guests wore their hair in elaborate styles wound around lengths of orange silk that sprayed out from their heads like bonfires.

What struck Thomas hardest though was that, without the benefit of trousers and skirts, he could not be certain which of the guests were men and which women and which lay somewhere in between. Did those tiny bud-like breasts belong to a young woman or a man? Was that a large clitoris peeking out from beneath a thick covering of pubic hair or a penis? Thomas began to wonder whether or not it mattered. The similarities between all those gathered here were far greater than their differences.

The crowd parted again and another litter was carried towards the centre stage. A woman. She was clad in a deep-crimson robe that clung to her body as if even the fabric itself desired to be near her skin. Her hair was a rich caramel brown, the colour of the Mississippi river in a shaft of sunlight, and it was cut close to her head in a style that emphasised her pointed jaw and sharp cheekbones. Her large, almond-shaped eyes dominated her face and made her small cupid bow of a mouth seem even smaller. She had the exaggerated features of a doll, but despite the smooth perfection of her skin, as she came closer it became obvious that she was not a young woman, though she was not an ancient one either. She was probably in her mid-thirties, perhaps even in her forties. Her breasts were large and heavy and her hips were wide and full. She looked like a cropped-haired Venus; radiant, beautiful and so powerful it would not have surprised Thomas if she had floated through the room towards him like an angel rather than been carried on the shoulders of servants.

As she drew closer, their eyes met and the fire that the servant woman had earlier sparked with the touch of her lips on his ivory phallus was ignited once more. But this time it was not an ember that had burst into flame, it was an uncontrollable inferno that scorched through his veins and left him with nothing but his awareness of the woman approaching him.

There was no riverboat, no Ball, no stage, no Thomas, there was only her body and her presence drawing ever nearer and being lowered onto the ivory phallus. His hips began to move of their own accord and he thrust the bull inside her harder than he had ever fucked any woman in his life and she wrapped her arms around him and clung onto his body and his cock as if the force that threatened to tear her apart was the same force that held her together.

When he came it was like a thunderbolt, as if every molecule of life force in his body had joined into one point that travelled from his scalp and into his chest and down through his body and into his groin and out through the head of the ivory bull and into this woman, the Mistress, who cried out as his energy visibly filled her and for one brief moment they were joined as if they were one being. Not man and woman, not lovers, but two bodies melded together through the sheer power of his release and her acceptance of it.

Then it was over. Thomas collapsed, spent, into the arms of the Bull's attendants and his eyes closed as he was lifted and carried away.

When he woke he was back again beneath the shady trees of Jackson Square and still wearing the travel-worn clothes that he had discarded on the riverboat.

His chest itched. He unbuttoned his shirt and peered down to check if he had been burned or injured. And there it was. An image of a bull tattooed in red ink over his heart.

He leaped to his feet and ran to the river, but the boat was gone, and he would never find it again.

8

Story of A

The next time Aurelia awoke, the heady scents of the forest and the Ball had faded and a weak light was struggling to breach the thin barrier of a set of net curtains. Shielding a window. Behind which a confused cocktail of muted sounds jingle-jangled as her hearing struggled to focus again and gain a foothold.

She opened her bleary eyes.

She was in a room.

In a bed.

A man's arm was stretched across her back. Warm. Firm.

Aurelia turned her head.

And recognised the tousled dark-brown curls of Andrei's head, his face buried inside lush pillows, his shallow breath a lullaby, regular, distant and reassuring.

Her initial realisation was not the fact that she had somehow been transported back from the island and the Ball where the last time she remembered she had melted away in thrall to the measured hunger of Andrei's fiery thrusts and lovemaking, but that for the very first time she was waking up in a bed in the arms of a man. And not just any man, but one she desired so strongly her heart could burst right here and now, as a surging wave of emotion raced like a torrent across her mind and body. This new feeling was just too overwhelming to process.

She held her breath, had a mad urge to pinch herself, to check whether this was still a fever dream and a byproduct of the night or actual reality.

But the rational part of her heart was screaming out that this was indeed no illusion. She was in a bed with Andrei. In Seattle probably, not that it mattered anyway. She was greeting a new morning with a man in her bed, something she had vaguely imagined for years but never thought would happen in this manner. A man she barely knew, but she was also aware this was no accident, no sexual whim, no meaningless fling. It felt as if it had to be, the inevitable destination for all the meandering roads she had been travelling along.

Aurelia watched Andrei sleep, taking care not to move and lessen the gentle pressure of his outstretched arms across her back, the connection of skin against skin, the subtle currents of warmth navigating between their bodies. It also dawned on her that she was naked and, for a fleeting instant, she wondered whether the initial flaming heart was now visible again, even though there were no sensations rising from that direction, unlike in the throes of yesterday night's embraces when its fire had roared with terrible strength. But had it been yesterday? Had only a single night gone by? She then remembered the image that Tristan had somehow conjured up on the underside of her wrist and turned her arms slightly to see if it was still present, while wary of disturbing Andrei's sleep. Yes, it was still there. Pale, like a shadow across the tightness of her skin. Curiosity then got the better of her and she shifted ever so slightly and delicately took hold of Andrei's extended arm and peered under his own left wrist, only to witness an identical image.

Andrei groaned.

Against all logic, Aurelia shuddered. She didn't want him to wake. Yet. She wished so badly right now to make the moment last, to record every single impression, every fleeting feeling and store it away in a memory cage of her fabrication.

The pleasant, musky odour rising from between the crisp white sheets of what appeared to be a hotel room with its geometrical and orderly lines and decor, the way the heat emanating from both their bare bodies coupled, the sound of two sets of heartbeats ticking the morning away.

She inched her way closer to him, hungry for his heat, the thrill of further contact. Their hips touched and a swell of emotions swept over Aurelia, and a million memories exploded of the way he had touched her in the forest, the feel of the grass under her arse, the taste of his tongue and the lilting ballad of his voice whispering in her ear as he entered her and more and more and more until it became too much to even evoke without her mind pitching into the bliss of madness.

And the images and emotions of their coming together at the Ball and their initial encounters, so briefly at the funfair and later the chapel in Bristol, all collided in the deepest pit of her heart and the fire within began to rise, like a river bursting its levees, flooding her veins with renewed desire and now she mentally prayed for him to awaken and make love to her again.

She rolled over and pressed her buttocks against him. In his sleep Andrei reacted, adjusted his position and spooned her, the soft velvet length of his cock lodging itself between the crack of her arse, fitting with comfortable precision. Aurelia squirmed with pleasure.

And as she did so, she felt him gradually harden, responding to her movement, slowly widening the welcoming valley of her buttocks.

She could feel her wetness already spilling from her.

Andrei moaned, his arm moved and a hand settled against her breast, cupping her, fingers lazily circling her nipple.

'Yes,' she said.

'Oh, Aurelia,' his voice emerging from clouds of sleep, unsteady, hoarse.

He shuffled, his now-hard cock rubbing provocatively against her skin and he adjusted its downward stance, his knee nudging her thighs open and squeezed himself inside her. Aurelia's heart seized; although she had been ready for him, the sheer bulk of him and the way he stretched her anew was a shock. Had he ever been so large before? He fitted inside her with the forced precision of a jigsaw piece entwining itself with another.

Noises outside the window faded alongside the rest of the whole wide world. Andrei was in her. He was fucking her. She was being fucked. And all was well. There would be another time for questions. She pulled her mental anchor up and drifted with the rhythm of his movements as he embedded himself deeper and deeper within her, spread, open, split, impaled but joyful.

Effortlessly riding the waves of lust as if it had been something she had been practising all her life, Aurelia aligned her rhythm with Andrei's. She began to float in space and time, her mind blanking anything that didn't contribute to the uninterrupted flow of sensations flooding her body, every single nerve ending on her surface and inside her processing the fiery current surging in all directions with explosive, impossible speed, savouring it as synapses opened and closed in rapid succession, stretching each moment to eternity. She greeted each stab of untold pleasure with her whole soul.

Her flesh was alive like never before, dissected from within and nothing else mattered. Would ever matter.

The calm authority of Andrei's hands moving to her shoulders and taking a firm grip shook her from her reverie. He pulled her up until she was on all fours, her back arched under the metronomic impact of his thrusts, every assault causing her to exhale as if she was out of breath.

His right hand reached her long hair and gripped it fiercely, a tangled knot forming in the hollow of his palm, pulling at her firmly but gently, like a conductor taking charge and adjusting the soar of a melody, every infinitesimal movement orchestrating a further wave of pleasure.

How could it be so good? Aurelia wondered. Did everyone feel the same? She pictured herself suspended between life and death, in a cloud of stasis, immortal, impervious, reduced to mere atoms of undiluted pleasure.

She felt like screaming, moaning, unable to contain the silence battering the tightness of her lungs, in an attempt to express herself however unintelligibly. But the sounds just wouldn't rise to the surface.

She closed her eyes, allowing the fire raging inside her and the scolding heat spreading outward from Andrei's body to consume her, blindly inviting oblivion.

'Welcome home, Aurelia.' As if cushioned by a wall of

air, Andrei's voice reached her, a reassuring breeze rolling against the shores of her consciousness.

The room was on the top floor of a towering hotel on 2nd Avenue overlooking Waterfront Park and once she drew the curtains, the window afforded a glorious view of the bay and its distant spread of islands beyond the ferry terminals.

Aurelia was taken back as she stepped out of the shower later that morning, waving the steam away to glimpse a sight of her nudity in the mirror, to note the third image on her body. In the midst of all the wonderful madness, she had briefly forgotten its recent appearance.

It was crazy, she knew. And she could not come up with any logical explanation, not that her imagination was lacking in talent or sense of wonder. But neither did it worry her any longer.

Barely bothering to dry herself, she pushed the bathroom door open with her toes and emerged back into the bedroom still naked. Andrei was lounging in the bed amongst the tangle of bed sheets, his arms behind his head, his curls a crown of untidy luxuriance, the angle of his jaw square and masculine and unshaven.

He looked up as she approached.

'You are fucking beautiful,' he remarked, his eyes lingering tenderly over her body.

And Aurelia realised for the first time, with a shiver of apprehension, that Andrei did not have the trace of an accent. He wasn't American, but then neither did he sound English, or betray any form of regional accent. His voice and spoken words were disconcertingly neutral, and she was unable to place him, pin him down to any specific locale.

She stood there, legs slightly apart, gazing at him, questions swirling through her head, oblivious to her nudity. Anyway, he had seen so much of her already, hadn't he?

'Where are you from, Andrei?' she asked.

'The Ball,' he said simply. 'Where I was born is unimportant. Ever since I was a child, I've travelled with the Ball.'

'Where?'

'Everywhere. Once a year it ends up somewhere different. It happens. Then it moves on.'

Aurelia paused, gathering her thoughts.

'Tristan, the man who brought me to the Ball,' she finally said, also remembering Lauralynn's possible involvement, 'he told me I was meant to attend the Ball. Insinuated that my presence was somehow preordained. And some parts of it seemed so strange . . . unreal, as if it were a dream. What is it, exactly?'

Andrei ignored her question. With a wave of his hand, he beckoned her back to bed.

'You'll catch cold standing there. Come.'

He raised the sheet, to make space for her.

'Won't you tell me?' she pleaded as she slid back under the covers. Having spent all night and morning enjoying blissful ignorance, it seemed important now. As if her whole life somehow hinged on this mysterious annual event.

'It's a long story,' he said.

'I'm not in a hurry,' Aurelia replied. It occurred to her that she wasn't sure what day it was, and that she now had a whole list of things she ought to do. Drop Edyta and her godparents a line, and write a reply to Irving, Irving & Irving. She mentally totted up and decided that only a few days could have passed. They felt like a lifetime. A little longer wouldn't hurt.

Andrei threaded his arm beneath her shoulder and pulled her against him. As she settled by his side, the heady smell of sex that still clung to his body wrapped itself around the soapy fragrance that now shielded her own skin.

'You are the Ball, Aurelia. You are the Mistress of the Ball, you always have been.'

She blinked, uncomprehending.

'No one really knows when the Ball began,' he said. 'Its origins are buried deep in time, but there has always been a Mistress, a woman whose destiny it is to overlook the Ball. There have been many Mistresses along the centuries, many fondly remembered . . .' His eyes lost focus and his voice took on a dream-like quality, as if he was reciting a story that he had told many times over, or perhaps had heard many times over in his own association with the Ball. Then he stopped, as if returning to the present and aware that his next words might not be welcomed by Aurelia.

'What do you know of your parents, Aurelia?'

Her throat turned parched dry in an instant. It was the one question she had not been expecting.

'Very little,' she replied. 'I was still a baby when they died. I was told it was an accident. I was raised by my god-parents. My father was an engineer but I've never known what my mother did.'

Did she now truly wish to learn more? Aurelia was unsure. She had stopped asking questions about her real parents out of respect for John and Laura, who she considered her family now.

'She was a dancer,' Andrei said.

'A dancer?' The whole concept felt unsettling to Aurelia, more so because of everything she had witnessed so far at the Ball.

'She was one of ours, belonged with the Ball . . . But I never knew her. I was still young then, and had been sent away to a school in Europe to complete my education.'

'What sort of dancer?' Aurelia asked.

'Not just a dancer. She was to be the next Mistress of the Ball. It was what she was born into.'

Aurelia's mind went blank. She felt unable to fully comprehend the revelation.

Andrei continued. 'She met your father at the Ball. He was a talented engineer and had been engaged to design some of the Ball's attractions in preparation for future events. They fell in love and she became pregnant. In the outside world it's a commonplace story, but for the Ball it proved a major disruption. He was an outsider and when he discovered the implications of your mother's destiny as Mistress, he couldn't find it in himself to accept it. He convinced her to elope, to flee. Which is what they did. The Ball officials tried to get her back but . . . it was too late. Ever since then the Ball has – how can I put it? – been orphaned too, without a reigning Mistress. It's something that had never happened. We were unprepared. A Protector was named to care for the Ball in the interim period until we could celebrate a new Mistress. This was my uncle, but he was already quite ill and I succeeded him shortly after.'

'I was always told they died in an accident,' Aurelia said, concern etched deep in her face, a cloud of suspicion shrouding her senses at the possibility the Ball might have been involved in her becoming an orphan.

'It was. We had nothing to do with it, I assure you,' Andrei said, as if he had guessed what was going through her mind. 'We were devastated when the news reached us. But then we learned through our investigations that they'd had a child before the tragedy. A girl. You. And thus you became our new Mistress-in-Waiting . . .'

'Why? Why couldn't you just appoint a new Mistress? Why did it have to be me?'

'It's in your blood, Aurelia.' He sighed. 'You can't escape your destiny. No one can.'

'I don't understand.'

He was silent. Waiting for the cogs in her mind to continue turning and make sense of it all.

'I'm not sure what this all means, Andrei.'

'The Ball is more important than all of us,' he pointed out. 'We are sworn to honour its traditions and, try as we may, we cannot escape its lure.' He sighed.

'So my arriving here was no accident? Lauralynn? Tristan? The chapel in Bristol?' Aurelia's mind was frantically racing in every direction, weighing up all the implications of Andrei's confession. 'The funfair in Hampstead . . . You were behind it all . . .'

'Yes,' Andrei admitted. 'It took us years to locate you. The Network, the organisation that assists us in coordinating each Ball and supplies many of our performers, had been investigating your whereabouts for years. Eventually they uncovered your adoption papers and informed us we might find you in England. I was sent to check whether you were truly who we thought you might be. We'd been scouring funfairs, circuses, celebratory events and such for ages, as we felt it was the best way to find you, that you'd be instinctively attracted to them . . .'

'It wasn't even my idea to go in the first place. It was my friend Siv's. Who's now with the Ball,' Aurelia told him with a pang of wistfulness.

'A wonderful coincidence.' Andrei smiled kindly. 'In fact, when I first set eyes on the two of you that evening I initially thought Siv was the possible Mistress-in-Waiting. The way she walked, dressed, laughed . . .'

Aurelia pondered. Distractedly passing her fingers through her hair as she often did without realising it, she caught a brief glimpse of the red heart on her wrist again.

'So you've been stalking me?'

'It was never intended that way. Truly.'

'And in Bristol, what happened, was it something you were ordered to do, out of duty to your Ball?' she asked, fearing the answer.

'No,' Andrei replied. 'It happened. The more I saw you, the more I wanted you. And then when I was near you – at the funfair – something happened. It was like electricity. I know you felt it too. I never planned for any of this. It was never deliberate. I wanted to be your first. As if a voice inside me said it had to be that way. It had nothing to do with the Ball, I swear. You were – you are – so damn beautiful and it felt as if everything was drawing us together, that I couldn't fight circumstances even I wanted to. There have seldom been Ball Protectors before these times; it's a function which is ill-defined. I've been improvising as I go along. I never planned to fall in love with you . . .'

Her heart leaped as he uttered those words, an intricate blend of fear and elation.

But why was he looking so despondent now, if he was in love with her as he affirmed, Aurelia wondered, a tight knot now weaving around her gut.

'The trust fund? You? The Ball?' she queried. 'Nothing to do with my parents?'

'Us. You are part of our family.'

'Lauralynn and Tristan?'

'Tristan is the next Protector in line, should anything happen to me. His family has been with the Ball for many years. And Lauralynn is merely a fellow traveller. Just a welcome visitor to the Ball, she sometimes works for it and the Network and we hold her in great respect, but she is freelance and has a mind of her own . . .'

Andrei took her hand in his, and the heat of his body rushed towards her in concentric circles of invisible warmth.

'I know it's a lot to absorb. But now we have found you and you have found us and that's all that matters . . .' He hesitated. 'And the decision is yours to make. Neither I nor the Ball will force it on you,' Andrei added.

'What decision?' Aurelia asked. Right now she didn't know what to think. About anything.

'Whether you wish to become the Mistress of the Ball. Assume your role.'

An imperceptible chill ran through the room and all four of her hearts, the three on her skin and the one inside her chest, were pulsing in unison.

'And if I do?'

'You will be trained.' There was a distinct note of sorrow in Andrei's voice.

'Trained?' Aurelia asked in a small voice. Her question was rhetorical. She knew exactly what he meant. Immediately she recalled the art exhibition that she had attended with Siv and the various displays that they had seen there, particularly the shrouded ballet dancers who had responded to Walter's bidding with such automatic precision it was obvious that for the duration of the performance he had controlled them utterly, right down to the tiniest movement of muscle and limb. They had responded to his commands as instinctively as if he had been orchestrating their performance through a direct link to their thoughts.

Because they had been trained, Aurelia saw now.

The marks on her skin continued to pulse although she was not aroused. It was as if her nervous system had begun to rule her brain. Rationally, it occurred to her that perhaps she ought to be upset with Andrei. He had misled her, perhaps not purposefully, but undeniably she had been merely a job for him, at least in the beginning.

And yet . . . She could not deny that the news he had imparted about her place in the Ball excited her. And that lying next to him, cuddled into his shoulder with the scent of his skin permeating her every in-breath, all that she wanted was for him to take her again and again. He was right, it had been like electricity, and if she was so powerless to fight it, why should she imagine he would be any different? What was the point in trying to fight biology?

All that Andrei had told her only confirmed her sense that she had spent her entire life being swept along by the winds of fate. Her adoption. The funfair. Ginger and the party at the chapel in Bristol. Her inheritance, which had ultimately led her to move abroad. Siv's disappearance.

In that moment Aurelia decided that her situation was no different to that of Walter's marionettes. It seemed to her that the only thing that separated her from those shrouded women whose voluntary subservience had been so disturbing was that they had accepted their fate – no – they were complicit in it, creators of their own destiny, not simply blown along by forces of which they were unaware and did not understand. She should probably be furious about the whole affair. With the Ball, with the Network, this bizarre organisation that had apparently controlled her life from birth, without her consent or even understanding, even permanently altering her own flesh somehow without so much as an explanation.

But behind all of her fear and confusion Aurelia was filled with a certainty, a sureness right to her bones that she belonged with the Ball. As if every molecule of her body and soul had been leading her here all along without the knowledge of her mind.

She had come home. And more than that, she belonged with Andrei. If she chose to become Mistress, then the Ball would become her life as it was his and she too would travel with it. Andrei would be her anchor, the stillness around which the rest of her world rotated.

She had just one question.

'Why? Why must the Mistress be trained? If it is an inherited position then surely it's just passed on at birth. Like a royal line.'

'But even kings and queens must be educated in every respect before they can adequately fulfil their office,' Andrei explained patiently. 'The Mistress of the Ball is the embodiment of all that the Ball stands for. It is a celebration of sexuality in all its forms. And until you understand all of those forms – truly understand them – you cannot be Mistress. And the only way to understanding is through experience. Observation alone is not enough.'

His words drifted gently into her consciousness like autumn leaves falling into a stream. It made sense, all of it, in a terribly crazy sort of way. But he spoke with a glum heaviness. A morbid depression seemed to have seized him. Aurelia could feel it in the way that his body was now sitting, all hard lines and stiff angles corresponding with the flat line of his mouth and downward cast of his gaze.

Automatically she sought to comfort him with her touch. She caressed his cheek with her palm and he rested his jaw against her hand and relaxed, as if with that one simple gesture she could absorb the burden of his fears.

They had spent so little time together. And so little of that time had been talking. She knew almost nothing about him, and how much did he really know about her? Until now, they had shared barely a word of their thoughts, their lives or their dreams. And yet all of that melted away when they were skin to skin. As if their physical connection was so strong it surpassed the need for anything else. When they touched, Aurelia felt as though a deep understanding passed between them like an electrical current and it carried with it the weight of all the words that they might ever have shared and made articulating them unnecessary.

And so she knew what had upset him.

'It won't be you, will it? Training me.'

'No,' he replied, cupping his hand over hers and holding her palm closer to his cheek. 'It won't be me.'

*

Becoming the Mistress of the Ball didn't feel like a choice for Aurelia. It was who she was, as simple as that. She had no say in the matter at all. She knew she had to accept its consequences, however much they conspired against all the beliefs in love and romance she had held in her previous life, her life before the Ball.

Nonetheless when she arrived at the Network's headquarters in Seattle, where her training would take place, she could not settle the racing of her heart or the nerves that pumped through her in a frenzy, more like a flock of savage, screaming gulls than delicately fluttering butterflies.

In his role as Protector, Andrei was responsible for advising the Network of Aurelia's accession to the position of Mistress and agreeing to the general scheme of her training, according to the traditions he himself had inherited. The Network, he had explained, was not the Ball but rather an associated organisation that worked silently behind the scenes, facilitating all of the tedious but essential elements of putting such an event together. For every circus performer, sexual gymnast, artist, wardrobe designer and hedonist who travelled with the Ball, there was an equally open-minded but differently skilled accountant or office manager shifting the administrative cogs behind the scenes like clockwork at the Network's headquarters.

They were also responsible for selecting and training many of the dancers, aerialists and other performers and ran certain sideline enterprises that were similarly themed but separate to the Ball. The whole operation was highly discreet and secretive, so even Andrei's knowledge of the Network's affairs was piecemeal.

He would accompany her to their offices but was unable

to provide her with any more details about what would happen next. Andrei had never witnessed the training of a Mistress and as Aurelia's mother had run away before her training commenced, such an event had not occurred for many years, though he had been told stories of how it had happened in the past.

Learning the history of the Ball, or as much of it as existed, was part of his education as Protector, but he was quick to point out that things had changed and developed over time along with sexual and cultural norms and what former Mistresses had undertaken in the process might not happen to Aurelia.

From the outside, the home of the Network looked like an ordinary office block and from the inside it was just as Aurelia imagined the interior of any corporate headquarters would look, as far removed from the fantastical setting of the Ball as she could imagine.

A middle-aged, dark-haired woman with large round spectacles met them at the front door, took their names and briskly punched numbers into a nearby telephone, alerting other unknown staff to their arrival. She wore a name-tag that simply read 'Florence', and might been a secretary in any downtown workplace if it hadn't been for the tightness of her pencil skirt that restricted the movement of her legs so greatly she was virtually hobbled, and the inward swoop of her waist that curved so sharply it was obvious that she was tightly laced into a corset.

Her shoes were like nothing that Aurelia had ever seen before. They were pitch-black and gleamed like light reflected on water, but had no base at all, so that when she stood she was forced onto her tip-toes like a ballerina. A long, thin heel held her feet almost vertical. Aurelia was amazed that Florence was able to move at all without falling over forwards, but somehow she managed it.

'Is that her uniform?' she whispered to Andrei as they waited to be introduced to whomever it was who had been called to come and get them.

'No,' he replied. 'It could be the way she has chosen to dress. Or she may have been instructed to do so by a dominant. But that's the same thing, really, in a way . . .'

'Why?' Aurelia asked. She expected that her training would incorporate these elements of restriction. If she was required to understand these things to be Mistress, her education may as well start now.

'There's a certain sort of freedom that accompanies restriction. Sometimes holding on can be another way of letting go,' he replied.

Aurelia puzzled over his words, but not for long, as it was only a few minutes before they were collected. The two women who came to greet them were as dissimilar from each other as night and day.

One was clad in a grey suit with a skirt that fell all the way to her mid-calf. Her hair was pulled back into a tight bun. She spoke and walked with the natural authority of a school governess and seemed to Aurelia like someone who in another age might have been referred to as 'ma'am' in hushed, fearful tones.

The other was dressed in a deep-red velvet gown that hugged the curves of her body as sinuously as a snake's skin and trailed along the linoleum behind her with each step. Her hair was as black as tar and hung loosely over her shoulders. There was a softness about her that was in stark contrast to the severity of her partner. In her left hand she held a flower pot that contained a delicately pruned miniature tree. The plant was in bloom and sprouting an unusual abundance of white and red blossoms that, in combination, resembled droplets of blood on snow. She extended her right hand towards Aurelia and, when Aurelia took hold of it, she was surprised by both the strength of the woman's grasp and the warmth that emanated from her palm.

'Aurelia,' the red-gowned woman said, in a voice so musical each word was a song. 'We're so pleased to meet you. My name is Madame Denoux. We will be overseeing your training.' She inclined her head towards the grey-suited woman who remained nameless. Both of them nodded towards Andrei, who stood wordlessly alongside Aurelia. It was evident that they had been previously introduced or knew of each other at least by their respective offices of Protector and Trainer, if not personally.

Andrei and Aurelia were then led through a series of seemingly endless monotone passageways that wound through the building like tunnels on a beehive until they reached a pair of wide double doors that opened onto a manicured garden.

The lawn was landscaped in minimalist oriental style with a series of neatly trimmed flora set amongst rock and water features that imbued the area with an aura of peace and precision. Surrounded by the gentle sound of water lapping over smooth stones and bright-green leaves softly swaying in the breeze, Aurelia took a deep breath and her shoulders relaxed involuntarily.

Andrei squeezed her hand. She was unused to the businesslike environment of the Network's office block, but the garden had a feeling of timeless rightness to it, as if every leaf was resting exactly as it should be. This was a place where she could feel at home.

In the centre of the garden was a large, single-tiered pagoda. It was raised from the ground and accessible by a few short steps to one side and empty of furniture, more like a bandstand or stage than a place to sit under cover and enjoy the surrounding garden.

In the centre of the pagoda was a round room walled entirely with glass, like a fish tank. They followed a stone path across the grass, stepped onto the pagoda and stood behind Madame Denoux and Miss Greysuit as they stopped in front of the wall of glass and each laid a hand flat against a section that did not appear to Aurelia to be any different from the rest. There was a soft 'shhh' sound as the sheet of glass moved on an invisible mechanism, sliding back to reveal a doorway. The women beckoned and together they stepped over the threshold.

'Your father designed this,' Andrei whispered to Aurelia. She absorbed this information wordlessly, wondering whether considering the nature of what might happen here she would have preferred to remain ignorant of that fact.

They had entered a very sparsely decorated bedroom suite. The bed was a low futon standing in the centre of the room and accessible only by four small, evenly spaced bridges that divided the room into quarters like the dial of a compass and punctuated the circular water feature that ran around the whole room like a moat. Steam rose from the surface of the water and one section contained a raised white bidet and toilet suite so artfully designed that at first glance Aurelia thought it was a sculpture. Light streamed in from all directions.

'This will be your living quarters,' Madame Denoux said to Aurelia.

There were no curtains, Aurelia observed. Whatever occurred in here would be visible to anyone who chose to linger in the garden outside or stare out of the windows that peppered the surrounding buildings. She was not to be afforded any privacy at all, she realised. Even while undressing or using the bathroom she would be on display.

'For how long?' Aurelia enquired.

'For as long as it takes,' Madame Denoux replied.

What it was that they would be waiting for or working towards remained a mystery, but as Miss Greysuit read a list of rules and instructions from a clipboard it became apparent that for as long as she remained in the Network building, Aurelia's body and her mind would not be her own but rather she would be the property of whomever was appointed to train her on any given day.

She would not be blindfolded, but she would be expected to keep her eyes closed to ensure the anonymity of her trainers and additionally because blindness would help to heighten her other senses and thereby render certain parts of her training more effective.

Aurelia was growing rather sick and tired of having her sight restricted, but she acquiesced to that item on the agenda along with everything else. It was made clear to her that at any time she could simply press a small white button that was fixed to the underside of the bed frame and a staff member would be alerted to the fact that she wished to cease her training forthwith and leave the premises and someone would be by her side in moments to escort her, unharmed, to the exit. If she was engaged in a training exercise and wished it to end then she could either say 'stop' or, if she was unable to speak, grunt three times and she would be immediately released.

She almost withdrew her consent there and then when she was advised of the conditions under which Andrei would be permitted to visit her. The Ball had required few full-time Protectors in the past, as bar current circumstances and a few other unusual and temporary periods of time, it had always had a Mistress.

Thus, no specific regulation prohibited the Protector from forming a relationship with the Mistress or Mistress-in-Waiting, but all those on the Network board of trustees agreed that such a thing was unexpected and highly irregular. More importantly, certain powerful members of the Network hierarchy had suggested that Andrei's presence would alter the tenor of Aurelia's training.

She might become too attached to him and unable to give herself fully to her trainers. As a result the process might be slowed or simply impossible, and they could not risk losing another Mistress. It was not said aloud, but insinuated, that Aurelia was after all her mother's daughter and running from destiny might be in her blood.

Aurelia would never know what Andrei offered the Ball committee in order to secure their agreement, or to what lengths he had debated the matter with them. She was advised that his presence would be guaranteed at certain training sessions and that he would be allowed to spend the night with her on occasion, but no more than once a week.

However, in exchange, she must agree to allow any other

visitors to enter her sleeping quarters at any time of the night and no matter who entered her room or what took place she must keep her eyes firmly closed from the time that she retired to bed at night through to dawn.

Andrei stood alongside her as Madame Denoux imparted this news.

Aurelia drew her eyebrows together. 'Do you mean that Andrei will only be allowed to make love to me if other men also can? And I will never know them?'

'Other lovers. Not just men,' Madame Denoux corrected, whilst nodding her head to confirm that the rest was true. Aurelia felt Andrei's hand tighten around her own like a vice, but he did not utter a word in protest.

Aurelia knew she had no choice in the matter but determined right there and then that no one would be allowed to steal her heart as Andrei already had done, even if they took possession of her body. Other lovers would not, could not, affect her feelings for Andrei.

They were granted the rest of the late afternoon and early evening together and they spent it curled up in each other's arms on the futon bed with the sliding door left wide open and the fragrant scent of the gardens wafting over them.

Not a word was exchanged until the moment came for Andrei's departure and they slowly rose from the bed and embraced again by the door in the manner of two people who could not bear to be parted.

He stroked her face gently and then, as he pressed his mouth to hers, he surrounded her throat with his hands as if he were marking her as his property and no one else's, no matter what the Network required.

As abruptly as he had grabbed her, he let her go again and walked away.

Aurelia felt as though he had taken her real heart with him and left her with only the tattooed likeness of a heart on her chest and below.

For the rest of that night a strange pressure lay over her throat, as if his hand was still there reminding her that she belonged to him. She welcomed the sensation as she slept, and when she woke to find her throat bare, she wept.

That would be her last night of relative normality.

In the morning, her training began.

9

A Game of Two Halves

When Aurelia began to rise the following morning, a hand flew over her face and gently held her eyelids closed. Her initial reaction was to scream. Then she remembered where she was. In the Network's headquarters, about to begin her training as the new Mistress of the mysterious travelling Ball. It hadn't been a dream after all.

She had been granted only a moment of accidental sight, just long enough to confirm that the space alongside her in bed remained empty. Andrei was gone. Her heart fell.

'Eyes shut while bathing,' whispered a voice that seemed neither masculine nor feminine.

The coverlet that she had slept under was swiftly removed, along with the cotton nightdress that she had been given to sleep in. She was led carefully into the stream of hot water that surrounded the futon and bathed.

Aurelia was now far more accustomed to displaying her nude body to others, so when the hands that washed her covered every inch, including soaping her breasts and running a soft cloth between the valley of her buttocks and the fragile indent of her slit, she was not motivated to protest.

After she had been cleansed, her companions dressed her in a simple white blouse and modest knee-length cotton skirt. Both garments were light enough to allow easy movement and having not been given either a bra or a pair of knickers to slip on underneath, Aurelia felt acutely aware of her vulnerability beneath the outer shell of her clothing. Despite the absence of any other stimulation, her nipples hardened as soon as they brushed against the stiff fabric of her shirt and below she felt deliciously bare without the cover of underwear.

Madame Denoux appeared the moment that her washing and wardrobe attendants had retired. She was accompanied by Florence, the woman who had been working on the reception desk the previous day, who was now wearing a black and white French maid's outfit and carrying a lightweight table and chair set and a basket full of gardening equipment.

Florence had been tasked with the initial stage of her training, Madame Denoux explained, as the other woman busied herself setting up the equipment, displaying regular flashes of thigh each time she bent over and her short frilled skirt rode up to expose her stocking tops.

'My partner or I will return regularly,' Madame Denoux explained, 'and you will be expected to report back to us regarding each task and aspect of your development. Your thoughts, feelings, and so on. Any questions you might have. And don't bother to hold anything back,' she added by way of warning, 'we will know.'

'If you already know how I feel, then why should I bother to tell you anything at all?' Aurelia responded with no small degree of irritation.

'Because talking will help you to understand.'

She was left with Florence, who explained in painstaking detail how to care for the red and white petalled Bonsai tree that had been her gift on arrival from her two trainers, along with all of the other plants in the garden.

'Gardening?' Aurelia asked incredulously. 'That's my training?'

'It is not my position to answer questions,' Florence responded.

Each piece of equipment that she had been provided with was ridiculously small, like something that Alice might have brought back from the Mad Hatter's garden in Wonderland. The watering can was the size of a teacup, so Aurelia was forced to refill it over and over again. The pruning shears were no larger than a pair of nail scissors so that trimming a hedgerow was a painfully slow and frustrating process.

She spent her first few days consumed by irritation and mind-numbing boredom and she wished that Madame Denoux or the nameless Miss Greysuit would finally show up as they had promised so that she could give them a piece of her mind, but neither woman materialised and Aurelia was left alone besides the company of her bathing companions each day and the presence of the plants that she tended.

By the third or fourth day the irritable humming of her mind quietened. Time slowed. She began to look forward to her morning and evening hygiene ritual purely for the human contact that her attendants provided and she also craved the time that she spent gardening because it was the only activity that she had been granted and the only period of time when she was allowed the benefit of sight.

She was even fed blind. At first Aurelia found allowing another to put food into her mouth as if she were a child a frustrating, humiliating and fearful experience. Her arms and hands felt useless by her side and yet she could not seem to help instinctively lifting them up to her mouth each time she sensed another spoonful of mystery food approaching her lips. She recognised few of the flavours that she imbibed. Whatever they were feeding her, it was not anything she would usually eat.

There were light soups that tasted of rosewater and tiny spongy cakes that smelled of lychee and dissolved into foam on her tongue and a thick, dark liquid that fizzed as it ran down her throat.

Each meal carried with it particular qualities and once Aurelia began to trust the unknown hands that fed her, her attention shifted to the changes in her body and mood brought on by each meal. Her breakfasts made her feel more alive than ever before and her suppers relaxed her and prepared her for sleep.

As soon as she began to find comfort in the act of receiving sustenance directly from her attendants, they disappeared and instead a dog bowl was pushed in front of her from which she was expected to lap. Rebellion rose within her immediately. How many people were watching her behave like a common animal? Aurelia wondered. Were they laughing? But she obediently lowered her head to the bowl and tentatively stuck out her tongue until she tasted a stew that was both sweet and salty, like licorice. Eventually, eating this way too became normal.

She noticed pomegranate was absent from the menu and no matter how relaxing a stupor was brought on by the warm, spicy drinks that were given to her before bed, she still spent her nights shifting restlessly under the covers and enthralled by her memories of Andrei. Often the burning sensation of the heart on her cunt would wake her and she would discover that she had orgasmed in her sleep.

Days and nights continued to slip away. She had no idea how many. Further tattoos appeared on her flesh, even without the benefit of any sexual contact besides the orchestra of her own fingertips expertly playing across her clitoris.

When her mind fell idle, she often thought of Siv and where she might be now. Still with the Ball? With Walter? Travelling?

Also unbidden came disturbing thoughts of Tristan and his ambiguous attraction, which she wanted to banish but was unable to do, evocations of him battling with her memories of Andrei in her waking dreams.

One morning, as she was lost in the beauty of the red and white petals unfurling, a trio of pale-pink buds bloomed across the underside of her unmarked wrist. On another day, as she was enjoying the attentions of her bathing attendants, she felt a familiar burning sensation on her calf and looked down to see the image of a bird in flight slowly appearing just below her knee.

Still, Madame Denoux and Miss Greysuit did not come to listen to her reflections and she took to analysing her every physical and mental response within the isolation of her own mind.

Though her attendants oversaw her comfort scrupulously, she often had the urge to open her eyes, far more than she ever did when blindfolded. Perhaps, she mused, that was because the choice to follow this instruction was now overtly hers. She hadn't had her sight removed, she had chosen to remove it, and fighting her natural instinct to see was much harder than simply agreeing to keep a blindfold on. Over time, though, she became used to keeping her eyes closed when instructed and eventually she began to feel as though her lids were weighted and she could not have opened them at an inappropriate time even if she had wanted to.

Then, out of the blue, one morning, she was informed she was being granted a day off, and would do so at regular intervals from now onwards and was allowed to walk out of the building into the thin rain that always seemed to cocoon the city of Seattle.

Her old clothing was loaned back to her for the occasion and the fresh aroma of sea air proved invigorating and disorienting. But with her eyes open again, everything around her now appeared grey and the city had few immediate charms.

Once she had mastered the art of voluntary blindness, her first night-time visitor arrived on the night of her first wet amble outside.

Time seemed meaningless now, but Aurelia felt as though weeks had passed since she had last made love to Andrei and her body responded instinctively to the touch of the firm hand that slid beneath the covers and cupped each of her breasts in turn before circling her nipples and then venturing further south with such deliberate languor that by the time the hand reached her cunt, Aurelia's insides felt sodden and she spread her legs wide apart without any further encouragement.

A finger slipped inside her and a long body pressed itself against hers. The body did not belong to Andrei. This man was leaner and totally hairless. He tasted different too; of fresh cigarette smoke masked with mint. His cock was long and thin and so hard that it throbbed, and when Aurelia wrapped her hand around it to ease the pressure of his arousal with her touch, she imagined that she could feel his heart beating beneath her fingers.

He was slow and gentle with her, perhaps knowing that he was the first of the strangers who would visit her room as part of her training. When their bodies joined, they fitted together as easily as a wave merging back with the sea, as if they had made love many times before.

He remained religiously silent throughout, his actions speaking for him.

He was the first of many men and women who fucked her within the glass-walled confines of her training room in the Network's headquarters.

The next night three lovers visited her, one after the other, and the night after that a group of men climbed into her bed together, ripping the covers away from her still-sleeping body, pulling up her nightdress and entering her so quickly that the first thrust felt like part of a dream. She almost instinctively opened her eyes when the light switch was flicked on and a sliver of brightness assaulted her eyes, but managed to keep them closed as she had been instructed and so could not be sure whether there were three, four, five or even more. There was just a tangle of arms and legs and cocks and hands that stroked her or grabbed her or lifted her up by the hair and pushed her face onto an erect penis or spread her thighs wide apart to aid the passage of whoever planned to penetrate her next.

The experience of being used by so many simultaneously was deeply relaxing for Aurelia. After so many quiet days spent doing nothing but bathing, sleeping, wandering the

Seattle streets or trimming the leaves of her Bonsai, her mind was in a semi-permanent state of relaxation and now being consumed by a multitude of dominant sex partners seemed entirely natural to her.

She did not need to think about anything at all, not even where she should next position any one of her limbs, because the men and women who had entered her bed simply moved her as if she were a lifeless doll who existed purely to give them pleasure.

Free from the mental distraction of thought and not even aware of who was fucking her, Aurelia was living through her nerve endings. Every touch of another's skin brushing against her own, every firm squeeze of her nipples, every thrust that filled her to the brim, seemed ten times more acute than any sensation she had ever experienced in what felt like a whole other life before. Everything became defined by before and after she had encountered the Ball.

When a man gently tipped her head back and helped her to take a sip of water from a glass, she imagined that she could feel each droplet pearling over her tongue and down her throat. The same man laid her tenderly back onto the bed and dropped his head to her cunt and lapped at her, licking her firmly but slowly, then twisting and flicking his tongue in a series of precise geometric patterns that orchestrated the rise of her arousal perfectly.

When she came, all of the tattoos on her body burst into life and burned so fiercely it was as if she did not exist at all besides in the patterns of the marks that seared her flesh.

When they finally left her, she fell immediately back into a deep and contented slumber. It was not until morning that her conscious thoughts returned and with them feelings of fear, guilt and shame.

The lights in the pagoda were as bright as stage lamps and the rest of the garden pitch-black in the darkness and Aurelia knew that every moment of the night's excesses would have been distinctly visible to anyone located nearby.

Had Andrei been watching? If he had been, what would he have seen? Unbidden images appeared in her mind as if she had been him, viewing the scene from outside her own body. The expression on her face transforming into a mask of exquisite pleasure with the onset of each new lover inside her. The curve of lips as her mouth opened to cry out when she orgasmed. The way that she had so eagerly allowed the men to shift her into whatever position they desired and had pressed her hips forward or back as if she were performing the mating dance of an animal to ease their passage.

Her body had been changed too. Thin tattooed bracelets now wound around each of her wrists and ankles. A length of delicate white pearls decorated the narrow circumference of her waist. Even if she could erase the sex acts that she had performed from her mind, she would not be able to erase them from her body. It appeared the Ball was painting its master opus across her skin.

Finally, as if sensing the change in her attitude and rapidly plummeting self-esteem, one of her training supervisors arrived.

It was Miss Greysuit. Bereft of any proper conversation for so long, Aurelia poured her heart out to the nameless woman who sat primly on a stool across from her, carefully jotting down every word that came from Aurelia's mouth on a yellow legal pad.

'Never be ashamed of sex,' her confidante said at last. 'Only be ashamed of violence.'

Miss Greysuit did not expand any further upon this remark and nor did she provide any other explanation or advice, but her few words soothed Aurelia.

When she reflected upon it she found that the nights that she had spent with other lovers had not altered the deep yearning that she felt for Andrei, nor changed the degree to which she longed for the touch of his skin against hers. Perhaps it would be possible for her to belong to both Andrei and the Ball. But she could not forget the look of sadness that had crossed his face as he had explained that she would be 'trained' by others.

More than anything, she wanted to hold him in her arms and make him know that, despite everything he might have seen, he still owned her heart. Her only comfort was that she knew that his arrival in her bed must be imminent, under the terms of her initial agreement with the Network.

The next night, he came and fucked her with the urgency of a man possessed.

His breath was hot on hers when their lips met and Aurelia recognised him in an instant. The heart of ink on her chest had begun to ache from the moment that he had approached, as if her flesh recognised the road map of his movements, the sound of his footsteps, the pattern of his breathing before their skin had even touched.

'You came,' she said.

'Yes,' he whispered, 'I came.' His voice was rough with grief and desire, but the intricacies of both emotions remained unspoken and communicated only through the way that he lifted her up and carried her to edge of the room and fucked her against the glass so that all in the Network probably watching could see Andrei take Aurelia.

He held her so tightly that his grasp was like a prison, but one that she would like to remain trapped in for eternity and, as the length of his cock pierced her, every marking on her body flared so brightly that Aurelia felt as though the sheer strength of her need for him would cause her to spontaneously combust and they would both be consumed in the fire of her lust and leave nothing behind them but ash.

The next morning she woke before dawn to find that he was already gone again and in that moment Aurelia understood why her mother had run away.

It was all too much for one person. She carried enough desire inside her small body to fuel an entire army. It would destroy her.

She could not bear it. But bear it she must, and she would.

And throughout it all, she treasured the idea of Andrei, his very existence metamorphosing into her own personal treasure at the end of the rainbow, the final destination of her journey, her training.

The sun was only just beginning to break over the horizon and cast its rays on the Network's gardens and her washing attendants would not be due for at least another hour. Aurelia knew that she would not find another minute's sleep, so she threw off the covers and hunted amongst her bathing supplies until she found a spare toothbrush and then she got down on her knees and began to scrub the length of the pagoda's whitewashed floor.

There was no sound in the room besides the dripping of water from the brush and the relentless scrape of the bristles against stone. Her knees began to ache. But she enjoyed the rhythm of the simple back and forward motion of her arm and hand moving the brush and she quickly became acutely aware of each and every bodily sensation. The way that her muscles extended and retracted, the dampness of the water on her skin, the pressure of her cotton vest top against her breasts.

She had the vague sense that she no longer existed as Aurelia. As if, since she had been with the Network, she had shed the skin that marked her as an individual and now she was a mass made up of flesh and bones and sometimes thoughts and feelings, but none of those belonged to her. The idea was freeing, and the strong emotion that had gripped her when she woke dissipated in the act of labour.

For the first time in her life she enjoyed simply being without worrying about what she should do next. With that realisation another tattoo bloomed: a red and black winged ladybird on the pad of one of her fingertips.

That evening, after a light supper of a warm liquid that was vaguely but not exactly tomato flavoured and reminded Aurelia of barbecues on warm afternoons by the seaside, Madame Denoux entered her bedroom and advised her that she was now ready.

Aurelia did not ask her for what. It now seemed unimportant.

Her next day's bathing routine took longer than usual. After being washed and dried, perfumed oil was massaged into her skin. Each time she moved she caught a faint whiff of her own scent. She smelled sweet and summery, like a combination of freshly squeezed lemons and the petals of a pink rose. Her hair was brushed out and left unadorned. Her attendants did not dress her and Aurelia waited expectantly for the sound of a decorative jewellery clasp snapping or the touch of a razor against what remained of her pubic hair since she had last shaved before her arrival in Seattle, but nothing came. She was led naked, with her eyes closed, out through the glass doors and into the garden.

The grass was soft and wet and Aurelia imagined that she could feel the pressure of each blade caressing the soles of her feet. She smiled as a gentle breeze ruffled her hair and she did not stop to tuck back the stray locks that flew over her eyes. Unable to see, she could not be certain how many people were around her but she believed that she had been led to the centre of a small crowd. There was a faint hush of inward and outward breaths and the occasional whisper of conversation.

And the faint but unmistakable scent of pomegranate.

The fragrance was like a bell to one of Pavlov's dogs. Aurelia's breath caught in her throat. Every cell within her came alive with desire. The tattoo over her heart burned even brighter. Her whole body began to shudder but, just as an orgasm was about to rock through her, a voice said: 'Stop.'

And she did. Aurelia could not be certain whether she had prevented herself from coming or if the voice itself contained some kind of power that had doused her arousal like an icy blanket. Her power and the power of the other had blended into one.

She knew, without being told, the owner of the voice: Walter.

'Get on your knees.'

Aurelia dropped down. The earth was damp against her legs. A cool draught brushed her skin as Walter stepped closer and loomed over her.

His palm was warm against her cheek. Then he pulled away and an almost imperceptible current of air drifted across her face as he lifted his arm into the air.

Without thinking, Aurelia braced herself but when Walter's hand came crashing down again and caught her cheek in a sharp slap she still exhaled in shock. She fought away the desire to blink and nestled into the pressure of his fingertips, which now rested gently against her skin.

She heard a sharp hiss in the crowd. Andrei? Was he watching this?

Thoughts like bubbles floated gently to the surface of her mind. The slap hadn't hurt, she realised. Nor had she felt any instinct to draw her own hand up to protect herself. She trusted Walter. Trusted all of them. She felt safe here. Accessing this knowledge made her even more relaxed. Aurelia sank into the earth. Allowed the blades of grass that she rested upon to take the weight of not just her body but her mind and any stray worries that arose as Walter moved around her.

'Get up,' he instructed. Aurelia rose to her feet almost before he had enunciated the words, as if even her limbs were eager to follow his instructions without needing the input of her thoughts. Her arms were raised over her head and bound at the wrists and her legs bound at the ankles.

Fingertips – still Walter's, Aurelia believed, not that it mattered – trailed softly up her ankles and over the crevices on the backs of her knees and the soft skin of her inner thighs. Her body responded to his touch and she felt moisture gathering at her lips and as he neared her opening. He did not enter her, though Aurelia struggled against the bonds that tied her ankles to indicate that she would like him to. She was steadily becoming more and more aroused and she longed to feel the wonderful release that followed being filled.

When release came, it was in a different form to any that Aurelia had ever experienced.

There was that change in air pressure again as Walter's arm rose into the air, but now it was not his hand that came crashing down but something else that felt both hard and soft at the same time and landed with a thud on her buttocks and then her back and between her shoulder blades. With every impact and exhale she felt as if some other part of her old life was departing her, disappearing with the vapour of each outward breath. Each blow was harder than the last and when Walter's whip fell for the final time with an almighty crack, Aurelia's whole body jolted forward and she cried out.

All of her thoughts and memories had drifted away and Aurelia felt nothing but the sense of existing in the present moment, a sensation of incredible lightness as if her body was floating in mid-air and not bound at all.

'Yes,' Walter said with a distinct note of satisfaction. 'Now.'

He rested his hands on the back of her neck and a rush of heat and energy bolted through Aurelia's body like an explosion that started at her feet and stopped as suddenly as it had begun at the points of Walter's fingertips and with no escape began to burn beneath her skin with the same fiery throbbing that had accompanied the arrival of the other tattoos.

She was unbound and immediately collapsed to the ground. Andrei was by her side in a moment. Aurelia's eyes remained closed, as she had been instructed, but she knew him in the same way that she had always known him. By his touch, his scent, the very particular way that he cradled her in his arms and rocked her back and forward, somehow absorbing all of her pain and confusion with the strength of his embrace.

Aurelia didn't need to glance in a mirror to know what had happened, but when she did, she was unsurprised to see the now faint outline of another tattoo, this time around her throat.

The marks resembled a thick iron chain, decorated with a coil of tiny red and white petals, just like the ones on her Bonsai tree. And she realised this signified she now knew the power of pain and the precise intersection of that pain with pleasure.

She slept like the dead, and when she woke the next morning Madame Denoux was sitting in her usual place at the foot of her bed, notebook and pen in hand, ready to write down Aurelia's thoughts as if the whole thing had been some sort of academic project.

No one had come to bathe her that morning, Aurelia realised. Unless they had sponged her down in her sleep. She raised her arm to her nostrils and sniffed. She still smelled faintly of the perfumed oil that had been massaged over her body the day before. The daily ministrations of her attendants had come to an end, then.

'Is it over?' Aurelia asked. 'Am I trained?'

'No,' Madame Denoux replied. 'You're only just getting started.'

Aurelia nodded. She had long ago surrendered her existence to the Ball. Whatever was planned for her next and however long it would take was irrelevant. She was Mistress and so she would do it.

She brought her hand to her neck. Touched the place where she knew that the iron collar with its chain of flowers encircled her throat.

'Does this mean that I belong to Walter?' she asked. Since her association with the Ball and its staff she had seen many men and women wearing collars of different descriptions, including the marionettes who had danced at the exhibition. Of course, she hadn't known what the collar had represented at the time. That it was a symbol of ownership willingly worn by a submissive and represented a heavy weight of responsibility to the submissive's dominant.

'No,' Madame Denoux replied, 'you do not belong to Walter. Nor anyone else. You belong to the Ball. The appearance of the collar indicates that you have surrendered fully to your responsibilities, to your place. That you have accepted your position and your future. You are now owned by the Ball, Aurelia.'

'Can it be removed? Like a regular collar?'

'It's not a regular collar, of course. It's etched into your flesh.' A bemused smile lingered on Madame's lips, as if Aurelia had asked a very stupid question. 'You will never be able to erase the Ball from your life, Aurelia, but all of these things only operate with your consent. The collar cannot be worn unwillingly. It is conjured from within. Not foisted upon you. So yes, if you decided to leave your position, you could do so. The chain of iron is a symbol of your voluntary surrender, not your entrapment.'

Aurelia nodded.

'What's next, then?' Laying in bed felt strange to her now. She had become accustomed to physical work and following instructions. Being idle made her uneasy.

'Now you must learn how to direct others.'

Of course, Aurelia mused. It must be her turn at domination, now that she wore a submissive's collar.

Madame Denoux dipped a hand into one of the pockets on her long robe and produced a tiny ornate brass bell intricately carved in the shape of a Chinese dragon's head. The tongue of the bell was also the tongue of the dragon. It produced the most beautiful sound that Aurelia had ever heard, like the echoes of glass raindrops falling into water.

Within minutes a young man appeared and immediately fell to his knees in the centre of the room with his eyes downcast. Madame Denoux motioned for Aurelia to get up and approach him. She did so, curiously.

He was naked from the waist up and in his bent-over position the muscles in his shoulders and back were clearly visible beneath the covering of his taut, tanned skin. From the waist down he was covered by a white, flowing skirt-like garment, something like a toga. His feet were bare.

Despite the nature of his submissive posture, there was an obvious strength about him that didn't just come from his physicality. There was nothing feeble about the persona that he projected. His manner resembled that of a soldier kneeling in front of a monarch.

Standing in front of him unshowered, barefooted and still

in her nightgown, Aurelia felt shorter and more foolish than ever before. She desperately wanted him to stand up.

She was not averse to the idea of dominating another, although she couldn't quite imagine causing a person pain, which she knew was sometimes involved in such activities. But if ever she mentally put herself in the role of a dominant, then she always imagined lording it over someone who was slighter than her either in stature or in presence.

She'd seen slaves and servants at the Ball and they hadn't seemed like this man. They'd seemed small both in size and in personality. Aurelia could have easily ordered one of them about, but she was not sure if she could do the same with the man at her feet.

She coughed and looked around at Madame Denoux for some sign of what she was expected to do next.

'He's awaiting your instruction,' Madame replied.

Aurelia looked down again at the back of the kneeling man. She was possessed by an instinctive desire to run her fingertips over the curve of his spine.

'May I touch you?' she asked.

'Yes, Mistress,' he replied without looking up. The tone of his voice was familiar. A dull memory struggled to surface in the back of her mind like a diver coming up for air. She knew him from somewhere.

Aurelia trailed the pads of her fingertips over his skin as if she could read his identity through his rippling muscles. He shivered in response to her touch and his response sparked a jolt of excitement within Aurelia. She brushed her hand through his dark-blond hair and then along the length of his jaw until she reached his chin and lifted his head so that she could meet his eyes with her own.

Then she remembered. 'Persephone,' she whispered. 'PJ.'

'At your service, Mistress,' he replied, grinning.

The last time she had seen him he had been dressed as Peter Pan and hand in hand with Siv at the party in the Bristol chapel, shortly before she had made love with Andrei for the first time. Reminded of Siv, Aurelia felt a pang of guilt. She missed her friend. Once she became Mistress of the Ball, would she be in a position to have her back by her side?

'You're the connection between the Network and the funfair?' she asked him.

He nodded. Aurelia was still clasping his chin and when he moved his head, the stubble on his jaw scratched against her fingertips. His hair was only just beginning to grow and the sensation was soft as well as prickly.

'Shave,' she said to him. 'I want you to remain shaved.'

Uttering that first simple command made her heart beat faster. She was trembling, but trying not to show it. Giving an order to another human being was at the same time deeply exciting because it seemed to Aurelia to be so forbidden, but it was frightening for precisely the same reason.

She exhaled with relief when he immediately stood up and walked to the bathing area. He knelt down and began to splash water over his face.

Madame Denoux approached her.

'You'll need to provide him with a blade,' she whispered into Aurelia's ear. Aurelia blushed when she realised her error. She knelt down and fished through the compartment cleverly concealed underneath the futon where she kept her personal belongings until she found a clean razor and a pocket mirror and she handed both to PJ with all of the authority that she could muster.

'Well,' said Madame Denoux drily, 'you appear to be getting the hang of it.'

Aurelia followed her to the door.

'Wait,' she hissed under her breath in an attempt to avoid letting PJ know how far out of her depth she was. 'What shall I do with him?'

'That's up to you to work out. Walter will be assisting you with some of the finer details.'

More questions bubbled to Aurelia's lips, but Madame Denoux had already walked through the door. Her long, deep-blue velvet dress swished around her ankles as she skipped across the paving stones that led from the pagoda to the Network's offices.

Aurelia let out a sigh and tried to banish the worries that crowded her mind. She needed to get on with the task at hand. Though at first it had been difficult to resign herself to being ordered around by others and truly find peace in submission, she already missed the ease and relaxation that came from simply following directions.

PJ was still kneeling on the hard stone floor and scraping the razor over his face, although by now she knew that his knees must be hurting and his face already smooth. She caught his wrist with her hand to stop him.

'Stand up,' she said.

PJ complied immediately. As he stood, the hem of his toga caught beneath his toes and slipped from his waist to his ankles, exposing the full length of his naked body. His knees buckled as he bent down to retrieve it.

'No,' Aurelia snapped. 'Leave it.'

He straightened up again, though this time with less surety in his movement, unnerved by his own nudity.

Observing the flush that crept into his cheeks, Aurelia stood stock still with her legs spread apart in the provocative pose that she had so often seen Siv adopt when she was at her most aggressive and let her eyes deliberately roam over his body.

He was shorter than Andrei, a little leaner and much more muscular. Wide in the shoulders and narrow in the waist with the strong thighs that come from regular exercise.

PJ did not have the perfectly symmetrical model's body that Tristan possessed, nor the overwhelming height and bulk of Andrei, but there was something distinctly appealing about the inherent imbalance in his physique that aroused her. As the flush on his cheeks deepened in response to her stare, his cock began to stiffen. Aurelia watched as he developed an erection that was straight and long and jutted out from his body at an impudent angle as if it had a mind of his own and refused to be governed by his thoughts.

He grew harder as he became more embarrassed and Aurelia took advantage of this interesting quirk in his psyche by making him walk laps around the room and watching his cock and balls bouncing awkwardly with each step.

She soon grew bored of this game, though, and commanded him to stop and face the wall as she bathed and dressed herself in the most regal attire that she could find amongst the rack of clothing that had appeared overnight now that she was tasked with dressing herself and no longer had her attendants to pick her costumes out for her.

She selected a floor-length, sheer robe in deep red, which closed with a single tie beneath her breasts but swept open to reveal the rest of her body when she walked. Wearing it made Aurelia feel both queen-like and deeply sexual. That feeling faded rapidly when she turned away from her make-shift wardrobe, glanced at PJ's back and remembered that she was at least temporarily in charge of him for the rest of the day. Perhaps even the foreseeable future. She had no idea what to do with him and so she turned to the place where she had begun.

And so Aurelia's understanding of domination began in the same way as her understanding of submission had. With the Bonsai tree. She explained to him how to care for the plant just as Florence had all those weeks ago and then left him to it as she considered what tasks she might occupy him with next.

She was relieved when Walter arrived that afternoon. PJ was now busily trimming a hedgerow outside and Aurelia was resting on her fold-out chair beneath the pagoda over-seeing his activity when she saw the older dominant begin to cross the gardens towards her.

He was accompanied by two attendants, one of whom had a firm hold on the crook of his elbow to guide him and the other who was carrying a large suitcase in each hand. It was the first time that Aurelia had seen Walter affected in any way by his blindness and the sight shocked her.

'Hello, Mistress,' he said to Aurelia when he was within speaking distance. It was a greeting of recognition rather than subservience. Although he had needed help to cross the garden, he seemed to know exactly where she was situated and how her body was positioned and the way that he managed to meet her eyes with his own sightless pupils was unnerving.

His attendants had entered the glass-walled room and

begun expertly and rapidly to set up an array of equipment, some of which Aurelia had seen before and some of which she was fairly certain she had been on the receiving end of without being fully aware of which tools and devices were being used on her.

A padded table had been erected, a little like a massage bench but with an additional lower section for an individual's knees to rest on, and on a bench to one side lay a paddle, whips with tails of various different lengths and materials, leather cuffs, bundles of coloured rope, nipple clamps and other items that she was unable to identify with any certainty.

PJ was summoned and instructed to bathe. Aurelia watched the warm water splashing over his limbs and the droplets that beaded and dribbled down his shoulder blades and she longed to take the sponge from his hand and run it over his body.

She stopped herself, uncertain as to the protocol. Could she serve and dominate at the same time? Was the act of dominating someone a service since the submissive so often found pleasure or release from it? Could she be both a dominant and a submissive, or was she neither and simply able to choose to take on either role at any given time? Aurelia wasn't sure, and the more she tried to puzzle it out the more confused she became. She filed the questions away for her next debriefing session with her training guardians.

'Get up,' Aurelia said to PJ once he had finished cleaning and drying himself, trying to imbue her voice with coldness although it didn't come naturally. The shape of the bench forced his legs apart and his buttocks into the air so that from Aurelia's viewpoint his cock and balls were clearly visible, dangling between his thighs like ripe fruit hanging from a tree.

Walter used the young man's body as a canvas to demonstrate his arts, beginning with a gentle flogging and, as the hours grew longer, moving into basic rope ties. Aurelia observed with interest PJ's reaction to it all – the way that he relaxed or tensed in response to different sorts of stimuli, the subtle differences in the sounds that he produced when moaning in pleasure or in pain.

That was the first of many technical sessions with Walter. Aurelia's mind was already primed for the meditative state that now came to her so easily when she performed any task that she considered to be submissive in nature and she was surprised to find that wielding a whip, drumming fire sticks or dripping wax over PJ had the same mental effect. When playing with his body she felt both exquisitely focused, but also deliriously carried away on the wings of sensation, maintaining just enough presence of mind to keep an eye on his arousal and safety.

At night he slept at the foot of the futon like a dog and Aurelia found that the awkwardness she had initially felt in his presence faded away and was replaced by a protective urge and a sense of peace that surrounded her when PJ was nearby. She spent many evenings stroking the nape of his neck as he curled up at her feet, as she might pet an animal. Whenever she took a few hours off to refresh her mind and enjoy the rainy Seattle streets, she would always find him in the same place and position she had left him in on her return.

When she had reached this state of contentment, her nightly lovers returned, only this time they fucked her in front of PJ, who was prohibited from taking part in the proceedings but forced to watch as men or women filled every one of Aurelia's openings in succession until she was left shivering in the throes of orgasms that became more powerful when they were witnessed, as if the sense of her simultaneous dominance and submission increased her arousal tenfold by satisfying her opposing cravings at once.

It was PJ who pointed out to her the appearance of the twin dragon's wings that now decorated her back, sprouting from her spine and spreading across her shoulder blades.

There was no mirror in the pagoda room besides the small vanity mirror that PJ used for shaving, so Aurelia was only able to see the tattoos that were within her normal range of sight. She made a mental note to request a full-length mirror from Madame Denoux or Miss Greysuit the next time one of them appeared to take stock of her training. She never had to do so; as if her mind was being read from a distance, a full-length mirror had been installed by the following morning, a step away from her futon.

Her training, she thought, as she watched PJ undertake his twice-daily ritual of shaving to ensure that his face was always smooth for her. Was she still training? Or had her life become an endless procession of fucks, her days to be spent in a glass-walled prison within a Japanese garden?

New Zealand 1964

Moana had always been a child of the sea.

It was the one and only thing that she had inherited from her parents, who had emigrated from London to New Zealand in the winter of 1947. Although she hadn't yet been born at the time, it was later said that Moana's love of water came from those six weeks aboard the *Rangitata*, most of it spent on the upper decks navigating the turbulence inside the belly of her mother who endured most of the long journey vomiting overboard, overcome by rolling waves and morning sickness. Her father had fallen overboard drunk and drowned on the way.

They had docked in Auckland and there they had stayed. Having travelled that far, and now husbandless, her mother refused to go any further, and Moana had been born eight months later and, although she didn't have a drop of Maori blood in her, she was named after the ocean and promptly placed into a Catholic boarding school as soon as she was old enough to be enrolled. Her mother visited her once a week, but each time they set eyes on each other Moana saw only the woman who had abandoned her and her mother saw only the waves that had swept her husband away.

She first heard about the Ball through Iris.

They had met, age seven, at Holy Communion. Having

opened her mouth and swallowed the dry husk that had been placed there by the robed priest, Moana had spied Iris through the curtain of her white veil, trailing her fingers through the Holy Water before an attendant had pulled her away. Moana had broken from the orderly queue of girls from the boarding school waiting to be escorted back to its cloistered walls and run after the little girl who had dared to touch the untouchable and managed to grab her hand before she too was whisked off by another adult. As they touched, the water had passed between them. Moana had carefully held her hand out from herself so as to keep it damp and not wipe the precious droplets away, but she could not prevent even Holy Water from drying.

The next week, they had introduced themselves, and from that day onward Moana began to look forward to Sundays, leading her tutors to hope that the strange girl who had never before demonstrated a pious bone in her body had finally found comfort in God.

Moana had not found comfort in God, but she had found a friend in Iris. The moments they shared were snatched between hymns or in the cover of darkened alcoves when they were supposed to be engaged in confession.

When she was seventeen years old, Moana was unofficially adopted by Iris's parents when her own mother passed away suddenly of a heart attack and left behind neither income nor provision for school fees. She became part of their family.

At the weekends, under the pretext of taking music lessons and keeping an old woman company, Moana and Iris were driven to visit Iris's grandmother, Joan, in Piha. Iris's father would drive them in his new Plymouth Valiant with its elaborate chrome-trimmed fender, with Ray Columbus and the Invaders crackling on the radio for as long as they could pick up reception.

The cream leather upholstery always felt cool against the skin of Moana's thighs as she gripped Iris's hand and tried to concentrate on not being sick. They'd be swung from side to side as the car accelerated around the sharp bends of the tree-lined road that led to the beach with its sand blacker than the night sky and so hot in the sun it was near impossible to walk across without scalding the bare skin of her feet.

Iris's father would spend the afternoons drinking lager with the boys at the surf club as Moana and Iris pried Joan for information about her previous life.

Iris's grandmother had once been a circus performer in London's music halls and it was rumoured that she could swallow fire and perform various unimaginable feats of sexual athleticism.

The girls would listen in fascination as she recounted tales of lewd events that had occurred in the back of hansom cabs when the twenty-two-year-old Joan had allowed herself to be wooed by the rich men who watched her.

She was still able to lift her leg over her head, she told them one day, before nimbly clambering onto the piano stool and demonstrating this remarkable feat by wrapping one slim wrinkled arm around her left calf and wrapping it around her right shoulder as if her hips were hinged and swung open as easily as any front door.

The stories they loved to hear most were those that concerned the Ball, a bizarre celebration that occurred just once a year in a different location across the globe. Joan told them that she had been recruited as a performer for the event by a tall and handsome woman who had waited for her in the shadows outside the Trocadero Music Hall in Piccadilly Circus. She had hair so long it reached all the way to her ankles, Joan said, and was so flame red that at first glance it appeared she was on fire. The woman had given her an enormous amount of money in advance to secure both her discretion and a lifetime of performances, just one night per year, and from that evening onwards Joan had travelled with the Ball.

Iris was disbelieving, but Moana listened with rapt attention as the old woman described her very first party on a burning riverboat in New Orleans where the walls had been set alight with flames that did not burn and half of the guests were disguised as human torches. She described another held in a mansion on Long Island in New York that from dusk to dawn appeared to be underwater and all of the guests swam from room to room in the guise of mermaids and tropical fish. And another in a vast underground cave beneath a frozen waterfall in Norway where a group of dancers had been dressed from head to toe in diamonds that stuck to their skin and gave them the appearance of glittering snowflakes drifting gracefully from a shimmering ceiling of stalactites.

Joan had never married, but left the employ of the Ball after conceiving a child under a rosebush with a man who she had met at a garden party. The life of a travelling performer was not well suited to child rearing, and so, with Iris's mother growing in her belly, Joan chose a new life with the pioneers who were emigrating to the Antipodes and she relocated to New Zealand. And there she gave birth to a child who would inexplicably grow up to be conventional in every way, aside from the genetics that had produced her mother and would eventually produce her daughter, Iris.

She had kept in touch with various other members of the Ball's staff who continued to travel and perform and so it was, shortly before Moana's eighteenth birthday, that Joan learned that the Ball would soon arrive in New Zealand.

'Are the stories true, do you think?' Iris asked Moana that evening.

'Every single word,' Moana replied, her eyes shining with the joy of it all.

When the invitation came, it was on thick, white card embossed with gold lettering and sealed with a large glob of candle wax. Joan had asked Moana to peel it open, complaining that her now arthritic fingers were no match for the heavy envelope although just that morning her digits had flown across the ivories with the dexterity of someone half her age.

Moana slid her fingernail along the surface of the paper, peeled off the seal and examined it between her fingertips. It was soft and pliable and smelled of marshmallows.

'Cape Reinga,' she breathed softly as she pulled out the card and read the invitation aloud. Moana rolled the words in her mouth as if they were a benediction. She had long wanted to visit the point that was often thought to be the Northern-most tip of the North Island, the place that in Maori was called *Te Rerenga Wairua*, the leaping-off place of the spirits. It was said that from the lighthouse that stood watch on the Island's tip, the line of separation could be seen between the Tasman to the west and the Pacific Ocean to the east as the two seas clashed in a battle of the tides. Along the way was Ninety Mile Beach, a stretch of coast-line so vast it seemed never ending to the naked eye.

'And what is the theme to be?' asked Joan, her bright eyes glowing with anticipation.

'The Day of the Dead,' Moana replied, reading further. 'A little morbid, don't you think?'

'Not at all,' replied the old woman, 'and I ought to know, because I have one foot in the grave already.' She lifted a wrinkled hand sternly to wave away the girls' polite protest-ations. 'Death is just another step on the way of life.'

That night, Moana and Iris lay side by side in the single bed in Iris's bedroom in her parents' ramshackle house on the North Shore. In another life they might have been sisters, but in this one they had grown to be something more.

It was only in the last few months that Moana had realised that she was in love with Iris. More than in love, she was consumed by her and consumed by the thought of losing her. Now that they had both finished school and Iris had begun working in the office of a local motor dealership, there were inevitable suitors. Older men, mostly, rich men, those who could afford to drive and very occasionally Moana suspected that their wives too admired Iris. With her thick, untamed, dark-brown ringlets that framed her face, eyes the colour of melted chocolate, who wouldn't?

Iris had a round doll-like face and a look of perpetual innocence that attracted people to her like bees to a honey pot. Moana felt herself to be the opposite. She wasn't fat, but she was stocky, her brown hair dull and straight, her eyebrows a little too thick and her features square and unremarkable. She avoided mirrors, because she found her appearance ordinary, and she often wished that she had been born a boy so that she did not need to worry about whether or not her hair was combed or her waist was becoming too thick.

As soon as she heard about the Ball, she had wanted to be a part of it, and take Iris with her. There was something magical about the way Joan described it. Moana felt it in her bones as surely as she felt that perpetual longing to be near the ocean, and when she discovered that the Ball was to be held in Cape Reinga, the place where one sea laps over another, she knew that they must go.

She had no way to secure an invitation, or so she believed before another thick, white envelope appeared through Joan's letterbox, this time addressed to Moana Irving and Iris Lark. Moana tore it open with shaking hands to find that the old woman had written to the Ball's organisers and recommended that both girls be offered positions in the kitchens. Neither of them could cook particularly well, but that, Joan said when they next saw her, was of little consequence.

All of the food and drink created at the Ball was unlike anything else that they might ever have tasted or would ever taste and consequently the recipes were exotic and heavily guarded. All they would need to do was supply the labour; peeling, cutting, chopping and stirring. It was believed that each dish would be imbued with the particular flavour of the person who prepared it and so the Ball selected only a few trained chefs to supervise the catering. All the other kitchen staff were chosen based on the vibe that they would be likely to pass onto the diners. A combination of personality, enthusiasm for the event and sexual libido. All things which Joan had advised the organisers Moana and Iris both possessed in abundance, each in their own way.

With the invitations secured, there was nothing else to do besides find their way there. Joan had declined to attend, stating that she preferred the memories of her youth to whatever inferior adventures her worn-out body might now be capable of.

Iris had convinced her father to loan her the car. She had little experience of the open road, but had learned to drive as part and parcel of her employment at the motor dealership and the necessity of opening up and closing down the shop and bringing the vehicles in from display outside to the secure workshop indoors.

They had little idea of what might be required in the way of costumes, but from everything she had heard about the ball, Moana guessed that any of the daringly short, brightly coloured shift dresses that she and Iris usually wore to parties wouldn't do. A brief note that had accompanied the formal invitation advised them that they would be provided with clothing suitable for their work in the kitchen and would then be expected to change into something more suitable once their duties had been completed and were free to enjoy the rest of the evening's entertainment. They would also be expected to attend a ceremony that would commence at dawn.

The drive was long and slow. Iris was cautious behind the wheel, all too aware of the eruption at home if she caused any damage to her father's prized Valiant. The vehicle was so roomy and she so petite that she could barely see over the steering wheel and anyone coming the other way might have suspected that the car was somehow driving itself.

At Moana's insistence, they stopped just west of Kaitaia to swim in the sea. Moana had never been able to understand the concept of a bathing suit. She always wanted to feel the lapping of salt water all over her body and particularly on the parts of her that a bathing suit usually covered. So, as soon as they had traversed the desert-like dunes that led to the ocean, she tugged her blouse straight over her head without even bothering to undo the buttons and slipped her skirt and undergarments down and over her ankles, tossed them aside and ran straight for the waves, not the slightest bit concerned whether her naked form was or was not visible to any bystander. Iris followed soon after her, though she stopped to carefully fold her dress and place it neatly over a bit of driftwood so that it would not crease or be covered in too much sand.

Moana's heart drummed in her chest as she watched her friend walk nude into the water. She had small breasts, her hips jutted out only slightly from her waist, and she had the long, slim legs of a wading bird. She was different from the majority of New Zealand pioneering stock who were mostly a hardy and rugged lot, accustomed to physical labour and rude good health. Her friend's slightness evoked a protective urge in Moana as well as a lustful one and when she entered the water and was close enough to touch Moana, she took her hand and pulled her into an embrace and their naked bodies tangled together in the waves. They laughed and splashed and kissed beneath the salty waves until the cold forced them to swim back to the shore.

*

By the time they reached the Cape it was just beginning to grow dark. There were no buildings besides the lighthouse, and they had expected no formal venue as such. Joan had told them that they would find the Ball once they arrived. The venues were always designed or located in such a way that the uninvited might walk right by them, but to anyone who was destined to be a part of it, the Ball would prove unmissable.

Moana heard the Ball before she saw it. They left the car parked on a grass verge near the point and as soon as she stepped out of it and her bare feet touched the grass, she knew where they were headed. The sound was a strange, keening-like whale song. She took the lead, and together they picked their way carefully down the steep embankment to the sea that stretched out on all sides of them.

Moana's heart leaped – it was exactly as she had imagined. Like standing on the end of the world. And there, by the headland where it was said that the dead begin their journey to the afterlife, a hundred or more large white birds flew, their wings beating in unison, diving off the edge of the cliff and then reappearing moments later, twisting, turning, joining with one another in mid-air, frolicking on the strong wind that blew across the Cape. But they were not birds, Moana realised, and she brought her hand to her mouth in shock. They were people dressed in elaborate feathered costumes. Both men and women and all of them naked besides the luminous paint that covered their bodies and reflected the light of the setting sun in a million coloured shards so that they were almost too bright to look at.

She could have watched these creatures endlessly, know-ing that they appeared to be floating free from the burden of any kind of harness or suspension device, but she was aware that she and Iris were expected in the kitchens, so continued onward, still following the whale song down to the shore line.

At first, the beach appeared to be empty. But as her eyes adjusted to the rapidly dimming light, Moana realised that what she had at first thought were rocks were in fact people clad in a skin-tight, silvery-grey and glistening fabric and curled up on the sand as still as corpses so that they resembled sleeping seals. As the young women approached, two of the grey creatures unfurled and stood to greet them. They were women, or at any rate they both had large breasts and erect nipples that were so prominent Moana found it difficult to meet their eyes as they spoke.

'Welcome,' the women said in unison, before taking both Moana and Iris by the hand and leading them a hundred yards further down the beach to a screen of ferns, which appeared from the outside to be a flat covering over a cliffside. But as they approached, the canopy of plants parted like a pair of curtains, revealing a high-ceilinged tunnel, as wide as a roadway. The sides of the tunnel were lined with lit candles, which stood in hollowed-out skulls set into the rock. Whether human, another animal or realistic fakes, Moana wasn't sure, but the effect was more restful than ominous. It made her feel as though she were stepping into another world as she followed the dimly lit pathway through to the vast network of caves within.

Music reverberated so loudly through the rock walls that when Moana ran her fingertips along the damp stone, she could feel vibrations as if she were inside a giant, beating heart. She caught only fleeting glimpses of the Ball's guests through openings that they bypassed on their way to the kitchen and the sights that caught her eyes were so bizarre she could not be sure whether she was here at all or if this was all part of some elaborate and mad dream.

Like the two attendants who escorted them and the acrobats who flew over the clifftops outside, the revellers were not properly garbed but seemed to be painted in such a way that their skin appeared almost transparent, as if they were ghosts; travellers who had already been to the afterlife and returned. They were unashamedly naked and some of them were joined in passionate embrace, a tangle of arms and legs and a corresponding cacophony of moans that were sometimes an utterly human expression of pleasure and at other times like the otherworldly cries of angels or demons. Iris caught Moana's hand and pulled her into an embrace, kissing her briefly on the lips. 'It's incredible,' she whispered. 'I'm so glad we came.'

They were ushered into the kitchens and were unceremoniously undressed before being ordered to bathe – not just their hands were to be washed but their entire bodies – and they did so in a shower area that resembled an underground waterfall set into the rock wall. Then they were provided with filmy dresses that served as aprons and were shown to their work stations.

Moana was given the task of assembling brightly coloured sugar flowers. She was assigned a mountain of pre-made petals in every hue of the rainbow and shades unknown and required to turn them into sprays of blossoms. The recipe card that served as an instruction manual did not contain the necessary steps to accomplish such a feat, but rather advised her that she should concentrate on evoking a mood of longing in order to fill the dessert and all who ate it with desire. With Iris squeezing cut mango, strawberries and banana between her bare hands on a bench in front of her and the curve of her buttocks and small of her back visible beneath the sheer smock that she wore, this was no difficult task.

The hours passed quickly and hypnotically, leaving Moana with no idea as to how many blooms she had actually created because as soon as she had finished a bunch, a white-gloved attendant would appear and whip her handiwork away on a silver tray to be consumed by the hungry guests. Eventually they were relieved of their duties and instructed to bathe and change again in preparation for the ceremony. They had been working all night and it was now nearly dawn. Before bathing they were given a plate of food. There were perfumed jellies in the shape of skeletons and flavoured with coconut, jam-filled pastries so light that they crumbled to pieces if Moana squeezed them too hard between her thumb and forefinger, a thin and bright purple soup that was supposedly carrot, but tasted of blueberry, and for each of them a bunch of the crimson flowers that bloomed on the Pohutukawa tree that Moana had fashioned with her own hands and a glass of the juice that Iris had squeezed.

The strange supper fed the hunger pangs that had arisen in their stomachs but left them with a new type of hunger, a longing for each other that raged so fiercely they barely made it back beneath the water spout of the shower before they set upon one another. Moana half carried Iris to the bathing area and in front of half a dozen other kitchen attendants she lifted her friend's skirts up to her waist, fell down to her knees on the wet floor and buried her face between Iris's legs.

The sound of Iris's moans was not dulled by the heavy trickle of the water that surrounded them and served only to urge Moana on. Her arms began to ache from the effort that it took to hold them and Iris's dress up around her hips. Her knees began to hurt on the rock floor but she ignored every discomfort. It was nothing in comparison to the joy that she took from orchestrating her friend's pleasure, running her tongue over Iris's sensitive flesh, flicking the tip over her nub, worshipping each crevice and fold as if she was a chalice that held the sweetest wine.

Moana could barely breathe as Iris wound her fingers through Moana's hair and held her firmly against her, pushing Moana's nose into her entrance and riding her face until she shuddered in orgasm and collapsed into her friend's arms.

Immediately they were both lifted and carried by a dozen hands who took them to one side, dried them, and with deft strokes painted every inch of their bodies in glittering silver so that they each resembled slivers of moonbeam or spirits.

Iris was smiling and laughing as gleefully as a child and Moana felt as though she was drunk.

'Dawn is coming . . . the ceremony . . .' whispered voices who urged them on and they blended into a flow of shining bodies exiting from the underground caverns and moving through the tunnels towards the beach and the growing light of day.

The sand was cool and soft beneath Moana's feet and she nearly stumbled, thrown off balance by the change of texture underfoot. They had emerged from the curtain of ferns and joined the congregation of revellers who gathered by the shoreline, all of them naked and all of them shining like a shoal of fish that had inadvertently stepped out of the sea and onto dry land.

They were all staring in the same direction and some were cheering and crying out, 'Mistress, Mistress . . .' Moana turned her head and gasped when she saw the carriage moving towards them. A woman was sitting upright on a chair that had been made from the bones of a whale and was being carried on the shoulders of half a dozen men who were a head taller and twice as muscular as any man Moana had seen before.

She was painted, but pure white rather than silver and in such a way that every bone beneath her skin was highlighted so that she appeared half angel and half flesh. Besides the paint, she wore an elaborate costume of feathered wings that moved in and out from the centre of her spine as if they were not a costume at all but a part of her.

The crowd stepped back, formed a circle, and the woman was laid down in their centre. She spread her arms and legs like a crucifixion and, for a moment, Moana felt she might laugh as the pose reminded her of afternoons spent on the beach as a child, laying on her back and moving her limbs up and down to create the impression of a flying creature in the sand. An eerie silence fell over the congregation and the only sound was the steady lapping and crashing of the waves behind them.

A man stepped from the audience. His hair was jet black and his body fit. His cock stood erect, proud, aloft, like a compass pointing north.

Just as the sun began to rise over the sea, the man fell to

his knees in front of the woman and she rose again and pushed him onto his back and then lowered herself onto his hardened flesh. As they were joined, her wings began to beat and the crowd began to cheer.

Moana cried out in astonishment as something moved over the woman's body. Her flesh was no longer pale, but now covered with images that flashed as brightly as the sun's rays roving over the sea. A landscape of spirals, hieroglyphs, creatures winged and land bound, fishes and reptiles etched across her flesh and all of them joined by a pulsing vine that wound around her entire body like a thin net joining them all together.

'The inking,' said voices alongside her reverently. 'It is done.'

IO

A Congregation of Pleasure

Aurelia threw open her dressing gown and looked at herself in the mirror. She had just sent PJ away on the pretext of needing some privacy. 'Thinking time,' she'd excused herself.

It was as if she had become a new person. Her body appeared leaner, stronger, more defined, underlying lines of increased power travelling like electric currents under her skin. There was no indication her hips were fuller or her waist any smaller than it had been previously, but the contrast in her outline was somehow sharper.

Unless she was mistaken, it had rained every single day outside her windows since she had been in Seattle, as well as during her rare daytime walks to Capitol Hill or the University District from her base in downtown, and her face now displayed all the pallor of a cartoon version of Snow White. Her eyes were automatically drawn to the areas where, in the right circumstances, the tattoos would regularly appear to both taunt and worry her slightly, unaccustomed as she still was to the language of lust – and the Ball – tracing a preordained path across the geometry of her body.

She closed her eyes and willed the images to appear. Her mind concentrating inexorably on memories of Andrei, sex, pleasure and the places and beds where their lovemaking had been given free rein. She tried to blank the world away and focus on recalling the ineffable sensations and the way her mind would invariably become divorced from her flesh and, at the same time, remain a captive part of it, a slave to instinct, animal desires, feral greed and the hunger within that craved to be fed by her being filled or exercising her will over others.

Her surroundings faded until she was just an antenna for a myriad neuronal stimuli, an empty vessel floating in space, calling for the flame to move nearer and consume her in its fire.

It felt like floating in space.

Free.

Feather light.

Complete.

She opened her eyes again.

She had willed them all back and heat rose inside her.

She contemplated the many marks, the images, the symbols, the drawings scattered across the horizon of her skin.

The palette of incandescent hearts, the collars and bracelets etched deep under her epidermis, the tree leaves, the wandering branches like snakes now encircling her pubis in a protective cocoon, the eyes, the hieroglyphs and sigils spreading along her flank, the words in languages she could not decipher drawn in a straight line on the underside of her breasts, the Chinese dragons lounging across the seat of her shoulders.

She turned round and peered at the taut expanse of her back. Graceful patterns crisscrossed its canvas, while lines of leaves intertwined with flowers danced down her flanks. She felt like an unsigned masterpiece.

Day by day, night by night, partner by unknown partner, fucked and fucking, controlled and controlling, experiencing bliss and pain and inflicting pleasure and possibly even greater pain when gripped in the storm of lust, she had become illustrated.

She blinked once and then twice, and as if she had given a signal, a command, the network of images adorning her body from neck to ankles disappeared in a flash. She could now control the power, Aurelia realised. Another step down the road. To what?

She threw aside the dressing gown and walked into the shower stall. Soon, she knew either Madame Denoux or the poised, nameless woman with the short-cropped grey hair would walk into her suite of rooms and proceed with the usual interrogation and ask her to offer her impressions on the latest session in the most minute of details, to help her focus on the way her body and heart had reacted. Yet again she would initially be lost for words until the something clicked, as it always did, and she relived the moment in every exquisite slow motion shard. Language would flow from her lips, words become flesh, skin become emotion until the relating of the often excruciating moments where lust had metamorphosised into transcendence no longer required speech and she found herself vibrating inside to the sound of her own voice and she could observe the wry smile of recognition and approval playing on the women's lips.

She had so often wanted to ask either of the older women supervising her training whether the responses she was evoking were right and proper, or if she was making progress, but that common, wry smile would never change, just a sparkle in their eyes providing a hint of a verdict before they nodded like ancient sages and left her alone to her day, to relax and prepare for the next session, or ordeal.

Aurelia had asked Madame Denoux about the many images she was sporting, but the woman declined to answer.

'How are the tattoos made? Is it a sort of invisible ink?' Aurelia had persisted.

The older woman had sighed.

'No, Aurelia. It's in your blood. You were born a Mistress-in-Waiting. It's the way the Ball works.'

'But I've seen others with a similar heart to mine on the underside of their wrist. Andrei, Tristan, sometimes when my eyelids opened a little during my training on the arms of others. But I also noted that was the only image they appeared to display on their body, not all those I now have. How come?'

'Because you are destined to be the Ball's Mistress. They are just servants of the Ball. It is what it is.'

And following that enigmatic statement, Aurelia knew neither Madame Denoux nor the grey-haired woman would willingly convey any further information about the nature of the tattoos or the way the Ball functioned. It was what it was.

After her shower, she sat by the desk, her eyes poring over the sheer delicacy of the Bonsai tree in its earthen pot, the small pair of scissors that she or PJ would use to snip stray leaves, the exquisite watering can that could have belonged in a child's toy set. The miniaturist intricacy of its branches, the quiet equilibrium of its upward and sideways growth was a form of silent meditation in its own right and, to her great surprise, Aurelia found she could watch it for long periods at a time, entranced by its formal beauty.

Time passed. Aurelia glanced out of the window. For a change it was not drizzling and the sky was a grey shade of blue. She had no watch to check the time of day, but realised Madame Denoux or the other benign interrogator with grey hair must be late today. Which was unusual. For months now life had become a predictable routine even if the nightly experiences all differed, and she had grown used to it, to the extent that as dusk loomed daily, her whole body was already in a tremulous state of sexual anticipation, welcoming the coming spectacle of flesh she would be presented with, even if in her heart she always saved a nugget of hope it would actually be Andrei on this occasion, or that she would recognise the smell of his breath, the hard softness of his skin or the characteristic way he would fuck her, regardless of position or situation.

There was a knock on the door.

The older women who had been supervising her never knocked.

'Come in . . .' she cried out.

Tristan came through the door.

Aurelia felt a pang of disappointment, although she was intrigued by his presence and this break in the orderly routine she had been following for what felt like ages now.

'Good morning, Aurelia.'

'Hello. I wasn't expecting you.'

'I know,' he said, his eyes running lustfully across the liberal amount of skin peering through the open flaps of the kimono she had slipped on after her shower and in which she was lounging in expectation of the women's visit.

Realising her parts were on full, impudent display, Aurelia blushed and instinctively pulled on the thin belt of the colourful silk gown and closed it as best as she could, even as the more practical side of her was all too aware that Tristan had already seen her naked, not only on the island at the Ball but, in all likelihood, many times during her training, and might well have been an active participant too. If he had, she had never recognised him in the same way that she always knew Andrei.

'Yes?' she mumbled.

'Andrei, the Ball's Protector, should be here instead of me,' Tristan stated, 'but he is out of town for another week, so it's my duty to instruct you in his absence.'

'What about Madame Denoux and . . . ?' How annoying that the other woman she knew as Mrs Greysuit had never revealed her name.

'Miss Morris.'

'Is that her name?'

Tristan nodded. 'That part of your training is now complete,' he informed Aurelia. 'They remain in situ, and will answer your command should you wish to consult them.'

He continued, 'But there is still a lot you must learn before you become the Mistress of the Ball, and I have been commanded, in the absence of the Protector, to put myself at your disposal to this effect.'

Why could it not be Andrei? Aurelia wondered. What more pressing duties could he have?

Instructing her.

Holding her in his arms.

Loving her.

Tristan was not always in a position to answer all of Aurelia's questions.

One of the most pressing ones she had concerned her parents. From the elliptic conversations she'd had initially with Andrei and later with Madame Denoux, she had learned that her mother was born to a previous Mistress and had, all along, been destined for the role. At the expense of the Network she had been privately educated in Europe but, when she had returned to the Ball on the death by natural illness of her own mother, the previous Mistress, she had quickly fallen in love with the design engineer who had been recruited from the mundane world just a few months earlier to contribute new sketches and ideas for the following Ball, which was planned to take place near Niagara Falls and would involve much play and improvisation on the theme of water. Aurelia's mother had not yet initiated her training by the time she passed away, and as the day grew closer, she rebelled against tradition and convinced the engineer to elope with her.

What could he tell her about her father? Very little. Just a name. No one now remembered him properly.

Considering the chosen theme of the Ball, it was sadly ironic that the couple's death shortly after Aurelia's birth had occurred by drowning. It was as if the gods presiding over the destiny of the Ball were taking a subtle if cruel revenge on those who had let them down.

There had been previous occasions during the course of history – and the origins of the Ball were lost in the mists of time, although many of its traditions persisted – when it had not had a proper Mistress, a function that ideally passed from mother to daughter through the blood. Whenever this had happened, a Protector had been appointed by the Ball's Council, and later by the Network.

'In the absence of a Mistress, what is the role of the Protector?' Aurelia asked, still puzzled by Andrei's true role.

'He looks after the Ball and . . .'

Tristan fell short.

'And what?' Aurelia continued.

'He is tasked to determine the next Mistress.'

'How?'

'He tests new women to see if they carry pleasure in their blood . . .'

Aurelia's stomach tightened.

'You mean . . . ?'

'Yes,' Tristan replied, a hint of cruelty painted across his full lips.

Aurelia fell silent.

'But there was no real need to test you,' he continued. 'Once we had tracked you down, we knew you were your mother's child and a genuine Mistress-in-Waiting.'

'How does one know? If a woman can be a Mistress, I mean. That is if the line of succession has been somehow interrupted or broken?' she queried.

'The burning heart,' Tristan said. 'On your pubis.'

'But you and so many others also have one,' Aurelia replied. 'A mark, at least, if not in the same place.'

'Just the one on the underside of our wrists. It's not a real one. It has to be tattooed. A real tattoo once we've been accepted into the Ball as one of the servants. We have many rituals. Too many if you ask me . . .'

'But mine?'

'Yours is genuine. The Ball flows through your blood and the mark will appear unbidden when . . .'

Aurelia remembered how Tristan had gone down on her in the antechamber of the forest on the island in the Puget Sound and how she had been unable to stem the inevitable flow of pleasure, the evidence she was joyfully wanton and a creature who was a willing slave to her senses.

The conversation paused as a crowd of thoughts jostled inside Aurelia's brain.

Finally she replied, 'You said you were born on the same day as me, if I remember.'

'So I discovered after we'd identified you. An omen, no?'

'And you've always been with the Ball, also born into it?'

'So to speak. I've always suspected Walter was my father. Like you, I never knew my mother.'

'Really?'

'You know that once you become Mistress, the Protector will no longer have a role to play.' Tristan seemed unwilling to elaborate on his own origins.

'Would that not be my decision?' Aurelia asked.

'Not really,' Tristan continued. 'Although by tradition the Mistress can choose a consort . . .' he added.

Aurelia reflected, just a hint of pain stabbing her heart on the thought of losing Andrei, that now that she had found him, although the knowledge of having shared him with all the other women he had 'tested' also triggered a pang of doubt, even if she knew that he had witnessed her taken by so many others as part of her training. That had never been kept a secret, though. Andrei had known before she had that this would be a part of her role. Why had he never told her about this aspect of his life? Was he still actively engaged in it?

'Where is he now?'

'Travelling.'

'To what purpose?'

'Only he knows.'

Tristan straightened his back as if he had taken a sudden decision and looked Aurelia in the eyes.

'Choose me,' he said.

'Choose?'

'Over him.'

'Why?'

'I am younger. We have more in common. I find you beautiful, uncommonly so. The two of us could run the Ball, make it shine again for future generations, assure its heritage. We were born on the same day. Some would call it fate, surely? Think how it makes sense, how it is meant to be.'

'And if I don't?'

'I will challenge him.'

'How?'

Tristan explained. Aurelia held her breath. After he had concluded his explanation, she remained silent. It made sense, in a crazy sort of way. By the strange logic of the Ball's magic, it would be a way to know for sure if her future really did belong with Andrei or if her obsession with him had been simply a crush. She was a different person now. And she had barely seen Andrei of late. Had he been prevented from visiting her? Or had he chosen not to? She

had no way of knowing, but the thought of his abandon-
ment left a bitter taste in her mouth. It was like picking at a
wound. She just couldn't help herself.

As she then said the words, she instantly regretted opening her mouth, but she was already too far gone. 'Tell me
about the other women Andrei has known . . .'

'I can do better than that,' Tristan said. 'I can show you.'

Aurelia noticed the hint of relish in his voice, but she
ignored it. However moral or otherwise his intentions were,
he had piqued her curiosity and she couldn't turn back
now. She followed him out of the suite of rooms and to the
elevator that serviced the administrative floors throughout
the building, for which he held an electronic key fob. A
prickling sensation ran up Aurelia's spine to the nape of her
neck as Tristan pressed the button to the basement. It was
an area she had previously not been granted access to and,
having spent so many months essentially living within the
enclosed perimeter of the garden's glass-walled prism, she
felt anxious about the prospect of going underground.

The soft hiss of the elevator's doors sliding open when
they finally hit the lowest level of the Network's headquarters made Aurelia jump. Tristan let out a low chuckle.

'You're not afraid of the dark, are you, Mistress?' he
teased. He used the title as if it were a joke and this irritated
Aurelia. She knew that she wasn't the Mistress yet and she
had no right to accuse him of disrespect, but that did not
prevent her from smiling to herself as she imagined all the
ways in which she could take him down a peg or two if
given the opportunity. Perhaps she would agree to make
him her consort, but only on the grounds that he agreed to
wear her collar. The thought of having Tristan bow at her

feet and perhaps even allowing her to take him from behind with the leather harness and ivory phallus that Madame Denoux had demonstrated using PJ as a subject during part of her dominant training made her immediately wet and also conscious of a burning sensation between her shoulder blades as her twin Chinese dragons began to flare into life.

Would she ever feel the same way with Andrei? She couldn't imagine it. He had never shown any indication of submissive traits. That part of her had never surfaced of its own accord during their lovemaking. Whether or not she wanted it to do so was another matter and one for which she had no answer. And perhaps there were as many aspects to his psyche that she would be unable to fulfil and for which he might always look to other lovers to provide.

The only thing that Aurelia was sure of was that she was unsure of everything.

The corridors that Tristan led her through were pitch-black. Not so much as a crack of natural light had managed to wend its way into the bowels of the Network's office block and Aurelia could not even make out the outline of his broad shoulders as he walked ahead of her. His hand was cool when he grasped her fingers to prevent her from stumbling. She was now completely disoriented and if he had abandoned her here, Aurelia was not certain that she could have found her way back to the lifts or if, without his key fob, she would even be able to access the upper floors. If they had passed a set of emergency stairs, she hadn't noticed.

Of course she knew that Tristan was aware of all this. It was the unspoken play of power between them that lit the spark of attraction that had never been fully ignited, but that lingered between them still like the embers of a fire that with a dose of the right fuel, might explode into a raging inferno at any moment.

He finally stopped walking, but so suddenly that she took one step too many and came to an abrupt halt against the firm pillow of his back. The warmth of his body and the strength that was barely concealed beneath the thin T-shirt that he wore was like an accelerant to the already flickering flames of desire that Aurelia was struggling to rein in. She didn't want to let him know the effect that his presence was having upon her and she knew that it would show if she let it. The markings upon her flesh were beginning to itch and, with little more encouragement, the road map of her lust would be seared across every inch of her exposed skin.

When Tristan switched on the electric light switch, the sight that met Aurelia's eyes doused her senses in metaphorical cold water immediately.

They were in a vast room – perhaps half the size of a football pitch – lined with shelves against every flat surface besides the far wall, upon which hung a huge screen. It was like a cinema without any seats. The shelves were covered with neatly stacked and labelled archiving boxes, books and miscellaneous papers that filled every inch of the cavernous space.

'Film?' Aurelia asked in surprise as Tristan approached the only section of the archives that was free from a liberal coating of dust and pulled down several large black cased reels.

'It's a dying art,' he replied. 'Retro, you know. I think it adds something. Digital just isn't the same . . .' He had lost the usual ironic tone that usually edged his words and there was a distinct hint of genuine enthusiasm in his voice.

Aurelia raised an eyebrow in surprise. She hadn't taken him for an artist.

'What is all this?' she asked, examining the frayed yellow bindings on some of the books. They were so old that the titles had been worn away and she was too afraid to pick up a volume with her bare fingers in case it melted into dust.

'Part of the history of the Ball. All the records that have been unearthed over the years.'

'I thought that there weren't any? Andrei always said that the Ball's origins had been lost . . .'

'Andrei is no supporter of the archives,' he said bitterly. 'He believes that the Ball should keep evolving, modernising, moving along with the current of the present . . . That getting stuck in the burden of past traditions will dilute some of the magic, the intuition of the revellers that keeps the Ball alive.'

'And you don't agree?'

'Andrei is correct to an extent. So much of our history has been lost, or was never recorded and what we do have is piecemeal.' Tristan lifted his hand in a wide arc indicating the sheer expanse of the material that filled the shelves. 'Some of these books only contain one line of reference to the Ball, and we can't even be certain that those lines describe the Ball at all and not some other hedonistic event.'

He sighed loudly. 'It's been my project since I became Andrei's second in command to carry on with the task of researching old material, preserving these records and making new ones. I come from a long line of librarians, you know. It's rumoured that I might even be related to

Casanova, who recorded all of his adventures . . . it's in the blood. He had a son, too, who unearthed much of the information that was thought to be lost.'

Aurelia choked back her surprise. The line of Casanova. What arrogance. She forgot her amusement as another thought dawned on her, the dots all connecting in her mind.

'You've been filming my training.'

'Yes,' he confessed. 'Not all of it. But much of it. We wanted to discover how the tattoos appear. When. If there's any relationship between the way that the Mistress's marks develop and the tasks that she is given during her training. If that power could be harnessed in some way . . . There are some in the Ball's hierarchy who believe that a Mistress could be created, tamed, not bred exactly but her responses moulded . . . And you are so beautiful, Aurelia, so beautiful and sometimes so terrible when you are fucking or being fucked. You have no idea. I was never one of your lovers, I regret to say. I was never assigned to you. But I was always caught like a fly in your web, so mesmerised by what I saw through my lens that I couldn't break my gaze away for even long enough to put my camera down and join you. And you burn so brightly that being in your presence is like being exposed to the fire of the sun. I sometimes feel if I looked at you directly I would be burned to ash. But if you were to name me your consort, Aurelia, then with you I could be like Helios. With your power and my knowledge, we could rule the Ball like nobody ever has before . . .'

He paused before continuing, 'But I did not bring you here to talk about the future. I brought you here to show you the past. Watch.'

The projector roared into life and flickering images

appeared on the wall in front of them. Andrei, half nude and the size of a Titan, blown up to fill the big screen. Bent over in front of him was a beautiful young woman with dark hair flicked delicately behind her ears and cropped into a chic bob, highlighting a pair of full red lips and the sort of cheekbones that would make any cat jealous. Her short denim skirt was bunched around her waist and red welts marked the soft tan skin of her thighs where the elastic of her white cotton panties had dug into her flesh having been hurriedly pulled down to provide access to Andrei's cock, the length of which was ploughing into her with the sort of uneven and haphazard rhythm that Aurelia recognised as born of passion. There was no ritual here, nor any kind of duty. This was fucking at its most basic.

Aurelia's eyes landed on the bright-red mark of twin cherries tattooed on the woman's hip, just above her pubic bone. For a moment her heart stopped. Then she realised the tattoo was a real tattoo, and not a very classy one either, she thought with a hint of bitterness.

Then her attention was caught by movement in the background. Lights. Streamers. A curtain of multicoloured glass beads flying into the wind from the tent of a fortune-teller. They were at the funfair on Hampstead Heath. It was still light, but the sky was showing some signs of clouding over and the wind appeared to be picking up. She and Siv had probably been on the dodgem cars then, minutes before the rain had started and they had sought shelter on the ghost train. Merely an hour later Andrei had pressed his lips against hers and changed her life for ever and here he was, rutting like an animal, with another woman who he had likely only just met. Testing her, Tristan had said, but it certainly didn't look like a chore. A distinct look of pleasure was carved over Andrei's face. Had he known who Aurelia was then, or had he been working his way through every pretty girl at the fair?

Aurelia swallowed hard, but she could not bring herself to look away. Her eyes were glued to the vision of their bodies slapping against one another, the cupid's bow of their lips open in cries of ecstasy, the hard angles of his muscled limbs contrasting with the softness of her flesh in a parody of opposites welded together by mutual attraction.

Tristan interrupted the film and then played another, and another and another. An endless montage of Andrei in his role of Protector making love to every sort of woman that Aurelia could imagine. Young, old, firm, soft, petite, large, beautiful, plain. Eventually she did not pay any attention to their features at all, but simply read the pattern of lust and requited desire that swam across their faces and across his. She'd seen that expression spreading across his features, that particular twist of his lips and the line of his brow drawing together so many times when he had come to her bed and entered her with all the fury of a man possessed in asserting his ownership over her flesh and she had not been able to resist disobeying the Network's instructions and opening her eyes for just long enough to catch a glimpse of the man she loved as he came inside her.

'Enough,' she said at last. 'I've seen enough.' Even Aurelia was surprised by the steady coldness of her voice.

Tristan switched off the projector, carefully returned the reels of film to their respective cases and orderly position on the racks and then escorted her back through the endless passageways to the elevator. Not a word was exchanged between them until they reached the outside world again and Aurelia immediately raced for the doors that led into the gardens where she breathed a deep sigh of relief at no longer being locked up indoors and waited for the sense of peace that she always found when surrounded by the clean lines of the neatly trimmed hedgerows and the gentle rustling of the leaves on the trees and the soft sound of water rushing over smooth stones to wash over her.

She'd almost forgotten about Tristan when he finally spoke.

'So,' he said. 'You'll do it? What I suggested? And choose between us?'

'Yes,' Aurelia replied. 'I'll choose.'

She turned and walked towards her glass-walled bedroom within the pagoda without looking back.

PJ was waiting for her with a warm infusion of rosewater syrup and honey served in a pale-pink teacup, and a plate of sliced mango that had been subtly flavoured with the smallest drizzle of lime and decorated with one of the vivid purple flowers that grew in the far corner of the gardens. PJ had become so devoted to his duties as servant and companion that he had developed an uncanny ability to sense her needs, desires and appetites that bordered on psychic. Often she was not even aware of what it was that she was in the mood for until PJ handed it to her.

Today, though, she did not impart her usual instructions.

'Fetch Madame Denoux for me please, PJ,' she requested.

He rushed immediately to do her bidding and returned a short while later accompanied by the dark-haired woman who had overseen the majority of her training.

'You summoned me, Aurelia? This is most unusual,' said

Madame Denoux, delicately rearranging the folds of yet another long velvet gown. This one was the same pale pink as the rosewater syrup that PJ had prepared. Madame's dresses all seemed to be cut from the same pattern but Aurelia was certain that she'd never seen her wear the same shade twice. She had as many different coloured velvet gowns as Aurelia had pairs of underwear. 'Though I must confess that I am curious,' she added.

The only sign of surprise that appeared on Madame Denoux face as Aurelia summarised the situation and explained her proposal was the barest hint of a smile playing across the usually straight-faced woman's lips.

Silence stretched out like an eternity between them until finally Madame Denoux spoke.

'It's an ancient custom,' she said, 'and one that has not, to my knowledge, been invoked in recent times. But you are correct. As Mistress-in-Waiting you may choose a consort, and if you feel, as you say, unable to choose then you are entitled to call upon the selection ritual. I will ask Andrei to return as you have requested and arrange the other necessities.' She gathered up her skirts and prepared to leave, before turning back at the last moment.

'Aurelia,' she said.

'Yes, Madame?' Aurelia responded, out of habit more than politeness.

'Are you sure about this? Once the selection ritual has occurred, it cannot be turned back. You may choose to cast your die, but you will be stuck with however they land. Or whomever they land upon.'

'I understand.' Aurelia nodded. 'And I am sure. It is the only way.'

*

Sleep evaded her that night and she tossed and turned, seeking the comfort of peaceful dreams that never came. Finally she roused PJ and asked him to give her release through his ability to pleasure her.

'Yes, Mistress,' he said in a tone that was full of adoration before gently lowering his head and pressing his lips to Aurelia's labia. She arched her back and lifted her hips and grasped him by the nape of his neck and pressed the tip of his nose against her cunt and held him there until an orgasm tore through her body and wiped every thought from her mind.

The release was like a drug and she slept through all of the following day. Her attendants arrived in the evening to prepare her for the ceremony that would be held at midnight. It had been deemed important that the future Mistress's choice should be made as soon as possible, paving the ground for the Inking to be concluded at the next Ball with no further delays.

She meditated as they busied themselves with sponging down her skin and then meticulously washing and drying her long hair and rubbing the usual perfumed oil over the full expanse of her flesh. This time she had requested a darker scent. Something woody, musky, reminiscent of the earth. A fragrance that would remind her that she was grounded and powerful.

When the moment came, she was blindfolded. Aurelia had asked for her vision to be obscured rather than rely upon the strength of will that it took from her to purposefully keep her eyes closed. She wanted to concentrate all of her awareness on her physical sensations without any other distraction.

The first man to take her was Tristan. She recognised him only because he was not Andrei. His breath was laboured with excitement and something else – the frenzied edge that comes from being too close to madness, perhaps – and he gripped her forearms so tightly that his embrace was like the confines of a straitjacket. She had been lying back, relaxed on a pile of soft coverlets and pillows with her legs spread apart waiting for one of her possible consorts to arrive and take her and Tristan had simply grabbed hold of her and flipped her over with a driven passion and thrust his cock inside her with little more warning than the pressure of his hands on her shoulders. He used her body as the anchor that allowed him to pierce her so fiercely that Aurelia thought that he might split her in two.

It was raw and wild, and yet . . . there was something equally feral within Aurelia, a passion that was as close to madness as Tristan's was and that had been simmering under the surface of her skin awaiting only the permission of a lover who defied convention to set it free. Aurelia screamed her rebellion and as she did so the heat of her markings burned across her flesh with familiar intensity. With an almighty burst of strength she pushed herself up onto her hands and knees with the weight of his body still pressing against her back and she flipped him off and straddled him, pinning his wrists down onto the bedding and then climbing back onto the straight length of his still-hard cock. He responded in kind and they wrestled and rolled like animals across the cushions that had been laid out, until they tumbled onto the damp grass lawn. Every tattoo on Aurelia's body flamed into life and burned as brightly as the stars in the sky.

Already her inflamed senses were screaming at her to choose him. Choose danger. Choose Tristan. Complicit in the lie that Andrei's affection and lovemaking were maybe too timid, too traditional, and that the way forward for her mind and body should journey through a road of fire and discord.

At the same time, the Aurelia of old counselled patience, and faithfulness to an earlier dream.

There would be time still to reach a decision.

Time to refresh her soul at the original source that had triggered the world of pleasure inside her.

A bell rang. Low, ponderous. A heavy note that tolled history and tradition. And, Aurelia knew, signalled the end of the first would-be consort's turn.

Andrei's touch, when it came, was as cool and soothing as a gentle breeze on a hot summer's day. He bent down and eased his arms beneath her and lifted her into the air, setting her down onto the coverlet again as if she were made of the most delicate china. He lowered his head to the scratch on her shoulder and pressed his lips softly against it. She inhaled the scent of his skin with each in-breath as if she was absorbing every element of his soul by osmosis. She sighed with pleasure and buried her hands in his hair, pulling him down so that he lay alongside her with his head tucked against her shoulder. They made a pair as easily as any of the birds that frequented the Network's gardens.

The whine of Tristan's voice floated into her ear as if in a dream. 'Hey . . . that's not how it's supposed to be—'

Andrei interrupted him with his own words.

'Your future is not written in the past, Aurelia,' he whispered into her ear. 'You can choose it. Carve your own path. Our path.'

'Yes,' she replied, and in that moment she knew what would come next. She took each of Andrei's hands in her own and gripped him tightly and then she focused all of her attention, every synapse in her brain and the tip of every nerve ending in her body, on accessing the power that she knew she now held within her and then she directed it towards Andrei, multiplying the current that always flowed between them when they touched by a thousand fold until she felt him twitch and shudder against her as if in the throes of orgasm.

The congregation around them hissed sharply. A ripple of shocked whispers passed through the crowd.

Andrei's body went limp in her arms.

Aurelia tore off her blindfold.

There it was, on his chest, clearly visible beneath the silvery light of a moon that was nearing fullness.

The bright-red outline of a tattooed heart, beating directly over his own. A perfect mirror image to the one that was etched on Aurelia's chest and was now pumping in unison.

Andrei opened his eyes and looked down at his chest and then up at Aurelia, who was bent over him, gazing at the mark on his skin in wonderment.

Tristan?

Andrei?

Even though her mind was still torn between the two men, opposites of each other in lust and personalities, it appeared that her heart had reached a decision. Her hearts.

'I am yours, Aurelia,' Andrei whispered softly. And Aurelia's hearts and body told her that all the women he had experienced in the past were only shadows that passed in the night and that, when dawn came, they would always belong together. The dark, inviting cloud that Tristan had briefly and tantalisingly become began to recede from her mind and his superficial marks on her body faded into insignificance.

She rose to her feet and there was a solemn hush.

II

The Illustrated Woman

The Ball came to Aurelia in a dream.

For five days and five nights she was consumed by images, as if being assaulted by the very fabric of her own mind. Her body was racked by powerful orgasms as she slept and she often awoke clammy, shivering and aroused well beyond any usual measure. Sex had become the focus of not just her life but her entire being and Aurelia fairly vibrated with it. She had now harnessed the power of her tattoos and with one focused thought she could evoke a tapestry of pleasure across her flesh or signal her mood, needs and desires by displaying a particular individual illustration but when she was in her bedroom, removed from her responsibilities and curled up in Andrei's strong embrace, then her skin was like a landscape across which every emotion and thought that entered her head also burned across her frame in bright pictorial form.

Sometimes they made love as they slept. So in tune were Aurelia's desires with her mind, heart and physical needs that she could not always discern which part of her it was that moved her limbs. It was as if her body and brain had married so completely that the notion of conscious thought or deliberate movement now seemed obsolete. When she was together with her consort and free to be herself without regard for convention or restraint then she behaved as an animal, and so did Andrei. Together they were like the eye of a storm. When her body was joined with his, then the rest of the world fell away. As he moved inside her, Aurelia felt at once as though she was flying, floating permanently on wings of lust and as if she had come home, grounded upon the island of his flesh. She was no longer just a traveller or a citizen of the Ball, permanently on the move. Andrei was her anchor and she his. Each of them was the axis around which the other's world revolved upon.

And so, when a still-slumbering Aurelia shuddered in Andrei's arms and he held her tight as the markings on her skin burst into vivid pictures that seared across her belly and her breasts and thighs, it was Andrei who read the patterns of the Ball aloud to her, as if the lines of her tattoos were a map that would lead them to treasure, or at least a clue to what the theme of the next celebration would be. The date had already been set and each day that went by without an answer from the Mistress-in-Waiting was another day lost that could have been used to make the necessary arrangements. Time was ticking by, as Madame Denoux never failed to remind her.

'You've been dreaming about rope again,' Andrei said to her when dawn broke and Aurelia's eyelids finally fluttered open. She was nestled into the crook of his arm, her head resting in the space between his head and his shoulder. Her arm was haphazardly slung over his chest and their legs were entwined. They often woke together to find that they had wrapped themselves up in each other's arms like a parcel in the night, as if their bodies sought the closeness that their souls had already found. Since the formal element of her training had been completed, Aurelia had been offered a much more elaborate suite in a central downtown Seattle hotel that the Network used as a base to accommodate its more exclusive clientele, but Aurelia had declined. She had grown used to the restful surrounds of the Japanese gardens, the light that streamed in over the bed through the expansive glass windows and the comforting presence of PJ, who still occasionally slept at the foot of her bed when Andrei was absent on business.

Aurelia blinked, shaking the last vestiges of sleep away and coming to her senses again. Her dreams of late had been so vivid, so all-consuming, that she wasn't always sure what was real and what had occurred only in her imagination.

'Yes,' she replied, snuggling up against him and planting a kiss on his cheek. Andrei hadn't shaved for a few days and his stubble was rough against her lips. 'But it wasn't a bad dream.' She tried to replay her night-time clouds back again, but remembering the images that had filled her mind as she slept was like trying to catch wisps of smoke between her fingertips and the more she grasped at them the quicker they dissolved again. The specifics evaded her, but she could always recall the feelings and sensations that had been evoked.

Andrei's hands were warm against her face as he threaded his fingers through her hair, his habit when she was distressed or needed soothing.

'A new tattoo appeared. A tree. Here,' he said, tracing the shape of a trunk from her belly to her chest and a series of sinuous branches over her breasts. Aurelia took hold of his hand and pressed it against her sternum. She knew that he had memorised the position of every mark on her body, as if the images had been burned onto his heart as well as her flesh.

The next night she dreamed of water. Of drowning and yet being able to breathe.

'Your parents?' Andrei asked her.

Aurelia shook her head. 'No. Not like that,' she said. 'Not a nightmare. I was swimming. Human but able to live beneath the surface of a lake. Like a mermaid.'

Another night, she imagined being suspended in mid-air on the wings of angels and the next of being set alight with fire that didn't burn. Each dream left her with a corresponding mark. On the fifth night she didn't dream at all but was overcome by an overwhelming urge to make love and she woke to find herself straddling Andrei's hips, his cock already hard in response to the urgency of her need. He opened his eyes and she guided him inside her and groaned as he placed a firm hand on either side of the base of her spine and moved her back and forward until she began to grind her clitoris against the base of his torso and she leaned forward and took hold of his shoulders and thrust herself against him until she was spent and then collapsed across his chest. Andrei held her flat against him and they fell asleep again still joined, not waking until the shadows that tumbled in through the glass-walled pagoda grew long and goosebumps appeared on their flesh as the air chilled.

'The elements,' Andrei said to her that evening. 'These dreams that you can't remember and the images that go with them. Earth, water, air, fire. And the last one, energy. Aether. It's the five elements.' He furrowed his brow in thought. 'I don't think we've ever celebrated all five elements. Aspects of them, of course. Legend has it that there was an inferno-themed Ball, on a riverboat, once. And the zodiac signs, which include water . . . But I don't think we've ever had the elements.'

'Then that shall be my Ball. Our Ball.'

She rang the bell to summon PJ, who in turn called Madame Denoux who, when advised of Aurelia's desires and decision, began to set the preparatory gears in motion.

Aurelia's input was largely artistic, and as the Mistress-in-Waiting she had the final say over everything, from the theme, the location and the guest list to the shape of the glasses and the flavour of the drinks and canapés. It was a little like planning her own wedding, something that unlike so many of the other girls that she had grown up with – with the exception of the ever-independent Siv, of course – she had given precious little thought to.

Initially the task had seemed overwhelming and she was conscious of the need to prove herself worthy of her title, but once she discovered that virtually every idea that she could dream up, even the most bizarre, expensive or down-right fantastical was somehow possible through the seemingly endless funds in the Network's mysterious coffers, the talents of the performers within their employ and that un-explainable and mystical element that Aurelia had come to think of as simply the innate magic of sex, then organising the Ball became a joy. Soon she devoted every moment to its inception, catching her sleep and meals in snatches as she worked through the process of turning her fevered dreams into reality.

It would be held in England, her adoptive homeland. Aurelia wanted to root herself in the Ball and for this one night to be grounded in not just the country where she had grown up but also a place with a history that stretched back through the ages, a place where she imagined that the ghosts of kings and queens would be smiling down at them as revellers danced on ancient stone floors.

A country house was located that was situated on expansive and secluded grounds to the north of London in the Chiltern Hills and belonged to one of the Ball's longest-standing associates. To Aurelia, who had travelled with Andrei to the location before confirming her selection, the house could be more readily considered a mansion with its opulent decor of crystal chandeliers, velvet carpets and an elaborately carved mahogany banister that wound alongside a staircase so vast it was practically a promenade. Her mind was made up when she noticed the wide French doors that swung open, as if by magic, when she approached to reveal a garden the size of a football pitch and leading onto a private wood.

'Perfect,' she said. Her host and the owner of the property, Thomas, a tall man in his late fifties with a brusque and overtly prim manner that was distinctly at odds with his eccentric hairstyle and the pair of leopard-print horn-rimmed spectacles that sat at the very tip of his elongated nose nodded, and the deal was sealed.

Throughout the duration of their guided tour, Thomas had walked ahead of them. He had the straight posture and deliberate gait of an aristocrat but far more striking was his companion, a young woman who was connected to him by way of a leash that was attached to the silver collar that encircled her neck. She was naked and crawling on her hands and knees but in the manner of a lioness rather than a dog, each sinuous swing of her hips moving her long legs forward as comfortably as if she were born to travel like an animal rather than on two legs like a human being. Finally, as they were ready to depart, she stood in order to bid them goodbye. She was no regular human, in Aurelia's view. Her eyes were a dappled green like the colour of a snake's skin and her lips as red and luscious as the apple that Eve had bitten, though seemingly free of rouge or any other artificial enhancement. Aurelia's attention was inevitably drawn lower. There, just half a finger above her completely smooth pussy, was the tattoo of a barcode, and next to it a number '1'. When her eyes met Aurelia's, an understanding passed between them. A realisation of the strength that they each possessed behind their respective positions.

Andrei had explained to Aurelia before they entered that the woman marked with the number 1 was what the Ball called 'the holy whore', a vessel for the enjoyment of others. She had been 'tested' for the position of Mistress before Aurelia's existence had been discovered, and her capacity for pleasure was found to be endless, but she desired only to be a submissive and possessed none of the streak of dominance that came so naturally to Aurelia and which was essential to the role of the Ball's leadership.

Number 1 had chosen to become a slave and to the surprise of everyone on the Ball's committee she had chosen Thomas as her Master. It was assumed that Tristan would be the natural choice but the holy whore had preferred the eccentric, bespectacled Englishman who now held the key to the golden padlock that secured the collar around her throat.

Aurelia made a mental note to add Number 1 to the guest list, and not just as Thomas's plus one.

*

Days were spent watching the potential performers demonstrate their talents. Aurelia had delegated a good portion of this task for the sake of time, but she insisted on selecting the ballerinas who would perform in the water act. She had chosen to recreate a scene from *Swan Lake* where the two lead dancers would experience a rebirth through drowning. It was morbid, perhaps, but her own way of mourning the manner of her parents' passing and bringing both closure and joy to it.

For the role of Odette, Aurelia nominated a Russian dancer named Luba who rose from the water so gracefully it seemed that she was a part of it, as if the very atoms that formed her flesh had melded together from the mist that hovers over the sea after a storm. Without being given any prior knowledge of the water theme she had even auditioned to Debussy's 'La Mer'. Aurelia was unsurprised to learn that Luba, who moved with such uncanny grace, had already been spotted by the Network's scouts and had also been tested for the role of Mistress before Aurelia's rediscovery. Andrei had danced with her and he had reported back that she was an exceptionally beautiful and talented woman, but not the next Mistress of the Ball. Her heart belonged firmly to another, and she would never be able to give herself fully in the way that was required.

Unlike her, Aurelia thought, though she no longer carried any regret or guilt over that fact. She knew that she possessed the rare skill of letting herself go completely, of surrendering her body, soul and mind to the needs of her flesh and she knew that with no regard to her relationship with Andrei, for at least one night of each year, she would allow herself to swim free on the currents of lust and not be burdened in the slightest by any tie that she felt to him during her regular waking moments. It was simply who she was.

Her mind turned to her coronation ceremony. That was the one element of the evening that would be arranged by others. Tradition dictated that she would be taken with ceremonial ritual in front of the Ball's revellers, but she would not know the identity of her partner until the ceremony commenced.

But as the Mistress-in-Waiting, she had already decided to break with tradition and knew that in the years of her reign, she would change much about the Ball. It would be both her desire and her duty.

The weeks of elaborate preparations passed in a blur until the fateful day finally arrived.

It was a clear night and the sky was peppered with stars that shone overhead like ethereal angels come to bestow their blessing on the proceedings. The sight heartened Aurelia and helped to settle her nerves as she took one final walk through the house to ensure that everything was in order, exactly as she had imagined, before the uniformed attendants began to welcome in the guests who would be arriving imminently.

She took Andrei's hand and together they stepped through the front doors and onto the lawn, which had been transformed from its former plain clipped grass into a tropical paradise, thick with the scent of frangipani and aglow from the light of a hundred flames that floated in mid-air like wingless fireflies, no doubt cleverly held in place by some invisible mechanism created for the purpose by the Ball's crew of skilful engineers.

Four tents had been erected in the garden, splitting the space into quarters with a fifth and final tent in the middle. The first was a homage to Aurelia's initial steps onto the Ball's path. Rope, with people suspended from it just as they had been at the exhibition she had visited with Siv, and trees that were close to life size but pruned with the same precision with which she had learned to care for her Bonsai. Walter had been recruited to assist with the technicalities and he had executed his brief with exquisite attention to detail. When they stepped into the space Aurelia smiled. She had asked Walter to capture that sense of peace and of groundedness that she always felt when she was tied and he had succeeded. In the centre of a forest of branches from which people hung, suspended in rope bundles like ripe fruit, was a tree that was not attached to the ground at all but rather tied to the ceiling with an elaborate harness. Tied to its base was a man and a woman embracing. The rope ran from them over everything, connecting all of the performers and all of the trees in one giant spider's web. To Aurelia, it symbolised both the holding on and the letting go, the tightrope between connectedness and solitude, the laser edge that ran between restraint and freedom. A sign blinked overhead that read: *Earth. What constrains us also sets us free.*

'It will be starting soon,' Andrei said, reminding her that any minute now her presence would be required to initiate the onset of the proceedings. She did not need to enter each of the other tents to know that the displays would be exactly as she had designed. That beneath an artificial lake a dozen dancers were submerged and awaiting the arrival of Luba who would lead them through a dance of life and death beneath the words: *Water. What drowns us also sustains us.* That fifty or more naked bodies would be held aloft on the wings of seraphs beneath the words: *Air. What makes us fall also helps us to rise,* and another darkened room would soon be bright with burning bodies and the note: *Fire. What burns us also brings us light.* The final cavern was dedicated to the revellers themselves. It would be empty until the night reached fever pitch and the massed party guests would create their own magic and, by doing so, bring the fifth element into being. *Aether.*

The Ball was a celebration not just of sexuality but also of humanity, its inherent duality and the imperfection that brings both joy and freedom to those who allow themselves to feel, to live and to experience pleasure.

Aurelia bid Andrei farewell beneath the open branches of the hanging tree. At that moment, no matter what the Ball would bring and her responsibilities to it, she wished for nothing more but to stand still there forever, held tight in his arms within the forest of peaceful bodies and the gentle sighs of inward and outward breaths that were indistinguishable from the gentle murmuring of swaying branches.

He pulled her against him tightly and lowered his lips to her ear. 'You'll be the Mistress of the Ball when I see you next,' he whispered. 'But you've been my Mistress right from the beginning, since the first time we kissed. Nothing will ever change that.'

'Nothing and no one,' Aurelia agreed.

She knew the time had come and so she kissed him again on the lips and then turned and walked away, back to Madame Denoux and her army of attendants who would lead her to be bathed, costumed and prepared for the ceremony as the guests were finally allowed inside to drink, play and be merry until the moment arrived when she would finally become Mistress, no longer in waiting, and be forever wedded to the Ball.

Hours passed. Aurelia's mind found that place of stillness that came to her so easily now and with her long hair washed and dried and streaming over her shoulders in a fountain of auburn locks and her oiled skin partially covered by the light robe that had been selected for her costume, so thin it was as gossamer as any spider's web, she rose from the dressing table and her companions escorted her through the mansion's passageways, down the velvet-covered steps and into the centre of the garden where she knew that all the Ball's guests and performers would be waiting.

Somewhere a signal was given and Aurelia felt hands grabbing her ankles, waist and shoulders and, in a single swift movement born of months of elaborate rehearsal, her body was raised to the heavens and held aloft, at one arm's length above the congregation. Her mind was in a whirl from the evening's events and disorientated by the strong, insistent rhythm of the industrial rock music still booming from the large speakers that surrounded the garden, the bass tones reverberating like a feverish heartbeat and bouncing relentlessly in a closed loop. Aurelia, for a moment, suffered a strong sense of discombobulation, as if her soul had exited her body and that her naked form, held high above the wave of dancers and worshippers, was not hers, had nothing to do with her. She had briefly become both an observer at her own coronation and a migrant soul inside a body over which she no longer had any form of control.

Life paused.

There was a break in the music, a jump in the rhythm and the industrial sounds of frantic rock played in overdrive faded into the sinuous line of a powerful, vibrant melody played on the electric violin, albeit still to the beat of an unstoppable drum machine dictating its metronomic speed and direction. Aurelia guessed the beautiful red-haired violinist she had caught a glimpse of earlier in the evening was at the helm, her spectacular mane of flame hair bouncing about with every successive new note. The melody sounded familiar, classical even, but speeded up. Devilish, like a runaway train on a night track, soaring and hypnotic.

The hands holding her adjusted their grip. Two offered support for her shoulder blades, another two took care that her waist did not bend, while yet another two cupped her arse cheeks, raising her pelvis upwards, and further anonymous hands flying up from the mass of the crowd offered extra relief from gravity at the back of her knees while the final pair gripped on her ankles and opened her legs wide, pulling them gently apart so that her sex lips were now held open, her shining, engorged labia internally pulsing with untold cravings. She was slyly caressed by the softest breeze created by the crowd beneath her, which stirred the humid air as they whirlpooled across the grass.

A hand moved below her body. Then another.

Soon she was in motion, travelling above the sea of the congregation like a magic carpet, every touch just fleeting until another set of fingers moved her a length or so forward. She was surfing the crowd, transported like a fragile embarkation atop a sea of waves. Aurelia offered no resistance. She attempted to loosen her body, liberating her muscles so that she would feel no more than a rag to them, a feather to all those who were now allied in conjuring her effortless progress. She abandoned herself fully to the moment, knowing all too well that the end of the journey would be truly unforgettable.

At first Aurelia thought that she would be born aloft in a circle, traversing the perimeter of the audience from her elevated status, round and round and round until everyone was dizzy and she would be lowered into the heart of the faceless throng.

But just as she felt the crowd sway beneath her and her body almost floating effortlessly along without the help of their combined hands, she found herself still six feet or so in the air being carried forward to an unknown destination.

The sky was losing its darkness, the moon receding beneath a herd of clouds, but the heat stored inside her naked body kept her warm, reserves of passion and overwhelming desire running through her veins and under her skin, and bathing her whole being in a cloud of satisfying heat.

The rest of the crowd – all those who were no longer carrying her aloft, although she knew that every single soul in the room had at one time or another been instrumental in the aerial progress of her journey – followed her.

The music faded in the distance as she was carried further into the heart of the dying night, the whole congregation trouping behind her, like a caravan of penitents at the climax of their pilgrimage.

Her carriers slowed down.

Despite their delicate care, the strain on her neck muscles was beginning to tell and Aurelia was obliged to move her head sideways and, as she did so, her gaze alighted on the group of Ball participants nearer to the carriers. She recognised Siv, who in a typically casual costume of pale-pink denim shorts and a tight black shirt stood out from the opulent satin gowns, chiffon and painted nudity that decorated the other guests. She was walking hand in hand with both Walter and Tristan. Her smile was beatific. There was also Madame Denoux and Miss Morris. And Gwillam Irving and Number 1 and Luba, the beautiful Russian dancer, and Florence, and so many faces she had no names for, but faces she had seen at some stage or another on her journey to here. Some were missing: Lauralynn, Ginger, Edyta; she tried to recall the names of those absent and those present, but her mind was in too much of a state of feverish excitement to concentrate.

The crowd parted and a path through the grass emerged. Aurelia was carefully lowered to the ground, the grass like a soft carpet under her bare toes. The carriers retreated, and as she steadied herself and her long legs renewed acquaintance with *terra firma*, on each side of her, like a military escort, Siv and Madame Denoux placed themselves alongside her and gently took hold of her hands. Silence fell over the nearby encircling crowd.

Aurelia was led forward.

There was a bed of white flowers draped over golden sheets waiting for her at the end of the brief journey down the garden, almost like an altar set inside a flimsy white wooden platform which creaked slightly under her as she cautiously set foot on it, her balance still unsteady.

She lay down on her back, half fearing the blanket of flowers might be rough and disagreeable to the skin, but it had all the softness and comfort of cotton wool.

'Part your legs,' whispered Madame Denoux before retreating.

Aurelia obeyed the instruction.

Closed her eyes.

The firmness of a man's warm and sturdy legs brushed against the inner skin of her thighs as he positioned himself between her legs.

The deep silence reigning over the garden where she now lay, legs open wide in offering, was disorienting, the loudness of the music, the tinkle of voices all banished to another dimension, as if the whole soul of the Ball had been suspended in time and space.

She felt the hard, fleshy tip of a cock pressing gently against her opening, rubbing against her, coating itself with her wetness. A man tenderly caressed one of her breasts. Aurelia shuddered.

From the moment she had been presented to the crowd, she knew she was going to be fucked and that it would be a fuck like no other.

The moment had come.

Slowly, the tip of the cock passed her lips, unstoppable, rigid with life and lust. Then it retreated briefly, almost hanging in wait before her cunt.

Then he advanced. Breaching her fully, occupying her fully in one rapid thrust, investing her, fitting as if he belonged there.

Aurelia kept her eyes closed.

It was Andrei.

The one she had broken with tradition to choose.

She recognised the way he filled her, as if she could blindly perceive the very contours of his shaft, its veins, its ridges, the way it beat like distant heart, the way her body wrapped itself around him, gripping him, holding in a vise of her own making. All the training she'd had to undertake had taught the nerve endings both inside her and throughout the surface of her skin to distinguish between different lovers with canny accuracy.

Her heart jumped.

His familiar scent suffused her. A low hum rose from the congregation, like a muted choir, a drone, an invocation as Andrei began to move inside her. Slowly at first and then with mounting energy, rough and rapid thrusts that bucked against her, every repeated contact orchestrating the rise of her desire and emotions.

Although this was not the first time she had made love with others present, she also knew there had never been such a large audience. More than a couple of hundred at least. But it no longer bothered her. Self-consciousness and words like shame or guilt had long been banished from her life. Instead it served to excite her more, something she had never thought would ever happen.

She opened her eyes.

Andrei's eyes were piercing, fixed on her. He was also naked, but wore a spectacular mask of peacock feathers that made him look like a king or a priest, she thought.

Already an earthquake was in motion and her heart felt it was dancing an animated, frenzied tango inside her chest, every tantalizing thrust catapulting her to a new, dizzying, higher level of sensation. Her breath grew short as the hum of the crowd rose to deafening proportion and her mind clouded.

Behind the ceremonial mask, Aurelia knew Andrei was smiling at her.

She smiled back.

On and on Andrei fucked her against the inchoate music of the congregation until she was just a mind and a body, both striving for holy transcendence.

Then Andrei bucked suddenly, as if electrified, and with one final, powerful thrust he advanced deeper forward to seemingly previously unfathomed depths inside her and she felt the fire of him beating like a wave inside her, bathing her in terrible warmth, burning her. And the path of the fire spreading at the speed of light through every vein in her body.

Aurelia roared with pleasure.

Andrei sighed.

The hum of the crowd fell.

Now she looked up at the man she loved and saw him catching his breath and throwing the mask to the ground, unveiling the luxuriant dark curls against which early rays of morning light stumbled.

She felt a tear she could not control run down her cheek.

He put his hand forward to pull her up. Initially she thought the strength of the orgasm she had just experienced had drained all the reserves of strength in her body, but his hand reached hers and she pulled herself up with an energy she never knew she had. Aurelia stood, let go of Andrei's hand.

She felt . . . new.

Strong.

Invincible.

At the front of the crowd she saw Siv, who was looking at her with awe in her eyes. As were all the other members of the Ball.

Aurelia straightened her back, adjusted her stance, legs slightly apart for balance.

'It's dawn,' Andrei said.

Aurelia felt an uncommon energy racing through her naked, exposed body. But also a tremendous sense of peace.

She looked down and her breath caught in her throat. Between every previous tattoo, word, sign and image, a network of branches, like poison ivy, was moving, like a film unrolling in slow motion, over the surface of her pale skin or what was left of it to see . . . It looked truly alive, animating her illustrated surface. And, inexorably, the animated tendrils began to join every tattoo to each other, inch by inch, branch by branch, leaf by leaf, word by word, sentence by sentence.

It was completing her.

Finally, the Inking ceased and she was fully illustrated. From the collar on her neck to the thin bracelet of sharp green leaves bordering her ankles.

Dawn broke.

Her body was outlined against the rising sun in the Ball's garden, a thing of incomparable beauty, and to the admiration of the audience, Aurelia looked as if she was on fire.

The Ball finally had a new Mistress.

Epilogue

Samarkand 21st century

Several years later, after the snows of winter had melted and the welcome warmth of spring had settled on the land and sea, the Ball arrived in the city.

It was a city once fabled in mythology and legend, beyond the desert and the steppes of Central Asia, and it had taken the Ball many months to reach its destination, its fleet of anonymous vehicles, trailers, lorries and sleek transportation roaring down the highways like a modern caravan, having assembled shortly after Christmas in a busy port by the China Sea, under the guise of a travelling circus. Andrei was in charge of the complicated logistics of the operation and revelled in the role, now that the function of Protector was to some extent superfluous since Aurelia had taken on the mantle of Mistress of the Ball.

It was Aurelia who now selected the destinations and the annual theme, although in truth the two of them conferred a lot and it had become more of a close collaboration, with the Network providing reliable administrative and financial support for the operation, once a consensus had been reached. Back in Seattle, the back-up operation was now led by Miss Morris and Madame Denoux, two women of experience and wisdom Aurelia fully trusted, who had both agreed to return to the headquarters at Aurelia's request, and were ably assisted by Florence.

The previous year's Ball had, despite obvious difficulties due to its remote and often perilous setting, been in everyone's opinion an outstanding success. The Amazon forest had liberated the imagination of the organisers and participants tenfold and it was generally viewed as one of the greatest balls to have been held in a generation. Which only made the next one even more of a challenge.

As a child, Aurelia had been something of a bookworm and now had full leisure to call on her sense of wonder and the books in which she had formed an idea of the world. There had always been something magical about Samarkand, a name and a place evocative of the *Thousand and One Nights*, and she was determined to make this Ball even more memorable.

It was to be themed on *Alice In Wonderland*, a prospect which opened up so many wonderful possibilities, devious scenarios and exemplars of beauty, Aurelia felt. For months now she had often woken in the heart of the night with her imagination unbound and exciting visions racing through her brain as she assembled the details of what she wished to organise and lead.

The followers of the Ball – the court of love, the guild of worshippers – had been travelling towards Samarkand, by sea, land and air ever since the word had got out. Some were rich, others were poor, some looked like accountants, office or factory workers while many were extravagant in appearance or behaviour, but to unknown observers they somehow didn't stand out from the crowd.

Alongside them came the dancers, the acrobats, the clowns

even, the contortionists, the wonderful freaks, the seam-
stresses, the animal and body tamers, the whip masters, the
beautiful and the damned, the holy performers, the caterers,
the maids-in-waiting and the studs, the cage-makers, the
light artists, the water crew, the painters and sculptors in
metal, flesh and colours, and the whole retinue of those who
lived for lust and love and joy.

To Samarkand they came in search of beauty and the
glorious ecstasy that would be reached on the stroke of
dawn.

On a recce the previous year, Andrei and Aurelia had
selected the grounds on which the Ball would take place,
just a few miles outside the city itself and discreet enough to
afford the Ball enough privacy for its activities, and initial
construction had begun in preparation for the event.

Following the Ball's arrival, the rehearsals began, overseen by Siv and Tristan, who managed to work together
despite the fire inherent in both of their natures. Walter had
retired after the last British Ball and now tended his garden
on the English south coast, which Aurelia found ironic
seeing that the place had been the departure point for her
new life and she could never envisage returning there
herself. But she had a smile on her face when she pictured
Walter sculpting his flowers and elaborately shaped bushes
and moving between them on the wings of scent and touch
alone.

Everything was now ready and the Ball was just days
away. As she looked into Andrei's face, like every year at
this time, she couldn't help but notice the thin veil of
melancholy clouding his eyes as he gazed at her, like a little
boy lost, a softness inside him that so rarely expressed itself

and was in such marked contrast to his manly, almost masterful, appearance, the hard chin and mass of dark curls, the swimmer's gait of his broad shoulders, the steady rhythm of his muscles under his skin.

'You mustn't,' Aurelia said.

'I know,' Andrei said and looked away briefly, his mind visibly torn, yet again, by the unassailable certainty of her deep love for him and the knowledge that others would touch her, fuck her, use her, worship her, at the Ball. As the tradition dictated. And only after the night had unrolled with its dizzy flow of excesses and pleasure would she fall into his arms again, carrying the scent of so many others, men and women, strangers and friends, infusing her flesh, inside and out, and she would finally find peace again in his embrace. Together they had chosen to disregard many of the Ball's traditions, but not this one.

'It is the way . . .'

For a fraction of a second, as she noted his sorrow, Aurelia understood why her parents had eloped from the Ball, unable to accept the idea that they could share their bodies with others.

But she also knew that Andrei would not love her as much as he did were she not the Mistress of the Ball. It was what tied them, held them together. The tradition, the inheritance of centuries of human pleasure.

It was what she had been born for.

'It is the way . . .'

Her whole life led to this.

This one night of the year.

Of ultimate pleasure.

Celebrating sex.

Celebrating life.

A smile returned to Andrei's face.

'You look so beautiful tonight. The quintessence of the Ball, my very dear Mistress.'

The shadows lifted from Aurelia's mind and she was overcome by a tide of tenderness for him, her man, her husband, her partner. For better or for worse.

And as every single invisible tattoo painted on her body began to pulse in readiness, she felt another small fire warming the pit of her stomach, and looked Andrei in the eyes and told him something she had been holding back for a few days now, waiting for the right moment, but knowing it should be before the Ball.

'I'm expecting a child,' Aurelia said.

Andrei's face lit up.

She watched him melt, a teardrop swelling below his right eye before it ran gracefully down his cheek.

'Oh . . . Aurelia . . .'

'It's going to be a girl. I know it. Everything inside me is telling me so.'

'I love you,' he said.

'And I want to call her Alice,' Aurelia said as Andrei took her in his arms.

'The next Mistress of the Ball,' he whispered, holding her body against his, hoping to freeze this moment in time, encased in amber.

'Possibly,' Aurelia said. 'That will have to be her decision.'

The early morning sun was drifting through the slants in the trailer window. Outside, the tents were dotted across the desert sands like flowers of colour.

Tonight Aurelia would stand, the centre of attraction, flesh made flesh, her body on fire, with every magical illustration fully incandescent, her light a blessing for the activities about to begin and she would say the words: 'Let the Ball begin.'

Acknowledgements

As ever, we'd like to thank our intrepid agent Sarah Such for her grand efforts on our behalf, as well as Rosemarie and Jessica Buckman who reign over our foreign rights front with talent and bravura.

In addition it's fair to say that this novel would not exist without the belief and encouragement of Jon Wood, Jemima Forrester, Susan Lamb, Mark Rusher and Jo Carpenter at our UK publishers Orion, and the valiant support of Christian Rohr and Linda Walz at Carl's Books in Germany.

Our other overseas publishers are too numerous to mention, but we are immensely grateful to have been invited onto their lists and become part of their family of authors.

Inspiration for this book stems from many sources, some of which we are aware of and others which percolated for years in our subconscious minds. They say that 'you are what you eat' and each romantic and erotic book and film that we passed in the night (and day . . .) can probably find an echo in these pages, along with a myriad of other influences as varied as the streets of London and sometimes as fleeting as the glance of a passing stranger who caught our eye for a moment and our imaginations for much longer. We hope our readers forgive our strange cocktail, a highly personal blend of ambiguous autobiography and sometimes perverse imagination and savour it with the same appetite that aroused us when we wrote the story and created its characters, until they felt so real to us!

One half of Vina Jackson owes a special thank you, as ever, to her employer for unending support and providing the best (non-writing) job in London, along with her colleagues who (totally unaware of the reason!) cover her frequent absences from work whilst she is glued to a different keyboard on another side of town. Thank you to Stephen Sallinger for kindly allowing use of his home 'The Chapel' within these pages; to TJMW for Persephone, reigning in my historical flights of fancy, and inspiration; to PB, for giving me pomegranate; and to Matt Christie, for being there right from the start, and the photos. Finally – this one's for Aurelie De Cognac. Happy Birthday – I'm sorry it's a year late.

While the other half of our two-headed writing creature wishes to profusely thank Charles Dickens, Lewis Carroll, John Irving, Angela Carter and Anne Desclos aka Dominique Aury aka Pauline Reage (all with mild apologies for the borrowings and profound inspiration). And, on a personal note, DJ whose husband was borrowed for long periods in the interest of the cause, SN for the writing on her skin and AH who supplied an essential body for the delectation of the eyes and senses.

We'd also like to add a note of caution and make it clear that our Aurelia is in no way connected to the dynamic Aurelia Szewczuk, press maven at our French publishers Bragelonne/Milady whom we only met for the first time long after the creation of our Mistress-in-Waiting . . .

And finally, a warm-hearted nod of appreciation to all our other family and friends without whom . . .

Vina Jackson

Vina Jackson is the pseudonym for two established writers working together for the first time. One a successful author, the other a published writer who is also a city professional working in the Square Mile.

Connect with Vina on Facebook/Vina Jackson, or follow her on Twitter @VinaJackson1.

www.vinajackson.com

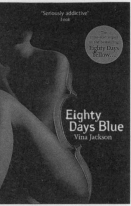

If you enjoyed

MISTRESS of
NIGHT & DAWN

look out for the other novels in Vina Jackson's
tantalising series.

Available now from Orion

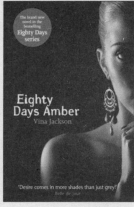
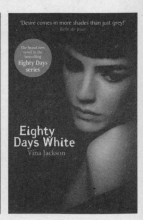